WHITE RUSH/
GREEN FIRE

WHITE RUSH/ GREEN FIRE

MARK McGARRITY

William Morrow and Company, Inc.
New York

It is the policy of William Morrow and Company, Inc., and its imprints and affiliates, recognizing the importance of preserving what has been written, to print the books we publish on acid-free paper, and we exert our best efforts to that end.

Library of Congress Cataloging-in-Publication Data

McGarrity, Mark.
    White rush/green fire
        p.   cm.
    ISBN 0-888-08658-6
    I. Title.
    PS3563.A296W48   1991
    813'.54—dc20   90-49906
                                                                                      CIP

Printed in the United States of America

First Edition

1   2   3   4   5   6   7   8   9   10

BOOK DESIGN BY M. C. DEMAIO

For Margie, Robin, and Liza. With the help of
Frank, Ralph, Greg, George, and George.
And Maddie.

PART I

ISLAND TREASURE

CHAPTER 1

PLAYERS 1 & 2

Brian Nathanson
David Creach

The Bahamas
Spring 1988

BRIAN NATHANSON GLANCED behind him. Over the Gulf Stream to the west a full moon was drifting at the edge of a storm front. It made the wake of the boat look like two jets of quicksilver dissolving in a phosphorescent sea.

Or twin silver snakes that kept rising from the water thirty feet out and followed them wherever they went, no matter how he turned the wheel or directed the surging *Tempest 43*.

Or a couple of lines of the purest Peruvian white that got fatter and and fatter and fatter until they merged and torched out in the silver wash of the moonlight. He was hot, yet his skin felt cool in the breeze that bucked over the top of the windscreen and beat on his face. It reminded him of the blinding, sweaty, chilling rush you got from free base.

Of the choice of images, Brian Nathanson liked the last best, given what now lay before them. His eyes fell to the afterdeck, where the larger of his two crewmen was assembling his weaponry, now pushing .500 sabots into the magazines of a Benelli 90, a slug gun that was configured to fire automatic and could shatter armor plate.

Up over the bow the sky wasn't much better. It was some deep purple shade that he tried to name and could only come up with mauve, which was a word a woman he couldn't take was always using, and didn't do justice to the brooding, turbulent cloud mass to the west. At some enormous elevation little horsetails of magnesium cloud were whisking into darker billows. He watched them curl, fray, and feather off into the ether.

Nathanson wished life could mimic that grace, and as the boat charged forward, he decided it was a sign. It was nature—whose side he was on—sending them a little message before the buy, a blessing. They would need it. When the two mountains of cloud met, there'd be a hell of a storm, but by then with luck the deal would be over and they'd be on their way back to Nassau, cloaked by darkness.

Brian Nathanson was a tall, broad-shouldered man with a deep chest and a mane of curly brown hair that the sun had tipped blond. With a Vandyke that framed large, even teeth and a ready smile, he looked like an actor cast for the part of Porthos, the largest of the three musketeers. It was a comparison that a friend had once made, and Nathanson quietly enjoyed. If he'd thought the stage or screen could have afforded him the variety of experiences he'd already packed into his thirty-nine years, he might have become an actor. As it was, Nathanson thought of himself and what he did as an artist—a director—of *his own life,* which was to him infinitely more rewarding than any mere career in film.

As a kid, Nathanson had spent vacations in the Bahamas. His stepfather had been a harbor pilot in New York; and with the profits from the little "this-and-that" he raked off in-coming ships, he'd made sure that every year until his death the family spent the last two weeks of January and the first two of February in the Islands. Later Sid had bought a grand old wreck of a house on Water Street in Nassau, but never got a chance to enjoy it. The second week of his retirement he—a man only in his late fifties who neither drank nor smoked, who ate carefully and exercised frequently—kicked off. Literally. Brian, who'd just been processed out of the SEALS, heard him gasping and got there in time to see his foot quiver.

For Nathanson his stepfather's death had been the irony of ironies: that a man so careful, so steady, and so . . . considered he was almost reverential got such little respect from Fate taught Nathanson what he still regarded as the most important lesson of his life—don't wait. Live now. And be thankful for every moment. Especially here among the—how many were there again?—680 actual islands and 2,378 other outcroppings of rock, corral, and mangrove thicket in the over 100,000 square miles of ocean that comprised the Bahamian chain. Facts such as that were important to Nathanson. They made him believe he was sharp; they might also keep him alive.

Beside him stood a small, well-built black man who now pointed toward the barometric pressure, which was displayed on the control console. It was falling. David Creach was from Newark, and had been Nathanson's partner since they had worked together on the Jersey docks nearly twenty years earlier. Their pasts, they had soon discovered, were broadly similar, and they saw things the same. Both had grown up during the sixties, when everything seemed possible. Both had gone on to college but had railed at its confinement and artificiality and dropped out. Both had fought in Vietnam, where they discovered how impossible life could be; back in Richard Nixon's Amerika, things weren't much better.

When his stepfather died, Nathanson inherited a small import-export business and the house on Water Street. He invited Creach down, telling him that the Islands were the perfect place to live. "Great climate. Clean air, clean water. Lots of women. Good food and booze. Dope galore. The only people who give a damn about who you are and where you come from, you don't want to know. The others are fuckin' free, man."

Only the dope proved wrong. Nathanson and Creach weren't dopers, but after their experience in Southeast Asia, it was part of their lives. And every time one of them wanted a little toot to party, he found himself with his wallet out, his thumb up his ass, and an obsequious smile on his face, watching people—bad people, mostly—getting rich on the business. How Nathanson and Creach began was with little deals, just for themselves and a few particular friends. Casually. Cooperatively. Communally, almost. Until the possibility of making a great deal of money got in the way.

Nathanson told himself, hell, he wasn't the guy who created

the demand, and opiates, dope, narcotics—call it what you will—had been around, far as he knew, since before written history. Booze, coffee, tea, and tobacco were narcotics, and didn't even birds have their special seeds? Like uranium, dope was just part of the natural order of things, and who was he to say the big *no*. It was out there, he enjoyed it himself, and what was he dealing with anyhow? Processed coca leaves? The natives of the Andes had had their cheeks bulging with coke since before the Spanish.

It was how you handled the stuff that mattered, which came down to individual freedom, which Nathanson didn't want tampered with. Ever. And laws? Laws were mainly self-serving bullshit made up by the rich for everybody else to follow. They were strict about dope because the profits were huge, enormous, immense. They wanted it all for themselves and their "drug" companies that were called pharmaceuticals. He'd read someplace that the world spent more on drugs every year than on food. Something like a half-trillion dollars. But only when Creach and he put themselves in the way of the coke miracle and it shit on their heads did Nathanson believe.

Two big runs and they had paid for their boat. A third and they were fat. As the years went by, the question became, how much was enough? And could Nathanson curb their greed—something he'd never had—and get out before the inevitable happened? "One more big score, no nickel-dime," Creach kept saying, "then we'll quit." And Nathanson, thinking of the aluminum flotation *suitcase*, for crissake, stuffed with G-notes and the bank accounts he'd set up on Grand Cayman for *retirement* at thirty-fucking-*nine*, imagine, got sucked in.

Nathanson eased off the throttle, and the boat, lifted on its own wake, began surfing toward the shore. They had arrived at the small, uninhabited island where he had dived for sponges as a child. It was shaped like a horseshoe and enclosed a deep-water cove that was maybe a half-mile long by a quarter-mile wide. The beach was flooding with frothy chop.

Nathanson adjusted the microphone of the headset that allowed them to converse over the roar of the engines. "What say? We going in?" He meant, because of the storm to the west. In the background a tape was playing "Ghost Riders in the Sky."

Also wearing earphones and a microphone, Creach paused

before turning to Nathanson a head and face that had the definite shape of a hexagon. His skin was dark, and he wore a neatly trimmed mustache that hinted at the care he took in all things that concerned him. With a good mind and a better memory, Creach now knew the Bahamas, its waters, people, and fickle weather almost as well as Nathanson himself, and his opinion carried weight.

Their eyes met.

"How long it take to set this deal up?"

Months, thought Nathanson. It was the big one, his absolute last.

"And we're here. Hell, they might not show themselves. If they don't, we just pull in under the mangroves and ride out the storm. If they do, they'll want to kiss quick and split, and so much the better. For us."

Nathanson nodded. Their experience had been, the quicker the drop, the safer the deal. A plane and boat meeting in an isolated cove was a dead giveaway, but with the storm it was unlikely that the Bahamas Defence Force, which patrolled the waters, would venture out.

"And if the deal gets done and the plane don't get back off, no skin off our ass. With no boat, they'll either still be here tomorrow, or—"

Dead, thought Nathanson. Maybe like us. He glanced down at the display on the control console. The lowest barometric pressure Nathanson knew about was 26.35 inches of mercury, recorded during the fabled hurricane of 1935. Twenty-seven-point-sixty-three was close enough.

Nathanson turned his head to catch a last look at that high, rare place in the heavens where storms could not reach and grace abounded. But it was gone. The sky was now a black, threatening, impenetrable mat.

He flicked on the infrared lamps that could expose the dark length of three football fields, then reached for the goggles that were strapped to his forehead. Playing one powerful engine against the other to regain steerage, Nathanson directed the dark hull toward the inlet.

Designed in the eighties for the Coast Guard to intercept "cigarettes"—the drug runners' boat of choice—the *Tempest* was sleek and fast with the difference that it could run at speed in most seas and was equipped with the latest electronics. With seven coats of muted black lacquer covering its production-line white epoxy, the *Tempest* was a stealthy and lethal gunship, perfect for the waters that it plied. Especially with the array of rocket launchers and side arms that Nathanson had mounted at various battle stations around the open hull.

S.O.P. was to arrive at the buy first, so they could conceal the boat and know what was coming at them. That way they could also secure any avenue of escape. As buyers, they had brought with them a boatful of money, and honor was scarce out here among the lawless. It was free enterprise—the free-est—and there was no telling what might happen.

But the delivery plane had already arrived. Raising binoculars to his goggles, Creach pointed to the end of the cove where an object was lit by their infrared lamps. "How you like that? They beat us here. How far they got to fly with the shit anyways—a thousand miles?"

"Two, if they flew around the picket." Nathanson meant the multinational cordon of naval vessels and AWACS planes that had been deployed off the South American coast to interdict drug shipments north.

"What about those markings? Where they from anyways?" The arrangements of the buys were Nathanson's, the logistics of how the deal went down on the spot Creach's.

"Bolivia."

"We deal with them before?"

Nathanson knew what Creach was getting at. Six years ago, a Bolivian transporter had stung them for over $200,000 with powder that had been packed pure around the outside of the bricks but cut deep within. How they managed that, Nathanson still hadn't figured out, but it had taught him, where dope was concerned, greed was surely the *mother* of invention.

"Greaser name of Romero, I remember right. You think that's Romero?"

Nathanson said nothing. Creach was the single most "concentrated" person Nathanson had ever met, and, once committed, he worked hard, was honest with his partners and loyal to his friends. His one failing, however, was his temper. He had a flash point lower than ether, and nothing touched him off like a cheat.

What Nathanson didn't like was the shape of the delivery plane. He had been studying seaplanes since he was a kid, and he had never seen a wing shape like this. It looked wrong; the wings were angled forward instead of swept back. Also, the cockpit canopy, lit by the infrared lamps, bulged out over the nose like a bloody, cracked eye.

"Russian?" Creach asked.

That was it, Nathanson decided, some sort of oddball Tupalev design they could have got via Nicaragua or Cuba or maybe on the open market. Nathanson didn't know. He never bought Bloc machinery; he heard it was functional and dependable, but in the Islands parts were always a problem.

"We still goin' through with this?" Creach turned goggled eyes to him.

"No rule says we gotta get here first. After all, it was us who told them about the storm, recommended they get here before it hit." When Creach said nothing, Nathanson added, "We *discussed* it, for crissake. What—you want all that product to go down in a storm? *Your* product?"

Creach again raised the binoculars to his eyes. "Well, I don't like them sneaking in here like this."

Or anything else that didn't go *according to form* by Creach, Nathanson thought.

He set the radio to the agreed-upon frequency. Before tapping in the code, he pulled up his goggles and glanced back at the storm. Sheet lightning was flashing but too distant for the thunder to be heard over the wind. It was gusting to 52 mph, said the console display, and fat drops of windblown rain were raking the boat. They had maybe a half hour tops to get things done. It was enough, if all went smoothly; he waved Bogan, his other crewman, to the bow.

Bogan was just another big, pumped-up pussy they'd been hiring in bars and off docks for deals like this. There was an army of them all the same in Florida and the Islands. For a quick score and a noseful of coke they'd go anywhere there was guns and not too much danger. Maybe it came from football, which most of them claimed they'd played, or looking in a mirror while pumping iron, but they had an awareness of their bodies, when they moved, that was total and didn't leave much for anything else.

Nathanson hoped Bogan was different and at least had balls. If they had trouble, he'd need them.

CHAPTER 2

BUY/BUST

◆

A KEVLAR FLAK JACKET made Bogan seem immense. He was also wearing a NATO-issue tanker's helmet that had been painted black and looked like something from a Fourth Reich. No weapon, no amount of potential firepower, could intimidate druggies, but you had to try. If they thought you were weak, you were dead.

"I don't know, I don't like it," said Creach, as they drifted near the plane.

Nathanson backed off the engines, then swung the boat around. A mestizo was standing in the open bay door of the plane, pointing a machine pistol down at them.

Raising a hand to the fuselage, Bogan kept the boat clear of the plane. With the other he aimed the slug gun at the man in the door.

"*What* don't you like?" It was important to keep Creach calm, but at the same time Nathanson credited his intuition.

"The infrared. What they doin' with infrared. And this plane. It's too fuckin' military for me. Look at that canopy there—" Creach motioned his chin toward the rear of the fuselage. "What's that, a gun turret?"

Nathanson beamed an infrared hand lamp at the tail of the plane; twin fifty-millimeter machine guns were covering them.

"What—their government in on this?"

Ultimately Nathanson suspected it probably was. Like most Latin American countries, power was purer and therefore life cheaper in Bolivia than in most other places. "Long as it's not Unk's government." That would put them in jail or make them dead, he meant. "Go easy."

"It's the only way," replied Creach, reaching for the test kit in the same resigned way he might have picked up his lunch box when they'd been working on the docks in Jersey. He stepped around the console and made his way toward the open bay door of the plane.

The money guy was an Indian, a short, round man with high cheekbones and quick, dark eyes. He wore a bright patterned shirt that was open to where his stomach ballooned the material tight. In the infrared glare the design looked like pink lightning bolts. He jumped down into the boat. Creach slid his test kit into the plane, then climbed up after it.

Nathanson passed the cash case to the Indian, so he would count it in the bow of the boat where he could be watched. Verifying $2.5 mil in thousand-dollar bills took about as long as the test for purity in cocaine.

A rocket launcher came next. Nathanson held it up for view from the plane. Stepping out from behind the wheel, he sighted in the bug-eye canopy over the cockpit. He wanted to let them know that, in case of a firefight, their controls would go first. They'd have no way out of there with the dope and millions except by boat, if they could take it.

The wind had picked up. It was now a hard, steady blast that made Nathanson feel suddenly cold.

Even the smell of the plane bothered Creach. It was the same old DOD drab lacquer that reminded him of Vietnam, scorching metal, blood, and death. He wondered if the Russians had bought the paint from the same company or if maybe they *were* the same company. You know, the way things were turning out so neat, globally.

Infrared overheads came on. Creach lowered his goggles and scanned the load.

It was divided into ten boxes wrapped in polyethylene for extra protection. The top of each box was open and the plastic pulled back to reveal smaller, plastic packages that looked like even pink bricks.

A scale had been placed nearby, but Creach had brought his own. As he bent to open his test kit, a fourth greaser stepped from the shadows and trained a machine pistol at the back of his neck. How many of them were there? he wondered. There was the money guy in the boat, the gunner in the turret, the guy standing over him, and a pilot. Four.

Glancing sidelong down the length of the plane, Creach wondered if the cockpit could contain another person, but all he could see was the shape of the pilot silhouetted against the lights on the instrument panel. The back and shoulders were larger than any Indian he'd ever seen. Could it be one of the Romeros? There were three of them. Brothers. What was the chance of running into one of them again, or was it too much to hope for?

The wind, howling past the open door, reminded Creach of his purpose. He lowered his head.

Coke. The cut in it could fool you. Crystals of pure cocaine hydrochloride were shiny, almost transparent, but even when powdered, they still held their sheen if you played a light over the surface. Generally the more sparkle, the purer the coke. Lactose dulled the coke bad, dextrose less so, and crushed crystal amphetamine least of the three. But none of that was much use under infrared in the back of a bobbing seaplane.

Taste was another giveaway. Cocaine had a bitter, distinctive, medicinal taste that you'd know again. If it was sweet, it was cut with dextrose. Slightly sweet, lactose. Procaine was just as bitter, but it acted like Novocain and numbed the tongue quicker and longer than cocaine. Then there was salt or Epsom salts, but both could be picked off too easy and weren't often used by pros.

Burning some was another test. You put a little in a square of tinfoil that you held over a lighter or a match. Pure cocaine burned clean or maybe a speck orange, leaving a couple of sandlike grains behind. Dextrose and lactose, being sugars, caramelized and were messy, and crystal amphetamine blew up, popping and cracking in the tin. The problem with burning was again procaine, and also menita and quinine. Some people claimed they burned different, but Creach could never see how.

Still others claimed they could tell pure product by snort, always trying to make sure they went into the buy straight and sampled the same amounts. Things like "head"—how quick it rushed you—and "freeze"—the numbing effect—were standard with pure coke. If it burned your nose and made your eyes water, speed was the cut. Sugar and salt made your nose drip, but pure cocaine was pure kiss. You were with it—and it loved you—and then you were without it, simple as that, with nothing left behind but the memory of the rush. And anyway, Creach never sampled a buy, and certainly not with five hundred kilos in front of him.

Finally there was a menthanol test that could pick off everything but procaine, and a cobalt-blue test that took time. Creach used none of those.

Instead he chose the second box of product and carefully removed all fifty bricks, placing them in five rows of ten the way he picked them out, top layer to bottom. Next he slit the surface of each kilo right in the middle of the plastic bag. With a long-throat lab spoon he dug deep into each bag and pulled out a small amount of cocaine, dumping it on top of the plastic alongside the slit.

Creach then opened his test kit. Inside were ten rows of test tubes sealed with plastic snap tops. Each contained a small glass rod and a mild solution of hydrochloric acid. Again using the lab spoon, he placed a small amount of product in each tube, and from a bottle added two drops of ammonia. Sealing the tubes, he closed the kit and shook it carefully but vigorously for thirty seconds.

Setting it down, he pulled a roll of Scotch tape from his jacket and sealed the slits in the bags. The Maclagen ammonia test was one of two principal tests for cocaine. It was based on the supposition that the amorphous alkaloids of coca could be set free by ammonia and deposited on the sides of a glass rod within five minutes. If the product had been cut at all, few crystals would form and the solution would remain milky. Creach had learned all that at Miami U. When he did a thing, he did it right—courses, library, and lab work included.

A cigarette came next. Lighting up, Creach blew the smoke over the array of plastic bags, scattering maybe twenty-five grams of coke. He glanced up at the greaser who was holding the gun. No flinch, no nothing. No coke jockey there. Just dark, watchful, jungle-Indian eyes.

Creach took another drag and turned his head toward the pilot, who now had his headset hanging around his neck. Could he be one of the Romeros? In spite of their name, they looked like krauts, and were probably the bastard spawn of some Nazi war criminal who had fled to Bolivia in the forties. One of them had said, "I want you to thank us for not killing you." And when they had, another had sprayed their boat with a subgun, shouting, "Louder! We can't hear you! Louder!" It took Creach and Nathanson two weeks to get back to Nassau. Broke. Even now it made the blood pound in Creach's temples. The loss, but mainly the humiliation.

Creach stood and took two quick strides toward the cockpit. "Romero!" he shouted over the howling of the wind. "Hey— Romero!"

The greaser scurried after him and poked the muzzle of the machine pistol in his ribs, but too late. The pilot had turned his head, and there it was—the high, balding forehead, blondish hair, and long face set in a smirk that said, *Assholes, we're going to take you again*. The guy was a Romero, and nobody but.

Creach flicked the cigarette toward the cockpit. He'd see about that. He turned to the Indian. Their eyes met, and with an index finger Creach pushed away the stubby barrel of the machine pistol.

Back at the test kit, he opened the top and lifted the rack that held the test tubes. Six of the fifty tubes were milky. The samples had been taken from the packages at the bottom of the box.

Creach lowered the rack back into the test kit and snapped it closed. He quickly repacked the box, then wrapped and tied all ten tight with the cord that had been provided. Stacking them at one side of the open bay door, he jumped back down into the boat.

Like a hostage exchange, the Indian, who had counted the money, climbed up into the plane.

"Love that shirt," Creach said. "You order the special effects?"

Behind a thick, surface fog, forks of lightning were blanching the horizon.

"Or was it Romero?"

The Indian's eyes swung to him. It was probably the only word he had understood.

Corroboration. Complete.

Back at the control console with Nathanson, Creach bent for the case with the money. "It's a fuckin' Romero, and they're ten percent light. Minimum. Packed down the bottom."

Ten percent was within acceptable parameters, since the product of most labs wasn't perfectly pure for openers. But to have a transporter tax them an additional 10 percent of $2.5 mil and have it be a Romero was something else.

Could they win a firefight? Perhaps—if Nathanson could swing the launcher at the gun turret and get off a first shot. But he'd aimed at the cockpit on the idea that the deal would go down as planned. Now he couldn't swing the weapon around without tipping them off. It was the crucial part of the sale, the exchange, and they'd be watching every move.

"Counting the boat we lost the last time we dealt with them, it makes seven hundred G's they're into us now. Whadawe *family*, for fuck's sake?"

Nathanson thought the cushion was there. They were buying at five thousand dollars per kilo and selling in New York at fifteen thousand dollars. As middlemen with clean, good dope, they stood to make $2.5 million *apiece* after getting back the $2.5 million they had in. The could afford to drop a few hundred here or there. How much was a bullet worth? Or worse.

The whole point from the start was not to get greedy. Greed kills, as Creach himself had said, but this was something different. The greed was coming down on the other side.

"Color hair?" he asked.

"Blond. Balding. The storm-trooper face. The honkie smirk. The fuckin' *works*." Creach snatched up the case. He sometimes forgot Nathanson was white.

A gust of wind rocked the boat, which shied into the fuselage of the plane. Bogan pushed them back; they were that close.

"David—why don't we play for *this* pot, long as it's on the table." Nathanson had used Creach's first name maybe once in the last year. "Now that we know who the Romeros run for, we can always set something up—something smaller—and come back on them then, when we're ready. Here, like this, now—" Nathanson shook his head.

In the darkness and the wind Creach seemed to nod, but he said, "That turret gun. Something happens, just make sure you get the turret. Don't miss." He turned and moved toward the stern and the plane.

A barrage of windblown rain stippled the windscreen. Thunder rumbled in the distance, and the bank of fog in front of the storm now appeared off the bow of the boat.

The Indian had reappeared in the doorway, but without his fancy shirt. As though too precious to mess up with blood, he was bare from the waist up. He looked like a tawny pregnant child of mixed gender—little splay tits, belly and all—or some *narcotraficante*'s primitive icon celebrating the god of the coca leaf. A fragmentation grenade, hanging from his eyeteeth, made it look as though he were smiling. The safety lever was up; it was ready to go.

Seeing it set Creach off. "Romero!" he shouted into the blast from the storm. "You fuckin' greaser. You wanna play rough? You wanna *fuck* with us? We'll see—"

Propping a foot on the gunwale, Creach slammed the money valise down on his thigh and snapped it open. *"This"*—he grabbed up a bundle of bills—"is for last time." He waved them at the cockpit. "—and *this* is for the fuckin' ten fuckin' percent you glommed from us here." He stuffed another bundle down the front of his jacket, closed the case, and with both hands lifted it above his head. Whipping his body, he tossed it over the Indian into the plane. He then began pulling the cartons off the plane, dropping them down into the boat.

The Indian with the grenade turned his head, as though conferring with somebody in the plane.

Nathanson's eyes flickered toward the gun turret. He would have to jump up, swing the launcher around, and sight in the dark shape through the night scope. A launcher was no rifle; its fire was not instantaneous. You squeezed the trigger, then waited through a pause that seemed interminable and could be deadly.

Standing in the stern beside Creach, Bogan now raised the slug gun to his shoulder.

Lightning splashed the bay door with brightness. Behind the Indian was the mestizo who was still training his machine pistol on Bogan.

It was then Nathanson heard the thunk and whine of the plane engines kicking in. When the Indian's hand came up, as though for the grenade, Creach grabbed the man's ankles. "You think so? You try that shit, and you go with us."

Their eyes met, and again the Indian paused. But when his hand jumped for the grenade, Creach pulled his feet out from under him. The Indian fell hard on the lip of the doorway, but the pin was out of the grenade. It dropped into the boat.

Creach didn't hesitate. He threw the Indian down on top of it, then dived on top of *him*.

Fuck it, Nathanson thought. That tore it. Now they had to take everything or nothing, or everything that would be nothing, he realized with strange dispassion.

Swinging the launcher to the rear of the plane, he aimed at the turret and squeezed the trigger. There was the pause—a fraction of a second in which he heard clacking and the *pow* of a slug gun— before the rocket spurted from the tube and filled the night sky with phosphorescent light.

The concussion was stunning and knocked him off his feet. He heard a second explosion and found himself on his back, looking up at a billowing orange fireball. Then came the pain. He felt wet and hurt bad, someplace low in his stomach, groin, or leg. He crabbed himself into the shelter of the control console and lunged for the slug gun there.

The entire tail section of the plane was now in flames. The most Romero could do was pull the plane away from the boat, but Nathanson wouldn't let him. Not after this.

He tried to lift himself up, but his muscles wouldn't work or he was going into shock. His whole body was jerking in painful, spastic throbs.

Still, he managed to raise the gun, which he fired again and again at the roaring port engine of the plane. Finally a sabot, ripping through the sheet metal, gushed something hot and steaming from a hole. The engine then sputtered, coughed, and died.

The gun slipped from Nathanson's hands and snagged on something that sent a galling pain through his side. Again he tried to raise himself up to check out the wound, but things—the control console, the wing of the plane, the sky that was now vivid with fire and lightning—had begun to go grainy.

He wondered if this was how it would end for him, and he tried to concentrate on who might be left. He knew for sure that the turret gunner was gone and the money counter and probably the mestizo in the bay door. He had heard Bogan's slug gun at least once.

Bogan himself? Not a chance; he was history.

The pilot who was a Romero? Maybe.

Creach?

Nathanson wanted to call out, but if Romero was alive, he would now need the boat. Nathanson would try to save himself for that.

Romero had done what he had to, once the fighting had started and he knew the money was safely aboard. He radioed his position to their monitor in Cuba, then tried to get away. When the weather cleared, a plane would be sent, but with all that coke and money, it would be best to get away as soon as he could.

Already he'd thought he'd seen a flash, like from a searchlight, at the far end of the cove, but it was probably just lightning. He didn't think anything could get through the strange fog that had enveloped the cay. He'd heard of such things in the Islands. It was storming all around him now, yet only wind and the occasional cloudburst had struck the plane.

Backup maybe? No—they were occasional runners, small-time smugglers, *piratas* in the strict sense, and they would work alone.

He'd return the money but not the coke. He'd make sure to blow up the plane before morning and say the buy went sour before the exchange could be made. But he killed the runners and took their money and what was left of the boat.

Londoño, the *cartellero,* would be satisfied. With the cash in hand, it would be a clean deal for him. The plane? Romero owned it jointly with his brothers; later he might even pay them their thirds.

It would be work securing the load, making sure the boxes wouldn't leak, then finding some weights to sink them where no pleasure boat or divers would find them. But think of the payoff. With the profit he might even go into business for himself.

In the open bay door Romero looked down at Manolito, whose corpse was spattered everywhere. With the head upside down, it was as if he were laughing at him. Romero glanced at the runner, a big white man who was sprawled over the side of the boat, his face raised to the heavy rain. Jerking the subgun to his chest, Romero touched off a burst of 9-mm fire, just to make sure. The body twitched and jumped.

The other guy, the tester, the one who'd known his name—where was he? Romero couldn't see a sign of him anywhere. Keeping a hand over his eyes, he tried to peer into the deep fog that was now rolling over the boat, like heavy smoke. Nothing. Not a trace.

Shielding his face with his forearm, Romero eased himself down onto the edge of the bay door. The boat below him was pitching and heaving now in the choppy water of the cove. Like stinging darts, the wind-driven rain tattooed his head and shoulders. He was wearing a new pair of flight boots with leather soles, and he didn't want to slip in the gore that was pooling in the stern of the boat. Slowly he lowered his legs toward a built-in seat. He would step from there onto the lockers, which were at least free of blood.

That was when Creach rose out of the chop by the side of the boat. He jabbed the slug gun toward Romero's ass and fired.

The sabot slammed up into Romero's body and burst, like a plug, from his chest. It actually blew him off his feet. Creach had to flatten himself against the flare of the boat. Romero jackknifed off the rail and pitched into the water.

Only now, with the immediate danger past, did Creach examine his hand, which was hurting like hell. Standing in chest-deep water, he held it before his eyes. He could feel—but he couldn't see—the four fingers of his left hand. Blood was streaming from the stumps.

Now *there's* a disability for you, he thought. He tore a strip from his ripped shirt and tied a tourniquet around his arm. From his earliest days on the streets of Newark he had known big money sooner or later brought big violence. It had caught him here. He also thought of guys he'd seen in combat in Nam who'd been so wired they didn't know they were wounded until they got back to base.

Which was a problem he'd gladly accept now. Base was ninety miles across open, stormy ocean. He had only one hand, and a partner who was hurt bad. More pressing still was the fact that they were not alone.

While in the water before the fog rolled in, Creach had seen a searchlight at the channel end of the cove. Later he had even heard voices and the rattle of a chain through a chock.

Romero's backup? Not by boat. Londoño, the *cartellero* who owned the dope, would hold the transporters responsible for its value, and without a doubt they would come tomorrow by plane.

The authorities? It was a possibility. The island was remote and little-visited, the inlet to the cove difficult to navigate. Who else could it be?

Tossing the slug gun into the boat, Creach waited for the thrust from a wave to heave himself up on the gunwale. With the next he tumbled into the boat.

The first thing he saw was a box of product—one of the ten—that had taken some damage. Powder was spilling from its side. The shit had gotten them into this, he thought. Wouldn't it beat his ass if it got them out.

Ripping open the cardboard with his good hand, Creach plunged the stubs of his fingers into the raw coke. The numbing effect was nearly instantaneous. It almost made him smile.

He raised some to his nose. Back when he was a kid, he had heard cocaine called "hero." For good reason, he hoped. He slipped a kilo into a pocket of his flak jacket and turned to Nathanson.

A big piece of plastic—fiberglass from the shattered side of the control console—was jutting from his side. His eyes were closed, but Creach could see he was breathing.

Raindrops, fat as nickels, had begun to fall through the fog. Creach knew what he had to do while the rain would cover the sound. He turned to the stanchions on the transom and began lowering the jolly boat. He would get them in under the mangroves. There, they could conceal themselves and wait out the storm.

And watch and see who the newcomers were. And what they wanted.

CHAPTER 3

PLAYERS 3 THROUGH 8

◆

Jay and Arlene Gelb
Bill Cicciolino and Gerri (McCann) Cicciolino
Tug McCann
Eva Burden

WHEN PROFESSOR JAY GELB surfaced from his plunge off the stern of *Whistler* the next morning, he got the surprise of his life.

The fog of the storm of the night before, which had caused the three couples from New York to seek shelter in the wide cove, was burning off, and there in front of him was a large, strange-looking, twin-engine seaplane. Beside it was a sleek black launch that was bobbing in a slight chop. Gelb raised the face mask onto his forehead and, pumping the flippers on his feet, lifted himself out of the water for a better look.

He could tell at a glance something was wrong. It wasn't only the tail section of the plane, which looked as if something big had taken a bite out of it, or the control console of the launch that was half blown-off. It was the noise of the gulls that were perched on the stern and in the open bay door of the airplane. They were fighting and squabbling, making a din that Gelb could now remember hearing through the fog when he had stepped out on the deck of *Whistler* earlier.

He also remembered something from the night before: the strange burst of orangey light that had appeared through the fog with what Gelb had guessed was thunder. It hadn't been repeated, and the incident had slipped his mind until now.

Cautiously he swam forward, moving his arms before him in wide, slow arcs, looking around in every direction. He didn't want to be surprised by anything . . . surprising, but he couldn't imagine what had attracted the birds, until he got close enough that his arm movement scared them.

They rose up from the stern of the speedboat in a bright, raucous cloud and exposed a form that Gelb couldn't quite make out. With all the red and white he at first thought it was a furled flag, then decided no, it was a large fish that hadn't been fully boarded. It would explain the sea gulls, a brave few of which now began to return. But why just leave the fish, and where were they, the owners or operators of the boat and plane?

Operators. Gelb took two further strokes forward and was just realizing what he was seeing when his hands struck something in the water. He jerked back. Adrenaline rushed through him. His flippered feet were pumping, treading water, raising him up. He stared at what he thought was some large sea anemone, until he realized it was a head facedown, the hair trailing away, like blond tentacles, in the bright blue-green water.

He glanced up at the boat. Nor was the fish a fish. It was a large white man, who had been crucified across a side of the boat. He was splayed there on the base of his spine. His arms were out, his neck back, his jaw pointed at the sky. He didn't have a face. Instead, he had a sea gull perched on his teeth, picking at the meat in the cavity of an eye.

Gelb tried to turn and flee, but he couldn't. There was yet another body, a face. As though framed in two shadowed thwarts of the boat, its nearly severed head was upside down, the tongue lolling out. The sockets had already been picked clean.

Gelb spun around and began thrashing off into the fog, but the clasp of a flipper caught on something on the dead man. He actually had to touch the corpse—the fat, bloated arm, the bracelet of the wristwatch—to get himself free. The skin felt soft and gooey, like cheese, and when he finally caught sight of *Whistler*, it was two hundred yards away.

By the time he climbed up on deck, Gelb was panting and trembling. He thought his heart would burst, and there was nobody stirring. Trying to outrun the storm, they had worked hard. Gelb himself had kept watch well past midnight, until he was sure the hooks would hold, and the brunt of the storm had passed. Who would he wake?

Bill, of course. A veteran cop—it was his kind of thing. Gelb suddenly relaxed, overjoyed that Cicciolino was along and he wouldn't have to deal with the horror of those bodies, you know, *himself*. Cicciolino, McCann, and he and their wives—girlfriend now in McCann's case, since his recent divorce—were on the final leg of their spring cruise, which had been an annual event for the past twenty years. Gelb, who loved boats and sailing, was always their informal captain, and it would be he himself who called the authorities over *Whistler*'s radio.

He could see the lead in the *Daily News,* which, if he was honest, was his newspaper of choice and not the *Times,* which he only made a pretense of reading. "Professor Jay Gelb of Columbia while sailing in the Bahamas, came upon . . ." He'd save all the *real* details, like the sea gulls feasting upon the eyes of the corpses and his flipper getting snagged on the wristwatch, for his colleagues. He'd take his own pictures with the waterproof Nikon that Arlene, his wife, had given him over the holidays.

As luck would have it, Cicciolino was already up, standing in the galley pouring himself a cup of coffee.

Reaching for the binoculars and camera that he had hung by the companionway ladder, Gelb forced what he hoped Cicciolino would later report as icy nonchalance into his voice. "When you get a moment, Bill, would you step up on deck with me? There's something I think you should see."

Gelb was a spare man of medium height who was handsome in what he understood was an unmistakably Jewish way. He had a thin face, a long, sloping but well-shaped nose, and deep, sensitive eyes of the sort that made other people want to confide in him. He was a good listener and, he hoped, a good friend. Whenever Cicciolino or McCann had a problem and needed somebody to "be there," they inevitably called Gelb. Now Gelb had brought them this further adventure.

The three men had been friends since their childhood on the Lower East Side. They had gone to elementary school and later Seward Park High School together. Although their colleges had been different—Cicciolino, Fordham; McCann, CCNY; Gelb,

Pratt—they had managed to stay in touch, and all had developed respectable careers in Manhattan.

After Fordham Law, where he met and married McCann's sister, Gerri, Cicciolino had joined the NYPD. He was now one of ten assistant chiefs and presently the official, uniformed spokesperson for the commissioner. Tug McCann had gone into the paper industry. Eight years ago he had started his own brokerage, and after some struggling and the recent divorce, had at last begun to make it pay well. Gelb's professorship at Columbia was in art. He was a photographer who specialized in platinum and palladium prints and pinhole photography. His wife, Arlene, owned a gallery on Third Avenue just off Fifty-seventh Street.

He was glad Arlene hadn't gone out swimming with him. Not that she was especially squeamish, but this was definitely something he'd rather share with Cicciolino.

Cicciolino wasn't thrilled. He woke McCann and stationed him at *Whistler*'s wheel. He had Gelb raise the anchors and start the engine, "Just in case. From the look of it, it's a drug buy that went sour. You sure that's all we got?" He looked down at the ancient, double-barrel shotgun that T. J. Monroe, who owned *Whistler*, had shown them with the flare guns and other survival equipment aboard the yacht. A Bahamian, Monroe had added, "Shells you supply yourself. They corrode aboard a boat in two days, and I'm tired, mon, of pitching them out." Gelb had decided they would not need any.

Cicciolino reached for a flare gun. He loaded it and slipped two spare rockets under his belt. "How dead they look?"

Gelb didn't know. Dead.

"I give you two the word"—Cicciolino waited until he had both Gelb's and McCann's attention—"you haul ass out of here." Cicciolino had a square, compact body with broad shoulders and short, powerful arms. His laugh could be quick and engaging, but when serious, as now, his face was an Etruscan mask. His eyes were light blue, his head a mass of tight black curls. "The bot' a' you. Don't hesitate, just go. And don't worry about me. I won't tell you 'less I have to. No sense in all of us getting wasted. Assholes might still be alive, and from the looks of all that shit"—he punched a finger at the wreckage—"if they are, they'll need a way out of here themselves, which means this boat."

Gelb winched the Boston whaler with its twenty-five-horsepower outboard over the side. As they motored closer, Cicciolino couldn't imagine what could have torn up the plane that way. Also, the superstructure of the boat with the dead white guy had big holes in it, like Swiss cheese.

"Remember last night that orange burst we saw? The roar?" said Gelb, cutting the engine to an idle as they drifted toward the boat.

Cicciolino nodded. That was it. It had happened last night. The sea gulls were eating only the parts of the bodies that had already been injured. And the eyes. None of the flesh stank or looked ripe. The gunwale of the whaler bumped into the side of the speed boat, and the gulls made a racket, lifting off into the crystalline sky.

There were two large cartons in the stern of the boat. One had been blown open and had spilled a white powder that Cicciolino guessed was coke. A machine pistol was lying in the sun in the open bay door of the airplane. Nobody alive or even wounded would leave it like that. Vaulting the gunwale of the boat with the flare gun out, Cicciolino made straight for it. Squatting down in what looked like a pool of coagulating blood that was swarming with flies, he checked the long, crescent-shaped magazine.

Half-empty—or half-full—depending on your perspective, though the man who had wielded it no longer had one. Another Indian, he had taken a blast of something big in the chest.

A slug gun maybe. Cicciolino now caught sight of one lying near the control console of the boat, he motioned Gelb to pick it up.

In the cockpit Cicciolino held the receiver of the headset to an ear. The radio was still on and set for the frequency that was noted down on a small pad clipped to the control panel. Otherwise the plane contained a crate of fragmentation grenades, another of 9-mm ammunition, an aluminum clamshell–style suitcase, and eight big cartons like the two in the boat. Cicciolino picked one up. Christ, he thought, it must weigh a hundred pounds.

Seeing him in the doorway, Gelb called up, "Everything all right, Chick?" It was a name from their youth when a teacher had made everybody in their first grade class say his Americanized name, "Chick-o-lee-no," until they got it right. The name was quickly adumbrated.

Cicciolino didn't hear him. At the suitcase he hunkered down and waited for his eyes to adjust to the dim light. Having been trained in nearly every major police function of the NYPD, including the bomb squad, he checked it for any sign of wires or trip devices. Drug runners who dealt in quantities this large were a whole other kind of animal, he knew. They made the street gangs who pushed the shit retail look like pansies, and you never knew what you'd find. Like the VC, they even wired corpses.

Drawing in a breath and saying a quick Hail Mary, Cicciolino popped the snaps. With his fingers he raised the lid slowly, as he'd been taught. "Fuckin' *A!*" he said under his breath. He'd suspected the suitcase contained money, but the sight of stacks of thousand-dollar bills with belly bands that said "$50,000 U.S." made him feel suddenly light, tingly, and happy, as if somebody'd goosed him. His mind flooded with possibilities.

Without even having to think, he asked himself when again would he find himself alone with this much found money. You know, just another American on vacation. He had no partners, other than his old buddies. No specter of Internal Affairs. He wasn't even in an indictable jurisdiction that he knew of.

He counted twenty-four-hundred thousand-dollar bills, or $2.4 million in greenback cash. Cicciolino shook his head. Could that be right? He clapped down the lid and moved to the open door of the plane. He looked down at the runners' boat.

There was no visible life raft or skiff, although he could see stanchions off the stern. Lines to hold a jolly boat were dangling in the water. Somebody had let it down fast and split, leaving all that dope and money behind. Why? Because they were afraid of losing more. Or couldn't physically take it away. Or both.

How many of them would there be? Cicciolino counted the dead white man in the water and the other one who was splayed across the rail of the boat. Then there was the dead Indian in the boat and another sallow corpse in the doorway. Say you put a third Indian in the remains of the turret at the rear of the plane, it only made five.

Would an Indian have been flying the plane? Cicciolino didn't think so. A run like this was big time with big money, and the pilot would have had to respond to a number of air-traffic-control challenges, mainly in English. No, the pilot was the dead blond guy in the water with the bomber jacket and flight boots.

That left only one guy on the boat, which was an impossibility. The Indians would have blown him away the moment he got in the door to test the product. Even two was chancy, since the tester could be done quiet in the plane, leaving the helmsman exposed. Obviously the big white guy with no face came with the boat, but where were the other two?

He handed Gelb the money case. "Put that forward, Jay. Stand it on the seat where it can be seen." It could be *Whistler*'s ticket out of the cove, Cicciolino decided. If the runners weren't dead and were out there somewhere in the mangroves, watching them, would they risk blowing away all that money and coke? He then began passing Gelb the ten cartons of cocaine. He added the crate of fragmentation grenades and the other that was filled with 9-mm ammunition.

For a big man Cicciolino moved fluidly and well, thanks to the weights he'd been boosting since high school. He believed that packaging—your image, what other people thought you were by the way you looked—was important. Given his chunky shape, it wasn't quite *la bella figura,* but one look said don't mess, which was more valuable as a cop.

Then, Cicciolino liked the idea of looking like a million. More, he decided, he liked the idea of *being* a million, or maybe a whole bunch of millions. Why look the part when you could be it?

It came to him that easy, the decision. Cicciolino had never been one who had to think things through. He either did a thing or he didn't. It was as simple as that. If he had to think about it too much, there was something wrong, and the point was he'd already lived half his life and come up a smidge short. In the second half maybe he could make up the difference.

His family was grown, his married life with Gerri wasn't much. Face it, his fuckin' *life* was blah, and his prospects worse, since he'd gone as far as he would in the Department. Without some radical change in the ethnic makeup of New York or his connections in city hall, the big plums of bureau chief or chief of department were beyond his reach. And commissioner? Forget it.

It might have been different if his name were Sanchez or Stokes. Ricans and niggers were the future in the politics of the city and therefore the police department. But after his present assignment, which was Public Affairs, he'd be shuffled around from one nothing desk to another until he got too bored or embarrassed to show up and took early retirement. There was no sight more pitiable than an assistant chief without a staff or a viable command.

Also, in going for the brass ring, Cicciolino had been extra careful, which meant dumb. "Mr. Clean, Italian style," was the way he once heard it put when he was head of Internal Affairs. "It's the one with the hair on the bottle." And no egg in the bank. He had been too ambitious, he had wanted to get ahead, until now.

Strategy. It would all depend on how he presented his case aboard *Whistler*. For the moment they would defer to his experience, but with about a thousand pounds of the shit, he would need their help or at least their silence. Except for McCann's bimbo, Eva, Cicciolino knew them well. In Gelb's case like the palm of his hand.

"What is it?" Gelb asked.

"Whadaya mean, what is it?" Christ—how was he going to get anywhere with a guy who refused to get real? Gelb's life had been one big escape. There was the marriage with no kids, his nowhere shtick at Columbia, and fuckin' *art* photography that the wife, Arlene, said they had willingly sacrificed their lives to. With her granny glasses, no makeup, and space shoes, she looked like a refugee from a sixties time warp.

"I mean, is it cocaine?"

Cicciolino pinched some crystals out of the broken carton. He rubbed them into the palm of his hand. "You tell me, Professor."

Gelb looked down at the white powder, then glanced back toward *Whistler*.

"Forget Arlene. Fuckin' broads can take care a' themselves. Gerri?" Cicciolino shook his head. "To hear her talk, you wouldn't think men were 'uman." Gerri McCann Cicciolino was a founder of UNION, the legal-aid group that focused on women's-rights litigation. "It's enough to make you believe in the tooth fairy, some of what she says. And what about Tug? You hear the details of his divorce settlement? Deidre cleaned him out good. It's like he's got to start over from fuckin' scratch."

Gelb thought it wasn't just Arlene, it was the entire *idea* of cocaine. Gelb had once become enamored of Incan design and had studied the civilization that, some scholars claimed, had developed around coca production. He had even toyed with the idea of flying down to Cuzco or approaching one of the Hispanics who flashed little pieces of tinfoil at people coming out of the Columbia gates on Broadway.

But the *risk*. The only policeman Gelb knew was Cicciolino, and none of the undercover cops on television looked like him. And finally there was the whole question of addiction. Gelb didn't want to be addicted to any substance, not even coffee. Ever.

Gelb appreciated, however, the camaraderie that he and Cicciolino shared on vacations and at occasional ball games. It was as if they were still kids on Hester Street or, better, two grown-up guys who did manly things together. With his careful Jewish shop-keeping background, Gelb felt cheated that he had missed all the fucking around that guys engaged in. Most of his life had been spent in classrooms, studios, libraries, and darkrooms. "How do you do it?" He felt dumb even having to ask.

Cicciolino raised an eyebrow. "Since wastage isn't much of a problem here, I'll show you the cop method." He dipped the tip of his index finger in his palm, twisted his hand around, placed his thumb on one nostril and snorted the powder with the other. It was coke, all right. Pure enough to launch his skull. "We gotta be quick about this."

He held the palm out to Gelb, who was sure Arlene was watching through binoculars. She had once made herself into a perfect bitch for six months when he had taken to having a pre-dinner martini. She said she didn't care to dine with anybody who had to drug himself to enjoy his food, even though she had earlier bragged that her cowboy father had been a quart-a-day whiskey drinker. Like most ignorant people, Arlene observed a double standard: one for herself, another for the rest of the world.

Even grazing Cicciolino's palm like this, Gelb found distressing. He hadn't actually touched many men before, not even his strict, ascetic father, who had left the care of his children to his wife. It made Gelb take too much. The coke scorched up his nose and filled his head with light and pain. But his thoughts became suddenly, miraculously, marvelously clear.

There it was, coalesced into what he thought of as a microdot moment—all the reading he had done on the Incas. He remembered *everything* at once: how the word "coca" came from the Incan *khoka* and meant "divine tree." How in Incan myth "Mama-coca" was the goddess of sexual desire, a beautiful woman who was hacked to pieces by other women jealous of her power over men. The pieces were carried to the farthest reaches of the Incan empire and buried. Wherever Mama-coca was interred, the coca bush sprang up. From that time Incans of high caste were forbidden to use coca until *after* they had serviced a woman.

How *huaca* was the power that allowed a person to do something, and it resided in the coca leaf. And how, since the rulers of Cuzco had most of the power, it stood to reason that they should have most of the coca leaves stored in great, quarried stone vaults, the building of which focused the activity of their society and became the monuments of their civilization.

Gelb remembered six whole months of research in a flash— the shapes, colors, designs, even the texture and *reality* of Incan culture—which, of course, he could never experience—and it frightened him. The power, the fucking *power* of the rush.

As suddenly, however, he was a mess of tangled emotions ranging from a crushing, paranoiac fear that something huge, formless, and horrible was going to smother him soon, through the suspicion that he now had such access to the drug that his life was ruined, to the terror that the coke was just what he needed to push him over the edge.

Throughout the trip Gelb had been thinking how wonderful it would be to throw over his professorship, which was boring. He would also give up his apartment, which was small and cramped. He would even leave Arlene for somebody like the young woman, Eva Burden, whom Tug had brought with him on the trip. And finally he would buy a boat like *Whistler* and take up permanent residence here in the Islands. All it would take was a little courage. Or, now, a little powder.

But they were back at *Whistler*. Gelb felt Cicciolino's hand on his arm. "C'mon—we're not out of this yet. I'll explain when we get the stuff aboard. Tell the girls they're wanted topside, then take the helm and get us out of here."

"Is it what it looks like?" asked Tug McCann, standing at the rail, looking down at them. With a deep tan, graying brush-cut, and trim, well-exercised body, McCann looked like an aging athlete. His clipped, aquiline features were set in concern.

Cicciolino nodded and handed him the aluminum clamshell suitcase. He then began hoisting up on deck the cartons of coke, which McCann placed in *Whistler*'s cockpit without being asked.

Cicciolino could count on McCann. It had something to do with McCann's being Irish, which Cicciolino thought of as smart/dumb. He had gone to school with, worked with, and had even married Irish, and he knew that, once convinced that what they should do was smart, McCann would take dumb to the limit. In some circles it was known as a stand-up guy.

By the time the women arrived on deck, *Whistler* was moving down the cove toward the inlet and the narrow passage to the sea. There wasn't a cloud in the sky. Everything had that bright, crisp look, like a snap from a travel brochure.

Cicciolino explained what Gelb and he had discovered, including his supposition that at least two runners had left hurriedly in the skiff of the drug boat.

"It's not our fault. We couldn't have known they'd be here. But now I guess the vacation's over, and we got three things to deal with, two immediate and one long term.

"The most immediate is the runners from the boat, the ones whose bodies ain't in the wreckage. I don't know what scared them, either us or the radio that I found on in the cockpit of the plane, or something else. I don't even know if they're alive or still in the area. But that plane there—see the tail?" With his dimpled chin he gestured toward the wreckage that was still visible off the stern. "Something big, like a rocket, took that out. Problem is, there ain't no launcher or rockets aboard the boat. Conclusion?"

Cicciolino waited for their eyes to return to his. He was talking cop talk, which was meant to intimidate. This was no discussion; it was a briefing. "They're out there somewhere in a small boat. They're probably banged up and need some means of getting clear of this island before the plane's backup arrives. That means us. Also, they possess the capability of blowing us away, which is the reason I brought the dope aboard. I figure it's about a thousand pounds of cocaine.

"There's also this money." Cicciolino bent, thumbed the snaps of the case, and opened the lid for all to see. "It's two-point-four mil." He showed the array of bundled bills around, then snapped the case shut. "It's also our ticket out of here. I don't think they'd risk blowing it up, not if they think they might be able to recover it later, say, in Bimini," which was where the Gelbs—who had arranged the vacation—had chartered the yacht.

Cicciolino pulled the machine pistol from under his belt and laid it on the desk. McCann's head was now turning, scanning the mangroves that lined the shore of the cove.

"But that ain't all. I think we might have a second problem that's the same as the runners from the boat. The radio I found on in the cabin? Maybe the pilot was in contact with his base when the deal went sour. Maybe he had time to Mayday backup before he got done. What time did we see that orange flash last night, Jay?"

"Twelve. It was twelve, Bill," Gelb rapped out in a high, tight voice. He was jacked up higher than the mast peak, and Cicciolino made a mental note to get him a beer.

He checked his watch. "So—if the call went out shortly before midnight, then they've had nearly eight hours to put a search team together. Again, I don't wanna scare nobody. I don't know where they're coming from or how long it'll take them to get here. But for a load this size they're bound to mount some sort of recovery effort, and the minute they see the condition of their plane and crew, they'll be mad as hornets. So the sooner we put some miles between us and this island, the better."

Cicciolino paused to gather his thoughts for the final point, when Eva—Tug's bimbo— spoke up. "I don't understand."

"You don't understand *what?*" Cicciolino liked her tight little body and the way her eyes were the same green color as her bikini. It made her look like a kind of mermaid. Then there was her restaurant, which Cicciolino considered better than any on Mulberry Street. Also, he had a little theory about women: Those who could cook, could *cook*. His own wife could hardly boil water.

"Why, if they're looking for all of this, we've taken it with us. And why we're displaying it out here on deck. Wouldn't it have been better just to leave it where it was and get the hell out of here, fast as we can?"

Just like at press briefings, Cicciolino tried to summon his patience, his tolerance, his *empathy,* for this little blond *person* in front of him. But he was in no mood for *dumb* questions that might slow them down. The money and dope weren't just their ticket out of there, they were his passport to a worry-free retirement. Or to a bimbo just like her.

Still, he managed to soften his voice. "For the benefit of the first group of people, the two or more drug runners from the boat who are still out there somewhere. Like I said, they ain't got a boat no more, but they've got a rocket launcher. Without this stuff, they might try to stop us any way they can. You know, for *Whistler*. But now, if they've been watching, they know what we got, so a blast from a rocket is out. They won't want to blow up all their money and all this dope. If they try to run up and board us from their skiff, I'll just drop one of these down on them and see how they react." From a crate Cicciolino pulled a fragmentation grenade. He held it out to Eva and smiled.

When she averted her eyes, he dropped it back in the crate and went on. "The second group of people will be the associates of the people from the plane. I had to study deals like this, I know how they're supposed to go down. And when they don't, what happens then. Whether the wombats in the plane were independent transporters or just mules for some cartel, they or their outfit or their heirs will be held accountable for the dollar value of the dope. It's sort of like insurance, and the reason they're paid up to a third of the value of the coke for a delivery. With a load big as this, I think they'll make some attempt to get it back. They could be here any minute.

"But as soon as we're out of here, we can decide what to do."

"Which is our long-term problem," said Tug, without taking his eyes off the shoreline.

Cicciolino nodded. Leave it to Tug. He hadn't lived on his wits all these years without being quick.

"You mean—we're *keeping* the money?" Eva asked.

Cicciolino hadn't wanted to bring it up until they'd got clear. "I don't know. I don't want to look too far. That's for everybody to decide. I'll tell you one thing, though. This money won't ever see no property room or evidence impoundment. The Bahamas Defence Force is notorious, and every last thousand-dollar bill will vanish between here and Nassau. Count on it."

"What about the dope?" It was the bimbo again.

"Like I said, I don't want to see too far. Right now, we got our own use for it, which is saving our lives. If you got a problem with that . . ." Cicciolino raised his broad shoulders and let them fall.

Eva waited for him to say more. When he didn't, she shook her head and looked away.

"Something wrong, babe?"

"Yes, there is. *Just* that—it's wrong." She stood and ran her hands down her bare, tanned thighs, which cupped her shoulders.

It was a nervous gesture, but it made her look good. She flicked a hand at the dope. "I know this stuff. I've been a victim of it, and I've seen what it can do. It ruins everything it touches, and I don't want any part of it." She turned toward the companionway.

"Not even the money? Your share works out to four hundred thou."

"Keep it, if you think you should. I don't want to know." Eva's movements were quick and graceful. Placing her palms on the cabin top, she swung her legs around Gerri and disappeared down into the shadows of the boat. Gerri followed her.

That was when Arlene—Gelb's wife, who had been looking toward the bow—tilted up her granny glasses, as though trying to see something more clearly. "Bill!" she called out, and pointed toward a tall rock on a bluff that overlooked the mouth of the cove.

Cicciolino shielded his eyes. But even with the binoculars that Gelb handed him, he wasn't sure what he was seeing.

CHAPTER 4

IMMANENCE

IT WASN'T DAVID CREACH'S problem, as he stared down at *Whistler*. He knew exactly what he was seeing—some greedy sucks on a charter boat who thought it was their lucky day. He shook his head. He understood how they could be tempted, but they didn't know what they were getting into.

Fuckin' stuff, Creach thought, looking at the stumps of his fingers that he had wrapped in bandages from the first-aid kit in the jolly boat. It was best dealt with quick; the longer you handled it, the worse off it left you. Nathanson had been right; they should have quit years ago. They had held on because . . . well, because every other way of making a buck just seemed like so much boring work. They had been good at what they did, and it had been fun. Until now.

Creach parted the gauze and nudged the raw ends of his fingers into the kilo in his pocket. He had come to maybe fifteen minutes earlier. Seeing the charter boat and what was going on, he decided to get himself to a spot where he could at least control the action. He chose the outcropping of rock that looked over the inlet to the cove. Sitting with his back against a boulder, he had the launcher in his lap and two spare rockets laid out where he could reach them with his good hand. Binoculars were hanging from a strap around his neck, which was now swollen and hurt from the sliver of shrapnel he'd taken in the throat.

Even medicinally, like this, coke stung at first, then numbed you good but left you fast and wanting more. *Lord,* he thought— touching the smallest amount to each nostril to get him up for what he had to do—*take me downtown.* It was a fragment of a coke-user's prayer, the other words of which Creach couldn't remember. Only the message, which had to do with addiction and was not inspirational.

And now there was *Whistler* to deal with. Creach raised the binoculars to the bridge of his nose. So far, he'd made "Mob," the curly-headed guy with the build who seemed to be running things. "Mob" had to know something. Displaying the dope right out in the open was smart. His sidekick was "Tennis," the only other male with a gun. "Tennis" looked like an aging jock and had on a windbreaker with CCNY across the front. Creach knew what that stood for. He had sent money north so a little sister could graduate from there.

Creach also counted "Hippy," the guy at the wheel with the John Lennon glasses, and his squeeze, "Granny," who was sitting by the foremast as lookout and had pointed toward Creach. Their specs were similar. "Mom" was the older broad who hadn't done anything about her hair. She was standing in the companionway, where the young one, the blonde, had gone below. Creach decided to call her "Daughter," even though she had to be with "Tennis." He could tell because "Mob" now turned to "Mom," as though for reassurance, but she too went below.

Options. Creach could try to pull them over, but he had forty feet of shallow water between him and the channel, and short of actually getting aboard where he could grab somebody and hold a handgun to their head, it wouldn't work. He could try and put a rocket in them someplace low where they'd only sink. But then what? Some sort of standoff with him demanding the whole package and them holding out for this or that, which would piss him off. Or he could crank up the jolly boat, which he had hidden under the mangroves, and overtake them when they got out into deeper water. But they were armed, and he had Nathanson, who was now flat on his back in the boat, dying.

Finally, he could put a period in the entire fuckin' deal, blow them away. The money was in a flotation clamshell suitcase. It was tight and could take a whole bunch of abuse. Also, the coke boxes were wrapped in plastic and stuffed with Styrofoam. Some would float, and not all of it would be lost. Even if it was, at least the deal would be over.

But at what cost? Creach how asked himself. Six more lives would be lost, if he didn't lose his own. And for what? The immediate gratification of not allowing some scavengers to rip off his money. Just glancing at the registration numbers on the bow of the boat told Creach *Whistler* was from Bimini. It wouldn't take much to run them down, *after* his hand and throat had healed.

Still, Creach raised the rocket launcher to his shoulder and prepared to walk down to the water's edge. Maybe he could bluff them into jettisoning the goods. If they fired at him, well, he'd have no choice. He'd leave the decision up to them.

It was only then that he realized what he had been hearing for the last several seconds; a plane suddenly appeared, sweeping out of the sun to the east. The pilot had to bank suddenly to clear the outcropping and the masts of the schooner. The roar was deafening.

The transporter's backup, Creach thought, scuttling himself to the other side of the rock where he wouldn't be visible to the turret gunner. Banking in at that steep angle, the pilot would have been looking at the boat and not seen him. Creach faulted himself nevertheless. He should have realized what he had been hearing. It was the shit again, which let you concentrate intensely on one thing but one thing only. To the exclusion of other things that could get you killed.

The plane was a duplicate of the wreck in the cove, right down to its bug-eye cockpit and olive-drab lacquer. Creach knew what they'd do: circle around again to check things out, then land in the cove and examine the wreck. Finding no dope and no money, they'd get the plane right back up. From the air they'd blast hell out of *Whistler* to stop her and soften her up. Only then would they land and make an assault. They'd want the dope and money first, "scalps" second. They'd leave nobody alive except maybe "Daughter." Creach had heard stories of what transporters had done to vacationers who had involved themselves in their deals. They'd probably toss her out the bay door at 3,000 or 4,000 feet. *After* they were through with her.

The boat was still in the channel, maybe a hundred yards

beyond him now, struggling against wind and tide. "Mob" had everybody aboard busy, hustling the suitcase and boxes below. Too late. An experienced transport pilot would have seen the load on first pass. As Creach had thought, the plane landed, taxied up to the wreck, and an Indian jumped down into the boat. It took him only a few seconds to check things out.

But the plane didn't take off right away. Instead it moved maybe a hundred yards off the wreck, then turned so the Indian would have a clear shot from the open bay door. The rocket flashed over the surface of the cove and struck the fuel tank where the wing met the fuselage. The explosion was immediate. Against the clear blue and sunny sky, the fireball looked like a crepe-black smudge. The backup plane swung around to begin its takeoff run down the cove toward the inlet, the yacht, and Creach, who guessed they'd pass almost directly over his head.

He raised the launcher, rested the tube against the top of the rock so it was nearly vertical, and fitted his right arm and shoulder into the web sling and against the butt. He had to slip down onto his back to manage the position, but like that, he wouldn't be seen. There would be no aiming here. As the plane swept over him, he'd have to guess, release, and duck. If he was lucky, the momentum of the plane would carry the debris away from him, out onto the beach or into the water.

The plane was nearly upon him now, its engines like two gaping mouths bearing down on him. It quaked the rock under his back, until with a roar that nearly deafened him the plane rose up suddenly and veered off to catch the wind sweeping in from the inlet.

Creach fired. The rocket scorched from the shelter of rock and passed within inches of the tail. But it missed and jetted skyward in a jagged white plume. The plane powered beyond the inlet and the beach, then banked to come around on the yacht.

Had the rocket been seen? Creach didn't think so, and he crawled back around to the other side of the rock. The turret gunner had been looking down into the inlet at the yacht, which was now turning to head out into open water.

But unless the plane passed his way again, Creach could do nothing to save his money and the dope. Or the people on the yacht, who, after all, had done nothing more than anybody else would have, faced with what they'd come upon in the cove.

And the transporters in the plane were Bolivians. More to the point, the pilot could be another Romero. But where could Creach go? Down on the beach there was no cover for maybe a half-mile in either direction. They'd chop him up for sure.

When Cicciolino saw the plane bank, then square off on the boat, he felt helpless. He looked down at the 9-mm machine pistol in his hands, which was useless at that range. The slug gun? A lucky shot might do some damage, but anybody standing up would be mowed down by whatever weaponry he could see protruding from under the wings and the canopy of the turret gun—50 mm's, he guessed.

Cicciolino considered telling everybody to hop over the side and grab onto the rail opposite the direction that the plane was coming from. But there was the turret gun. The fuckers would blast them coming and going.

Hell, what had he gotten them into?

Not a thing, he decided, pulling the slug gun out of McCann's hands. "Here—I'm better with that." He had chosen, and so had they.

He pushed the machine pistol into McCann's chest. "Ge' down!" he shouted as the plane leveled out and began its killing run that would rake fire along the length of the boat, stern to bow.

At the wheel Gelb glanced back at the plane, then forward at Cicciolino. "What do you want me to do?" he asked in a calm voice that distracted Cicciolino momentarily. Gelb was a weird bastard. Cicciolino had expected him to jump over the side.

"Wait till the fire nearly hits the boat, then swing the wheel hard and get down. And remember, they got a turret gun—" was all Cicciolino managed before the guns opened up and began "walking" a pattern through the wake of the boat. The fire sent up bright spumes of silvery water that sparkled in the morning sun, until it struck the stern.

The heavy, jacketed shells thwacked into the old wood of the schooner, making it shiver and sway. Fragments and shards of deck flew everywhere. A single round split the mainmast. Another—right by Cicciolino's foot—bit through the floor of the cockpit and rang off something metallic below. The engine coughed.

Cicciolino popped up and jacked out the entire clip of the slug gun at the nose of the plane. But the withering fire continued, riddled the cabin roof, the foremast, and bow, until the plane was beyond them. Then the turret gun took over, again "walking" a pattern toward the bow, which it chopped up. What looked like a cloud of dust, slivers of wood and bits of metal burst from *Whistler*'s foredeck.

"Arlene!" Gelb shouted, but his wife was nowhere to be seen. And the plane, which was now over the beach, had begun to turn. It would come around on them again.

When the fire from the plane struck them, Eva Burden and Gerri Cicciolino were below deck. Eva was standing in the galley, trying to decide what to do—continue on to Bimini with *Whistler* or just get off while they were still close to the island.

Really. It was no act, she wasn't pretending to be pure. Dope had caused so much trouble in her life that she didn't want to be on the same boat with it. Plenty of people sailed in the Bahamas; somebody would eventually come by. After the storm and rain of the night before, there had to be some fresh water someplace, and she could live off shellfish.

Didn't she own a restaurant that served little else? She'd equip herself with a knife from the galley, and she was just about to reach for one when she heard the unmistakable whine of a plane diving at them. Cracking followed. It sounded as if somebody were taking an ax to the back of the boat.

A bullet exploded through the deck and smashed into the engine, stopping it. Others began chunking down through the cabin top. Eva knew combat from Vietnam and threw herself across the salon table, out of their path. She fell into a berth and flattened herself into the ribs of the boat, which lurched suddenly, turning to port. The cracking stopped for a moment.

The plane roared overhead, but just as Eva was about to launch herself from the berth and scramble topside, another burst of heavy fire riddled the bow of the boat. From a turret gun, she thought, like the damaged plane they had found in the cove at dawn.

Now the cabin of the boat was filled with steam and smoke. She could smell diesel fuel, hot oil, and bilge water. And she could hear the plane in the distance, snarling as it banked to come around on them again.

Eva pushed herself out of the berth. She'd get off the boat now, before it was too late. She'd find a way off the island. It couldn't be that remote. Anything was better than this, but she tripped, and in picking herself up, she saw Gerri.

The older woman was standing in the door to the master cabin. "Don't go up there. Bill was right. They're here."

A stellar explosion staggered the boat. It was the loudest single noise that Eva had ever heard. The floorboards cascaded beneath her feet, and she was knocked onto her knees. The boat shuddered and listed, while pots and pans clattered around the galley. The chimney of the lamps over the salon table had burst, and glass spangled her bare arms. Her hands and knees were cut and bleeding.

Eva no longer had to think. Fighting her way through the debris on the companionway ladder, she jerked back the hatch in time to see a large section of the plane—the nose with two men still in it—plummeting on a collision course with the stern of the schooner. Other fiery pieces were falling into the sea, as though it had been struck by a rocket.

Creach had waited until the plane began its banking turn before he fired. He figured that was when it would be closest to him and moving slower, but at the last moment the rocket dipped and slid under the belly of the plane.

Windage, he thought. The in-shore breeze would be stiff there above the mouth of the channel and had caught the rocket, forcing it down.

He slammed the final rocket into the tube, primed the arming mechanism, and decided to take the chance. He couldn't just sit there and watch those fuckin' Bolivians clean up on him again.

Turning toward the beach, he began jogging through the storm wrack of loose stones, shells, and seaweed, until he hit the hard sand. There, he sprinted into the water, pushing himself out to the depth of his chest. He wanted to get as close as he could. Also, he might be able to hide underwater, if he missed yet again and they came back for him.

But he didn't. Having to bank a second time to correct its approach, the plane passed nearly overhead. Creach loosed the rocket, which struck the belly of the fuselage, breaking the plane into four fiery parts. The wings and tail plummeted into the sea, but the nose spurted forward and, like a torpedo, skipped on two waves toward *Whistler*'s stern.

When it struck, everybody on deck went down, their legs jarred from under them by the impact. Glass from the canopy sprayed the afterdeck.

The pilot and copilot, constrained by seat belts, were sitting there stunned amid the tangle of wreckage.

Cicciolino didn't hesitate. He snatched the machine pistol from McCann and scrambled up on the taffrail for a better angle. Like a dentist with a drill, he leaned over them, pocked their upturned faces with bursts from the automatic weapon.

"The ax," he called over a shoulder to McCann. "Get me the goddamn fire ax. Under the stairs." He meant the companionway ladder.

McCann turned to Eva. "You all right?" But he didn't wait for an answer.

Snatching the ax off the cabin wall, he passed it to Cicciolino, who began hacking at the smashed metal, trying to disengage the plane from the boat.

Inside the twisted cage of the plane canopy the wounds of the two stiffs looked like dozens of red, oozing eyes staring up at him. Letting out a roar of frustration—at the complication of the damage to the boat; at having to commit himself so early to violence—Cicciolino swung again and again, loading all his strength into each blow.

Finally the tangled mass, groaning over the wood of the stern, quit the boat, taking with it a smashed section of rail.

Gelb appeared at Cicciolino's side and peered down into the water. It looked like the battered, decapitated head of some huge fish, sliding back into the sea. "What do we do now? The auxiliary's gone. One mast is split. I don't know what-all might be wrong with the hull."

Cicciolino didn't know himself. He straightened up and looked around. *Whistler* was a mess. It looked as if somebody had taken a pickax to the deck and cabin top. A crack of white wood spiraled the mast, and they were drifting toward shore.

His eye caught on something in the surf—the little nigger with the rocket launcher, who was now making his way toward the beach. He was dangerous. Cicciolino didn't want him coming back on them, now that they were stopped and would need to make repairs.

He pushed by Gelb, ejected the spent crescent clip, and grabbed up another. Pushing it up into the machine pistol, he raised the weapon to take aim. The nigger was maybe seventy-five yards away, pushing through the surf toward the shore.

"But didn't he help us?" Gelb asked. "But for him we'd—"

But Cicciolino cut him off. "I have to explain everything? He don't give a shit about us. All's he wants is the money and the dope. He wouldn't a taken the plane out, 'less he thought he could. Later."

Cicciolino sighted him in, allowing for distance and windage. He'd have to get him on the first burst. Guy'd only have to flop in the water to hide, and they had to get away from the island quick. The plane could have been one of several.

Cicciolino squeezed off the full clip, holding the gun tight and patterning the burst to saturate the area around the nigger. He went down right away, and not—Cicciolino judged—because of the report, which would have reached him last. With a fresh clip, he waited, but the guy was just no place, and Cicciolino figured he'd got him.

Turning to Gelb, he said, "Drop an anchor and see about the mast. I don't care how, just get us out of here quick."

Cicciolino began to move toward the companionway to see what damage they had taken below, when he found Arlene in front of him. She was soaking wet, her glasses were off, and she looked . . . fetching, which was the first time Cicciolino had thought of her like that.

She was a tall woman with deep red hair and starburst gray eyes. "Bill," she cooed. "You know Eva?"

'Course he knew Eva, for fuck's sake.

"She slipped over the side."

Confused, Cicciolino looked down at her dripping clothes and realized Arlene had big, well-formed tits. Jesus, he was horny; action did it to him everytime. In Nam he'd come back from the field and spend three days in a cathouse.

"I was in the water myself, holding on to the rail, and she dived right over my head. There she is."

Cicciolino followed Arlene's finger and saw the little blonde in the surf, digging toward the shore. "The fuck she doing there?"

"I think she's abandoning ship."

"*What? Why?*" Turning, he bawled, "Tug!"

McCann didn't know why either, but he said, "We can't just leave her."

"But we should," said Arlene. She had found her glasses again and was standing with Gerri, who was noticeably shaken. "That plane. It could be one of several. I think we have to think of ourselves. First."

Arlene, *baby,* Cicciolino thought. She was as cool as she looked, but McCann vetoed her point.

"No, Jesus! She's scared, is all. Terrified. Could she be hurt?" He glanced at Gerri.

"I don't think so, but—" Gerri glanced toward the companionway, out of which a steamy diesel-fuel funk was now spewing.

It was no time for indecision. "Tug—pull in the whaler and we'll go get her. Jay?" he called out to Gelb, who was on the foredeck deploying an anchor. "If you get this thing up and running, don't wait for us. Just go. Tug and I'll catch up to you."

"But what's our destination?"

"Bimini, of course." Cicciolino had already worked out several approaches to dealing with T. J. Monroe, who owned *Whistler,* and to getting the shit north. They might have to jink and jibe a bit, but the general details were in place.

If he could get the others to *cruise* along; he figured it would be the operative word.

By the time they reached the shallows and pulled the whaler through the pounding surf up onto the beach, Eva had vanished. All they could see were footprints leading into the tangled foliage.

McCann plunged in, but rubbery vines snagged and netted him, and he kept stepping into sudden sinkholes, once up to his waist. After a couple hundred yards he lost her footprints, and he had had enough. Christ, where could she have gone to in this stuff? "Eva!" he called out. *"Eva!"*

Cicciolino eventually caught up. "Look—we're getting nowhere. Let's walk up the beach. That way we can call out for her *and* keep an eye on the whaler. We don't want to have to swim."

Anything sounded better to McCann, and they discovered a duny area from which they could survey most of the horseshoe-shaped island.

There she was, walking along the beach on the other side of the narrow island about two hundred yards away. The wind was blowing in her direction, and when McCann called out, her head turned to them.

"Eva—come on back. It's all over. We're gonna leave." He tried to wave her in.

She only turned and began running away from them, up the beach.

McCann started after her, but Cicciolino called out. "You faster than her?"

McCann was. They had jogged together.

"You think you can make up all that distance?"

Eventually he would, and he owed her that much. He had to try.

"What happens when she ducks back into the undergrowth?"

McCann was running now, and he found he could sprint on the hard-packed sand at the fringe of the plunge step.

What did he know about her? Little, which was how he preferred his relations with women since his divorce. He had had too much . . . intimacy in his life, and now that his family was grown, he preferred to keep his relationships light. And fun. After a couple of dates when Eva had said she just couldn't see herself getting romantically involved again with a man, *"ever,"* McCann had decided she was just the girl for him.

He had met her at O'Casey's, his favorite haunt just off Madison Avenue near the business he owned; her daughter was attending a private school a few blocks away, and sometimes Eva would have lunch there. McCann flirted with all pretty women, but there was something about her diminutive good looks and angular body that had attracted him right off. Just ten years younger than he, she had an interesting oval face and unlikely green eyes. McCann glanced at the azure water he was passing.

There was the space between her front teeth, and her smile seemed to suggest that she knew his secret, which was that he liked her a lot. After a few fleeting conversations he asked her name, which he put in the pool for the Monday Night Game. She—or, rather she and he—won, but when she refused to take her half, the other guys at the bar insisted he take her to dinner. She refused. "Lunch?" Not lunch either.

It became a running joke that she refused his every advance, until one day she asked *him* out. He could tell his friends envied him her small, tight, angular body, but he also found her to be good company. First there was the restaurant that she owned in Soho. Though small and out-of-the-way, it served fantastic dishes, and he could always get a table for a particularly important client. Also, Eva was cheerful, agreeable, intelligent, and fun to be with both in and out of the sack. He could take her anywhere. She knew how to behave, she did not judge, and she fit in with his friends, high and low. Until today.

She was about seventy yards away now. "Eva!" he yelled.

She ran faster.

Sure, the whole episode had been terrifying, but the other women had come through it all right. McCann didn't know enough about her to understand why she'd freaked.

And Jesus, she was running toward a big clump of slimy sea grass that grew down to the water and covered the beach for maybe fifty feet.

McCann stopped. He had bare feet, and he didn't want any part of that gunk. "Eva!" he roared. "Come back! It's all over, they're gone. We gotta leave now. Eva!"

She didn't turn her head, and was gone in the brush.

Back with Cicciolino, McCann said, "Christ, Chick—we just can't leave her."

"No? I don't see we got a choice. Those people with the planes—they come back, we won't stand a chance. When we get to Bimini, we'll tell the authorities about her. They'll send a boat. She'll be all right," and we'll be gone. With everything, he meant. With Tug he didn't think he had to say it; since kids they had been on the same wavelength.

"Yeah?" asked McCann, hoping to be convinced. But he wasn't. "If we're being honest here, I gotta tell you I don't care how much it is, or can be. It makes me feel low, running out on her."

"Whadaya talkin' here? Who ran out on who?"

"You know what I mean."

"I do? Don't I got eyes? Didn't I just see her sprinting up the beach like a fuckin' gazelle? There's a lot in life you can't know about. And can't control."

McCann only shook his head and looked back to see if he could catch sight of her again.

"And you, of all people, should know about luck. Tell me I'm wrong. Tell me we ain't been hit here. Big time."

McCann was an inveterate gambler, or rather, a smart, lucky inveterate gambler. Even what he did for a living—paper brokering—was like gambling, and he was good at it.

"The cops got patrol boats. You saw them in Bimini. They can't have tourists coming down here without providing something for emergencies. Hey—I know about these things. It's my business, right? People get lost all the time, one reason or another." And permanently, which would be most convenient.

After Eva watched the whaler leave the island, she searched for a source of fresh water, which, she imagined, would be her primary need. The cove and bay would be filled with oysters, clams, mussels, and crabs.

But all she could find among the pocked and pitted ridges of corral and calcareous marl were fetid pools teaming with little fish and worms, and the thought of actually drinking from one repelled her.

And bugs. They were everywhere: flies, stinging gnats, mosquitoes in swarms that made her swat at her arms and legs, her head, her face. They didn't give her a minute's rest until she actually ran down to the shore and threw herself into the surf, where she remained for most of the sunlit hours.

Around dusk, before the sharks would enter the shallow waters of the bay for the carnage from the plane, she climbed around the outcropping of rock and moved toward the cove. There, mangroves, growing away from the bank toward the sun, had created a long, shadowed tunnel beneath which she discovered clumps of mussels and beds of oysters, some the size of her hand. Now if she could only find something sharp and hard, like a piece of metal, to open them. She was famished, not to mention parched in spite of her afternoon-long immersion.

But turning a corner where the foliage was most dense, she was startled to find a small boat. In it was the small black man who had saved them with the rocket and another, large white man. In shock or coma, only the sclerae of the black man's eyes were visible. One hand was wrapped in gauze. There was a puncture wound in his throat, and his thigh was bloody.

The white man, having heard her gasp, opened his eyes. He

had a blonding Vandyke, and his mane of curly hair was also bleached from the sun. There was something jagged sticking from his side, which somebody had tried to wrap in gauze. The entire area was covered with white powder, through which blood had seeped and dried.

His eyes were glassy, his voice weak. "You alone?"

She didn't know how to answer; his right hand was gathered loosely around the grip of an assault rifle.

"Can you take us out of here? It's far, but I can direct you. A couple hours. Maybe three. Don't worry, we won't—" He tried to laugh, but it came out as a wet cough. Blood appeared on his lower lip. "If you don't, we'll die." He paused to gather breath. "If you don't, you'll die."

CHAPTER 5

CRUISING

◆

It took Cicciolino and McCann an hour of hard pounding in the whaler to overtake *Whistler,* which had set off without them as per Cicciolino's order.

Gelb had lashed two oars and a short spar to the mainmast, and with a thirty-two-mile-an-hour breeze driving them from the port quarter, the battered boat sailed as well as she ever had.

Once aboard, Cicciolino asked McCann to take the wheel, and he turned to Gelb, who because of his sailing abilities would now become the key man, if he could be convinced to cruise along. "Well, Cap'—shall we make a survey?"

Gelb liked the sound of that, Cicciolino could tell, and he imagined Gelb's share of the money in the suitcase alone would change his life. He hadn't thought about it before, but the Gelbs had probably been stretched all of their adult lives, which might explain why they were childless.

First they'd gone to graduate school forever, it seemed, getting one worthless degree after another. Once, when scanning Arlene's résumé, Cicciolino had pointed to something she'd got at some university in England. "What's a B. Litt.?" It sounded like something chemical companies did to flies. "It's a Bachelor of Letters," she had replied. "But I thought you already had a bachelor's degree." She had nodded. "And you went back and got *another*?" They were living in the same city, but not the same world.

Next came the succession of no-pay, low-pay university jobs: teaching assistant, adjunct professor, and finally the litany of lousy salaries on the tenure track for Jay but not Arlene. During her political phase she had pissed off some important academic. No recommendations for her, and therefore no appointments and no career. Even as a full professor at Columbia, Gelb couldn't be pulling down more than sixty a year, which was bare subsistence for two in Manhattan. And it was an open secret that Arlene's ginchy photo gallery was scarcely breaking even.

Gelb showed him the engine first, which was destroyed. A fifty-millimeter round had bucked through the afterdeck and shattered the cylinder head. Likewise the table in the main salon had been split, several of the cabin-framing pieces were broken, and the mast step of the foremast had suffered some damage. Miraculously, however, the hull remained unbreached. It was work, constantly altering the configuration of sails to allow for fluctuations in the strength and direction of the wind, but as the afternoon progressed, they made time.

Below decks Arlene and Gerri cleaned up the damage, while Cicciolino and McCann under Gelb's direction pulled out an inventory of old, blown-out sails that they spread over the visible bullet holes topside, as though drying canvas after the storm. The radio had been knocked out, so they could keep only a visual watch for planes, and they agreed on a contingency plan of evacuating to the more mobile whaler, should they be attacked again.

But with every passing hour the likelihood of being stopped grew more remote. They saw three planes in the distance—one suspiciously low and dark—but none ventured in their direction, and at around sundown, when by Gelb's estimate they were some thirty miles west of Bimini, they began to relax.

Dinner was served on the afterdeck, another passing yacht hailed them and they waved, and they ate greedily, ravenously, almost in silence. All seemed to be playing over the details of the day and pondering what had happened to them and why, except for Cicciolino, who had moved on to the next step in his plan. The best-case scenario required a firm commitment from each and every one of them, which might be hard to get. Failing that, he at least needed their silence.

"I don't know about you guys, but I think the worst is over. I'm going to have a 'smash,' " He stood. "Anybody else?"

Four hands were raised, and McCann said, "Jay—let me spell you at the wheel again. You've been great, and you must be beat."

"Yeah . . ." Cicciolino echoed, picking up a handful of dishes as he made his way down the ladder. "What you doin' up at Columbia anyways? You ought to get yourself a boat and come down here. Do the Hemingway bit. Didn't he write a book about an artist who lived here in the Islands? George C. Scott played in the picture, I remember right."

Gelb preened, and Cicciolino saw him glance over at Arlene, as if for her approval. She smiled, and Gelb did too, which confirmed Cicciolino's opinion of who ran things—even emotional reactions—between the Gelbs.

Back up on deck with a pitcher of strong drinks, Cicciolino poured five glasses and took his to the rail, where he looked out at the stars that had begun to appear in the east. After the heat of the afternoon, the wind was now pleasantly cool. All they could hear was the wind soughing past the foil of the sails and the heartbeat regularity of *Whistler*'s hull thumping through the waves.

Cicciolino waited for the rum to work its magic. As usual Gelb, who seldom drank, spoke first. "Did it actually happen? If it weren't for details like this"—stretched out against the cabin trunk, he was playing an index finger into one of the holes that the 50-mm guns had gouged from the deck—"I'd think of it as a dream. You know, a kind of—"

Adventure of a lifetime, the others supplied for themselves.

"I mean, how would you even go about telling somebody what happened? But, of course—"

With $2.4 million dollars on the line, you wouldn't.

"And the crazy part is with all the spectacular and"—Gelb swirled his glass, searching for a word—"*stunning* violence, none of us got hurt. Those who did were—"

Drug runners, and deserved what they got, the others filled in.

"I don't know. It was all so bizarre. So . . . Hemingwayesque, like Chick suggested earlier."

Even to the payoff.

"Anybody for another drink?" Standing, Gelb staggered a bit before moving toward the companionway.

"What about Eva?" Gerri asked.

Leave it to her to think of the down woman, Cicciolino mused. "What about her?"

"Will she be all right?"

"What—for a day, maybe two? Sure, why not? Isn't seafood her bag? And then, didn't you tell me she used to be some kind of hotshot nurse, Tug?"

McCann nodded. "A physician's assistant."

"Which is what?" Arlene asked.

Said Cicciolino, "Closes up operations. Emergency med care. Outpatient surgical procedures. Way I understand it, some of them babes are better than most doctors."

They listened to the wind and the waves for a while longer.

"I mean, mentally. Psychologically. She must be terrified."

Cicciolino saw his opening to soften any misimpression they might have formed after the action in the bay. "I don't want this to sound unmanly or nothin', but I think maybe we all were."

McCann's laugh was quick and nervous, but it broke the ice. He said, "I'm glad *you* said that, Mr. Wayne. Me—I was *petrified*. Jesus, what must combat be like?"

Cicciolino, who had seen combat, said, "I think you saw it, soldier."

Gerri interrupted. "No, I mean to have just jumped over like that. Sure, she was terrified, but what must she have been thinking about, what must have been going on in her mind to want to just escape into . . . nothing? Being alone on that island—now that, to me, would be *truly* terrifying. Not that what we went through wasn't, it's just, as Jay said, we—"

Got away with everything, Cicciolino thought.

Gelb reappeared on deck with another pitcher of drinks. "Maybe it had something to do with her father. Didn't she tell us he was in prison?"

"And that her husband had been murdered," Arlene chimed in. "Tug, where do you come up with these people? The one before her you picked up on a plane. She was a stewardess, if I remember correctly."

And a sword swallower in her free time, thought Cicciolino. Tug had all the luck.

"But still—to be so frightened that she could just watch us sail away." Gerri shook her snowy head. "That takes guts."

"Or something," Arlene said.

"I just hope she'll be all right. Up until then she seemed so . . . normal, in spite of. . . ." Murder and prison, she meant.

"Finish what you got in your glass first," Gelb said, before pouring the women refills. "I'm not going to be the only one smashed here."

"Aye, aye, Captain Bligh," said Gerri, who, like Gelb, had a capacity that could be measured in thimbles. Gelb hadn't finished with McCann's glass before she asked, "What are the figures again?"

"A' what?"

"You know—what we found on the boat. Just for interest's sake. Who'll get it now?"

Cicciolino straightened up. "Wait a minute—the money or the stuff? I thought we were agreed on the money. It's just going to disappear if we turn it in, and there's no sense in giving some lucky nigger cop or politician a spectacular payday he don't deserve. The people who claimed to own it are dead. Now it's up for grabs. We didn't ask for it, but—hey—because of it we had to defend ourselves. We put our asses on the line back there on that island. I don't think it's stretching things to say we could as easily be dead now."

Cicciolino waited, and when nobody said no, he went on, "So much for the money, which is two-point-four mil. Split three ways, that breaks down to eight hundred thou, tax free. If any of yous don't want your part, tell me. I'll take it myself."

It was the fish Cicciolino was throwing McCann. With Eva gone, five shares was fairer, but McCann's participation would be crucial later. Cicciolino respected his savvy. McCann knew the city and had connections, people who could and would do him favors and keep quiet, and Cicciolino would need a "beard" to carry the thing off successfully, once they got it back to New York. "Minus whatever it'll take to satisfy Mr. T. J. Monroe."

"The other part—the stuff—we can do three things with. One, dump it. Two, turn it over to the authorities, who might just finger who we are to the runners and give the police a huge *mothah* of a payday. Three, we can get rid of it ourselves. Compared to what we could get for it, the money—two-point-four million bucks—is like chump change. Say the cartons weigh a hundred pounds apiece. It's better than that, but say a hundred. That's around a thousand pounds of product, which breaks down to roughly four-hundred-and-forty kilos. Down here in the Islands the price is around five thousand per kilo. In New York it's fifteen grand for a clean, no-nonsense, hello–good-bye deal. And that's what? Another six-point-six million, if my arithmetic is right.

"Done another way—say, shares with some midlevel dealers, who'll step on it two, three times, it could be more." And yet another way, $250,000 a kilo or $125 million. But figures like that scared people, and there'd already been too much publicity about crack, as far as Cicciolino was concerned. People had been doing free base for years. "And I'm talkin' *real* here. It happens every day. I know the guys. I know how it's done. And we wouldn't get caught."

Cicciolino watched his wife's tanned brow furrow, and he raised a palm, staying her. He had his summation left. After that the others could have the floor, say anything they wanted. The reality of the situation was in the boxes in the forward cabin, and he already knew what he was going to do, Gerri or no Gerri, with or without the others.

Except for his youngest daughter, who was so severely retarded she needed full-time supervision, his family was grown and gone, and Gerri with all her causes and so forth had turned into a sullen—kind of mannish, even—bitch. He couldn't remember when they last, you know, *really* got laid. All that kept them together was Karen, and would all that money be good for Karen? It would make sure she—his own flesh and blood—would never have to undergo the indignities of public institutional care, which was like jail, and something he, *not Gerri,* knew about.

"Look, we talked about it the other night at Arlene's birthday." The day that the sailing holiday had begun, Arlene had turned forty-three. The men were forty-eight. Gerri was fifty-one. "Life is short. We blinked, and here we're fifty. If we've learned anything, it's opportunities like this don't come around too often. What am I talkin' here—they don't come around for most people. Ever. It's like hitting the lottery. This is our lottery. It's staring us in the face. If you can't see it, it's your business, and I'm not going to try and change your minds.

"Way I look at it, if people want dope, they're gonna get it, one way or another. And don't think the government, *our* government, ain't in on it. In Vietnam all you had to be was an *anticommunist* drug dealer, and you were immune from prosecution. In South America with the Contras it was the same. The shit I seen? Scumbags let off for reasons of national security or some ongoing investigation. The CIA. Some CENTAC or other. And all the while they're telling us, 'Just say no to drugs.' If they wanted, they could stop it. Meanwhile, what am I—a one-man revolution?"

Cicciolino took a sip from his glass. He was standing with a leg braced against the taffrail, a hand on a shroud. He looked out to sea. "Far as I'm concerned, it's just chaos out there, smoothed over with all sorts of bullshit telling you it ain't. Look at the fuckin' Kennedys, for crissake. How holy they became, once they got theirs. It's the reason they got whacked. Their old man—Joe—scored with the Mob, bootlegging out of Cuba during Prohibition. Booze was the cocaine of their time. Thirty years later his kids forgot and went after the guys their old man had made money with. They had to be reminded of their past.

"Alls I know, this is a kind of crossroads in our lives. And if at fifty we ain't learned nothin'—hey—we don't deserve to be flush."

Cicciolino finished his drink, then turned and faced the others. "Now I want you should know, so you understand. I do this thing"—again he glanced at Gerri, but he couldn't read her face—"I do it with my eyes open. I'm no dope dealer, and the reputation I got for being straight is right. I never considered any other way till now, and after this goes down—hey—I'm out of the Department. Out of law enforcement. The works. I quit, I retire. End of career.

"Then Gerri and me got Karen to think of." Cicciolino watched his wife's chin fall to her chest. She looked down into her glass. "One thing I learned—you don't take care of you and yours, nobody else will. Not in New York. Not where we live."

He was quiet for a while, and the others respected his silence. Finally he added, " 'Course, this is nothing that should be decided like this, after a big day. But in the morning I'll need to know."

*   *   *

After a while Tug McCann spoke up, "Just *how* would we go about it? What would we have to do?"

Cicciolino smiled. "That's the pretty part. Not much. I don't want to go into details right now, but the three of us would kick in, get ourselves another boat in Bimini, and put it in Jay's name. He's the sailor, and he'd keep it as, you know, a perk. We'd also have to deal with Monroe, but the rest would be just a long sail to New York. How long you think it'd take to get ourselves north, Jay?"

"Inside or out?" By inside Gelb meant the Inland Waterway, a system of estuaries, canals, and bays that traced the shoreline of the eastern United States. Out meant the ocean.

"Which would be safest?"

Gelb tried to think. "Once we got in, probably in. But cutting in farther north would probably be safer."

"How 'bout Long Island Sound? How long that take?"

Gelb didn't know. It would depend on the boat and the wind and any problems they might have, and the second drink had hit him hard. He felt dizzy and tired, as though his blood had suddenly sludged. Just the thought of another day like this nearly made him nauseous. Gelb wanted most to get to someplace quiet and dark—his berth, preferably—where he might play over all that had happened and how it might have changed him. At the same time he was intrigued by the possibility he might soon own a yacht capable of sailing to and from the Islands. And the $800,000! Christ—did Arlene and he need that? It was almost too much to contemplate. "Two or three weeks out. A month in."

"After that, I won't need much. Some arms and legs. A few phone calls. A meet. Maybe a pickup and delivery. Like I said, once we get it there, I know what to do.

"Whadaya say, Jay? You in?" Without him they'd have trouble getting the stuff there, and Cicciolino would probably have to devise some other plan.

Gelb didn't know what to say. It was too much to take in, much less decide, and hadn't Cicciolino said they could wait until the morning? Gelb now needed sleep desperately. He set the glass on the deck, glanced up at McCann as though for help, then turned his face into the breeze, hoping it would revive him.

"Well, you can count me in, Chick, regardless of what Jay

decides." It was Arlene; every head turned to her. "I don't expect an equal share. I know you'll be taking most of the risk, and without your knowledge of how things work, it probably wouldn't be possible. But I think you'll find me useful. I'm brave, and often women can go places and do things men can't. Also, I'm part of this thing. They shot at me too. I want in."

Gelb was stunned. And floored, when she announced almost—was it?—insouciantly, "I've never liked New York. Not from the very first day. I wanted to be an artist, and New York was where artists went to show their work. I think that was what I liked most about Jay, when I met him in Albuquerque. He was from New York. I'd never really met anybody from New York, and he seemed so . . . different.

"But now that I'm pregnant, I don't want my child raised there. This is my chance to get out, to go back to New Mexico where I belong. You offered, and I'll take you up. I think you'll find me more—what is that military term?—*resourceful* than you imagined. One of the first things my father taught me was how to shoot a gun. I can help you." Feeling a strand of hair straying in the breeze, Arlene raised her arms and tucked it back into her bun. "I will, if you'll let me."

"Good, I can use you. And will."

Gelb watched Cicciolino's eyes play over Arlene's breasts and move down the rest of her body. Gelb glanced down at the empty glass that felt almost hot in his hand. It was like a one-two punch. First, that she'd never really loved him for himself. Ever. All along it had more to do with his being from New York and, as she had said, *different.* Did that mean Jewish?

And *pregnant?* When could it have happened? He tried but couldn't remember any specific recent occasion. They hadn't had sex in months.

Said Gerri, "But aren't you concerned about children, or at least your own child, and what the stuff might do—"

"Frankly no." Arlene's tone was almost cheery. "I think Chick was right in what he suggested earlier. We're back to Social Darwinism and the survival of the fittest. If we ever left it, it was in *words* only, and the *stuff,* as you call it, has only made things clearer. You know, the quick and the dead. Wouldn't it be downright ignorant not to take the lesson? And here I'm very much thinking of the children—especially yours and mine. They're going to need that money. In the next century it'll be necessary to be rich."

Gerri shook her head. "But isn't that a jaundiced and simplistic view of things?"

"It's a jaundiced and simplistic society. Even UNION recognizes that. It's why you go to court and fight issues on a case-by-case basis. Goodwill, moral suasion, trust?" Arlene expelled some air between her large lips. She had a wide mouth and big, well-formed teeth. "Nothing works but law, and only when penalties are enforced."

Slowly Gerri stood and, placing a hand on the small of her back, straightened up. "I don't know. It's late and I'm tired. I'm going to bed." But she stopped in front of her husband. "I *think* I understand why you're doing this."

"Karen," he said.

"Whatever." She looked away, as though she really didn't believe him. "But don't expect any help from me. I'll keep my mouth shut because you're my husband, Tug is my brother, and Arlene and Jay are friends. But I hope you've thought this through. You know, what it'll mean, if . . ." If it goes wrong.

"It won't just be a crime. Given how visible we are, it'll be a scandal from which nothing and nobody—not UNION, not our other kids, not even Karen—will recover. We'll lose everything, and you and she will find out about state institutions firsthand."

"But it won't." Cicciolino reached for her shoulder, but she moved away from him and went below.

They had raised Bimini. Gelb caught sight of a navigation beacon at the southern tip of the island, and summoning his last reserve of strength, took the wheel. The trick would be to find an anchorage that contained other boats, but far enough from the harbor that customs would not be likely to board them. And all without auxiliary power in the dead of night.

A mile or two from the Alice Town Harbour breakwater, Gelb noticed a spray of white thirty-two-point lights that turned out to be a flotilla of yachts at anchor near the beach of a resort hotel.

"Didn't we anchor here before?" McCann asked, as Gelb studied the chart and searched for a buoy or a can to guide them in. "Remember, maybe six, seven years back? Deidre got food poisoning, and we got her a room there."

And under the guise of the caring husband, you played every skirt at bar, Gelb thought. Even got yourself a second room for action. Like a sudden hazard in the water, Arlene's pregnancy flashed into his consciousness. And her infidelity.

Nevertheless, Gelb discovered the channel, and then, playing *Whistler*'s split mainmast and sails against both wind and a swift, countervailing current, he managed to ease the schooner into the anchorage among the other boats. There, scarcely making way, Gelb doused sail quickly, waited for the current to halt the boat's momentum and begin backing her up. Only then did he signal McCann to drop the hook, which held.

Other sailors on a nearby boat, not knowing the *Whistler*'s auxiliary engine was out, thought it an act of nautical brio and began clapping. On any other occasion Gelb would have reveled in their applause, but he felt terrible. It was without a doubt the worst day of his life when—a little voice was telling him—it should be the best. When was the last time somebody gave him $800,000, offered him the promise of much more, and his wife said she was pregnant?

Problem was, he'd probably be too dead to enjoy it. Or, worse, in prison. Gelb could never put up with prison. He valued his freedom and his—could it be?—lifestyle, as presently lived, too much to put up with any change even remotely resembling fucking jail and the notoriety that would go along with it. Then there was homosexuality and AIDS.

What about *Whistler* and the dream he'd had of throwing everything over and taking off? It was just that—a dream. Gelb needed other people, he couldn't exist without them. They even made his decisions for him, and always had. He remembered suddenly how Arlene and he got married. He said he was going back to New York; she said she was going with him; her father said they'd have to get married first.

The pregnancy, the *baby*? Even thinking about it was painful, and he knew for sure it wasn't his, but that didn't matter either. What mattered was that the marriage was still an actuality. They had shared over twenty years of their lives together. He couldn't see himself getting married again; his wife was pregnant, and the baby would need a father. He told himself that in at least one major way the situation was better than any other possible scenario. He had been spared having to decide that he would become a father.

Below deck, he tripped over one of the cartons of cocaine. Reaching out to locate their position, his hands fell on the open box. Why not, he thought, listening to Arlene's steady breathing no more than a few feet from him. What did he have to lose?

Like a fuse, the powder smoked up his nostril and burst in his head in a vivid flash. Dusting the other nostril, he thought:

When the Spaniards discovered that their Indian slaves could work for days on nothing but coca leaves, they began substituting it for food. Coca was plentiful and cheap. A wild shrub, it grew everywhere along the high slopes of the eastern Andes from present-day Colombia through Peru, Bolivia, Ecuador, and Argentina to Chile. It was estimated that when around 1500 the Spanish arrived in the Andes region there were some 10 million Indians. By 1572 there were no more than 2 million, much of the decline attributable to the malnutrition brought on by coca abuse.

Arlene was calling out in her sleep. When Gelb moved closer to hear what she was saying, she took hold of him. With a deftness that seemed remarkably practiced, she quickly had him out of his swim trunks and in her hands, her mouth, and finally into her deep.

She rolled him over and crushed him against *Whistler*'s ribs. "Oh, Cal," she called out. *"Cal!"*

PART II
NUMBER ONE

CHAPTER 6

CLAIM MANAGEMENT

◆

Medellín, Colombia

WHEN BY NOON of the next day Pachito Londoño Vasquez still
had not heard from the brothers Romero, he began to make phone
calls.

First he phoned the airport in Remedios, ninety miles northeast of Medellín. A contact on the Compañia payroll told him no
TU-454 with Bolivian markings had touched down there today.
Nor had any plane from Pando Provincial Airways made radio
contact with the tower. Presently he had nine aircraft on the scan-
ner, none of which had indentified itself as Pando.

Next Londoño phoned another source in Teléfono Colombi-
ano and gave her the Romeros' number in Bolivia. Since the phone
systems in both countries were primitive, he had to hang up and
wait. Londoño was concerned, but he was not yet worried. The
storm, which had been predicted, or some other problem might
have grounded the *transportadores'* plane. He had known it to
happen before in the six years that he had been an associate of

what he and his colleagues called Medellín & Compañia and the rest of Colombia referred to simply as "the mafia."

Problem was, this was no Compañia shipment, but rather a deal that Londoño had fronted himself. Through hard bargaining that had resulted in a deep discount, he had bought excess Compañia product, that had had no buyer, and arranged a deal with a wholesaler in the Bahamas by the name of Nathanson. He had dealt with him before.

The *transportadores,* however, were another matter. The complaints about the Romeros ranged from light delivery weights to coke that had been reprocessed and cut. Londoño had tried to find some other deliverer in time with no luck. It was either Pando Provincial or no deal. Nathanson said timing was essential for *his* buyer on the other end. If Londoño couldn't do it, he'd go to somebody else.

Instead Londoño had put the Romeros on notice. He told the older one, Gerardo, that the run was a test, that they were on probation with the Cartel to prove they could deliver pure product on time as arranged. The man had insulted him. He said maybe Londoño was a mafioso, but if the deal were truly mafia business, the mafia would have used mafia transporters. And if Londoño was a mafioso, he was a small mafioso. Big mafiosos made big money, and didn't have to resort to side deals, such as this.

"And get something else straight—you threaten us again in the name of the mafia, I go straight to the *pesces gordos.* Don Pablo and me go way back." He meant Pablo Escobar Gaviria, who was the biggest of the three big fish and the acknowledged head of the Medellín Cartel. Londoño didn't doubt what he said. Escobar had begun his career as a pimp and a petty thief, and Romero sounded just the type.

More to the point, Romero had spoken the truth. Londoño was truly a small mafioso. He needed the money to pay the mortgage on his family's *finca* in the country. He had thought if he could only get through this one deal, the $2 million or so he'd get from it would at least buy some time. Finca Los Llanos had been in his family since the sixteenth century, and was perhaps the premier gentleman's working estate in all of Antioquia. But over a forty-year period, his father had squandered just about $11 million on horses, women, and a costly search for emeralds. The notes were long-since due.

Londoño touched a button on the console by his desk and asked his maid to bring him a *tinto,* the strong, dark coffee that Colombians drink throughout the day. He carried it out to the balcony of his Medellín pied-à-terre that overlooked the city, but he had only raised the cup to his lips when the phone rang.

"Señor Londoño?" said the operator. "Your party in Bolivia answers but keeps hanging up."

"Did you tell him who it is?"

"I think that's why he's hanging up. He says not to bother him, he's expecting an *important* call."

"Well, try it again. And *keep* trying until you get him. Tie up the line if you have to. Remember, we *pay* you." Now he was worried, and that he again had to threaten somebody with his tenuous connection to la Compañía filled Londoño with shame.

If nothing else worthwhile, Pachito Londoño had been taught by his father to be proud no matter what. Even in his decline, when his reputation and habits had made him such a ruin that people had begun calling him facetiously "Don" Pacho, his father had at least maintained his sense of self. He didn't change one iota. And something he never permitted was people stealing from him. Not a centavo.

The phone rang again, and when Londoño picked it up, a drunken voice said, "*Hijo de puta,* you're in my hair. I got two planes, two crews, and my brother out there somewhere. Maybe down, maybe dead. And you want what?"

"My money."

"Your *money,*" Romero said sarcastically. "Is that all you Antioqueños think of?" He meant the people who had settled the Departmento de Antioquia, of which Medellín was the capitol. They were known as the Yankees of South America, and had the reputation of being aggressive, hardheaded businessmen who held their money closely.

Londoño leaned back in his desk chair, and stared up at the ceiling that needed paint. The entire apartment—which at least was his and not nominally his father's—had become so shabby that he could no longer have people in, not even a woman. He had to take them to hotels where he could charge the cost of a decent room and worry about paying later. He was no longer a man, he decided, but a juggler, passing debts from one hand to another, then tossing them up in the air into a financial limbo, hoping they'd go away. Every couple of months they fell back on him, heavier each time. Even the $500,000 for this deal he had had to borrow. La Compañía no longer extended him credit. He had to pay for everything up front.

Half a mil would break him. He'd have to get his father—who, like old evil, would not die—declared incompetent so at least he might save something for his mother and two spinster sisters. And if he himself was to have nothing, he now decided, he would have nothing proudly. "In this case, yes."

There was a pause on the other end, and then, "Why *this* case?"

"Because you are *un hombre sin vergüenza*, Romero. And if I don't get my money within a day, you'll be a dead *hombre sin vergüenza. ¿Comprende?*"

It was a revered, perhaps even an antique phrase, which was laden with understatement. Literally it meant "man without shame," but to Antioqueños it connoted much more and was tantamount to calling Romero scum. Londoño only hoped the idiom and the threat it intended wasn't lost on the Bolivian.

Beginning as a low cackle and then rising to a wet roar, laughter filled the receiver. "Tell you what—*when* I get your money, *if* I get your money, I'll give you a treat. You can call it a bonus *sin vergüenza.*"

Londoño could scarcely hold the phone to his ear. He thought he heard somebody else in the background also laughing. "Sure—without any shame at all, I'll stuff it up your ass. Bundle by bundle. From what people say about you, you'll enjoy it." The laughter rattled in the receiver, and Londoño smashed it down into the yoke. It missed. He tried again, and the whole works toppled from the desk onto the floor, from which the laughter continued.

"Maria! *Maria!*" he shouted, and pushed himself from behind the desk.

Standing, he discovered he could hardly walk, he was so enraged. His blood was pounding in his ears. The floor quaked beneath his feet. Out on the balcony, the *tinto* spilled from the cup and spoiled the front of his shirt.

Londoño didn't know what to do, where to turn, how to deal with the insult and what now looked like the loss or theft of his profit from the deal. Even if Romero had been telling the truth and the plane had not returned, would he now pay him, when and if it did?

So much depended on respect or, rather, fear. Maybe Romero hadn't planned on paying him from the start? And without la Compañía behind him, or money for *sicarias*, the professional assassins who could be paid to eliminate cheats and thieves, he was powerless to do anything.

Londoño spun suddenly and threw the *tinto* over the railing. He watched the fragile china demitasse cup and saucer tumble out over the tops of the cypress trees below the balcony, then almost sail in a breeze that was sweeping up over the edge of the cliff on which the high rise had been built. It was part of a set *de café* that an ancestor had purchased in Cádiz at the beginning of the last century, and the two objects seemed to hover there, the delicate floral pattern frozen for a moment in the sunlight before plunging into the gorge of the Medellín River below.

But the waste of what was now for the first time in nearly two centuries a broken coffee set was not complete. It gave him an idea.

The city of Medellín sits on a five-thousand-foot high saddle of rock that spans a valley between two ridges of the Andes. Through it runs the river that as much separates two worlds as two parts of a city. On this side is El Poblado with wide boulevards, esplanades, and avenues lined with mansions, fashionable apartment buildings, restaurants, and shops. On the other is Barrio Antioquia, the worst of Medellín's several slums and perhaps the most notorious crime zone in all of Latin America. It is from Barrio Antioquia that La Compañia recruits its mules, its enforcers, and its killers.

For as little as fifty U.S. dollars, you could get an unimportant person done. This was called a *trabajito* or "little job"—all you needed was a photograph and an address. For more, you could target somebody like an attorney general or a Supreme Court justice, who would be taken out with a bomb or from the back of a motor scooter while his Mercedes was stalled in traffic. Londoño knew the details of such murders. In Miami, in Louisiana—for the proper money nobody was safe from the sting of a *sicaria*. With enough money you could keep paying *sicarias* until your idea of justice was done, even in the jungles of Bolivia. Or the streets of Nassau.

Londoño might be broke, but it was only because he didn't have any money *that he could put his hands on.* The phrase was key. Success was just a way of thinking about things. Even failure. Hadn't his father only the other week bragged that he had drunk more wine, fucked more women, and broken more horses, banks, and Indians than anybody of his generation? When Londoño had mentioned the old man's debts, he replied, "Don't pay them. I certainly don't intend to. And when I die, you'll see. You'll be all right, if you smarten up."

The cryptic comments of a failed man-of-action? Perhaps. But now they were just the ticket. If Pachito Londoño was going to fall too, he'd go out in a blaze that would be all the brighter, could he get at least some Compañía help.

In the study, where he found Maria holding the phone, he began making further calls. There would be a "sit-down," as they called it in English, in two days, and he phoned the El Poblado restaurant three blocks distant and made reservations. He also phoned a limousine service and arranged for them to take him there. It was no time to run scared.

Londoño glanced at himself in the mirror by the desk. Just thirty years old now, he was a tall man with what he knew were classic Antioqueño good looks. He had a long face with a thin Roman nose. His mustache was dark and full, his skin white and untinted by any bastard strain, and his eyes hazel and clear. Londoño had no bad habits. Yet he had trouble now even holding his *own* gaze.

At the sit-down, he reminded himself, look Escobar in the eye. Forget that he looks like your father, forget that he's the most powerful man in Colombia. Tell yourself he began his career as a pimp, truly a man *sin vergüenza,* whereas you carry two of the most ancient and revered names in all of Antioquia. And you know how to cut a figure. It was perhaps the only valuable lesson his father had taught him.

The most important call he saved for last. A situation like this had to be handled quickly before both money *and* product disappeared. It was a Barrio Antioquia number that had been inscribed on the cover of his telephone index but that he had never before called.

In a very real way it—or, rather, she—was his ace in the hole.

CHAPTER 7

SLIDING

Bimini
The Bahamas

TUG McCANN HAD a little theory about decisions. If they didn't involve buying or selling, they almost never got made. People liked to put things off or let them slide.

In this case there was a lot of money already in hand, and it was hard to think it was real. If Eva had been in the berth beside him when he woke up, McCann might have forgotten the whole thing. Only the damage to *Whistler* was there to remind him it hadn't been an ugly dream. And the eight hundred thou. Thinking about that in the second second he was awake had brought a smile to his lips. And how maybe it could be much, much more. Enough for a lifetime.

Could they pull it off? Chick had said it wouldn't take much, but McCann hadn't believed a word. Money didn't come easy, otherwise lazy, dumb, unlucky people would have a bunch. And money like Chick was talking drew sharks. It was a lesson he hoped they'd learned yesterday.

But why decide now? Far as he was concerned, they could slide for a while longer, see how things stood. With a mug of coffee, McCann climbed the companionway ladder to the afterdeck and looked across maybe five miles of now-placid water at Bimini. In the fresh light of the newly risen sun it looked like a wafer of pearl on a bolt of Kelly-green silk. He lowered himself down onto the deck and eased his back against what was left of the taffrail.

Gerri, his sister, was the next up. She poked her snowy head out of the companionway and asked him if he wanted some breakfast. He smiled and nodded, then remembered it was Gerri and said please.

Cicciolino looked great—tanned and trim, even his eyes as clear and sparkling as the sky—but he said he felt sore. "I must've used muscles I forgot I had. All the lies they hand you in the weight room don't mean nothin' on the street."

"Or in the Islands."

Cicciolino joined McCann at the taffrail. There was so little of it left, they had to sit close. He looked around at the damage. "Can you believe it? Waking up just now, I had to pinch myself to know it was real. Christ—the luck of it. I mean, that we got through." He lifted his mug of coffee. He drank, paused, then turned to McCann with a smile on his lips. "Not that two-point-four mil ain't luck too. You make up your mind about the other stuff?"

McCann hunched his shoulders and dipped his head a bit to the side. It was a New York street gesture that said maybe, he'd see how it worked out.

Cicciolino agreed. "That makes sense. It came to me when I was waking up. Why press? We'll make some moves, see how it goes. How many days we got left on the charter?" He reached down and felt a splintered hole where a bullet had pierced the deck.

"Two."

"Then we got that much time at the outside. I figure it'll take at least a couple days for all the wreckage and shit to be found. In the meantime we can take the whaler into Bimini and poke around. I'll mosey over to the cop shop and do what we should about Eva. I think we should take care of the dough too, you know, put it 'south' the easy way." He glanced over at McCann, who only regarded him. Where money was concerned, McCann fancied himself as something of an expert.

"You got an account with Citicorp?" It was New York's largest bank.

McCann nodded.

"Business or personal?"

"Business."

"Good. They got a branch on Bimini. You give Arlene a business card, and we'll have her take the suitcase to the bank, less what we'll need for our purchases and walking-around money. She'll ask for a check made out to your company. That way, when she gets back to New York, she can deposit the check in your account, where—I assume—no eyebrows'll be raised at its size. Sometime later you can issue us checks."

McCann tilted his head, right away seeing a problem.

But Cicciolino raised a hand. "You mean, the extra taxes you might have to pay? I hope you're not getting greedy on us, Tug. You should remember your share." Which was $400,000 better than the others.

" 'Course, there's the remote possibility that the check might trigger an IRS audit. But the way I understand it from a check-kiting scam we busted a few years back, the IRS can 'request' an investigation of a Bahamian banking procedure, filled with all sorts of legal and bureaucratic pitfalls, and they only go after big, *big* fish. Nothing as small as this, and certainly no one-shot deals.

"If, on the other hand, you object, I can take the check over to Jersey City to a check-cashing guy I heard about. For one percent, maybe two, he'll split it up, but then we're left with the problem of explaining cash again, and the possibility that if he ever gets busted, he might rat."

McCann considered Cicciolino. How could he have known a guy all his life and not really ever *known* him? He had always thought Cicciolino kind of . . . obtuse, but what he had suggested was perfect. It smoothed out at least the problems McCann was having with the money. As an established paper broker, McCann received in his office each week many checks far larger than $2.4 million. The difference was, he took only a decimal percentage of profit from each before sending the money on to the manufacturers whose paper he had sold. In that way he couldn't agree with

Cicciolino more. He had never thought of it before, but he was ideally set up to launder money.

"What about the dope?"

Cicciolino smiled. "At least you didn't call it *stuff*."

McCann raised an eyebrow. "It's time to be real."

Cicciolino nodded. "In a nutshell, *Whistler* has got to disappear. It's, you know, physical evidence that we were somehow involved in the busted deal. Next, we've got to get ourselves a boat to transport the . . . *dope* to New York. We'll put Jay on that. And finally, if it all works out, we'll need two capable people who have the time to get it there."

McCann closed his eyes and raised his coffee cup. Cicciolino meant Gelb, who was on sabbatical, and McCann, who owned his own business that could run itself.

Cicciolino touched his arm. "Hey—by the time you arrive, I'll have everything set up. I've worked it out. Minimum ten mil. Twenty is what we're after. We'll see."

Perfect, thought McCann—we'll see.

Arlene appeared on deck. "Gentlemen . . . sorting things out, I hope?" She sat down to her twig tea and her wedges of *mochi* that she'd lugged all the way down from New York for her breakfasts.

And did McCann see her wink at Cicciolino before she sat against the cabin trunk? He thought he did. In his pursuit of the "weirder" sex, as McCann had dubbed his preoccupation, he'd met women, like Arlene, who were all hormones. He didn't think they knew themselves what they were going to say or do next. They were just chemicals reacting.

Finally Gelb appeared, and he looked terrible. Drained. His hands were shaking so bad he had to use both of them to get the mug to his lips. "Cold up here," he explained. "I better go below and get a sweater."

Arlene's smile was superior, as though she was sharing a private joke with herself, and when Gelb returned, he seemed better. He stretched. He touched his toes. "I'm going to miss this air," he said. But no sweater. Instead he had a beer.

"Maybe you won't have to," said Cicciolino.

"That's right, isn't it?" Gelb sat where he was, folding his legs under him.

Said Arlene, "Jay—why don't you tell Chick what you told

me last night. You know, what *Whistler* was probably worth before . . . The fair market price, so he'll have some background to
approach our Mr. Monroe."

Cicciolino turned to McCann, glanced at him, then looked
off, as though to say, Here we go.

Gelb seemed glad to unburden himself of the information. He
spoke in a rush. He said there really wasn't a market per se for an
older, wooden boat like *Whistler,* so much depended on its condition and the avidity of the buyer. Gelb didn't think himself competent to make an actual survey of the boat, which would really
require pulling it out of the water to check the hull, but she seemed
in reasonably good shape topside.

"But below, remember how every morning I had to pump the
bilge? There's a rule of thumb for wooden boats. One year in the
tropics is like ten in more northerly—"

"Jay, how much?" Arlene said evenly, her eyes narrowing
down on a piece of *mochi.*

Gelb's hand darted at her. "I just want to make this point, all
right? They advertise Gilchrist's Water Sealant as lasting—I don't
know—two, three seasons up north. Here? Nine months at the
outside, and don't believe any disclaimer you hear or read."

"How *much?*"

Gelb sighed and looked away. He raised the beer can and
drank. "A hundred thou tops, if she's been down here any length
of time."

Asked Cicciolino, "And if not?"

"A hundred and a half. She's old and probably needs to be
refastened. Then her deck would have had to be recaulked soon,
and her winches are creaky."

"May I say something?" It was Arlene. Having finished her
mochi, she rubbed her hands together and turned her head to
Cicciolino. "You know how Monroe is when we've dealt with him
before—always looking for a little here and little more there?
Don't let him give you a song and dance about the charters he'll
lose. I know he's booked for this month, since I tried to get us a
later date. But that's it. It's the end of the sailing season. If Jay is
right about the *Whistler,* I doubt that he could get another complete year from her without major work.

"Also, it's a buyers' market. The wharves are stacked up with
boats on the block. Were I he, I'd be overjoyed to get a buyer,

especially one who might be willing to pay a premium for *all found,* which is how it should be expressed. That way, he won't have to see it, at least up close."

Cicciolino nudged McCann and nodded. "Anything else, 'pardner'?"

"Yes—don't be *too* generous. We have uses for that money, and Monroe's a . . . barracuda. We don't want to tip him off."

"And what about you, Tug?"

McCann waited.

"You in with us or you out?"

"I'll slide along for a while, see how things go."

"Then let's do it." Arlene stood and waited until the three men had got to their feet.

Gerri met Cicciolino and McCann at the bottom of the companionway ladder. She had a plastic cooler in her hands. "I packed you a lunch, just in case you don't want to—" She didn't know how to say, Eat in public, which sounded as criminal. She pushed the cooler at her husband. When he reached for it, she added, "I only hope you've thought of *everything,* Chick. And I mean *everything,* both here and there."

From the deck they heard Gelb say, "Tell me one thing before we get going, Arlene—who the hell is Cal? Do I know Cal?"

"*Cal?* What do you know about Cal? Are you trying to embarrass me? I don't want to hear you mention that name again." There was a pause. "Am I understood?"

There was another pause, and they heard a footstep on the ladder and looked up to see Arlene's ankle.

Cicciolino had never liked Bimini. He thought of it as the Forty-second Street of the Bahamas, and motoring the whaler into Alice Town Harbour reminded him why.

It was the beginning of the high fishing season, and with Florida only forty-five miles away, the approaches were jammed with gaudy, towering high-tech sportfishing boats from the spreaders of which pennants bragging of their kill were flying. Alice Town's single business street was similarly crowded. Everybody moving was white and had a tan, a blond girlfriend, and some kind of package in their hands. Everybody standing was black, poor, or looked poor, and had watchful, hungry eyes.

The crowd in the Conch Inn, which T. J. Monroe also owned,

was maybe worse. It was made up mainly of two types. The first were beefy, mustached Americans who looked as if they were trying to relive the Hemingway experience. Some were talking loudly at each other about barracuda, tuna towers, and "the Stream," while others were affecting the laconic, surly-professional Fisher King attitude of the later Hemingway right down to gray beards, potbellies, open-neck sports shirts, and eyeshades, no less. Cicciolino shook his head. He had written his senior thesis at Fordham on Hemingway, and he knew whereof he judged.

The second dominant image was pirate/drug runner. Up until '87, when U.S. Customs and the Bahamas Defence Force stationed new, fast interceptors off Bimini, the island had been the last transit stop for coke bound for Florida. Some of the runners had remained. Their quick, incredible profits had made them welcome in Alice Town, and some still managed the occasional run in spite of the blockade. Generally they were a quiet, circumspect if not inconspicuous lot, and Cicciolino's eyes, sweeping the crowded barroom for seats, now snagged on touches of gold. There was a neck chain here, an oyster-shell Rolex there, even a large single earring under a pirate's tricorne, for crissake. *FELONS*, he thought without blinking. *FUCK YOU, COP*, their eyes flashed back.

Monroe himself was sitting where they had found him when they had chartered *Whistler* two weeks earlier. The Conch Inn was a thatched-roof affair, open on three sides and filled on the fourth by an ornate Victorian bar. From one corner Monroe could lean his back against the wall, keep an eye on the cash register, and get ready service from the four bartenders who were plying his custom, which was brisk.

Monroe was a small man with dark sunglasses banding a face that had fallen and was now a system of prominent bones and loose black folds. Cicciolino had heard that Monroe had made his fortune fronting drug runners. He'd put up buy money for a risk-free third of the profits, provided something *real* was advanced as collateral: property, gold, guns, jewels, boats. T. J. Monroe was now one of the wealthiest men on Bimini, but over the years that they'd been chartering from him he'd got the shrunken, "pickled" look of a man who spent too many hours on the wrong side of his own bar.

Above Monroe swirled a paddle fan. In front of him stood a tall, opaque glass and a leather cup that contained four dice. For five dollars you could roll Monroe for the price of your drink. If any combination of dice produced the numbers of the exact amount of the charge, you got the drink free. If not, you slid Monroe "a fin," as he called it, gleefully showing a good set of teeth as he folded the note into the wad that he kept in the pocket of an always-colorful sport shirt. Around his neck hung another thick gold band, the links of which had been shaped into small three-dimensional conchs. Pushing toward the bar to order a drink, McCann wondered aloud at its value.

"Or his life expectancy on Forty-second Street," said Cicciolino.

But the dice game lent itself to the buying of rounds, since the wager was the same if you spent five dollars or ninety-nine, and the action with the leather cup made the atmosphere of the Conch Inn sporting and festive and today almost rowdy. Some drinkers, it appeared, had never gone back to their boats last night. Others, nursing visible hangovers, seemed to wish they hadn't. In front of them were glasses the size of cocktail shakers filled with thick reddish fluid.

Cicciolino, seeing a seat at the bar, motioned McCann to sit down, but McCann held off until two came free near the corner where Monroe was sitting. "Remember two weeks ago when that drunk rolled the dice and lost but couldn't pay?" Monroe had blown up. "Would you have drunk that drink, had you rolled the num-bah?" he had roared. "Nothing I despise more than a cheat. *Nah*-thing!" He personally had thrown the man out. "I got an idea," said McCann.

"What, back so soon?" asked Monroe, when they had taken their seats. "You have—let me see"—with a thick, quaking finger he traced down a column of names in a pad that he took from a back pocket—"two more days."

"The girls wanted to do some shopping, and we ran out of booze. Care for a pop with us?" McCann flashed his wallet, as he laid a fifty on the bar.

"Ah, yes—the *girls*," said Monroe, his sunglasses turning down on the soft kangaroo leather of McCann's thick pocket secretary. "And, of course, I'll have a 'pop,' as you call it. I'd be honored to drink with you two gentlemen." He waited only a moment before asking, "Care to try your luck this morning?"

Again showing his teeth, Monroe slid the cup toward McCann, who obliged and lost.

While the drinks were being set before them, McCann turned to Cicciolino and said in low voice, "This might take some time. I'll have to soften him up. Maybe you ought to see about our other matter." And stay sober, since McCann obviously didn't intend to. He was at his gambling best slightly in the bag, and Monroe was almost there.

"You go easy," Cicciolino advised. McCann could be wild when he was drinking *and* gambling.

"Double or nothing?" Monroe raised his glass.

"Well—why not?" McCann replied jocularly. "Did I tell you I'm feeling lucky today, Mr. Monroe?"

"That's good. That's very good. *Feeling* lucky is important to a mon. I seldom *feel* lucky." Monroe smiled.

"Cheers." McCann raised his glass, which was filled with Absolut.

But his second roll was no better, and he placed ten dollars on the bar between them.

The police station was an official-looking building with stone steps. A Bahamas flag, adorned with a Union Jack in one corner, was beating above the door, and somebody had just swept the sidewalk and washed the windows so they sparkled in the hard, tropical sunlight.

But inside was the same as every other precinct house Cicciolino had ever been in. There was the same complaints desk, the same glassy-eyed stare from the desk officer, even the same "feel" of you, as an individual, suddenly having to confront something huge, ungainly, and only occasionally purposeful called Law and Order. The modus operandi was the same too. You waited. It was the big advantage the State had over people. It would make you wait so long you'd decide the whole thing—a complaint, justice, a life of crime, even life itself—wasn't worth it.

Cicciolino presented himself at the desk, said he wanted to report a missing person, and then took a seat against the wall with maybe a dozen other people who, he assumed, had queries, complaints, or more likely family who were prisoners to visit. Most of them held bags and wicker baskets that smelled as if they contained hot, spicy Bahamian concoctions that Cicciolino couldn't place. Suddenly he was hungry.

But there was a difference too. Here, for the first time Cicciolino sat very definitely on the other side of the great divide between law enforcers and law breakers. Had he actually broken a law yet? It was still debatable, since they had only actually failed to report a crime with due speed, which, he assumed, was required of a person here too. Had he sequestered evidence? Had he confiscated for his own use money not belonging to him? Had he engaged in drug trafficking? Not yet, for here he sat, waiting. He could report the whole thing the moment he was called, and nobody would question his actions.

He'd often thought that the "going over" happened for people with a personality snap. He likened it to the urges he sometimes got. Not often, but once in while, he'd be talking to somebody he'd just met and knew nothing about and didn't either like or dislike or anything, and he'd get the urge to punch him in the face. Just for the hell of it. Or he'd be driving down some highway and he'd imagine he'd just jerk the wheel and pile the car into an oncoming car or bridge abutment. You know—how that would change things, and what it'd be like to suddenly decide to be dead.

But it didn't happen with a snap to him. Sure, there was the moment in the plane when he looked down on all that money and dope and decided it was his. Or could be. But really the decision had come long before that, and it was nothing sudden. No snap.

No, it was more like tiny grains of sand. Somehow, seeing day after day how impersonal, arbitrary, and dumb things were, he decided that of all the lies, the biggest was that people as a group knew what they wanted and how to go about getting it. Sure, they made laws, but not all of them were good, and most were ignored. When laws were enforced, often it was for reasons other than justice. After a while Cicciolino saw it didn't matter if he ever made commissioner, since politics just made the job a sham and without politics he'd never get it.

Sometime around then he decided all that mattered was getting through his career unscathed with enough interest in life to at least have a few good days somewhere. Here in the Islands? Cicciolino looked down at the floor that was gleaming except under the bench across from him where the buffer wouldn't fit. No—he couldn't live with a bunch of *mulingiannu*. But he'd find a place somewhere, he was sure.

He then heard something like his name being called, and he looked up to see some big smiling nigger in a starched khaki uniform and gleaming shoes bearing down on him. The man stopped. He was holding what looked like a telegram in his hand. His smile fell. "What—no Mr. McCann or Mr. Gelb?"

Cicciolino didn't know how to respond. What could it be? Had Eva *bought* it? Or, worse, turned them in, and the telegram was an order for their arrest? Cicciolino had never been in the position of having to watch his words or phrase a lie, and suddenly he could feel sweat trickling down the crack of his ass. "They're—" He waved a hand to mean outside, somewhere on the island.

But he managed to force himself to his feet. He wanted the man to know who he was *before* the hammer fell. That way it wouldn't seem as if he was hiding behind his badge. "Actually, I'm *Assistant Chief* Bill Cicciolino of the New York PD." He pulled out his wallet and handed the sergeant his chief's shield, which was contained in a small leather folder. "And I'm here to report a missing person."

The sergeant studied the ornate hunk of gold that looked like a sunburst, and his smile reappeared. His eyes flashed up at Cicciolino. "Miss Eva Burden, by any chance?"

Again Cicciolino didn't know if the question was a trap, but he had no choice except to continue. "Yes, we had trouble in a storm and—"

The man waved him off. "Well, I'm hah-py to inform you that she's well, suh. Through our Nassau headquarters, she sends this message, saying she's there. She's sorry she"—he turned, so Cicciolino could also look down at the tan piece of paper. His finger pointed—"overreacted." The finger quickly traced the rest of the message. "Evidently she's met some friends there, and will get in touch with you when she gets back to New York. She asks if you can send her her bag and 'effects' via an interisland flight." The sergeant turned his head to Cicciolino. "You can do that out at the airport. She also says she'll explain when she sees Mr. McCann back in the city. I assume she means New York Ci-ty.

"Have you been a police officer there long, Chief?" he asked, but Cicciolino hardly heard him. And as the man continued to try to make light conversation about the police profession, Cicciolino only smiled and nodded and tried to get away as soon as he could.

The luck of it. The fucking luck! Somehow she had got herself to Nassau, rethought the entire event, and gone to the police, where she'd been as good as her word. Instead of mentioning the boat, the planes, the money, and the dope, she must have told them something innocuous that had to do with "overreacting." Overreacting how? He didn't know and couldn't guess—a spat with McCann, the storm? Something safe, otherwise the sergeant would have questions and not just chatter.

"How much longer will you be with us, Chief?"

"Just two more days, I'm afraid. I only had two weeks."

"That's a pity. If you had longer, I'd take you out to see our drug-interdiction effort. Perhaps you've heard about it?"

Cicciolino said he had. "It's made all the papers." And begged off. "I better get back to my friend McCann. He's shaking the leather cup down at the Conch Inn."

The sergeant's expression sobered. "With T.J.?"

Cicciolino nodded.

Furrows appeared in his brow. "Be sure to call me if there's any problem. And tell T.J. I said that."

Working his large body through the milling crowds in front of the shops, Cicciolino stopped suddenly and pulled out the telegram that the sergeant had given him. ". . . bumped into some friends . . ." What friends? From New York? From what Tug had told him, she had none. From California? How many Californians vacationed in the Bahamas?

He glanced up and saw Arlene entering a tourist agency across the street. She no longer had the aluminum clamshell suitcase in her hands, which meant she had already done the banking.

Now she would be getting their return plane tickets changed to tomorrow. Motoring in on the whaler, Cicciolino had explained why. "We want to be set up to split, if we have to. If by tomorrow things haven't worked out, we'll change them again and keep changing them until we have to leave." It cost fifty bucks apiece each time the change was made, but reserved seats might be important.

"But why all five of us, if Tug and Jay will be aboard the boat?"

"Because when you, me, and Gerri get to the airport, I'm

going to stand by the ticket line and offer two men a real deal. Cheap tickets for anonymity. That way there'll be a computer record of all five of us leaving Bimini. *Capisc'*?"

Arlene had lowered her sunglasses, and her starburst gray eyes locked in his. "*Capisco,* Chick. That's brilliant. You have a natural bent for intrigue, or is it something that can be learned?"

Gelb had looked away.

Now Cicciolino thought about getting her alone someplace and finding out how hot she was. He'd give her a lesson, all right. He'd make her keep on the white wide-brimmed sun hat and sunglasses, maybe even the flats and bobby socks that made her look like a little girl. She could meditate on his cock.

Cicciolino wasn't a pig about sex, he wasn't greedy. He always made sure the woman came too, no matter how painful or how hard he had to work. It was part of the deal, and would set things up for when they got to New York.

But he remembered McCann back at the Conch Inn. Jesus— he could ruin everything with all his supposed bar smarts, especially now with the telegram from Eva that she hadn't linked them to the wreckage on the island.

Cicciolino stuffed the telegram into a pocket and began pushing his way through the crowd.

CHAPTER 8

SUBROGATION

◆

Pando Province
Bolivia

IT WOULD BE a stunning, cruel rain, she could tell. It would be a rain that could occur nowhere else but a tropical rain forest. It would sting the skin and bite right through ponchos and hats, but it would also do something else. It would blanket the area and distract their quarry. And in that way it would be a good rain. It would provide them cover.

For three hours now, as the boat struggled against the swift current of the Madre de Dios River, they had watched the dark clouds, laden with moisture, stack up against the Andes to the west. The captain had said the cloud mass would climb only to the top of the mountains. Then, driven by the cold air off the icy peaks, the cloud mass would curl around on itself and form funnels, spires, and great black avalanches of wet cloud that would hurtle east toward them. "And then—*cuidado!*" His thumb had touched his forehead. "We'll feel God's wrath."

The woman had asked him when?

"About the time you get where you're going."

She had not told him where she and her entourage of seven Boyaca Indians were going, and she looked away from his lips, which she had been reading, saddened that he would have to die. The man had intelligence and humor, and she had enjoyed speaking with him. He had helped her pass the time. "Where am I going?"

"To Puerto Heath, or at least some miles south of there. To the airstrip run by the *transportadores*."

"How do you know that?"

"Because I have never seen you or your retainers before." His eyes shied, as though he would look behind her. "From the way you speak and . . . look, you are Colombians. You could be going nowhere else."

"Retainers" was an overly nice turn of phrase. The Boyacas were mountain Indians from the *páramos*, the high barren plains of the Colombian Cordillera Oriental around Chivor where years ago her father had employed them in his emerald mine. They were small men—none more than five feet tall—with powerful shoulders and enormous chests from having lived for countless generations at altitudes above ten thousand feet.

They had high cheekbones, Mongolian slant eyes set off by reddish, coppery complexions, and lank black hair. Most notable, however, were their legs, which were short and bandy but powerful. It was not unusual for a Boyaca to traverse sixty miles over two mountain ranges of fifteen thousand feet in one day. For weeks at a time they had trotted beside her father's horse with a backpack and a thirty-inch *penilla* bush knife dangling on a cord from their belts. And loyal. Once you gained a Boyaca's respect and trust, he was yours for life. It was as though he decided you and he had merged fates; what happened to one happened to all. And what happened would be good or at least safe, a Boyaca would make sure.

Here in the tropics, however, they were decidedly out-of-place. Their skin glistened with sweat, and they could wear nothing but loin skins and their *penillas*, which they were never without.

The woman herself was dramatically different. She was tall, taller even than the boatman, with a powerful, angular body. Her cheekbones too were high and sharp, but they revealed a racial mixture that was recent and pronounced. She had deep red hair that was almost blond along the temples, and large dark eyes that appeared green at one moment and brown at the next, depending upon the light. Her nose was long, sloped, and definitely Indian; her lips prominent and Negroid; yet, in all, she appeared nearly European and was as strikingly beautiful as the Boyacas were strange.

Nor was she dressed for the jungle. She was wearing white—a sleeveless blouse and slacks, covered usually by a white cotton poncho and in the sun a wide-brimmed white hat of the sort a lady would wear to tea.

"Why are you telling me this?" she now asked the captain, who turned the wheel sharply to avoid a large tree trunk that was bobbing in the thick, swirling mud-colored water of the river.

"So you won't kill me."

"Why do you think I will kill you?" Her green eyes flickered down on his lips, awaiting his reply. Then fell to his belt to make sure he wasn't carrying a gun or a knife. She leaned back to feel Maluko's presence behind her: the heat of his body, his odor, which was distinctive and familiar and comforting. She moved her hands, as though to clasp her elbows, and under the poncho let her fingers rest on the grip of the automatic under the sash that wrapped her waist. She had not survived in her profession by being careless.

"Because the *transportadores* have moved their base. Their planes, the one that is left. Everything. I have been told they've lost much. Eight of them are believed dead. There's nothing there now, at Puerto Heath. Instead they are in another base outside of Puerto Maldonado. They fear something. Or someone." His eyes met hers briefly, before turning back to the river.

She waited.

"I will take you there."

"Why?"

When the boat had swung back into the channel, shuddering in the grip of the current, he touched the throttle and continued speaking. "Last month they took my woman. They have money. They give her expensive presents from La Paz and Medellín. Habana. And cocaine."

"And by this you will pay them back?"

He nodded. "With interest."

"Did you know who we were when you picked us up in Sena?" It was the town thirty or so miles down river. When the call had come from Londoño, they had left immediately, flying there in a plane and sending it back. In a matter such as this, early speed was essential. Cash money and narcotics disappeared fast.

"It occurred to me. And when you didn't get off the boat earlier at the usual stops—"

She waited, now scanning the wide, rubbery leaves of the foliage that wreathed the banks. She had known men who in their fear or arrogance had actually announced their intentions before striking. Though not in so many words. "Did it also occur to you that you still might lose your life?"

He only looked at her. His expression seemed to say he had, but they had spoken together, and he did not think she would kill him. Not now that he had helped her.

The woman removed two cigarettes from a case, lit them, and handed one to the captain. "Tell me—did she leave willingly? Your woman."

He looked away, then nodded.

"And you still want her back?"

Again.

Pulling in the smoke, she thought perhaps she might do him a favor. If what he had told her about the transporters was true.

The rain punished them. At a point not far from the transporters' new base, they waited and watched for it.

Sweeping down the river in a visible, dense cloud, it struck the boat a stopping blow, then pushed them toward the bank. Like enfilade or saturation ack-ack, it flattened back leaves and roiled the water of the river. It made the jungle earth under their feet greasy and slick, but with rubberized ponchos now to protect their weaponry they moved as quickly as they could, the captain before them, leading the way. With a hand signal Maluko sent two of the six Boyacas on points to either side and advised a third to hang back.

The camp was new, the airstrip recently cleared and still rough at each end. Not all the tree trunks and stumps had burned, and the charred slash had been pushed to the margins of the narrow open field. Apart from a porched house, which had been positioned at a corner nearly under the tree cover, the woman could see no other habitation.

The captain touched her shoulder and waited for her to turn and face him. "They sent the Indians off, after they got it cleared. They gave them another project miles away, far beyond Puerto Maldonado, so they'd forget about this."

But they'd have guards, she thought, a cadre of followers who for small money or drugs or both would be loyal up to a point. Again Maluko directed the others to reconnoiter while the three of them waited under a kind of shelter formed by the slash and overhanging foliage. A rain like this would be that point, she imagined.

She was right. A Boyaca returned to say there were no others on the periphery of the camp besides those at the house, which had two parts: the living quarters proper, the largest room of which was a kind of office, and servants or crew quarters to the rear. There was a white man in the office, three women in the kitchen and living areas of the house, and at least five, maybe seven, Indians in the building to the rear.

She asked the captain if he would like to come along and watch. He declined, saying he would wait for them there.

"But if we're successful, we won't return. You'll have to come in to get your woman." There was an airplane parked under the tree cover near the edge of the strip.

He smiled slightly. "I'll wait here until then"—which was the reason the woman had left him, she assumed.

There was a puddle of water a foot deep in front of the door. The rain was exploding off the corrugated-metal roof of the house. She tried the handle, the latch moved back, and she took a long step into a dim room. Maluko slipped in behind her.

She could see movement in the large hammock that had been slung along a wall of shuttered window. It was swaying, the burden it carried at the bottom of its yoke was rocking. She turned her attention to the man who had his head on the office desk near what looked like a nearly empty bottle of *aguardiente*. His arms were spread before him.

He had long blond curly hair, and would be one of the three brothers Romero, or so she assumed from what Londoño had told her.

She moved farther into the room, pulled a chair to where she could see both hammock and desk, and sat. She removed her hat and shook off the rainwater. She placed it on the floor and took out a cigarette, which she lit.

Maluko had completed his transit of the room. In a corner near the desk he had found an assault rifle. He checked the clip, then moved in back of the hammock where he could watch the doors and the desk.

She rested her neck on her shoulders and watched the hot smoke from her cigarette rise to the eaves and fall in stratified layers toward the hammock. Here they were, she thought: five people at rest or play or whatever was going on in the hammock. People had two few moments like this. Soon everything would change, more for some than others, but that was life. Or death.

She glanced at the form of the man at the desk. In his sleep saliva had dribbled from his mouth and stained the blotter on which his cheek was resting. Control was everything.

Finally the smoke reached the hammock, and when she saw renewed movement there, she stubbed out the cigarette and folded her arms under the poncho.

The mosquito netting opened, and the face of a pretty young Indian girl appeared. The Indians were different here. They were tall and thin with pale skins and delicate, almost Oriental features. She assumed it was the boat captain's erstwhile "woman," a term that she knew from personal experience could be applied to girls as young as eleven.

The face disappeared, there was some more movement, and another appeared: a white man who, although somewhat younger, was obviously related to the man at the desk. He had the same features and blondish hair. "¿Quién es? What do you want?"

"Dos milliones dollares. United States. Or five hundred kilos of cocaine, whichever is easier. For you."

He looked around the room, everyplace but in back of him, and, seeing nobody else, began pulling himself out of the hammock. "What's this—they send us a woman, a—" He pulled himself out of the hammock. He was a tall young man no more than twenty-five. He had a strong build, with long, well-formed legs and a surprisingly large, uncircumcised penis, the head of which was now retracting into its sheath. His stomach, however, was fat and distended, and made him look like a pregnant woman. It had the shape and even the yellowish color of a ripe pear.

He stepped toward her, "—*puta?*"

She wondered if in her former career he had once been a client. His face was long and Teutonic, as the brothers Romero had been described to her, but she could remember more than a few men like that.

"What do they take us for—?"

"Thieves," she said evenly, which stopped him.

"What did you say?" He was now nearly leaning over her.

She again reached for her cigarette case. "I said you are a thief, your brothers are thieves." Without looking at him, she tamped a cigarette on the case and placed it between her lips. She clicked her lighter and held the flame to its end. "Which thief are you? Roberto, Gerardo, or Helmut?" She exhaled the smoke and glanced up at him. "Helmut, I should imagine. The baby of the family. Did anybody ever tell you you look like a baby? Or maybe you look like you're going to have a baby?" She smiled.

Helmut straightened up. He again scanned the room and, now seeing Maluko, was suddenly conscious of his nudity. He reached for a pair of shorts that were draped over a chair.

"Leave them off."

"What d'you mean?"

"I mean we might have to operate on you, and we'd prefer to see what we're doing. Rouse your brother now, please. I understand he makes the decisions around here, and I wouldn't want him to miss the procedure.

"Look—your *macho*. It's got to be the best thing about you. Or at least the smartest thing. It's vanished completely. Isn't it tragic you couldn't too?"

Helmet tried to glance down at his cock. But his eyes flickered up at the woman and then moved to the girl, whose head alone was showing in the folds of the hammock. He turned to his brother. "Gerardo." He shoved his shoulder. "*Gerardo!*" He reached for the bottle, but a hand came off the desk and seized the neck.

An eye opened and looked from Helmut to the woman to Maluko and the assault rifle he was holding. "*Maricón*—I thought I was dreaming."

"You *hoped* you were dreaming," the woman corrected.

Did he smile? She thought he did, slightly. He pushed his younger brother aside and raised the bottle, as though to ask if he could drink from it.

She shrugged. "Why not?"

"I don't know, *señorita*. What is your name?" When she didn't answer, he went on, "You come in here like a *víbora*. I respect vipers. You find yourself in the company of a viper, you watch your step." He tilted back the bottle, drank off the three or four inches that remained, and again eyed Maluko before lowering it.

Except for his beard, which looked dirty, his hair was gray and curly. His face was netted with small ruptured veins that seemed to have spread from his eyes, down his nose, and onto his cheeks. "That's better," he said. "Not *much* better, but at least it appears I'm alive." He smiled. One front tooth was missing.

"Now, then—your business again?" He pushed himself back from the desk, as though he would open the top drawer, and Maluko raised the barrel of the assault rifle. Displaying his palms, Gerardo went on, "If we're to talk, I'd prefer to be awake. I've got a little something here to perk me up, if you know what I mean."

The woman shook her head. "Place your hands on the desk and leave them there." But it explained their need to steal. It was control again. Control was vital. "I say this for the last time. I have been sent for two million U.S. dollars now. Or five hundred kilos of *pure* cocaine. Failing that, I take *everything,* and leave you with nothingness. Am I understood? You are thieves, men who are"— she paused—*"sin vergüenza."*

"Nothing-*ness?*" Gerardo questioned his brother. "Did she say *nothingness?* Who is this bitch with her *tertulia* manners? Us without shame? *Us,* when it is we who have been stolen from? *Us,* who have lost our brother, eight of our people, and two of our planes? Those *sin vergüenza* are the gringo bastards who stole from *us!*" Again his eyes fell to the desk drawer.

"It strikes me you're not convinced of my sincerity." From under her poncho the woman drew an automatic pistol with a long black maté barrel. It was the tool of her trade, and she waited until they understood what it was. She then raised the barrel toward them, but turned quickly and fired. The bullet hissed from the silencer and smacked into the middle of the forehead of the girl in the hammock. As though more surprised than injured, her eyes widened and her mouth dropped. The hole looked like a smudge of holy ashes. Her head then fell out of sight into the material of the hammock. The hammock swayed.

Helmut started. His arms came up, and his body jumped

toward the hammock, but Maluko stepped in front of him. He had his *penilla* in his hands, the long blade glinting in the light from the lamp on the desk.

"I said I would not ask you again."

"We have *nothing* but what you see. One airplane that will allow us to carry on, this poor building, and—" His eyes shied toward the door to the back rooms where his Indians were billeted. And then Gerardo's indignant expression fell, as he seemed to realize what must have happened there.

The woman nodded to Maluko. The blade of the *penilla* flashed, Helmut gasped, and something wet and heavy fell to the floor. It was the favored knife stroke of the Boyaca: a stomach cut that began horizontally, just under the ribs, and curved around, finishing on the other side without contacting any bones that might snag the blade. In one deft stroke it freed but did not severe the contents of the stomach from its cavity.

It wasn't a killing stroke, not immediately. Nothing as nice as that would do a Boyaca. Killing was an art, and had to be effected in such a way that the victim could understand for as long as possible that he was worse off than dead without being able to do anything about it. Killing also required a spectacle that could be appreciated by the killers, since taking a person's life was a pleasure that should be memorable.

Helmut looked down at his former paunch, which now lay on the floor by his feet. He seemed undecided about what he should do—lunge at Maluko, who of course still held the *penilla,* or reach down and try to pick up what had fallen from him. Instead, he turned and ran toward the door, dragging the bloody mass of his intestines after him. He pulled the door open and fell down the stairs into the puddle and the pounding rain.

There, the other Boyacas were waiting for him, and began howling and yipping like a pack of feeding wolves. Helmut picked himself up and tried to run away. The tube of his large intestine, having been washed of its blood in the deep puddle, was bright pink. One of the Boyacas put his foot on it, and Helmut, after a few steps, was brought up short.

He shrieked and fell. His body shuddered. They could only see the whites of his eyes. But when he still moved forward, he was allowed in his agony to crawl off. He would not get far.

The puddle was a bright, almost iridescent red for perhaps the minute it took for the rain to dilute his blood.

Before Gerardo was turned over to the Boyacas, he showed the woman a consignment of two hundred kilos of product that had already been loaded aboard the plane. He swore on his mother's grave it was not part of the delivery she was after, and named a mafioso as its owner. He also surrendered $52,347 U.S. and a cache of small arms. The Boyacas then swept the base clean of every other item—radios, handguns, transmitters, antennae, automatic weapons, chain saws, dynamite, flare guns—that might prove useful or be resold in Medellín.

Salvage was what they were after. Anything after $2 million U.S. was hers. The cocaine would not count. It would be held by la Compañía until the named mafioso made a claim. If not, it would be sold, and Londoño would get his standard 30 percent and give her half. She herself was careful about such things and maintained excellent records. But with the plane, which had to be worth something, and the money, she had made a good start on the project.

While the plane was being loaded, she dispatched Maluko with a rocket launcher to locate the boat captain and his vessel. There could be no witnesses.

She then searched through the Romeros' radio log of two nights earlier and found the entries that concerned her: At 10:51 the Romeros had received a radio relay from Cuba saying that contact with the buyers had been made. At 11:15 trouble was reported. She could barely make out the scrawl, but it looked like, *Heavy damage. Boat out. Crew dead. Send backup.* And then at 9:11 the next morning: *Wreckage sighted. No product, no payment. Schooner nearby. Will engage.* And no more writing.

Instead there was a long page of doodling, mainly of naked women performing impossible contortions with snakes and firearms, which would have to stand as Gerardo Romero's last testament, she concluded.

So—the buy had gone sour, and the pilot had survived long enough to radio a Mayday. Then nine or so hours later a backup plane had spotted a pleasure boat sailing away from the wreckage with the product aboard. The boat was engaged, obviously unsuccessfully. Otherwise they would have heard from the plane by now. How would that have been managed, if not by design?

It made her think of one Mr. Brian Nathanson of Nassau, the buyer of record. He had the reputation of being a hard, tough, but honest trader. And not stupid.

Could the money or the shipment or both have been confiscated by the authorities? Could the Romeros have been deceived by their brother? Plainly she did not know enough to form any conclusions. Yet.

When Maluko returned, saying he could find neither the captain nor his boat, she was pleased that the man was a fool only with young Indian women. She had liked him, and he had done her a favor.

CHAPTER 9

STIFF

◆

Alice Town
The Bahamas

CICCIOLINO WAS TOO late, he decided, when he got through the door of the Conch Inn. The place was packed, and everybody focused on Monroe and McCann at the bar. Even the bartenders had stopped serving. With arms folded, they were quiet, until Cicciolino heard the dice rattle in the leather cup and hit the bar. A number was announced: "Six fifty-two." It was McCann's roll.

With pen in hand, Monroe had to concentrate to write the number in his dog-eared notebook. He then scooped the dice into the cup and rolled. "Six sixty-five!"

"T.J.!" somebody shouted. Some others cheered.

Monroe's head went back, and the black band of Monroe's sunglasses winked in the light through the open sides of the bar. Having won the roll, he dropped his jaw and showed his teeth. It was supposed to be a smile, but looked like the first movement of a shark feeding. Or a barracuda.

"How much that make?" somebody shouted.

Monroe's head moved within inches of the pad. "I make it eighteen t'ousand, four hundred, and twenty-two dollahs. So fah! Double or nothing, Mr. McCahn?"

The crowd quieted quickly, waiting for the answer. McCann reached for his drink and, finding it empty, signaled the closest bartender to fill both of their glasses.

Cicciolino almost had to fight to get close, saying, "The white guy—hey, he's my buddy. I'm his backer." When he finally got there, he found a stack of thousand-dollar bills in front of McCann and what looked like a checkbook in front of Monroe, who now pushed a palm at the bartender, as though to say make the drink light.

"What—?" McCann inquired loud enough for the crowd to hear. "We can gamble together, but we can't *drink* together?"

One of the Hemingway types picked up on it. "Go on, T.J.— loosen up. When was the last time you had a *real* goddamned drink?"

"Don't matter no-how. It's all a big act," said somebody else. "All day long he walks around here like he's half-gassed. Ain't nothin' in his bottle but tea."

Monroe spun around to see who had spoken, and Cicciolino judged Monroe was either drunk or a good actor. Finally he returned his gaze to McCann and said, "Suh—what are you drinking?"

"Absolut on the rocks."

Monroe popped two fingers at the bartender. "Doubles"— turning to McCann, his stern expression fell to a sudden smile— "or *nothing?*"

McCann smiled. "If you like, but I have my own wager, one that I know you won't refuse." He turned on his stool so that he was speaking to Monroe but could be seen by most of the people in the bar, and his voice would carry. "How 'bout I pay you the eighteen-fifty I owe you now?" With deliberation he picked up the stack of thousand-dollar bills in front of him and, one at a time, snapped nineteen down. "And we get down to some *real* gambling."

It was so still that the two fresh tumblers of vodka smacked like hammer blows on the bar.

McCann pushed the money toward Monroe and reached for his glass. *"Salut?"* he asked.

Monroe reached instead for a thousand-dollar bill, which he held to the light. His head canted this way and that, his teeth showed, and then he replaced the bill and squared the pile. Lifting his glass, he touched McCann's. "*Ab*-solutely."

The crowd appreciated Monroe's humor. A murmur of approval rippled throughout the large, airy room.

Clinking glasses, the two men tilted them back. When Monroe had finished his, he turned to McCann. "You were saying, suh?"

"If you'll pardon me for a moment?" He turned to Cicciolino. "You go to the bank?" Again his voice was loud and meant to be overheard.

It took Cicciolino a few seconds to realize that McCann was merely trying to obscure the source of their cash. "Oh, yeah. Yeah," but in an undertone, he added, "Tug, I hope you know the fuck you're doin'. This ain't easy come, easy go."

But McCann ignored him. "I propose we roll for *Whistler*. I've become enamored of the boat and would like to make it mine. The easy way." He pointed to a framed photograph of the schooner that hung among five others on a mirror of the back bar under the advisement MONROE CHARTERS, CASH IN ADVANCE, BY THE WEEK ONLY, NO CREDIT CARDS ACCEPTED WHATSOEVER.

"Whoa—" a voice was heard in the crowd. "This is getting heavy." People began closing ranks around the two barstools.

Monroe's sunglasses were focused on the ice cubes in his vodka tumbler. "Let me get this straight. You mean, you would like to roll me for *Whistler* and not—" He pointed to the stack of nineteen $1,000 bills.

McCann nodded.

"Then—may I?"

McCann nodded again, and like a five-headed snake, Monroe's dark hand palmed up the roll, which disappeared in a trouser pocket.

"You owe me five hundred," said McCann.

"Seven hundred and eight, to be exact. Bring my new friend a drink. In fact"—Monroe waved a hand—"get all my friends a drink."

But the diversion did not work. Only the bartender closest to them moved to fill their glasses, and the crowd, if anything, pushed closer still.

Said Cicciolino in McCann's ear, "Tug—you're shitty. You're gonna fuck yourself up. Even if you win, you lose. This guy won't let you walk away with his boat."

"Tell me—how would we go about this wager?"

"Walk the fuck out of here with me now, please?"

"With seven dice," said McCann evenly. "One roll. If my roll is higher, I own *Whistler*. If yours is higher, I pay you that amount. There is a condition, however. Each of us can take one die from the other's cup."

Two refreshed tumblers appeared.

"Jesus, Tug—can I show you somethin'?" Cicciolino pulled Eva's telegram from his pocket; he would try anything to distract McCann now.

Monroe looked down at his glass, but did not reach for it. After what seemed like the longest time, his head jerked slightly, and he turned to McCann. "Let me understand you perfectly. I assume that you are a gentleman."

McCann nodded.

"And a scholar."

McCann wiggled a hand. "Let's say, after a fashion. I got by. Just."

"Well, let me ask you this way—are you a university man?"

Again McCann nodded. Monroe was blitzed; he was sure of it.

"I am myself. Kings College, London." With the tips of his fingers, Monroe touched his chest, then pointed to a framed diploma that was hanging with the photos of his charter fleet.

Two years back, McCann had checked it out and thought the parchment a phony.

"So, now that we've established we are men of honor, let us go through the terms of the bet one final time so that you and I and"—his hand swept out—"*everybody* understand perfectly what you propose. You are suggesting that we place seven dice in this cup. We roll. Whichever six-digit figure is higher wins. If you win, you win *Whistler*."

"Papers, future charters, all found. The works."

Cicciolino thumped the heel of his palm on the bar. "*Look* at this, for crissake!" He pushed the telegram in front of McCann's face.

McCann lowered Cicciolino's wrist and stared down at it for a few moments. "Fuck Eva, and fuck her friends. I never really dug her anyway."

Christ—he was drunk and didn't understand what it meant to

them. Cicciolino had seen him like that before and maybe too often. He dropped the telegram on the bar and looked away. He thought of all the "good news/bad news" jokes he had ever heard and how the day—hell, the vacation—was shaping up like that. McCann had to be crazy. Dice were numbered 1 to 6, therefore the worst Monroe roll would be $666,666, and they'd be out over a half-million bucks. Correction. *McCann* would be out the half-mil. Cicciolino would be fucked if he'd pay for McCann's drunken stupidity.

Said Monroe, "Pardon my inquisitiveness, but *how* will you pay me when you lose?"

"I won't lose, but have you any objections to cash?"

"You have cash like that . . . hahn-dy." Monroe's hand moved to his glass.

"Of course. I wouldn't propose such a wager if I hadn't. As proof and for ante, I'll put a hundred thousand in the pot. My friend here has just gone to the bank for me." McCann turned to Cicciolino, who only blinked.

"C'mon."

"C'mon, what?"

"Put two down." Two packets of fifty $1,000 bills, he meant.

Cicciolino shook his head. "You gotta be fuckin' nuts. Or drunk."

McCann smiled. "Maybe both. C'mon, while he's hot."

Cicciolino felt somebody press against his back and, swirling his shoulders, fended him off. But he reached into his windbreaker for the waterproof pouch he had tucked under his shirt. There was no going back now. Cicciolino plunked two on the bar.

Monroe's hand again moved forward and picked up one of the stacks.

The crowd began buzzing. Somebody shouted to a boy who now bolted from the door toward the harbor and the boats, "And tell him to bring his camera. Mr. T.J. will want pictures."

With a practiced gesture Monroe fanned the end of a stack and slowly let the notes break from his thumb in a quick count. He tried the other. He then slipped a note from under the band and held it up to the light. Satisfied, he placed it back on the stack; McCann then slid both stacks back to Cicciolino.

"And you have more?"

Cicciolino, replacing the stacks, glanced at Monroe and pat-

ted his windbreaker. He then turned and swept those behind him
with his practiced, dead-eye stare.

"My question to you is, do you in fact own *Whistler*?" Mc-
Cann asked.

Monroe nodded.

"It's a documented boat?"

Again.

"You have her papers."

Yet again.

"May I see them?"

Monroe raised the tumbler and drank the icy water that remained. "Why *seven* dice? Why the discard?"

McCann spilled the dice from the cup. With a finger he separated one from the others, and began rolling it. In a series of ten
quick rolls, it came up six eight times.

Somebody behind them in the crowd said, "What I tell you?"
There were shouts and hoots. Others began laughing. "Fucker
caught 'im. He caught 'im!"

McCann glanced at Monroe, whose body jerked before he
said, "You saying I cheat?"

"No, no. Not at all. What makes you think that? How long
you own this, is all I'm asking?" He rolled it again, and once more
it showed six, which McCann guessed was a number that didn't
figure in a cash-register sum as often as, say, five. It could also be
that Monroe had instructed his bartenders not to ring a six if it
appeared that somebody wanted to roll him for the price of drinks.
A $6 charge could always become $5, $16 could become $15; $26,
$25; and so forth without complaint. How often would a round of
drinks cost $60 to $69? Probably never. McCann had never gam-
bled in a house where the house didn't have some advantage, and
from what he could see, that die was Monroe's.

But Monroe was still quick and seized upon the out McCann
had given him. "Long time. Long as I can remember. Forever."

"And these others."

"The same."

"They're worn. Shot. Finished."

Monroe waved his hand over his head. "Then throw them
out," he ordered a bartender. "Throw them out this minute."

"And give us six fresh dice," McCann added. "And the papers
for *Whistler*."

But after the bartender dropped the dice in the trash, he straightened up and looked at Monroe for further orders.

It was his play, and McCann imagined that Monroe would either gamble with him or have to give up the scam of gambling for drinks, which he obviously enjoyed. His number had been called when he had least expected it, and he now stood an even chance of losing the flagship of his charter fleet.

Said Cicciolino to McCann, "You got him where you want him?"

McCann only kept his eyes on Monroe, who was staring down into his drink. It was the crucial moment. If Monroe swallowed his pride and said no, McCann was out eighteen thousand bucks.

"You're the real Napoleon of the dice cup, you are. A Stonewall Jackson. A Guderian." Cicciolino slurped from his drink. "Can I ask you somethin'?"

Still McCann didn't move. Smiling slightly, his heart pounding, he was *willing* Monroe to take the chance. He hadn't had this much fun in years. Going head to head with a guy for really big stakes, seeing who had the bigger plums, was better than sex even, and McCann enjoyed sex a whole bunch. Half-drunk now but feeling the sweet pressure of the action, he could imagine whole days like this. Days and days. Somehow it put everything into perspective for him. It made everything seem either worthwhile or worthless, he didn't know which, but *pure* and *clear*. It was what life was all about. Ultimately. The chance of having been born. The chance of when you would die. And all the chances—the *big* chances—in between.

Cicciolino went on, "So, you change dice. So, you roll 'em. What's keeping him from rolling a higher number? You got money like that to throw around? Let me tell you something"—Cicciolino waited until McCann's head turned and his eyes locked on his—"I hope you do, 'cause I ain't payin' none of it, un'erstand? This is fuckin' nuts, and you're on your own."

McCann only smiled and nodded. Voices around them were now speaking to Monroe, some taunting, others urging him on. The place was suddenly noisy; everybody had something to say, some advice, some observation, the need for that free drink Monroe had promised. Again the bartenders were hopping.

Of course, McCann *had* thought about it, if *thinking* it was.

Monroe, like McCann, was a gambler, and what McCann had done by questioning the dice was attack Monroe's strength—his luck or confidence or aura of invincibility, call it whatever. Gamblers believed in such things. McCann did himself. And if you didn't "feel" right about a bet, you simply did not lay your money down. It was going against the grain of everything intuitive, visceral, extraconscious, that was involved in the urge to gamble.

Again McCann didn't have a word for it, since there was none, but he knew it was real. The feeling. And in this situation, if Monroe did not have it, he would not roll a winner. McCann was sure.

Why? He didn't know. Did it make sense? Not a bit. Mathematically Monroe still had an even chance to win much more money than Gelb had said *Whistler* was worth. He wouldn't roll six snake-eyes. There had to be at least a two or maybe a four or five or six in the configuration, but Monroe would not win. McCann was certain. More, he knew Monroe, as a gambling man, would know it too.

On the other side of the question, McCann himself was on a roll. He could do no wrong. He'd been in a position like this maybe once or twice in is life, when things . . . conspired so that it didn't matter where he turned, where he stepped there was *shit,* as the saying went, and both his Sperry Topsiders were in it right up to the ankles. Great, glorious green shit.

He picked up his tumbler of Absolut and turned to Monroe. "What say, Mr. Monroe—are you a *gambling* man?"

He could see Monroe struggling: with the voices behind him, with the vodka, but mainly with his greed. If he won, it would be a quick, delicious killing that would become legend on the waterfront of Alice Town. It would boost his ego, perhaps attract other fat "fish," and certainly increase interest in the Conch Inn, which would be good for business.

But if he lost . . .

Suddenly Monroe's body jerked. He leaned back, gazed up at the photo of *Whistler,* and said, "Jason—go get the papers to my schooner."

Pandemonium broke out. Jason immediately left the bar through a back door. The new dice were casino-regulation and still wrapped in security plastic. McCann himself broke the seals and tried them out. Perfect. Like tossing baskets, he popped them one at a time into the cup and pushed it toward Monroe. "You first?"

Monroe nodded, then scraped back his barstool. With the help of the rail, he got to his feet. Raising his glass, he looked around until he had everybody's attention. "To *Whistler*," he said. "To a lady."

"Hear, hear!" somebody shouted.

"T.J!" another said.

Monroe did not hesitate further. He drank off the drink, reached for the leather cup, shook it once, and spilled the dice on the bar. Without looking down, he turned his back and said, "Jason—tell us the good news."

And truly it was good news. There was a 6, two 4s, a 3, and two 2s. 644,322.

"You can pay that?" somebody asked Cicciolino. "In cash?"

He ignored the question. The less said, the better. One way or another, it'd be a miracle if they got off the island with their lives, and it looked like the other. Booze and Irishmen, he thought: Whoever told them they could drink hadn't been a friend. He wondered how he could get in touch with that sergeant at the constabulary without tipping anybody off. He couldn't see a phone anywhere.

The number cheered Monroe. He smiled broadly and resumed his seat. "Pretty as a pict-chah," he said to McCann. "Pity I don't have a camera."

From behind them now a strobe bleached the top of the bar. "Got it, Mr. T.J., suh!"

Monroe resumed his seat and smacked the heavy bottom of the rocks glass on the bar. "You to play," he said to McCann, who had maintained his composure and was still showing his slight grin.

"The fuck a' you smiling at?" Cicciolino asked. "How you gonna beat them numbahs?"

"Easy. Watch."

He flicked the dice into the cup, raised it to his ear like a bartender shaking a cocktail, and saying to himself, "Hail Holy Queen, Mother of Mercy, our life, our sweetness, and our hope," he let the fucker fly.

Bodies, leaning forward, pushed him into the bar so at first he couldn't see the dice himself.

"Son of a bitch!" Cicciolino complained. Anchoring his hand

on the bar, he shoved himself back so they could get some room and watch the fucking dice. Out of the corner of his eye he'd seen a fucking 6 and one, two—he pushed McCann back—*three* fucking fours! He couldn't believe it. The fucking Mick had pulled it off! He shot an arm around McCann's shoulder. He gave him a fucking kiss on the ear, and—look at that—there was a five in there too. It had come to rest on the side of the nigger's rocks glass.

But McCann's expression didn't change. He'd been in this position before. It was one thing to win, another to walk away with your winnings, especially when the stakes were high and the turf not your own.

And even Cicciolino in his joy noticed something else. The place was probably as quiet as they had heard it all day long.

McCann turned to Monroe. The move had to come from him. He was sitting again—the papers for the boat, the dice, and the two stacks of thousand-dollar bills before him—and he seemed to be struggling with his emotions.

Cicciolino saw his opening, and pushed away from the bar. McCann had his talents, but Cicciolino hadn't been a cop all those years without being able to sense a situation that was about to explode. This wasn't New York; it wasn't even the States, for crissake. No way was Monroe going to let them walk out of there with the papers for *Whistler* and all that cash. The guy was a thief, a fuckin' bandit. He wanted it *all*.

Cicciolino palmed up the two bundles of bills and zipped them into the windbreaker. He reached for the papers for the boat, and Monroe's hand fell on them. "Hey—they're ours. You rolled with your own dice, you lost."

Monroe said nothing. He only kept his hand and the black sunglasses riveted on the sheath of papers that were contained in a plastic pouch.

Fuck him, thought Cicciolino. He might have a gun or a knife, but they were too close for that, and the guy was a fuckin' boozer. Gone. Shot. He reached for the package, but Monroe held on, and suddenly Jason, his bartender, had a long, ugly truncheon in one hand.

Said Monroe, "You came here this morning to steal *Whistler*. You stole *Whistler*."

McCann stood. "Wait a minute—anybody, I mean *anybody*, in this bar think I didn't win *Whistler* fair and square?"

The bar was again quiet.

"And *anybody* here now think *Whistler*'s not mine?"

Cicciolino yanked on the pouch, but Monroe held it, and the bartender stepped closer. Monroe's notebook fell to the floor.

"Then fuck the welsher. I don't need his papers. I know it's mine."

Monroe's head swung to McCann. With his other hand he pulled off the sunglasses and laid them on the bar. His eyes were opaque and had the surface sheen of old, veined marble. "You are thieves," he began saying, "and—"

McCann broke in, "Oh, yeah. We know, we heard the rest. 'Would you have drunk that drink if you had rolled the num-bah?' Nothing I despise more than a thief. *Nah-thing*!' " His parody of Monroe was deft, and the largest of the Hemingway types began a big, deep-chested laugh that was picked up by most of the people around him.

"Probably not worth a shit nohow," McCann went on, "from a deadbeat. A fuckin' *stiff*!" He took a step toward Cicciolino to help him, but his foot slipped on something. Looking down, he saw Monroe's little dog-eared notebook. He picked it up and slipped it in his back pocket on the idea that at least they'd go away with something. Their names in the charter book.

Cicciolino wanted the papers to *Whistler*. They might be important later, if Monroe complained and tried to say they stole the boat. How many of the witnesses here would they be able to round up? How many would Monroe get to?

But out of the corner of his eye he saw Monroe flick his other hand to what seemed like the only people not on their feet. There were eight or nine of them, young, mean-looking, mostly white with the gold appointments—in the ear, around the neck—that showed they'd scored. They were sitting at a table off in a corner. When the closest one suddenly got up and began making his way toward them, followed by the others, Cicciolino decided it was time to back off.

"You know the word *stiff*, Mr. Stiff?" McCann was now shouting drunkenly. Cicciolino grabbed him by the arm and pulled him away from the bar. He shoved him toward the door.

"You're a fuckin' stiff! Worse, you're a hypocrite! And you want another bet? I bet you never laid eyes on King's College, London."

The lead guy from the table was nearly on them now. When his arms shot out for McCann, Cicciolino dipped down, pivoted, and hooked a punch up from his shoelaces. It burrowed so deep in the guy's stomach, he lifted him off his feet. He was a big, strong-looking nigger with a gold front tooth, and with a sweeping left Cicciolino aimed at that.

The punch drove him back into the others, and he fell all in a piece, like a hunk of dead meat. The others just looked down at him; nobody moved for maybe three seconds.

But when they did, a uniform stepped between them and Cicciolino and McCann. It was the sergeant from the constabulary, the one Cicciolino had spoken with earlier. He had one thumb hooked under his Sam Brown belt, the other resting easily on the flap of his holster. "What's going on here?"

Said Cicciolino, "My friend here rolled Monroe for *Whistler* and won. Now Monroe won't give up the title."

"Gambling is illegal without a license."

"What about welshing?"

"That, sir, is between you and him."

"Really? Then now that you're here—" Cicciolino stepped toward Monroe. The others, wary of him now, moved back. When his arm darted for the papers on the bar, Monroe cowered. "Boo!" Cicciolino said. Monroe flinched, and Cicciolino pulled the papers away.

Some of the Hemingway types began laughing, and McCann and Cicciolino pushed toward the door.

Arlene was waiting for them outside. "What have you been doing in there all this time? Jay's beside himself. He's found just the boat, but the man refuses to take our check, can you imagine? And our bank closed at three."

Cicciolino glanced behind him, trying to match some of the people walking behind them with the faces in the bar. The Conch Inn had open sides, and it'd be easy to slip out.

And Monroe would make a play for them before they could leave. He just knew it.

CHAPTER 10
CLAIM TERMS

Medellín, Colombia

EPIPHANY, PABLO ESCOBAR Gaviria thought when he lowered his snifter of cognac and found Pachito Londoño approaching his table. It was like a miracle, or at least a miraculous coincidence. Londoño had never once before deigned to lunch with them, and only a moment past somebody had mentioned him as a case in point.

In light conversation over their food, Escobar and the six men with him had been discussing Medellín and Antioquia and the advantages of living here, the chief of which was the present immunity from extradition to the U.S.A. The disadvantages were many, but mainly its isolation. And now that he was a billionaire at least twice over, Escobar could barely stomach the self-satisfied provincialism of Antioquia.

It would be one thing were Antioqueños manifestly superior human beings who made, built, or produced something—*anything*—better than the rest of the world. But apart from growing coffee, which had more to do with ground and climate than agricultural expertise, they seemed deft only at the unbridled exploitation of any and all, their own included, who could be squeezed for a centavo.

They had even taken to publishing a magazine called *La Raza*—as in, *la raza Antioqueño*—in which things particular to the *departmento* were celebrated, discussed, or invented, including racial characteristics. An Antioqueño was tall and dark with large, piercing eyes, an aquiline nose, and high forehead, and he kept his "hair and mustache resplendent." Ideally an Antioqueño was *blanco* but could also be among the *"gente de color,"* for otherwise there would be few veritable Antioqueños.

And there he stood before them, Pachito Londoño—*"de pura cepa"*—"the real thing," even down to the English suggestion in his surname and what he had chosen to wear. Unlike the capos to either side of Escobar, with their solid-gold watches and silk suits, their alligator shoes and designer shirts open at the neck, Londoño was wearing a plain white linen suit. Every cut and stitch followed the lines of his tall, angular body. It spoke to Escobar, who had been born in the slums, not of wealth and taste but rather of fear and subservience. Somebody had labored desperately long to make that suit, and when not squandering their money on "gentlemanly" passions, the Londoños were mean and niggardly.

The shirt was some strange but entirely appropriate silver color. His tie a black four-in-hand that only somebody like a Londoño would wear. All he needed was a dark cigar to complete the Antioqueño archetype. He raised it now to the carefully clipped line of his mustache. "Don Pablo." He nodded to Escobar. Then said, "Gonzalo" to Gonzalo Rodriguez Gacha and, "Jorge Luis" to Jorge Luis Ochoa. Although Escobar was definitely *primus inter pares,* the three men controlled the Medellín Cartel. Ochoa was also Londoño's cousin on their mothers' sides.

There were five other men—all associates, like Londoño—also seated around the large table. At other tables, situated at strategic points leading to and from all doors and the kitchen of the Spanish-style restaurant, were Compañía security teams of two men each. Except for the tables at the windows, the lighting was dim. Tapestries and thick rugs absorbed voices.

Said Escobar, who owned the place, "You should have told us you were here. We only just finished eating. Sit. Have some champagne. Waiter!"

"Thank you, Don Pablo. But *tinto* will suffice. I'm in company." Londoño inclined his head toward a table near the large window at the front of the restaurant where sat a redhaired woman whose back was to them. "I'd like to have a word with you, if I may."

Escobar pointed to his own chest, as though to ask, Me, personally?

"No, it's business."

"But of course." It was the reason they gathered there at least once a week. After-lunch petitions were always entertained.

Londoño sat, the coffee was poured, and Escobar tried to imagine who the woman was. Londoño was unusually discreet about his private life.

"It's a matter of the purchase I made last month. The five hundred kilos."

Escobar nodded. He himself had personally negotiated the sale, or, rather, had been worn down by Londoño's doggedness. Over Ochoa's objections, Escobar had surrendered the load on the idea that it did none of them any good to have one of their associates so plainly needy, no matter who.

"I believe it's lost. In the Bahamas."

Escobar eased himself back in the cushions. "When?"

"Yesterday. Or last night."

That explained it. Escobar had received word from a contact in the Islands that officials in Nassau had been notified by a passing cruise ship that the wreckage of a plane and a boat had been spotted on an uninhabited island. The plane had Bolivian markings, and their contact, thinking Medellín would be interested, had sent the message on. "How do you know?" Escobar was always interested in how his associates gained their information.

"I phoned Gerardo Romero. He as much as told me he had no intention of making good the loss. That he had probably lost a brother, two crews, and two planes, and I was out of luck."

At the table eyebrows were raised. One of the reasons *transportadores* were paid so well was their guarantee of delivery or return of product. Otherwise they did not work for la Compañía. For long.

"What were you paying him?"

"Five hundred thousand."

The standard was one third, but it was a large load, and

Londoño, being Londoño, had doubtless beat them down. If they had trouble, it was probably because they had been trying to make up the difference with the product. The Romeros had the reputation of taking a little here and there. "Was Gerardo drunk?"

Londoño nodded.

Well, it was no excuse. "And what would you have us do, Pachito?"

Londoño gathered himself. His future and that of his family could be riding on his pitch. Without Compañía help, he and his *sicaria* probably wouldn't be able to recover enough to make it worth her while, which meant she'd stop. With it he might at least save face and be permitted the chance of another deal.

Nevertheless, he paused dramatically. He raised his cigar to his lips and drew on it, then slowly let out the smoke. Gently he touched the ash to the edge of an ashtray to disengage only burnt and not glowing tobacco and to demonstrate his command, which he would never lose, not even if they denied him. "I won't dissimulate. I present this matter because I myself have suffered a personal loss. One which I can ill afford." He allowed his eyes to sweep the table, so they would understand that he was being frank with them.

"It strikes me, however, that losses have been increasing of late. La Compañía has had several. Señor Gutiérrez has had one." He nodded to one of the men at the table. "Señor Silvestre another." He raised the *tinto* to his lips and lowered the cup back into its saucer. It was some modern design, the edge thick and ungainly, entirely unlike the delicate set he had ruined three days earlier. "I bring this up *not* to complain. It is the risk we take. I accept it. And I despise . . . whining.

"Theft is another thing. Theft strikes at the heart of what we're about. Here." A finger of the hand that was holding the cigar thumped the table. "I was not an associate of this Compañía when it first began, but lest we forget, it was the threat of thieves that first brought us together." Londoño again scanned the group.

The story was legend throughout Colombia: how in 1981 the Medellín Cartel had been formed in reaction to the kidnapping of Marta Nieves, the daughter of drug kingpin Don Fabio Ochoa, by the revolutionary group M-19. When a large ransom was demanded, Ochoa refused to pay. Instead he assembled 223 other drug lords and convinced them that any attempt to extort drug profits from one of them posed a threat to all. He asked them to contribute operating funds of $4.4 million (U.S.), and to assign ten of their best men each to an action group.

A reign of terror followed. Homes were broken into, houses searched, dozens of "suspects" kidnapped, tortured, and shot. M-19 soon negotiated a settlement with the mafia that not only released Ochoa's daughter but also conscripted M-19 guerrillas to guard drug caches and landing strips and to act as assassins in return for money, drugs, and guns.

But the lesson was plain. In numbers there was a strength so compelling that the government lacked either the power or the will or both to stop their trade in cocaine, and three of them decided to corner the market. Gacha would monopolize the supply of coca leaves and paste, Escobar would consolidate the manufacture of cocaine hydrochloride, and the Ochoas would see to it that the powder got where it was going safely and in tact.

In such a way the three became known as *"los Dueños del Cupo,"* or "the Holders of the Quota." It meant that in addition to their own drug activity, they dispensed excess coca paste to others to be processed or finished product to be sold.

"It has been my experience," Londoño went on, "that every so often people must be reminded not to take what is not theirs. If they think we are weak and lack will . . ." Londoño let the silence carry his conclusion, which all certainly endorsed. Weak meant dead, or, worse—at least to Londoño—enslaved.

But Jorge Luis Ochoa, his cousin, glanced dismissively at his wristwatch. "What are you proposing, Pachito? Exactly." As far as he was concerned, Londoño should have processed the order through la Compañía for the standard 30 percent commission rather than trying to get as much as he could on the open market. That way, the product would have got where it was going, and Londoño would have $750,000 in his pocket now instead of nothing, and they would have been spared his plea.

"That the wolves are grouping. It's again time for us to make the point."

"With *your* loss, you mean?"

"With *all* our losses, Cousin."

It was too much, the play for Ochoa's support, and Escobar straightened up. "What would you have us do?"

"Deal with them, of course."

"With Security?" Escobar meant the enforcers of la Compañía, who comprised a small, tough, and well-armed fighting force that had skirmished successfully with a number of national armies.

Londoño blinked. He tried to assess the mood of the three men, which somehow had changed. "No, that would be too strong. And it would expose us to adverse publicity. Unnecessarily."

"Then you think we should chip in for *sicarias*." It was the usual procedure in such cases, to assure shared responsibility and therefore silence.

Londoño raised the cigar to his lips. He drew on the fine, mild tobacco that had been grown on an erstwhile family property that he wished, from the bottom of his soul, he still owned. To have them all contribute to a fund would be the best case, but it never served to seem too anxious. "It was my thought, in broaching the matter."

Escobar smiled. "And tell me, Pachito—how did you come by the five hundred kilos?"

Londoño looked away. The man knew as well as he how he had got the product. He motioned the cigar toward Escobar, meaning from him.

"For a good price?"

Londoño nodded.

"I'm sorry. I didn't hear you."

"*Sí.*"

"And if the buy had gone through, who would have profited?"

Londoño felt like a child in school called up before the master with the class looking on.

"How much would you have profited?"

Londoño could now feel color rising to his cheeks, being questioned like that by a man who had begun life as a petty criminal.

"*¿Quanto?*" Escobar demanded.

"Around two million, U.S."

"And had it gone down according to the arrangement, would Pachito then have sent us all"—Escobar paused—"a *pacheta*?"

Some of the other men, who had been smiling, now laughed outright. In the muted light of the restaurant, their eyes were gleeful, and Londoño imagined it would be all the gossip in the bars in the neighborhood. Not that he cared. Not having the money, he never visited bars himself, and they were all *canalla*, his associates.

"*Would you have?*" Escobar was a big, ugly man with a long, uneven face and no chin. Although generous to friends and the poor, he was ruthless with anybody who crossed him, including Supreme Court justices, attorneys general, and army chiefs of staff.

Londoño shook his head.

"And now you want us to pay for your *sicarias*? Tell me— how much for that? Who would you get? Guhl? *Las Arañas?*" It was a gang—"the Spiders"—that was associated with the Cartel but that sometimes jobbed out its services when the money was right.

Londoño again kept silent. He had promised he would not reveal the name.

But Escobar had had his fun and was satisfied. He had made the point that la Compañía was neither a welfare nor an insurance agency that would cover associates' personal losses. That it came at the expense of a blue blood, like Londoño, was a plus. It now occurred to Escobar that Londoño was the only man in the organization who had never invited him to his *finca*. Why? Was he afraid maybe Escobar might want it? It was an idea to pursue.

"So—this is what we'll do for you and also Señores Gutiérrez and Silvestre. Since you're associates, and this is, after all, business, we'll allow you to use the Compañía network for information, reconnaissance, contacts, and the like. But the *sicarias* you'll pay for yourself. *Comprendeis?*" He glanced from Londoño to Gutiérrez, who nodded.

"Our *own* losses, the ones la Compañía has incurred collectively, we are dealing with. Expeditiously. Now—is this settled?"

The other men murmured their assent.

"Pachito? Is that fair?" Escobar asked.

Londoño summoned a smile. "Oh, yes, Don Pablo. More than fair, and I thank you very much." He stubbed out his cigar in the ashtray, and pushed himself up to leave. His arms were quaking.

After the other men had left, Escobar, Ochoa, and Gacha remained as usual to confer. Eventually the matter of Londoño came up, and Gacha asked, "Isn't he broke? How much is he into us for?"

Said Ochoa, "He borrowed three hundred thousand to buy the five hundred kilos. The rest was his own, or at least somebody's."

"Then wouldn't it be in our interest to back him?"

Ochoa's eyes met Escobar's before he said, "Not with his assets."

There was a pause in which three pairs of eyes were directed to the table in front of the windows where Londoño and the redhaired woman were still having lunch. They appeared to be lingering over *digestivos*.

"Have you ever seen Finca Los Llanos?" Escobar asked.

Gacha was from Bogotá originally. He shook his head. "He never had the good sense to ask me. Maybe if he had . . . ?" He let his voice tail off.

"It's . . . well, it's the *estancia* you'd choose, if you had had first choice, how many . . . ?"

"Three, four."

"—four hundred years ago."

"*He* owns it? What about his father? Isn't he still alive?"

Escobar turned to Ochoa, who, as Londoño's first cousin, knew something about the family.

"Wasted, now. As good as gone, but—you know—a real fucker in his time. Mention him to my father if you want to hear stories. They're the same generation." He did not have to add, "same family."

And the son, all three men were thinking, was like a duck out of water. But a sitting duck? There was that possibility.

"Who's he going to get?"

"For a *sicaria*?" Ochoa was smiling now. "That's already been arranged. He thought he was being cute here with us this afternoon, that maybe none of us would know. Maybe he thinks we're in this thing for our health or, like him, pocket money to keep things afloat."

Londoño had stood and now stepped around the table to take the chair of the red-haired woman. She was a Creole, woman nearly as tall as Londoño, with an angular, powerful body that was wrapped closely in a silk dress just the amber color of her hair.

"You're looking at her," said Escobar.

Gacha's brow furrowed. "The *woman*?"

"I hear they make the best assassins. Think about it—if somebody was coming after you, you'd assume it was a man, right? And a woman like that? You're in a bar having a drink. 'Is this chair occupied?' You say no, sit down, what are you drinking? It leads to dinner, a bottle of wine, some sweet talk, and your guard is down. You make your proposition, she says, 'Well, why not.' And in bed she slices your *macho* off, feeds it to your face. In the morning, long after she's gone, they find your corpse.

"Or here. All our security, all around us. If a *sicaria* tried to approach this table, he wouldn't get ten feet. Her? She'd probably have all of us done before we got our eyes off her ass."

Londoño and the woman had begun to make their way through the tables, Londoño nodding or stopping to say hello to this one and that. The woman's smile was pleasant and contained, but her eyes kept moving about the room. They now fell on Escobar, Ochoa, and Gacha.

Said Gacha, "What's her name?"

Escobar answered. "Solange Mercier La Guatavita. She's the best. For the right money, she'll go anywhere—London, Paris, it doesn't matter—and do just about anyone. We've tried to put her to work ourselves, you know, on a permanent basis. But there's more money in being an independent."

"Salvage," Ochoa said, and all three men nodded. Sometimes a skilled *sicaria* could make more in salvage than the deal had been worth. It all depended on the resources of the thieves who had stolen the load.

"She's Bogotaña?" To the Chibchas—the dominant Indian tribe around Bogotá at the time of the Conquest—the Guatavita had been king-priest, the representative on earth of the sun god.

"They also call her *la Sorda Roja*."

"She's deaf?"

"Since childhood. People say it was Londoño's father. A blow to the head. *After* he murdered her mother and father, who had been a partner of his in an emerald mine." Escobar glanced at Ochoa, but he added nothing.

Not with the possibility that Finca Los Llanos might soon become available. For over a year now he had been quietly buying up Londoño debt.

"But there was no proof," said Escobar.

That *you* know of, thought Ochoa.

CHAPTER 11

SHIP BUY

Bimini
The Bahamas

THE NEW BOAT for the passage to New York was a fifty-four-foot
Frers ketch. She had an owner stateroom, a full galley, a circular
table in the main salon that could seat eight, and so much interior
mahogany and butternut that she looked like a wooden boat. She
was also equipped with Mercedes diesels for auxiliary power and
lighting, Monel tanks, and nearly all new sails. She had a six-man
life raft, a sea anchor, and all the electronic goodies including a
satellite-assisted navigation radio that could contact Mars, Gelb
thought.

More to the point of their immediate needs, she had full fuel
and water tanks. Even her lockers were crammed with canned
goods and dry foodstuffs, as though recently prepped for a world
campaign. But what sold Gelb was *Trekker*'s hull, which was not
wood; it was aluminum and as immortal as he would ever be. It
meant that, if and when they got through all of this, he'd be
fucking free and could sail wherever he wanted without fear of the

tropical bugs, worms, and leeches that ate into hulls. Gelb was obsessed with decay. In his present frame of mind he didn't think he could actually own a wooden boat out of fear for it.

Of course there was a problem. The boat had been marked, said the man who was selling it, by, "*La policía nacional.*" He was a big Cuban with yellow skin, a walrus mustache, and large, tired eyes that a rum bottle, which graced the exquisite butternut salon table, did nothing to enliven.

"It can no longer sail in the Bahamas. You know sneef dogs?"

Gelb's brow knitted. "Know what?"

"*Sneef* dogs. *Peritos.* Cops now have them. How you say, *sabuesos*, in *inglés?*"

"Beagles."

"You speak *español?*"

Gelb wiggled a hand to mean a little.

"*Los pecados en la mierda de los angeles los sabuesos pueden oler.*"

Gelb smiled at the nicely turned hyperbole, which translated literally to "Sins in the shit of angels beagles can smell." "And so?"

"And so, like I say, *La hermosa Trekker*"—he spread his hand to indicate the boat—"can no longer sail in Bahamas waters. I don' know, maybe some guest of one of the owners brought a little marijuana to smoke, or maybe in rough weather some pills in a bottle got broken. Not one roach was found, not a bit of powder. Crystal?" The man shook his head. "But the sneef dog whined, and *Trekker* got marked."

"Which means?"

"Like I say, she can't sail here. Is the same for the other boats up and down this dock. Bahamas say you must load boat on some other ship, take away from the Islands, and never come back. But if you leave quietly, is not necessary."

"And how would you do that?" Gelb asked.

"Night. Bimini is two islands shaped like a horseshoe, facing east. Nobody is bothered sailing east. I would sail east to the edge of Grand Bahama Island, then thread the needle and point northeast." He meant the passage between Grand Bahama and Little Abaco Island. "Then run two, three hundred mile to sea, like you' headed for Bermuda. You' a gringo, no?"

Gelb nodded.

"*Nueva York?*"

Again. Gelb's Lower East Side accent was ineradicable and harshest when, like now, his concentration was most complete. But the Cuban's knowledge of the American idiom was revealing.

"I know these waters." The Cuban smiled slightly and raised his glass to his lips. "I know that passage. *Intimamente*. Is the way to go."

Suddenly Gelb's paranoia squalled. What was he hearing here? A voice of experience, or the lead man in some complex DEA or U.S. Customs sting operation? He wished the packet of powder that he had stuffed in his ditty bag was nearby. For better or worse, it made him decisive, something that he had never been. Better, he decided, reaching for the drink that the Cuban had poured him. "Where would you cut in?" he asked.

"Once away from Bimini, anywhere. Is only here that *Trekker* is known. In other places the cops might suspicion, but they won' be prepared."

"To plant something, to set me up?"

The man canted his head and regarded Gelb closely before continuing. "Well, maybe, but I had in mind no *sabuesos*. No sneef dogs."

Gelb tried to think. Had he given away why he was interested in *Trekker,* what they were up to? He couldn't remember exactly what had been said, and he decided to chance it anyway. "Where did *you* cut in?"

"*Me?*" The man smiled. "I never been more north than Little Abaco, like I say. But stories I heard—New Jersey is the place. Is like Florida with barrier islands, lots of lagoons and small-boat traffic. And people and roads." He finished the drink and poured himself more. "Few cops." His eyes rose to Gelb's. "From what I hear."

Then came the matter of money, about which the Cuban was adamant. "A t'ousand a foot, I been tol'. Cash. U.S. If you know boats, you know is a deal. This boat—I don' know how much it worth. A quarter-million, a half."

Three-quarters, Gelb thought. Especially equipped as it was.

"I don' care if I never know you' name. You remember mine?" The man had not offered it.

"Papers?"

"All you wan'. You wan' more, you tell me."

*   *   *

Five minutes later, Arlene returned to *Trekker* with Cicci-olino and McCann. Gelb explained about the boat, then took Cicciolino forward where fifty-four thousand dollars was counted into his palm. Back out at the salon table Gelb watched closely while the Cuban signed the documents with the exact same signature as the person who had taken delivery of the vessel from the manufacturer. They then shook hands, clinked glasses, and drank farewell.

Gelb could scarcely believe it. It was like his zaniest wish come true. *Whistler* was a lovely old boat, perfect for a couple of weeks in the Islands, but *Trekker* was something else entirely. *Trekker* was a veritable *dream* boat that could take him anywhere in the world in a style that only corporate leaders and heads of state could duplicate.

But Cicciolino brought him out of the dream quick. He laid it all out: the action in the bar, Monroe and *Whistler*, how it was now general knowledge that they were carrying big cash. "We might be challenged from some quarter. Monroe. Them scumbags in the bar. We showed too much green, there's no getting away from that." He glanced up the companionway where McCann was on watch, scanning the docks and the harbor front. "But it all seems to be working out."

"The sooner the better," said Gelb. His new life couldn't happen too fast.

Cicciolino agreed. "Monroe is probably out of his mind by now, and he'll start searching for *Whistler* and us right away. He knows these waters, and I don't doubt he'll be able to raise a navy of 'friends' who'll want a piece of our green.

"It's imperative that one of us get back to *Whistler* without revealing where she's lying. Gerri should be warned, and maybe the boat moved. Then we've got to arrange a rendezvous with this boat, which we should begin immediately. Who knows who that Cuban might tell?

"Finally, we've got to transship the stuff, scuttle *Whistler* someplace she'll never be raised, and get ourselves clear. You and Tug in this boat headed north. Arlene, Gerri, and me back into Bimini on the whaler and then to the airport and New York.

"The problem is the whaler, which we left at the public dock. Like I said, we're going to need it, and it's the fastest way one of us can get out to Gerri. After this morning, Monroe knows what

Tug and me look like real good, and he's been seeing you, Jay, for years."

"Then I guess I'm your woman—" said Arlene. "*Senza* disguise." Cicciolino was wearing mirror sunglasses, which he had raised up on his forehead. Arlene reached up and flicked them down over his eyes. Using them as a mirror, she removed her sun hat, her own sunglasses, and quickly, deftly bound up her deep red hair that she had been wearing in a bun at the nape of her neck. Out of her purse came her granny glasses, the bows of which she fit over her ears. She turned her head to either side to assay the effect.

And then, *then*—Gelb could scarcely believe what he was seeing—she undid the buttons on her yellow blouse and pulled it off. Below, she was wearing some black skimpy and lacy brassiere that Gelb had never seen before. It made her breasts look full and sassy, the way they had that first time years ago back in New Mexico when without a kiss or anything she had lowered the bodice of a party dress and then pulled Gelb's face down on them. Now, in the mirrors of Cicciolino's sunglasses, she straightened the straps and, smiling slightly, pulled the sleeves of the blouse inside out. It was reversible, and the other side was red.

"Like what you're seeing, Chick?" she asked, pushing the blouse toward him so he would hold the sleeves.

"I remember what the nuns taught us. You know, when everybody was wearing shiny shoes to look up girls' dresses. 'Custody of the eyes,' they called it.

" 'Please help me, Holy Mother, to keep my eyes pure and my thoughts clean.' I'd look away, 'cept you need my glasses."

The brassiere and the whole . . . look of Arlene was something you saw in ads in *Vogue* or *Harper's Bazaar*. It was something expensive, designed to be provocative, and Gelb found it very, very sexy.

"Useful when you were little boys." She slipped her hands through the sleeves in the graceful, feminine way that Gelb had been watching for years. It made him realize how much he still loved her. "Let's hope this experience will help you two to grow up."

And she was gone, up the companionway ladder where she had to squeeze past McCann's legs. They heard her laugh and say something flirtatious to McCann who, when drinking, reached for all women.

"What's with her?" Cicciolino asked Gelb.

Gelb didn't know what to say, but he came out with, "I guess money changes people," and Cicciolino began laughing.

"How 'bout yourself, Captain?" Cicciolino glanced around the cabin, reaching out to touch the leaded-glass doors on the lockers above the chart table. "Jesus—this is some scow you got yourself. At some price," he added. "You fucker. You done good, Jay." He raised his hand so they could high-five.

Gelb smacked his palm into Cicciolino's large, strong hand.

Cicciolino nodded. "Real good."

It made Gelb feel like a million. Or, rather, several millions, if things kept going as they were. Once it was over, he'd sort everything out. With Arlene, with himself.

As Arlene made her way through the crowds dockside and along the main street—circling the harbor and having to pass directly in front of the Conch Inn—she was surprised that fear made up only a small part of what she was feeling. It was there, certainly. What had happened to the men in the boat and planes had been no fantasy. Their deaths had been brutal and terrible, and the same could easily happen to them.

But mostly she felt a kind of elation; her life had changed totally, irrevocably, and so much for the better. All she had to do was follow her emotions.

Logic-chopping meant nothing to Arlene; what good was knowledge without feeling? And from all that she could judge, she was on a roll. Like her reprobate father, Arlene was a gambler. He, however, just never knew when to cash in. You had to watch for the signs.

CHAPTER 12

SHIP BURIAL

THROUGH BINOCULARS MONROE caught sight of the woman only when she was well beyond the harbor. The anchored and moored sportfishing boats, which were crowding the harbor mouth, had obscured his vision, but he knew the skiff. It was from *Whistler*, and the woman at the tiller was the wife of Professor Gelb.

Monroe was crazy-drunk. He'd been that way before, and it was a dangerous condition. In it he could concentrate on one thing for short periods of time with an insight and clarity that was denied him at any other level of intoxication. Trouble was, the next level was drunk-drunk, where he couldn't think at all. More than once drunk-drunk had nearly killed him.

He turned to the man beside him in the tiny kitchen of the marl-and-driftwood shack he'd been born in fifty-two years before. Monroe could afford to pay cash for the finest house on Bimini, but it was not his way. Monroe's single, maniacal pleasure lay in contemplating his *liquid* capital, by which he meant not only his bank statements, money-market accounts, cash, gold, and jewelry, but also the inventory of his bar. The phrase seemed to sum up everything in life that he enjoyed, and he now decided that he would get both things: *Whistler and* the money that the Americans had flashed.

He handed the man the binoculars. "There, off the jetty, Sidney. The woman in the skiff. How long would it take to round up your crew and follow her?" To *Whistler*, he meant.

Sidney was a tall, dark-skinned younger man with a pleasant face that a receding hairline made seem long. He glanced at the horizon to the west where the sun was now declining and raised the glasses. "There are only two anchorages in the direction she's heading. She won't outrun us." He turned his glasses toward the docks where he caught sight of his crew of four lounging near his boat, a big, rangy cigarette that was reputed to be the fastest launch in Bimini. "Shares?"

"*Af-tah* I get my bet back." The one they cheated me out of, he did not have to add. Sidney had been in the bar. It had been one of his crewmen that the New York cop had dropped.

It was nightfall when they found *Whistler* in the cove of a cay some six miles southeast of Bimini. She was standing there at anchor, looking like a ghost ship in the bluish beam of the searchlight. "She's abandoned," said Sidney. "You frightened them off."

"Nonsense. You think scum like them frighten easily? They're sewer rats. New Yawk!" Monroe spat, the alcohol driving his tongue. "We'll see how rats fare on the high seas." Idle and drifting now, the cigarette boat rocked on a wave, and Monroe staggered, an empty glass clutched in his right hand.

One of the four younger men standing behind him said something, and the others laughed.

Monroe spun around on them, but Sidney, who was at the wheel, said, "Then you think they'd just sit here? Where's your whaler?"

Monroe had no idea. Yet. "Put out the lights." They had to wait until their eyes accustomed themselves to the darkness again. "See that glow in the galley port? One or another of them is in there now, waiting for the whaler to return."

"Sleeping perhaps," Sidney suggested. It made no sense at all. Anybody aboard the schooner would have heard their noisy approach. The intensity of the lights alone would have startled a sleeper awake.

"Or drunk. That one—Mc-*Cahn*," Monroe intoned, his voice dripping with hatred. "He's probably passed out." He smiled. In Monroe's scheme of things passing out was a definite sign of weakness, and he would treat the son of a bitch accordingly. He would keel-haul him. He'd make him gargle and drown in seawater. Or Absolut. Why hadn't he thought to bring some along?

Sidney switched the searchlight back on. He had wasted enough time on Monroe's empty promise of shares. At least now Monroe would have his schooner back and owe him a favor, for all that would mean to Monroe. He'd probably have to be reminded. "Well—you to play," he said, appropriating one of Monroe's expressions.

"You mean you're not coming aboard? Where's your sense of adventure? Your courage?"

Sidney put Monroe off on *Whistler*. "You can handle her yourself?"

"Yes, of course. The boat. The scum. *Everything*." Monroe had a large, old-fashioned automatic pistol in one hand, the empty glass in the other.

"Shouldn't we wait, see if he gets under way?" one of Sidney's crew asked.

Sidney shook his head. He'd had enough of Monroe for a day. Drunks were predictable and therefore boring. All that really concerned them was their next slosh of grog.

Good boat, strong boat, true boat, Monroe thought as he stepped aboard *Whistler*. His eye caught on the damage to the taffrail and the cabin top. He tried to understand what that might mean, but it was beyond him. He set the glass down.

And then there was the source of the bluish light that now glowed from the port and looked almost fuzzy on the deck by his shoes. He tried to bend to peer in, but the boat was rocking on its anchor, and he nearly lost his balance. He placed the gun next to the glass and, holding on to a shroud, lowered a knee to the deck.

There now, he thought, I can't be *that* drunk. A genuflection so graceful on a swaying boat was worthy of a saint. Or at least an accomplished sinner.

It took him a moment or two to understand what he was seeing, the light seemed so odd and eerie. There was the stainless-steel edge of the sink, there the teak floorboards, there the corner of the cooker. He also made out what appeared to be the shadowed edge of some large pot, and the illuminated base of the cooker itself.

Yes—that was it; they had put something over the burners to cook. It meant they—some of them, one of them—were below. Another possibility was that they had gone away for a short while and hadn't yet returned. Leaving something on to cook, like that, wasn't a safe practice, and certainly nothing that he himself, who had been raised on boats, would ever think of doing. But he knew there were those who did.

By means of another sustained, concentrated effort that cheered him, Monroe made his way to the companionway, which was locked from the outside. What? With something cooking in the galley? Did they expect brigands, or was it just the way people from that pest hole, New York, acted as a matter of course? Locking up everything, the car, the house, the bicycle. Monroe had seen them in movies.

Back at the port, Monroe had just begun to lower his knee to the deck again, when it occurred to him that he had been smelling something now almost since he had come aboard.

Gasoline. They must've run her hard, getting her there to the cove anchorage.

But *Whistler* had a *diesel* engine, Monroe thought, as his face moved into the blue glare from the gas jets. He would never let gasoline aboard any boat that he ever owned, apart from gasoline contained in the gas can of an outboard engine. Gasoline was lethal and really couldn't be trusted. Its vapor was explosive.

It was then that he noticed the gas can in the cockpit, a big shiny thing with a word printed neatly across its side. Monroe squinted. *Trekker,* it said. The name of a boat, perhaps?

Monroe returned his gaze into the cabin, where the fluid in the pot had now come to a rolling boil. Monroe watched it rise up toward the brim and realized suddenly that he had had his last drink. Drunk-drunk had got him, and he would never shake the leather cup again.

Well, he could jump, but would it matter? In spite of all his years on and around the sea, Monroe had never learned to swim. He hated even the thought of water, and drowning? It was his most abject fear.

He turned to watch the gasoline bubble up out of the pot. It would catch on the flame of the propane burner, and all those fumes. . . . Monroe had once been burned rather badly across a forearm, and he now remembered the agony it had brought him for whole sleepless nights.

Pivoting suddenly, he hurled himself overboard just as *Whistler* went up.

The explosion filled the night sky with a ball of orange light. The tremor came next. It rocked *Trekker* and was followed a split second later by the report, which riffled the sails and made Gelb's hand jump to his face, as though expecting debris to rain down on them.

"Yeah!" Cicciolino shouted and punched a fist at the night sky. "*Awright!* That asshole got his!" Which Cicciolino had explained was "Bronx soup"—a bucket of accelerant left to boil on the burner of a rent-controlled apartment house—but Gelb knew was called "Jew stew" by the arson squad of the NYPD.

No matter, they had followed Monroe's arrival on radar and had watched his transferral to *Whistler* through binoculars. The white light of the search beams of the other boat had been achromatic and cold, different from the greasy red light that now enveloped the ship.

"There's two lessons in that," McCann said.

Cicciolino and Gelb turned their faces to him. Arlene was sitting behind them on the cabin trunk, watching the conflagration that was flickering in the lenses of her octagon glasses.

"One, never drink rum. You go up like a Roman candle."

They laughed.

"And two?" Cicciolino asked.

"Welshers burn good."

Cicciolino wrapped his arm around McCann's shoulder. He tilted his curly head back to the dark sky and laughed and laughed. It was New York humor, black and almost always pointed at losers.

Another explosion tremored the boat. They looked up and saw a fireball floating above the burning ship. The blast made them flinch.

"Wow!" McCann said. "That was—what's the word kids are using now? You teach them, Jay. You know what it is. It was—"

"Awesome."

"That's it. Awesome!"

"No, no—" Gelb corrected. "You gotta say it right." Gelb

raised his arms and gestured his hands at the fire. "Awe-some. Really *awesome!*"

Cicciolino and McCann joined him, and with hands raised together they shouted, "Awe-some. Really *awesome!*"

Looking back to see how Arlene was taking it, Gelb thought here they were on the bounding main, just three ordinary guys from the Lower East Side. Just imagine what they could do when they got back to the city. The deal was virtually in the bag.

Gelb hadn't felt so . . . vital since he still considered himself an artist and had immersed himself so totally in a project that he lost all sense of self and time. Here he had given himself over to the process of making them all richer than their wildest dreams. It didn't matter what happened or what they did, as long as they got through and won the final reward. Then he'd go back to being Jay Gelb—good, caring, thoughtful, considered, Nouveau Jew. Humanist. Professor of fine arts.

Arlene was still staring at the fire, smiling slightly as though it was a pleasant, warming sight. And it occurred to Gelb that not only had he never really known her, he *couldn't* know her. She was inscrutable, like some sort of Far West Sphinx. Using the excuse that he wanted to get his camera, Gelb nipped below to powder his nose.

Gerri was at the salon table, packing Eva's bag in a large cardboard box.

Up at the helm Cicciolino could look down into the boat, and when he saw Gelb's legs disappear into the toilet, he asked, "Jay got something wrong with his kidneys, Arlene?"

Her eyes only flashed up and met Cicciolino's briefly, then returned to the blaze in the distance.

Cicciolino turned to McCann. "It's something you better watch."

McCann raised the glass in his hand. Each to his own addiction, he thought. Who was he to cast the first stone? And then he'd heard it gave you energy, helped you stay up. When he had tried it himself, it made his heart beat so fast he didn't sleep for two days. Sure, he'd got a hard-on, but coming off he found nearly impossible; when he did, it hurt. Which was the end of any cocaine story for him. McCann would tolerate nothing—not even rare, aged malt, which he loved only slightly less—to get between him and carnal pleasure.

But Gelb had only just laid two fat, shimmering lines on the edge of the sink when the door burst open and pinned him against the sink.

It was Gerri, her face a tear-streaked, tragic mask. She had a drink in her hands. "Just what I thought," she said, glancing down at the powder. "Is it worth it? Does it help?"

She had shocked Gelb, barging in like that, and the adrenaline rush made him angry. "Help with what?" he demanded.

"Help with the fact that we've just killed . . . *murdered* another person," she nearly screamed. She raised the glass in her hand. "This doesn't." She tossed the rest of the drink into the toilet.

Gelb didn't know what she meant. That *person*, like the others back on the island, would have gladly killed them. They had got caught up in this thing, and now all that mattered was getting out. Properly.

"Here—" He handed her the rolled up thousand-dollar bill he had taken from the damaged, drug-runners' boat three days earlier. Somehow it made everything classier. "Put this in one nostril and close the other with your finger. Now lower your head. . . ." The boat was heaving in a following sea, and he had to guide her face down to the bright powder. "Try to take each line in one pass."

There was so little room in there that it was as though he were directing her down on his penis, and he wished he had snorted first. In some ways Gerri had always reminded him of his mother, who had been born in Berlin and had had real—as opposed to *arriviste*—style.

When she straightened up, her eyes were distant, but her anguished expression had eased. There was a perfect white ring around the edge of her nostril. After a while she said, "Oh, Jesus. Oh, Christ."

She moved into him and rested her head against his shoulder, and they just stood there for the longest time, rocking with the movement of the boat.

PART III

THE TWO AMERICAS

CHAPTER 13

REAL

The Bahamas

FOR EVA BURDEN, the night with the two dying men in the open boat had been hard—like a test to see if she had the courage and skill to survive and keep others living in what was without a doubt the real world.

After nearly eight years, her medical skills were rusty, but she turned her attention first to saving their lives. The short, stocky black man had lost four fingers on his left hand. A bullet had severed an artery in his left thigh. Having bled profusely, he had lost consciousness, and his pulse was thready. He also had a puncture wound in his throat.

She sat him up to keep blood out of his lungs, then secured the tourniquets on arm and thigh. In his jacket she found a kilo pack of cocaine, which she stowed in a locker. Blood-soaked powder crusted the stumps of his fingers, and she would allow him no more. In his condition cocaine toxicity could kill him more quickly than his wounds.

Coke had also been sprinkled around the stomach wound of

the white man. Large and leonine with a mane of curly hair and a Vandyke, he was wedged between the forward seats of the small boat. A barb of what looked like black fiberglass was jutting from his side. He was lapsing in and out of consciousness, and Eva judged that she wouldn't move him if she could. As he was situated, he didn't appear to be bleeding externally. Both men needed intensive medical care as quickly as possible.

It was twilight and low tide. She had to hop out into the shallow water and pull the launch from the mangroves where it had been concealed. But the outboard engine started on the first pull, and in her small hand the boat felt quick and sure.

Eva swung wide to avoid the wreckage of the drug boat and plane. In the gloaming it had the tangled, fire-charred intricacy of modern sculpture. Flotsam—tufts of yellow insulation, a flight jacket, and a landing tire that was still inflated—was bobbing through the narrow passage that linked the cove and bay.

There, the chop was manageable, but entering open water, she had to ease off the throttle to keep the boat from vaulting off the rollers from the storm of the night before.

The pounding brought the white man around. "Go. Go!" he shouted over the snarl of the outboard engine and the gusting wind.

"Go where?"

He struggled to raise his head above the rail. "There." His hand shot out in the general direction she was headed. "South. After a while you'll see the lights of Nassau." His eyes closed, and his head fell back against a seat.

"But I need something more. A compass and a compass bearing."

It took a few minutes, but he came to again, which was a good sign. "What?"

"I need a compass or something. Anything."

He kept regarding her.

"I mean—here I am in a small boat with two dying men. One wants to go *there*. *There* is open ocean for at least fifty nautical miles that I know of. Wouldn't *you* want a compass and a bearing or a chart? Wouldn't you want to know how much fuel we have? Or if there are things like flares, a life raft, a radio. How about a radio or—more to the point—a radio direction finder with an azimuth heading? And running lights. Shouldn't we at least show a light so we don't get run down?"

"No. Not until we're well away from the island."

His eyes, which were glassy, were nearly the same unusual bluish-green color of her own. They moved down the work shirt and denim cutoffs she was wearing, then focused on the duckbill cap she had found in the bottom of the boat and put on. "You a cop?"

"No, of course not."

"Then what? You're something. Coast Guard? Navy?"

"I was. Once."

"Navy?"

She nodded.

"What, a—?"

"Nurse." Had she not got married, Eva might have made the navy a career.

"OCS?" He meant, had she gone to Officer Candidate School?

"I processed out as lieutenant commander."

He tried to laugh, but it sounded more like a cough. "Who'd 'a' thunk it? Off that charter boat, out here? A navy nurse with OCS training. Well, it's something anyway, and I thank whoever sent you."

"Don't. Yet."

Again their eyes met, and an understanding passed between them. He knew how badly he was hurt. "Try the foredeck hold. You'll find everything you'll need there. When we get within sight of the inner harbor, wake me. If you can't"—he attempted to pull the wallet from his back pocket, but it dropped into the boat— "call a man name of Denny at my number. It's in the wallet. He'll get a doctor. But *no* cops. Please. No hospitals. If we"—his eyes searched hers—"go out"—he hunched a shoulder—"we bought it. But cops—" Again he shook his head. "And don't worry about us, Commander—we're beholden."

Which was an odd word from a drug dealer, Eva thought, lowering the speed to an idle and heading up into the wind. But then, what words were drug dealers supposed to use? Her own husband had had two degrees in clinical psychology, and he had dealt but mainly used drugs with the best of them. Or the worst.

In the dark, pitching boat Eva made a foray into the narrow

foredeck hold. She had to climb over the two men and then brace herself to open the hatch. With the aid of a flashlight that was fixed by a U-clamp to the underside of the deck, she discovered a veritable ship's store of supplies. Hanging from hooks were coils of line, auxiliary lights, buckets, a sea anchor, several types of bottom anchors, lengths of chain, etc.

In wooden niches along either side of the hull and even labeled with black-and-white intaglio plates was an array of other nautical spares and emergency equipment, including a battery-lit compass that mounted in a bracket near the helm, a flare gun, and a box of flares. There were three deck jackets and sou'westers. After tucking a set around each of the men, she discovered nautical charts of Bahamian waters. They had been reduced in size, laminated, and were stored in a waterproof wooden locker that seemed to have been constructed just for that purpose.

She switched on a portable radio–direction finder and placed it by her feet. And in fixing the compass to its yoke, she caught sight of the fuel tanks, which had been shackled under the seat midboat. They were full. According to the IDs in the wallet, the large white man was one Brian Nathanson who lived on Water Street in Nassau. He might be a drug dealer, Eva thought, but he was a neat, orderly, and well-prepared drug dealer. It did not make him better, but it might keep him alive.

As she sat back at the transom, her hand touched a switch that had been concealed under the seat. Running lights, she guessed, but she left them off. Instead she pulled on the remaining deck jacket and, wrapping the sou'wester around her legs, set off.

Again the little boat wanted to vault the waves, and running blind without lights made Eva uneasy. But a moon was rising in the storm-washed sky, and she kept a close watch for any patch of unusual phosphorescence in the water that might signal an uncharted cay, some submerged hazard, or even maverick waves, which were not uncommon after cyclonic storms.

She had run hard in small boats through rougher seas than this on fishing trips out to Santa Catalina Island with her father and mother and, later, her husband. But with the two critically injured men slumped in front of her, the time wore on, and she thought of many things.

Brian Nathanson had mentioned luck. Eva didn't know how much luck went into a successful life, but certainly hers with men had been bad. Right from the start of dating in high school, she had gone out with a succession of "romantic" losers that culminated in the debacle of her six-year marriage to a man whom, she discovered, she didn't know. There had been a superjock, a motorcycle monkey, even a plant endocrinologist—all obsessive men.

Was she attached to such types because her father himself had been driven? At the Long Beach Naval Shipyard where he had worked, he had been known as *the* mechanic. There hadn't been anything he couldn't fix, from immense marine diesels to gyroscopes, nuclear heat-transfer systems, air-conditioning systems, outboards. How things worked had been his life, and once presented with a problem, it had been as if he couldn't help himself. He had to dive in headfirst; he became consumed.

But was that bad or wrong? No. Had it ever got in the way of his being a good father and husband? No again.

Was it possible, then, for a good woman to have a succession of bad relationships with men? Why not? she laughed to herself— there she was, living proof, since she knew she was a good woman in the best sense. When she finally realized why her husband had quit or been fired from one job after another, she got him help time after time, slip after slip. When he was no longer employable, she brought him into her own business, a restaurant that she had begun with her mother in Long Beach.

Everything seemed to go along fine until one night, after hours, he was found dead by her father, shot with the handgun they kept in the safe. It was registered to her father, who phoned the police. They arrested him, said they'd been surveilling the business for a month and had tapes of them arguing, which they did. Unknown to Eva, her father had been trying to get her husband to leave and had even threatened him. SCAG SELLERS' FALLOUT, the headline said. A jury agreed.

Next there had been Tug McCann, whom Eva had been *sure* was a good man. And now here she was in a small boat with two dying drug dealers. Well, at least I'm consistent, Eva thought. And look at the bright side: This Nathanson and she had something in common besides the color of their eyes—a dislike of cops.

An hour later she began to see the blush of lights on the horizon that could only be Nassau. She flicked on the running lights.

The wind off the land was blessedly warm, and she could hear laughter from moored boats, the occasional car horn, and the general low roar that any city gave off over water at night. From a mile or so out, Nassau looked like twin mountains of shimmering light: one the city itself, which was stacked up the side of a hill; the other all the towering, modern hotels of the resorts that had been built on Paradise Island. While on R & R from the navy, Eva had once stayed in Nassau.

Between the promontories was the harbor, which had deep water and was open on both ends. Under a nearly full moon it looked like a sheet of silver broken here and there by the looming shapes of docked cruise ships and large, moored oceangoing yachts and pleasure boats. Drifting with the wind at her back, Eva could hear other outboard and marine engines, and she watched the lights of what she guessed were ferries or nightcruise boats plying the waterway. She moved forward and tried to rouse Brian Nathanson.

Only the cocaine worked. Wetting a finger with seawater, she rolled it in the powder and touched it to his lips. His face wizened at the bitter, medicinal taste, and he tried to turn his head away. But his eyes opened.

The other man was now delirious and moaning.

Eva helped Nathanson raise himself up to look around. "Cut in after the last cruise ship starboard side. There's a small dock there. Tie us under it, and go for help." His eyes moved to hers. "It's right across the street. Cover us now, and"—a large hand fell on her wrist—"thanks." She helped him pull the hood of the sou'-wester over his face.

The dock was indeed small, just four pilings and a ramp leading up. A small sign said, B. NATHANSON. KEEP OFF. KEEP CLEAR. She tied the skiff in deep shadow and checked the black man, whose fever seemed to have worsened.

The dock led up to a small lawn bordered by trellised vines. There was a table with chairs and an arched picket gate, which she opened. Stepping out onto a sidewalk, her eye caught on another sign that repeated the advisory of the first.

The house across the street looked so big that at first Eva thought Nathanson must have meant some other place. To one side was a narrow street that climbed the hill and to the other a large side yard enclosed by a high stone wall. Even at the late hour the street was teaming with traffic, and while waiting to cross, she studied the house.

Two immense sycamores stood behind the wall in the front yard. Each had been carefully trimmed so no limb blocked the view from a second-floor porch. There, she guessed, you could look out over the harbor when the shutters were pulled back.

Now they were closed, and the only light she could see over the high wall came from a multipaned window at the rear of the house. She rang the bell at the gate, and immediately a dog began barking. She heard a screen door slap, and suddenly the spotted snout of a Dalmatian appeared in the gap between the gate and its jamb.

"You get back in here, Bert. Who appointed you to the welcoming committee?" The voice was that of an old Bahamian man, who now asked, "Who is it?"

"Are you Denny?"

"Yes, ma'am."

"Brian Nathanson sent me. He's hurt and needs help. He told me to tell you he needs a doctor, and he and his partner—"

"Creach," the man supplied.

"—they'll need some way of getting up here from the dock."

When Denny opened the door, the Dalmatian bolted, turning down the sidewalk toward the street and the dock below.

"Come in." He ushered Eva into the deep shadows of a leaf-covered walkway.

"Oh, Lord," he continued, leading her to the house. "Oh, mercy—I knew it. I did. I told him, I said, what you need go taking chances? But he said Creach gonna do it, and it couldn't be alone." Suddenly he stopped and turned to her. "How hurt?"

"Hurt. They need help fast."

Eva waited in the kitchen while the man made several phone calls from what looked like a pantry.

The house was an old, graceful Colonial design, its kitchen large with a patterned brick floor and an array of tall arched windows near which tropical plants had been grouped. The room contained the standard kitchen items along with a sweep of built-in counters and a long kitchen table with a small stack of books at an end.

One was open. There was a coffee cup nearby, and in all Eva found it an inviting, peaceful setting and quite different from what she had known for the past two weeks aboard *Whistler* and what she had expected of a drug dealer.

They found the dog on the dock pacing back and forth by the ladder. Two young, strong black men soon arrived, and without saying a word climbed down the ladder into the boat. Following them, Eva directed their efforts to carry the man named Creach up to the house—"Watch those tourniquets. They can't be loosened in any way"—and then Nathanson.

"I want you to carry him as though he's sitting in a chair. Don't stretch him out." But he was a big man, and all four of them had to ease him up the ladder. Stopping traffic in both directions, they trundled him across the street with the dog weaving around their ankles and leading them toward the house.

By the time they got him into the kitchen, they found that a doctor had arrived and had examined Creach. "David must be put in hospital immediately," he announced. "An artery is severed in his thigh, and his hand—" A white Bahamian in his mid-thirties, he shook his head.

"And as for you . . . ?" he turned to Nathanson, who had been struggling to keep himself from crying out from pain. "What're these?" He waved two banded stacks of thousand-dollar bills that he had found in Creach's jacket. "I thought you told me no more, you were too old for this"—he considered the sodden stack—"*shit,* was your word. What do I do with it now, Brian, order David a prosthetic device? He'll need one, you know."

But Nathanson was beyond responding, and there was no time to waste. When she saw the two young men glance from the money to each other and then back at the money, she took it out of the doctor's hands. Giving it to Denny, she said, "Count it, dry it, and put it in a safe place. They'll want it later." She turned back to the doctor.

"Can't we work on them here?"

The doctor began shaking his head. He was a tall man with dark, glistening hair that had been combed back and made him seem older than his thirty-five or forty years. He was wearing a blue blazer with gold buttons, white duck trousers, and white shoes. Obviously he had been called away from some social occasion.

"Wait—hear me out. I'm a certified surgeon's assistant. I served on hospital ships and MASH units in Vietnam. Later I was chief surgical nurse ICU at L.A. General. What do we have here?

"One man"—she pointed to Creach—"has a severed artery. He'll need blood, and we can't tell how weak he might be. But the bullet passed through, and the procedure won't be terribly complicated. Same with his hand. The fingers are gone. We'll clean them up, do some preliminary grafting, but—" She shook her head. "His throat? We won't know about that until we get in, but if it was mortal. . . ." He'd be dead.

"Same with him." She meant Nathanson. "Do you know these two men?"

The doctor nodded. "Brian nearly all my life, or at least since his father bought this house. I only live down the street. Creach maybe twenty years."

"Do you want to see him lose it?" She meant the house, which might happen if the police could tie the busted drug deal to him.

"Better than his life."

"What are prisons like here in the Islands?" Because of her father, prisons were something Eva knew, or at least *thought* she knew from her few visits and the tone of his letters.

The doctor closed his eyes and shook his head, as though to say Bahamian prisons were not good.

"How would either of them fare locked up? Maybe this *is* their lesson, their—" She did not want to say punishment. "Why don't we take the chance?"

"Where? It can't be the hospital, it can't be my dispensary, which is closed now. The lights would draw the police."

"Then here," said Eva.

"Where, here?"

"That table." She pointed to the large kitchen table.

The doctor sighed and looked away.

Nathanson raised his head. "Darrin—try."

"Which is easy to say. I'm no surgeon, and if it doesn't work, my career goes with you."

Nathanson raised his large hand to the doctor. "Darrin—if it doesn't work, Jared and Deke will take care of the problem." He meant their corpses. Nathanson turned to the two young black men, who nodded. "What about it?"

The doctor thought for a moment. He shook his head. "The things I get involved in, knowing you." But he clasped Nathanson's hand.

Turning to the two young men, he said, "Here's what I want you to get from the dispensary." He pulled a pen from his blazer and turned to a kitchen notepad on the sideboard.

Eva asked Denny where she might shower and get a change of clothes. "Anything that might come even close to fitting." Her shirt was stiff from dried seawater and blood, and she had sand everywhere, it seemed.

Leading her up the wide front staircase in the house, Denny explained that over the years they had collected, ". . . some lady's this-es and thats. And then Miss Nattie, Brian's mother, her things still here, if you don't mind dated. Know what?" On the landing he turned to her. "I believe you and her just about the same size." He led her down the hall to an enormous bedroom. "Both fine-boned ladies, if you don't mind me saying."

Nearly five-and-a-half hours later, Dr. Darrin Southworth held out his hand to her. "That was some performance. You certainly know what you're doing."

"I'm out of practice," Eva said, only now realizing the sun was out. She pulled the surgical mask from her face and the rubber gloves from her hands. The muscles in her shoulders, arms, and neck were galling her.

"Not that I saw. Breakfast? I know a nice, quiet place overlooking the harbor where we can talk."

It was the last thing Eva wanted, and Denny stepped in. "We gotta get them two boneheads up to the porch bedroom where there's air." He added that he was about to serve "a full breakfast for all hands," which he had cooked in the butler's pantry off what turned out to be a large, cool dining room. "No nicer *quiet* place in all Nassau. To talk," he muttered with obvious disdain for Southworth's suggestion. "And then where we gonna get you two, if we need?"

Only able to nibble a slice of toast, Eva excused herself and walked out through an open French door into a garden that seemed to contain every type of tropical plant. Each tree, bush, and plant had been labeled with the same white-on-black intaglio tags that she had seen in the foredeck hold of the skiff. The garden was scrupulously maintained. There were no weeds, the bare ground had been freshly raked, and the grass cut to a putting-green regularity.

It led to a boxwood maze that Eva skirted, and at the corner of the large house she found some other French doors that were also open to the morning breeze. Inside she found a kind of living room that was filled with tasteful and expensive-looking antiques or at least vintage furniture that looked well-cared-for but well-used. Here was a serpentine leather couch with shining brass tacks, and there an oval ebony table with raised, hinged wings that had obviously been taken from a ship. Underfoot were Oriental rugs, and the walls carried paintings mainly of ships, seascapes, and nautical scenes.

Eva moved from that room into a kind of den or study with a well-used fireplace and a pigeonhole desk. A narrow door opened on a library that was filled with light from seven tall windows. Newspapers, magazines, and a few books that looked new had been set out on a central table, as though to be read. And with several other stuffed leather chairs grouped around yet another fireplace, the entire feel of the place was more that of a gentleman's club than a house.

It made Eva think of Tug, who had a weekend house in Connecticut with a similar, if smaller, room. She should make an attempt to contact him so he wouldn't worry or send the Coast Guard or police or whoever searched for missing persons in the Bahamas. She didn't want that now. All she wanted was sleep and to get herself together, so she could decide what to do next.

She had taken a month off, so she had just about two weeks left. She had left Thermidor, her restaurant, in the capable hands of her chef, who was a woman about her own age. Now that they were established, the place virtually ran itself, but in spite of how hard Eva had worked over the past four years to get things going, she didn't know if she wanted to return to New York permanently. Somehow the entire thing on the boat had soured her on the idea of staying there.

Only Denny remained in the dining room when Eva found her way back. He was loading dishes onto a tray, the Dalmatian dog by his side, waiting for scraps. "Dr. South' left. He said he be back in a few hours to check how they doin'. He said you should sleep long as you can, like any fool can tell. *Dr.* South'—hmmh—he ain't worth much. And you' only a nurse?" He shook his head. "You can take the missus's bedroom, if you like."

"Denny—how would I get a message to Bimini?"

"There's a telephone just inside the door there. In the pantry. You got a number, I'll put it through for you."

Without revealing too much, Eva explained that she would like to reach some friends who were cruising on a yacht and probably thought she was lost.

"You just write down what you want to say, and I'll send a telegram. When they get to the constabulary, it'll be there."

After reading the message, Denny glanced up at her. His eyes were suddenly serious and intense. "No matter how Mr. Brian come by you, he sure was lucky. What you done for him and Creach is much appreciated."

As Eva turned and began making her way along the wide hall toward the staircase, he said it again, louder this time, as though to himself. "Much appreciated."

The dog's nails clicked on the tiles as it followed him into the kitchen.

CHAPTER 14

ANGLING

WHEN ASSISTANT CHIEF Bill Cicciolino got to the mauve stone building at One Police Plaza that was NYPD Headquarters, he did not stop at his office on the twelfth floor. Instead he went directly to the commissioner's level on the fourteenth floor. There he waved to a patrolman secretary, who waved back, and he walked right into the first deputy's office without being announced.

Bob Brant, the first dep was peering into a file cabinet. When he glanced up and saw who it was, an immediate smile appeared, which pleased Cicciolino. He had done the job good on Brant, whose cover he would need in the next couple weeks. The guy really liked him, and it wasn't just an act.

"What happen to you?"

Cicciolino stopped in the middle of the floor, held out his arms, and looked down at the new light gray worsted suit that an uncle on Mott Street had tailored to his sturdy frame. With a silk tie and handkerchief in the pocket to match, it gave him the on-camera credibility of a corporate CEO. "Me? Wha'?" he asked. "Whaz' a matter with me?"

"Plenty. People'll turn on their television, they'll say I thought this s'pozed to be the Bob and Bill Show. Now look—" Moving to

Cicciolino's side, Brant held out the back of his hand until Cicciolino did the same. Cicciolino's skin was darker. "It's the Bob and Bob Show. Don't you read the papers, *The Science Times, The New England Journal of Medicine?*"

Brant was a mulatto with white features, freckles, and kinky reddish hair combed back in glistening finger waves. In all he looked like a cross between Nat King Cole and Sugar Ray Robinson, with the difference that he had a Ph.D. in criminology from Michigan State. He had also been a fellow of the Rand Corporation, the warden of the largest state prison in Tennessee, and the chief of police of Worcester, Massachusetts, before being called by Police Commissioner Ben Ward to the first dep post.

More telling, his tailor was nearly as good as Cicciolino's uncle, which, Cicciolino knew, was important. Taste communicated, and Brant and he had hit it off from the start.

Holding out the papers in his hand, as if reading from a script, Brant said, "In a dunk experiment conducted in some twenty-three-thousand major cities across the country, Hoboken-based scientists discovered that Man Tan is bad for the skin. Carcinomas, melon-nomas, with you people grape-nomas, which are the worst. They're the big wine-colored splotches that prove Raisa Gorbachev once had an Italian lover." Brant glanced over the top of his tortoiseshell half-glasses and began to crack a smile.

It was a nice turn, but Cicciolino did not laugh. "Where'd you get these X-rated political jokes? The *National Review?*" Cicciolino was the straight man of the two, and he only shook his head. Out of the corner of his eye he could see the office staff gathering in the open door. Brant and he went through a routine like this every once in a while, and it was talked about for days. "They won't have no trouble telling Bob from Bill."

"Maybe you're right." Brant still had his hand out. "They'll see all that hair when you reach for the large appendage in the middle of"—Brant paused slightly—"your face."

The back of Cicciolino's hand was covered with dark, curly hair. Taking two quick steps, he moved behind Brant and grasped him by the elbows. "Nah," he replied, boosting the trim man off his feet. "No trouble. Bill's the one can press skinny little first deps. What you eat anyways—marshmallows?" Extending his arms, Cicciolino moved Brant toward the desk and set his feet down on the blotter.

Brant looked ludicrous—his back to them, a sheaf of papers in a hand. The two men and the woman in the doorway began laughing.

"Oh, hi, Frank," Cicciolino said, winking to the staff as he took a seat by the door. "Good to see you."

One of the men, picking up the gambit, said, "Can I get you a cup of coffee, Mr. Commissioner?"

Brant's head snapped to the door.

"Gotcha, baby. You're slow. You oughta take a vacation, get some color back in your face," said Cicciolino, and everybody laughed.

Their first meeting had come over two years earlier, when Brant had called Cicciolino up to his office "for a chat."

"Oh, yeah?" Cicciolino had asked. "About what?" He had a resignation already typed up in triplicate in a drawer of his desk, and he wasn't going to let any little half-nigger try to tell him how things were.

"I thought we might kick things around a little. See where we stand."

Cicciolino had an idea of who would get kicked, and he had folded the resignation and slipped it into his suit coat.

At that time Cicciolino had been an assistant chief for nearly five years. It was by no means record time to be stuck at that level. With over twenty-two thousand uniformed and plainclothes officers in service, it was a significant position with a salary of sixty-two thousand dollars and a guaranteed pension after twenty years of half that amount. The problem was Cicciolino could not survive on so little, and he still thought he could run things better than anybody he'd seen since Patrick Murphy, and he had been without a definite command for nearly two years.

The rank was equivalent to field general in an army. Assistant chiefs commanded areas, which were: the Bronx, Queens, Staten Island, Brooklyn North, Brooklyn South, Manhattan North, and Manhattan South. Because Manhattan South contained City Hall, Wall Street, the United Nations, and the heart of the city's commercial and entertainment districts, it was considered the plum, and Cicciolino had commanded it for thirty-nine months. Everybody—himself included—thought that at forty-eight he would soon be promoted to one of the five 3-star bureau-chief jobs or even be named to the 4-star position of chief of department, which was the final uniformed rank. Commissioner, then, would only be an appointment away; with thirteen years to wait, even that might occur.

But none of it would happen, through no fault of his own. It was the end of the Koch administration, and from all Cicciolino could see the new mayor would not be white, which meant his commissioner *couldn't* be. Even Koch had had a black commissioner. As far as the other top spots were concerned, Cicciolino found himself passed over by blacks, the ever-present army of qualified Irish cops, and now Hispanics. His own "rabbi" in the department had recently retired. And with an Italian population that was in the thick of several racist incidents and was fleeing to the suburbs by the day, Cicciolino's prospects for advancement were dim.

As Brant said when Cicciolino got to his office that morning, "You tired of bullshit, Bill? We don't know what to do with you. In spite of your years of exemplary service and your obvious qualities, there's simply no compelling reason to promote you." Whereas there was reason, he meant, to promote a nigger, a Rican, or even a Mick, since the Irish were still powerful in Queens and police politics.

"Then the book on you, as I hear it, is you're a dem-dese-dose kind of guy. You're gruff but very experienced, maybe overqualified, and smart as hell. You being white too scares hell out of all the characters they jumped over you. One look and they think Joe Hoffman or Patrick Murphy, and who wants somebody around reminding them maybe they're not competent?"

Face it, Cicciolino thought he was going to say, you should put out résumés, work someplace else, and maybe get hired back, as commissioner or first dep, like Murphy and Hoffman, if the New York political situation changes.

Instead he asked, "You mind a question?"

Cicciolino shrugged. He'd had two whole years of silence with everybody above him covering their ass, afraid of bias charges if they were candid. As far as he was concerned, the NYPD always was and would remain a racist, sexist organization until the city itself changed, which it wouldn't. And his experience had shown him that blacks and Hispanics had learned well. When it could work to their advantage, they were the most profoundly prejudiced groups he had yet encountered.

"How'd you get on the cops?"

Cicciolino looked at Brant close. The guy was from Detroit originally, but he had the New York phrase right, which meant details were important and he had a good memory. Cicciolino liked that. Maybe they could do business. "Took the tests, like everybody else."

"Have any help?"

Cicciolino tilted his head. It was so far back it was hard to remember. "Sure. Like everybody else," though it would not have mattered. He had scored first on the mental test, second on the physical. He was a college graduate, a lawyer. He'd passed the bar, and looked like a heavyweight contender.

"And coming up—you have a hook?" It was another word for "rabbi": somebody to make sure you got your boost every chance you could.

Cicciolino nodded. "And you?"

"You mean, did it help to be black?"

It was what Cicciolino had meant. Exactly.

"Well—I'm qualified, but it didn't hurt, which is really what I wanted to talk about this morning."

Cicciolino regarded the man. Had somebody in his office ratted? Were they going to use a pretext to force him out? Every once in a while—to his driver, to his secretary, or somebody he knew for a long time—he'd drop a "nigger" or a "spic." Kike, Mick, Harp, hunky, it was street-cop talk, and Cicciolino enjoyed posing as a street cop, though he knew he was far from it. These days, talk like that could kill a senior officer's career.

"For the last couple of years, being—you know— conspicuously white and bright hasn't helped you, but maybe it can now."

Brant went on to say that there was a growing perception among the white population, but more particularly among white businessmen and corporate leaders, that maybe New York was no longer the place to be. "It's the whole 'browning' of New York thing. Services are expensive, and quality help scarce. With all the crime caused by crack, people no longer feel safe in the streets."

Corporate flight, of course, was nothing new. Recently, however, the issue had become cloaked in racial terms. With Bernhard Goetz, Tawana Brawley, and Howard Beach it had become *white* corporate flight, and New York without its corporate base would be just another dirty, poor, black, and decaying American city.

"Which is where you come in," Brant said. "I want you to listen to something." Brant then switched on a tape of a meeting of the Citizens' Crime Commission of New York City. It was a highly regarded group formed in 1979 by forty of the city's major corporations and utilities to evaluate the police and criminal-justice program. He heard somebody say, "What about Chick? You know, the big guy who did such a good job in Manhattan South. Chief Chick—"

"—o-lee-no," somebody supplied.

"Can't we bring him back? I know a lot of us would feel better with him on the job. When you called about something, he came over himself and brought some blue uniforms with him. Made an impression, which is important to people. Then later he made sure everybody—cops, the mayor, the papers—got a report. What's he doing now?"

There was a pause, and a voice that Cicciolino recognized as Commissioner Ward mumbled, "He's on special assignment to the chief of department."

Yeah, Cicciolino thought, seeing how long it would take a grown, white man to go crazy around a bunch of incompetent *mulingìannu.*

Brant switched off the machine. "Whadaya think?"

"Do I want my old command back? Sure, but—" Brant wasn't offering that.

"How about something else? Something a little more public?"

Cicciolino waited. He liked offers. He hadn't had one in five years.

"You become the department's up-front guy. Our ambassador, so to speak. If there's a situation or an 'Unusual,' you're there to explain it, make everything all right. You go meet with the people on the mayor's committees or precinct or neighborhood groups that have a beef. Or we need somebody to speak at the Union Club or butt heads with Gabe Pressman? You're it. You know my press conference every Saturday morning? We'll give you equal billing. Wherever there are cops in action and the press, you're our guy. The commissioner says he'll stand behind you—your judgment, whatever you say—a hundred percent."

Until Cicciolino made a mistake. Cicciolino knew politicians and political appointees all too well. They were the reason he had short eyes.

Brant had leaned back, as though to say that was it, and Cicciolino asked, "Sounds like press secretary to me," which usually had been handled by a civilian deputy commissioner, some woman reporter hired away from a local television station for a two-year stint. The last had just quit.

"Not as we see it. What did those"—Brant glanced toward the open door and lowered his voice—"women know about police work? Half the time they were saying things that pissed cops off. And they couldn't make decisions or give orders. You'd be handling the big stuff, only major operations and . . . opportunities." For good cop PR was the implication.

"What about the new dep for public information? Or community affairs, for that matter?" Directly beneath the police commissioner were seven deputies for adminstration, community affairs, trials, public information, criminal justice, and legal matters. Each had large staffs and therefore constituencies that were not messed with successfully, Cicciolino knew from experience.

Brant's smile was wan. "You look big and fast enough to me. We give you the ball, you run right over them. I'll do the blocking. If they complain?" Brant pointed to his own chest, then raised his fingers toward the ceiling. The deputies of those agencies reported to the first dep, who reported to the commissioner, and if, like Ward, the commissioner was more interested in politics than the day-to-day operation of the department. . . .

But something else Brant had said concerned Cicciolino more. A certain territoriality went with an area command, which could only be breached by a superior officer, and usually not without ruffling feathers.

"We'd make that plain in a written memo signed by the commissioner. You'd be his roving assistant chief, able to step in and command, if necessary."

But not his roving *bureau* chief.

"Think of the possibilities for showcasing yourself, your talents, who you are. In three years' time thousands of other guys, like the one on the tape, they'll know who you are. Presidents. CEOs. Chairmen of corporations. Maybe you'll want a security job in private industry? Or voters? Maybe you'll want that? Three years, anything could happen."

Even a political reversal? Cicciolino doubted it. The city was going down the toilet, no two ways about it, and he liked the sound of a security job at, say, the Trump Plaza, the Waldorf, or the World Trade Center. A decade-long sinecure would round out his career nicely, he had thought. And then? Fucking Florida or someplace where the assholes were at least mainly white assholes.

But that wasn't *this* deal Brant was talking, and Cicciolino was enough New York to argue downside. Far as he was concerned, Brant had offered nothing real except the chance to fill in for a broad, and he told him. Worse, he was asking him to be a token white, and visible, senior cop. A shill. The correlative of what they used to call an "up-front" nigger, and he told Brant that too. "Like"—Cicciolino waved a hand and glanced out the window at the superstructure of the Brooklyn Bridge—"a kind of pross."

Brant shook his head. "There's no *kind of* whore. You' either a whore or you ain't." He smiled, not nasty but real. They were talking here, and beginning to understand each other.

"What about loot?"

"Whadaya mean, *loot*?"

"Is there more? Whadawe talkin' here, make-believe? You guys here in the Commissioner's Office, for you it's all like a chessboard. Move this guy here. That guy there. This hump, he's been sitting on his ass so long he'll jump at the chance to replace a civilian broad." He shook his head. "For me you gotta do *better*." Cicciolino sounded suddenly pissed off, but he knew Brant knew the tone, and Cicciolino liked that most. If he could talk open with the guy, it'd be easy to work with him.

Brant shook his head. "You know we can't do that."

"Why not?"

"Civil Service is why not. You get what you get. It's all down in black and white. And I hope you're not talking *better* better."

Cicciolino hunched his shoulders, as though to say he tried, but he also liked Brant's knowing the words, the code that cops used in speaking to each other. It made him different, and not just another bureaucratic cunt. "Better position?"

"Whose? They're all filled." With men it would be embar-

rassing to bump, he meant. "And unless somebody gets flopped
. . ." Again it was cop-speak for what happened when a command-
ing officer was reassigned under pressure or demoted in rank,
which was embarrassing for everybody and seldom happened.

"What would I have to do? Specifically."

"Tit city," said Brant, referring to the phrase "on the tit,"
which meant headquarters work. "You float. You keep informed
and available. We'll give you a staff. Twenty more men," which
would still make Cicciolino at least a hundred shy of the next least
important assistant chief in the Department.

He already had thirty-two. "Make it forty and I'll think about
it. I'd want them to keep on top of what's happening citywide.
And the memo to the area commanders—I'd want to write that
myself, giving specific examples of situations I could step into and
issue orders."

Brant had inclined his head. "I guess. I'd have to see it."

"And one more thing. A boost to bureau chief"—Brant began
to object, but Cicciolino raised a palm—"sometime near the end,
if only for a day."

"For retirement purposes?"

Cicciolino hunched his broad shoulders. "Something like
that." There was no way he could hold them to it, but at least he
was planting the seed. And then, hey—he had thought—if he became real visible and that visibility was important, they'd *have to*
do something for him.

"I don't know."

Cicciolino liked that too. Somebody who would say he didn't
know with no false promises.

"I'll see if it'll clear. That and the manpower."

"Shields," Cicciolino corrected, already sounding like a
spokesperson.

It did, along with thirty additional men, and "Assist Chief Bill
C." (Chick, to his intimates) had begun the task of selling a new
"brown" NYPD to a frightened, increasingly angry white minority
New York populace.

In the memo, RE: *COMMISSIONER'S TASK FORCE ON PUBLIC
INFORMATION AND PUBLIC SERVICE*, Cicciolino wrote that the intention in setting up the task force "was in no way to compete with
your policing of your area," but rather, "to elaborate police pres-

ence in areas of high visibility," which had been double-speak
Department policy from the time of the reduction of forces during
the budget crisis of the Beame administration.

"From time to time," the memo went on, "Asst. Chief Cicciolino's task force may find itself engaging in standard police activities. It may have to pursue perps, make arrests, or engage in
crowd control, surveillance, etc., but will always endeavor to make
its presence known to Area Commanders before, during, and with
a full report to the Chief of Patrol after any task force action.

"ALL COMMANDERS AT EVERY LEVEL ARE TO CO-
OPERATE WITH ASSIST. CHIEF CICCIOLINO WHO RE-
PORTS DIRECTLY TO COMMISSIONER WARD."

Cicciolino closed the memo with the telling line, "Task Force
size 63 POs," which put everything in perspective and, he imagined, provided area commanders relief. While not quite a "white"
wash, it was just another trick with mirrors, moving cops quickly
from one area to another, to provide the illusion of a significant
police presence. Other commissioners had done the same, the difference this time being that Ward was now institutionalizing a
flying squad for the purpose, which could in itself be bad publicity.

But Cicciolino made sure it wasn't, and he didn't care what
anybody thought or said. Brant was right. Having a big white
well-dressed cop like him, and not some dink-ass, non-cop reporter broad, fronting for the department was good politics, and
went over well. Cicciolino, who neither drank nor caroused and
didn't mind having his sleep broken, tried to make himself available to the press twenty-four hours a day, and he returned every
call himself personally. Interviews, photo ops, press conferences,
multiplied, and in his second year in the command the *Daily News*
named him to its list of the "Ten Most Admired New Yorkers."

The squib, written by Liz Smith, who had a contact at police
headquarters, noted his dedication, his strength of character, his
patience and tenacity. She also mentioned Gerri, who with her
NOW thing was so prominent, and their dedication to their inca-
pacitated daughter. It ended with, "And all New York would like
to know the name of Bill's tailor."

Bob Brant's name was several behind on the *News*'s "Most
Admired" list. Together every Saturday morning, Brant and Cicciolino looked like two healthy, competent, qualified, early-
middle-aged American professionals—one black, the other

white—who had joined forces to defeat crime and the crack menace. They were serious when it came to the problems facing the police department and the city, but both smiled readily and could joke with each other and the press, which was always important in New York.

It was as though they were saying that no matter how dire the problem or how bad things seemed, they could deal with it, and life (and therefore business) would carry on as usual. And when the mayor cited the commissioner's task force on PIPS (Public Information and Public Service) as one of the accomplishments of his administration, Cicciolino knew he had salvaged the wreck of his career. "In other words," said his buddy Tug McCann, from his pulpit at O'Casey's on Forty-first Street, "you're not the berries, you're the PIPS, Chick. Check it out." He had pointed down the bar where half the patrons were smiling and the other half looked vaguely uncomfortable in the sear of Cicciolino's practiced cop stare.

And while he still couldn't hope for any promotion that might seem to judge the administration's earlier choices for bureau commands, Cicciolino was approached by police-chief search committees of several large cities and by Bell Labs in Jersey, a sprawling scientific and defense-research facility that was looking for a director of security.

Cicciolino politely declined, saying that he was looking for a position in town. In the back of his mind he had this vision of something easily doable and profitable, something that would give him some "quality time," as yuppies were always saying. Something that would allow him to live leisurely at his own pace.

And he believed he had. If he had gleaned a single lesson from New York and his former command of Manhattan South, it was to grab as much as you can, as fast as you can, and go after anybody who will take it from you.

Now, in Brant's office, he pulled a seat closer to the desk and asked, "So, Bobby—how goes the battle? Miss me?" The desk held so many files and yellow legal pads Brant had to step carefully before hopping down.

Brant outlined what had occurred in his absence, which was the usual, and stroked Cicciolino's ego by saying the three Saturday morning press conferences he'd missed had been tough. The reporters had come at Brant from every angle. "And you're out there on your own. It's like having to do the funky chicken when you're used to fox-trots. You'll see." He meant during his own vacation, which was approaching.

They then moved on to department gossip. With forty-four hundred duly-sworn police officers under one roof, the headquarters rumor mill was a powerful engine, the speed and direction of which it was stupid not to be aware. They discussed who had announced plans for retirement, who was on sick leave, who was spending his credits in the favor bank to position himself for the next round of promotions.

Before his vacation, talk like that would have depressed Cicciolino, but not now. He asked questions, he drew Brant out until Brant finally said, "Enough of this crap. Let's get down to the important stuff. Your vacation. How 'bout the boat you chartered? Everything work out?"

Calling into the outer office for coffee, Cicciolino took his time with that too. He knew Brant worked too hard and seldom got out of the office. He was basically an intellectual, but like so many other cops, he was divorced, and, Cicciolino suspected, their conversations gave Brant a feel for white New York and the streets that he could get no other way. Every once in a while on some pretext, Cicciolino had pulled Brant away from his desk and then refused to take him back. Instead they had had an afternoon of drinks with McCann in O'Casey's or an eight-course meal in Little Italy, and even once an enjoyable spring sail around Manhattan with Gelb.

The phone kept interrupting them, their coffees were refilled by the sergeant who supervised the office, and finally Cicciolino, who wanted to make it obvious he was in no hurry, got down to his business. "What about you? Where you headed—when is it?"

"Three weeks."

Perfect timing, Cicciolino thought. In three weeks the boat would definitely be there, and Cicciolino would have everything set up and ready to roll. "For how long?"

Brant tried to look coy. "Only three weeks."

"Oh, gee—*only* three weeks." It was a shame Cicciolino couldn't be named acting first dep, but it was a civilian position, and he would have to resign as a police officer first. No matter, whoever was named to fill in wouldn't dare countermand one of his orders. All the public exposure and the praise from the business community and the mayor had given him too much clout for that. "Where you going?"

Brant sighed. "Hartford, I guess. You know, the kids."

It wasn't far enough for Cicciolino. "*All* three weeks?"

Brant only looked away. His relations with his ex were still stormy. She even made him take a motel room when he visited his kids.

"You know, you ought to think of going to another country for at least part of the time. You know, someplace that you got to fly to get there, someplace with another culture. Looking at all that different shit and, you know, eating different food and so forth, it's relaxing, really. Also, it gives you perspective." Cicciolino let that float on the idea Brant was an intellectual and anything to do with perspective would interest him.

But Brant only shook his head. "The kids. Jesus—they're growing, and I never see them anyhow."

"Loosen up, for crissake. Take them with you. Don't they pay you around here? Try the Bahamas. I'll arrange everything. You don't even need a passport, and the money's the same. You know, the currency."

Brant glanced up from his blotter, and Cicciolino thought he had him. He'd lean on it, even buy him the goddamn tickets if he had to. He'd say Tug got them on a scam. Brant liked Tug. Sometimes they met for a drink without Cicciolino.

"The Bahamas," Brant said, as though trying the word out. And liking it. The corners of his mouth moved up. "You see that ad on the tube? The one with the broad in the blue bathing suit. She comes out of the surf all wet with this big smile looking like Florence Joyner-Kersee, saying, 'Come to the Bahamas—' "

Cicciolino shook his head, "Nah. First, that broad's a big, fun girl. She's got tits. Second, she's singing, 'Ooo, Jamaica.' That's the place with all the *ganja* and *posses,* not pussy. You don't want to go there. Bad politics, if anybody found out. The place you want is—" Cicciolino then sang a few bars of "Come to the Bahamas." He had a good singing voice, and his falsetto and accent were perfect.

Brant began laughing. "You sure you took your wife?

How"—he twined his fingers behind his head, which usually signaled a leading question—"how do they feel about blacks there? I mean, American blacks."

Like Cicciolino, Brant had been in Vietnam, and he had told Chick his experiences as a black American in Japan and Australia had left him cautious about ever leaving the country again. How had he put it? "At least here I know the mind-set and the rules."

"Feel about black Americans?" Cicciolino asked the ceiling. "Jeez—I don't want you to take this wrong, but pretty much with their fingers, when they get permission."

Brant smiled and shook his head. "Whew, that reeks." Then he glanced at the clock. "What's this about perspective?"

Cicciolino smiled broadly, glad he hadn't been wrong about Brant. He stood. It was something he didn't want to discuss; he only wanted Brant's okay, so that if later things ever got checked out hard, he could say it was just something they discussed in passing. And agreed upon, mutually.

"I don't know. It's just that, when you're really away in some totally different place, it helps you to see things here more clearly." Cicciolino paused, as though he had to think. "For instance, there I was in a dive in Bimini, having a drink with Tug. I turn around and I see this group at a table. One glance, and cop sense tells me *felons.* You know, each of them's showing a little gold, and they all got tans, a certain cut to their khakis, same kind of boating shoes, and hard, wary eyes. And that look. You know the look?" Brant really wasn't much of a cop, but Cicciolino was willing to bet he knew—or wouldn't admit he didn't know—the look.

"Tug's yackin' away, and I go to myself, I go—I bet there's some kind of look or something that's shared by the major street-level drug lords in this town. I know, I know"—he waved a hand—"the gold chains, the Reeboks, the BMWs and Mercedes. But not just that."

Cicciolino paused again, as though laboring to form his thoughts. The dumber he looked here, the better; later he would want Brant to think it was an idea they had worked out together. And if push came to shove? Hey, he'd hang the fucking little nigger out to dry. Cover your ass—it was rule number one in the NYPD. In the Apple. In life.

"I mean, I wonder if we ever assembled in one place all the

data—heaps and heaps—that I know we got in Intelligence, the Narcotics Division, OCCB, TNT, DDT, and so forth, and tried to correlate just what it is about them fucks that's like the gold earring in the ear of them modern-day pirates on Bimini. You know, some MO, some common thread or inside handle on who they are or how they operate. Or even just the way they go about things. Buying and selling, day to day."

Brant untwined his fingers from the back of his neck and eased himself toward the desk. "Like what, specifically?"

"Everything from how they apportion the time in their days. Is it similar, is it different, could there be a pattern? When do they get up, when do they 'work,' when are they away from their cribs? Stash houses. You can't tell me they don't check traps regular. When does that happen and how? Also there's associates, girlfriends, goombahs.

"I mean, 'product' controls their lives more than, say, law enforcement controls ours. It has to. Cocaine is illegal, and felons that they are, they're dealing with felons themselves, usually twenty-four hours a day, which is dangerous and exhausting. It's something they just can't put to bed. Hence my idea that there must be some life pattern, common to all of them, that allows them to get through.

"Then there's things like tax records. I wonder if anybody in our department has ever checked if one of these humps paid his taxes. I know, I know"—Cicciolino held up a hand before Brant could object—"it's Mickey Mouse and most of it not our jurisdiction. But as you and I both know, there's now an NYC income tax, and—hey—are we going after these guys or we going after these guys? If not, we round 'em up, line 'em up, snap their pictures. The media will have a field day. You know, 'Drug Dealer Tax Cheats.' Front page guaranteed in the Post and the News. I can also think of hospital records, motor-vehicle records, welfare records, property tax, civil actions. We'll brainstorm the thing and get every scrap we can on these assholes.

"It's a long shot, but what's it gonna cost? A couple weeks of phone calls, some computer time, some analysis, and, if we find something, whatever it takes to get out the report. I could also make some inquiries with the guys I came up with, maybe even touch base with my contacts in Brooklyn and Manhattan

South. You know, my old area commands. Make a tour or two.

"Then there's the other commands I had, like IAD. I don't know now and couldn't tell you what we're looking for. Nor do I think we'd have to commit anything more than the manpower we already got in my office, and—"

"Wait, wait," Brant said, holding his hands out in a *pace, pace* gesture, "I like it. I like it. You never know where breakthroughs might come from. What will you need?"

Cicciolino hunched his shoulders. "Like I said, for the moment nothing but okays." He meant orders from Brant directing the chiefs of other agencies to cooperate.

Brant tilted his head, wrinkled his brow, and nodded. "Okay. You got 'em. Tell the sergeant to step in. Good to have you back, Chick." And before Cicciolino could leave, he asked, "What travel agency did you guys use to get down there?"

"Didn't I tell you I'd do it for you?"

"No, no, no. That smacks too much of patronization. I'm a big *boy* now, remember?"

Just as Cicciolino had been thinking.

After greeting his small staff in his offices on the twelfth floor, Cicciolino assembled his three key aides and told them what he wanted. Calling it Brant's idea, he spoke quickly in a no-nonsense manner, detailing how they would go about the search. They had received an order from the first dep, and they were going to carry it out quickly and efficiently.

The others took notes. Only procedural questions were asked. Cicciolino's approach to police work was exclusively authoritarian, which was how most cops preferred to be led. There was his way, which was by the book, or no way, and nothing to think about but getting the job done right. Cops who were left on their own too long without direction, he had noticed early in his career, began doing things their way, which inevitably led to trouble. Those under his command who dared regretted it. One way or another he got them. It was his reputation, of which he was proud.

"The first dep thinks there might be some way to line up the dossiers of all these assholes and find something or some set of somethings that links them. If we do, and it helps put them away, hey—" He did not want to seem too enthusiastic, but at the same time he wanted the search to be real and in-depth so it could never be questioned.

Cicciolino already knew how he would proceed himself, but the more cover the better. What if—*what if*—he could get out of this clean with the money *and* a major score to cap his career. As he saw it now, there was the possibility.

Striding toward the hall, Cicciolino signaled to his driver who—according to his orders—spent his non-car time clipping articles that pertained to the NYPD from all city newspapers and magazines. His name was Nunzio D'Amato; like McCann and Gelb, he had grown up with Cicciolino on the Lower East Side. D'Amato, however, had limited book smarts and even less ambition, and had remained a patrolman, even though he had joined the Department six years before Cicciolino.

Cicciolino had thought of cutting him in, since he didn't know how he'd keep him out. For all his supposed simplicity, D'Amato was knowing, sly, and useful, and it wouldn't take him long to figure it out. But he'd wait until then. Too many people were in on it already, and not all of them reliable. Or deserving.

In the car he pointed to a shop with a pearl-gray awning and framed art photographs in the window, and D'Amato pulled into the curb in front of a fire hydrant. "Ain't this Gelb's wife's place? Why didn't you say so, Chick? We could a got here quicker up First Avenue."

"Afterthought," he explained, stepping out. "Gerri's birthday's the fourth of the month. I thought maybe I'd get her something different. A little art."

"How they, anyhow? Him and—what's her name again?"

"Arlene."

"What a stick. Dale fucking Evans from *Home on the Range*." D'Amato shook his head. "Some guys—" Having watched his friends' marriages closely for thirty years, D'Amato viewed what he now called his "decision" not to get married as the biggest victory of his life. Maybe even bigger than Cicciolino's being named assistant chief. "Me, I want to get laid," he kept telling Cicciolino, "I call Sal," who was yet another of their early friends, and now a high-priced pimp. "I don't care what it costs, pluggin' a different bimbo every time s'got to be cheaper than what all you chumps go through. And better."

*   *   *

Cicciolino was hoping, but luck seemed to be against him. He had no sooner stepped out of the car than some guy walked up to the door of the shop and pulled out a key, as if he was going to open it and walk in.

He was maybe thirty with a modish haircut, Buddy Holly sunglasses, and an expensive speckled overcoat with the collar pulled up. With a nervous sweep of a hand that made Cicciolino think *fairy,* he pulled a Walkman headset from his ears. He glanced both ways before inserting the key in the lock.

Feeling Cicciolino behind him, he turned. "Can I help you?"

"I want in."

"Sorry, sir, the gallery is closed." His voice was deep but his tone pissy, and a chickenshit manner kept him from turning to face Cicciolino.

"Work here?" The door was open, and over the wide, padded shoulder of the overcoat, Cicciolino could see a light and hear Arlene on the phone. From what Jay had told him, the place couldn't support even a single employee, which was why Arlene spent so much of her time there. And suddenly he understood the scene.

"Really. We're *not* open."

"You are now." Cicciolino pulled out his shield, flashing it at him. Out of the corner of his eye he could see D'Amato step out of the car with his right hand stuffed under a lapel, and he waved him off. "You Cal?"

"Excuse me?" The guy flicked the sunglasses down on the bridge of his nose. His eyes were such a strange purple color. Cicciolino was willing to bet it was from tinted contacts.

"I said, sweetness. You? Cal?"

The eyes worked down Cicciolino's body and back up, not liking what they saw.

"Because if you are, I got a message for you from Jay Gelb. You ever heard of a paternity suit?"

The guy gave him nothing, only kept staring, and suddenly Arlene was in the doorway, one hand clasping a robe tight to her neck. "Chick?"

"Maybe you got it all figured out, and you're the same genetic match as Jay. But if you ain't, I'd hit the trail. You're pretty, I'll give you that, but somehow you don't seem the steady type to me.

Over the long haul, I'm talking. In this state it's twenty-one years of monthly payments. You understand what I'm sayin'?"

Cal's head snapped to Arlene, as if blaming her for Cicciolino, but he pivoted with dancerlike grace and took one long stride away from the door. Quickened by a stutter step, he was soon up to speed.

Before he could fit on his Walkman earphones, Cicciolino said, "Love them designer irises. You get an AIDS test recently?"

"Cal. Cal!" Arlene called after him. But he did not even glance back. Cicciolino pushed her into the gallery, then closed and locked the door.

"Jesus—why did you do *that,* Chick?" she asked, backing away from him.

Cicciolino shrugged. Maybe because of his protective nature. In his own way he liked Gelb, and it was one thing for Arlene to be putting out. Another for Gelb and him to be sharing her with a fruit. "Because if we're gonna get fucked, we don't need a witness." And the other stuff, he was thinking: They had to keep that tighter still. He knew how it went: Lots of things that should not be said got divulged after a good screw.

Arlene shook her head, so that a strand of her reddish hair became freed from the bun at the back of her head. She still had her hand to the neck of the robe, which was black, and Cicciolino could see she had nothing on under it. And she looked different than he'd ever seen her: wild, as though she'd done something almost . . . theatrical with her eyes. They were darkly shadowed, and her eyelids had been painted orange, like her hair. Then, the eyes themselves were shimmering, glittering, sparkling, like from belladonna. They were the same color as the light through the curtained windows and her lipstick, which was silver. He wondered if the lipstick was greasy and how it would feel, sliding down his dick.

"That the guy?" he asked, still walking her back toward the dim glow he could see coming from the office.

She nodded.

"What's he to you?"

Arlene did not know what he meant. Her eyes flickered down at his crotch, which was bulging, and for a moment she almost felt fear. She had always thought of him as such a big, rough man.

"I mean—what's he mean to you? Outside of being the guy."

She shrugged. Maybe it had been the danger, and all that they had gone through down in the Islands. But suddenly she had become a different person. Like a kind of white, flameless fire, her emotions had escaped her. They were burning intensely somewhere beyond her consciousness and could only be sensed in situations like this, when her feelings flared. As for Cal, he was merely the father of her unborn child and meant nothing, especially now that Chick had run him off so easily.

"I don't want you to see him again until we get this thing over. Un'erstand?"

She had her hands up now, as though she would try to dodge or fend him off. Her head was shaking, and for a while she had been making little noises in the back of her throat.

"After that—you want to support him? That's your business. Because with a guy like him, that's pretty much what you'll have to do. For the moment, though"—their eyes met—"it's you and me."

And then, as in a flashback, Arlene remembered something from childhood when, just at puberty, she had spent a summer with an aunt up in Colorado. They had a camp on a lake just high enough to be cool without being cold, and her first night there she awoke with a start to harsh, loud, horrible—mechanical almost—clacking. As she listened to it for whole minutes, she realized it was actually a vicious, threatening growl interspersed with the most plaintive mewling that sounded like sheep being led to slaughter. There followed a savage chase and fight with shrieks and different, enraged growling, all around the guest cabin where she was sleeping alone. Arlene, used to the wild life of semi-arid New Mexico, thought for sure one of the animals was a mountain lion claiming prey. In the morning her aunt explained it was racoons mating.

"Filthy old things in rut. They'll carry on like that for hours, night after night, as long as the bitch is in heat. The dominant male fights off all the rest, and then services her sometimes till dawn." Her aunt, who was a widow, had drawn in a breath while pushing her palms down into her lap and looking away. "I'll put Butch out on them tonight," which was their large yeller dog. "He'll enjoy the sport."

But now Arlene was nearly at the beaded door that led into the office. She was still objecting, but her tone had changed, Cicciolino noted, as he pulled off his jacket and loosened his tie. He had heard other women make sounds close to that when they were coming, and he wondered if Arlene was a screamer. Cicciolino liked screamers, and he imagined it was the reason they'd been meeting here, she and Cal. So Arlene could howl and bitch and scream.

Out of habit he looked around the shadowed corners of the gallery, even turned his head to check the windows and doors to make sure D'Amato could not look in. It wouldn't do for him to know there was some change in his relationship with the Gelbs. Cicciolino's cock was stiff now, rock hard and even aching, for crissake; he hadn't really *had* it in so long. And his breathing—Christ, it was like he was pumping tons.

Hand on her chest now, he pushed her back.

Again he shoved her, harder this time, through the beads, into the office.

"Is this rape? Are you going to rape me, Chick?" she almost cooed.

Cicciolino said nothing. He couldn't. He was nearly dizzy, and he had swallowed his voice. He had hoped the office was tiny, where they'd have to fight to get it in. Gerri and he once worked for almost an hour to rip one off in a telephone booth back when they were in law school. When Cicciolino came, he thought the booth was going to explode at the seams, and he was all bumps and bruises afterward.

But this was heaven, no bigger than a shoe box. Set high, maybe a foot above his head on a shelf, was something like a red votive candle before the blaze of a gold or at least a brass icon. It gave the tiny room an eerie glow and made Arlene look like some sort of evil sorceress. Her eyes—Christ, what had she put in them?—they were like glowing from within.

It was then Cicciolino remembered Arlene was Russian, or her mother had been, and his hand darted for the belt of the black robe and pulled it open.

"Don't be too rough with me. Please, Chick," she said, but her tone said different. Two patches of the brightest red had appeared on her cheeks, and he could see that she had been ready for it. She was wearing black stockings and a garter belt and was enough pregnant that she was just beginning to swell. "Cal like this stuff?" he asked. He pulled back a garter strap and let it smack against her thigh.

Arlene took a step toward the cot, but Cicciolino spun her around and threw her up on the desk. He snatched up her ankles, pushed them back, and then set her feet down on the top of the desk. With his body he forced her knees apart, and suddenly in one hard shot he was in her. Deep.

"Oooo-h!" she said in the back of her throat.

He pulled out, then hit her with it again. Cicciolino knew this about himself. He was big, everywhere. More to the point, he was also wide.

"Oooo-h!" she said again, and then sighed. She twined her fingers around his neck, threw her head back, and tried to pull his head down onto her breasts. But he didn't move, and it only drove him into her deeper. She rested her head on one of the shelves where she could watch the candlelight flicker on the ceiling. "Chick—" she asked, "what about Jay?"

Aw, Christ, Cicciolino was thinking, what was this? For some reason she really turned him on. Already he was about to come. They'd have to go again, just to make it right, and he had D'Amato waiting for him outside. "What about him?"

Arlene had an idea, which was not good. But it could wait. She could feel Chick pulsing inside of her, and there she hadn't done a thing to him yet.

CHAPTER 15

REAL REALITY

◆

EVA BURDEN SLEPT so deeply that she awoke with a start, not knowing where she was or why. It took her whole seconds to recognize the wooden shutters covering the windows and the antiques, curios, and whatnots of "Miss" Nattie's bedroom.

In that same moment, however, all the details that had arrived her in the room in Nassau came flooding back: the downed plane and damaged boat, the dope and the money, the attack of the other plane, and her—deciding wasn't quite the right word—to jump ship. Then there was Tug trying to get her to return, her discovery of the drug boat with the two injured dealers, and now here.

Had she done the right thing? Without a doubt. Eva wasn't one to second-guess herself, and she knew this much: The consequences of right action were always better than wrong, even if in the short run it didn't seem that way. She wasn't particularly religious, but she did believe that ultimately you paid or were rewarded for what you did, one way or another.

The moment she tried to get out of bed, she began paying. At first she could barely raise herself up. Unlike a surgical table, the kitchen table downstairs was not adjustable, and her back still ached from all the bending and close work over the two men. Also, there was a weal of bruised flesh on her thigh from the rail of the pounding boat. When she tried to step out into the hall and find a bathroom, she discovered that her right heel was bruised from where she had braced her foot against a seat in the boat.

The parquet floor was warm, however, and she imagined—glancing out a window—that she had slept through the day, for it was nearly dark again. When she found the toilet, the tiles were warmer still. Glancing up, she stopped short.

The toilet was dry and hot from an infrared lamp glowing on the ceiling. Hanging from the track of the shower curtain, from the edges of the tub, sink, window ledge, and even from the top of the water closet of the john were thousand-dollar bills, evidently from the two bundles that had been taken from the jacket of the man named Creach, and she had handed to Denny.

Each had dried in its hanging shape and was water-wrinkled. Before showering, she gathered them up into a semblance of a stack. All one hundred were there, which said something about Denny and the household he ran. And only after a good ten minutes of intense, steaming hydrotherapy, did she begin to think about her "patients," if they could be called that. Or rather, Dr. Southworth's *private* patients.

And how hungry she suddenly was.

Taking the stack of bills back to the bedroom, she dressed herself in the most acceptable of the dated, musty, casual clothes she could find—a red polo neck jersey and pleated Bermuda shorts—when she heard from the hall the metallic race of ball bearings. Looking up, she found Nathanson standing in the doorway, one hand on the jamb. The other hand was grasping the stanchion of a movable intravenous drip. "Where'd you get that?"

"Southworth." He was pale, his forehead was beaded with sweat, and she did not give him long on his feet. He was wearing a clean, pressed pair of tennis shorts, and he looked as though he had somehow bathed. He had shaved and brushed his long brown hair back from the temples, where he was beginning to bald. The blonding curls at the back looked as though they'd been combed and clipped.

"Here's this." She waved the $100,000, and not finding anyplace on his person that she could put it, slipped it in the deep pocket of the Bermuda shorts until she could get him back to his bed. "Did he also say you could take strolls with that thing?" She meant the drip. It was sound medical practice to rouse a patient from bed as soon as possible after surgery, but usually it entailed a few careful, assisted steps. Nathanson was at least fifty feet from the room in which she had left him, and where was Southworth, or Denny?

"I thought we should talk. It's time for us to get out of here." One of his legs began to tremble, and she reached for his arm, turning him so she could lead him back to his bed. If he fell, he was too big for her to raise alone.

"Out of where?"

"This house, and soon. I don't want to frighten you, but the people from the plane? Either they or the guy I bought the dope from will be here soon. They'll want either the dope or the money or both. Worst case is for them to send a *sicaria*. Know what that is?"

She had him as far as the doorway to the porch, which was a long, cool, screened-in room that seemed to be set in the bows of the sycamores that framed the front of the house. "No, but go on." Nathanson was heavy on her shoulders, but they would make it to the bed.

"It means assassin, but they're more than that. They're employed by the cartels partly for recovery of whatever's been lost, but mainly for punishment and to line their own pockets." His head turned to her. "You know, to make the worst sort of example so others won't be tempted."

She helped him up into the bed, then swung the stanchion around so the drip line would not be pulled from his arm.

"First they'll go for the *transportadores*, the guys on the plane we had the problem with. Next they'll come for us."

"But can't you phone the person you dealt with, tell him what happened, and talk it out?" Eva asked, showing him the thick stack of rumpled thousand-dollar bills and putting them in the drawer of the nightstand. "It seems to me both of you were losers. What if you could make him whole? Some way."

Nathanson waited until she looked at him again. He had a long face with a thinly bridged nose that had a kind of bump in the middle. As he spoke, a dimple appeared in his right cheek. His eyes were green, and a deep tan made his teeth seem very white.

"I've tried. The number I have for him doesn't answer, which means it's probably too late. A thing like this goes fast. Money and dope can just disappear quick, so the source arranges for *sicarias* the moment he knows things have gone wrong. And they . . . swarm.

"You wouldn't happen to know where it is, would you? The money and the dope?"

Eva looked away. Like on the boat, she did not want to get involved. "But say you *could* get in touch with the source, isn't there some way you could work it out?"

"You mean, if I could have contacted him, say, within a day of the deal going bust, before he arranged for *sicarias* and set them loose? Sure, if I had managed to get him the agreed-upon price immediately. By that I mean I would have had to dig up another two-point-five million fast and have flown it to a meet, most likely in Colombia.

"There I would have had to beg his forgiveness and assure whatever coked-up crazies he brought with him that it would never happen again. You know, a pilot, his plane, and me. Or a pilot, his plane, me, and Creach, standing out in some jungle airstrip alone." Nathanson shook his head. "One, I don't know a pilot that dumb. Two, neither of us is either. Three, if I did, I would have paid for the dope twice and—"

Gotten no dope, Eva concluded.

"And four, I wouldn't have, if I could have, not with this," he pointed to his side, "and that." The hand swung to the other side of the room where Creach lay in another bed; he appeared to be either sleeping or still unconscious.

The man who had saved everybody aboard *Whistler*, Eva thought. For that, her accomplished, urbane, upper-middle-class New Yorkers had stolen from and then nearly killed him. Worse still was what they had stolen. From Eva's point of view, it was death, and not just for a few.

"We've got a whole lot more than money in this thing now," Nathanson went on. His green eyes were now angry. "What does the source have in it but his product? Also, he should've checked, should've known about the *transportadores* by reputation. Even Creach and I did, but too late. And we're . . . we *were* strictly small time.

"Now, like I said earlier, we have his *sicarias* to worry about. Their game is salvage. The best way to describe it is sharks. You ever hear of a feeding frenzy? Look around at what you see here. Anything left after the recovery figure, they'll glom."

Eva thought of the house and the library and all the paintings, furniture, and obvious antiques. She also wondered about the man's past and background. His accent was New York, and "glom" very much a New York word.

"Look—what I want to say is, you saved our lives." He reached for the drawer of the nightstand. "And I want to thank you."

Knowing what was coming, Eva tried to move away from the bed, but he grabbed her wrist. "No, really. That's not necessary. I sent a message to my friends, and my clothes and things will be arriving soon."

"Listen to me. Without you we would have died, there *and* here. You know that. You worked with Southworth. He means well, and he can be good company. But his practice is mainly society matrons, and we couldn't have had anybody else without too many questions. Publicity. The police. He as much as told me this morning you should be a doctor. Or rather, a surgeon."

Eva cocked her head and summoned a smile. "But don't you know you probably saved my life too?"

He released her hand and regarded her, waiting for her to continue. "I was"—she pulled her eyes from his—"marooned there. Another boat might not have come by for weeks."

"Then you saw everything that happened?"

She said nothing; she glanced over at Creach.

"Were you part of it?"

When she still said nothing, he went on, "Here—I don't know what saving somebody's life is worth in New York, but around here a fire run to that island and back is worth five. I figure what you did for us surgically and so forth, five more. Apiece." He had some difficulty snapping off fifteen of the wrinkled bills, but he placed them on the night stand and looked up at her.

"Take it. You earned it." When she made no move for the money, he shrugged. "What do I know? Maybe you're rich and don't need it, maybe you do the Samaritan bit every once in a while for personal gratification. But—can I tell you something?—if you're not rich—" Nathanson paused, it seemed, for emphasis, "you're gonna need it."

Again he waited, his eyes tracing her face, the line of her shoulders, the way the Bermuda shorts, which were a bit too long, were crimped by the linen belt. He liked what he saw—her green eyes, her wide mouth, her teeth with the space in the middle. She looked . . . together and strong, in her own small way, and she was competent. He himself was living proof. "To run. To escape. If they have your name and know who you are. Understand?"

She thought she did. She understood feeding frenzies, or at least the kind of greed that resembled it.

"You don't believe me? Let me show you something." He again reached for the nightstand, and slid two pieces of paper from under the telephone there. "Here I lie in a sickbed, right? I been out of it, unconscious—what?—most of a couple of days. I'm weak, I'm dopey from the painkillers. I got Creach, who can only write me short notes. And a phone.

"What do I find out?" He tossed one sheet of notepaper so that it fell neatly on top of the money he had placed on the nightstand. In large, shaky letters the writing on it said, "The Dr. is 'Daughter.' Blond girl from the charter boat. *Whistler*. Topsail schooner."

"That's from Creach. Sure, he was there, but he's nearly dead. This"—Nathanson tossed another sheet on the pile—"is from five minutes on the phone. No special number needed. No insider information or paid informer. I called Tourist Information and told them I'd once seen a certain charter boat, a topsail schooner, that I'd like to book for a few weeks and could they help me. I gave them the name. I didn't even have to hang up the phone before the woman told me *Whistler* is owned and chartered by Mr. T. J. Monroe of Bimini. Or, rather, *was*.

"I tried to phone him, but a man name of Sidney answered. I asked him if *Whistler* was presently available for charter. He didn't answer. I asked him if he could give me the name of the last person to charter her. He was evasive, and rightly so. Denny showed me why." From the table on the other side of the bed, Nathanson pulled a newspaper and handed it to her. BOAT TRAGEDY, banner headlines read. BIMINI BUSINESSMAN PRESUMED DEAD IN CHARTER BOAT EXPLOSION.

Eva scanned the article that mentioned no other victim by name but T. J. Monroe.

The charred remains of the vessel sank five miles south of Bimini in thirty fathoms of water. The accident was reported by Capt. Sidney F. O. Thomson of Bimini, who was returning to port when he saw the flash. The heat was so intense that he was unable to approach the site until after the wreck had sunk. He found no survivors.

Sergeant G. S. Moss of the Bimini Constabulary is investigating. The explosion was heard throughout the Bimini Islands. An attempt will be made to raise the wreck.

"I wouldn't worry about your friends, though. McCann and Cicciolino and Gelb." Nathanson placed the sheet of notepaper on which Eva had written the telegram message for Denny. "Or their wives—let's see." Nathanson flipped the sheet over. "Geraldine and Arlene. They left on Chalk's International flight to Fort Lauderdale early this morning. When I called Chalk's, I said, 'Gee—I was supposed to meet some friends and fly back with them yesterday, but I couldn't make it. I wonder if they went on without me.' "

He shook his head and waited again until they were staring at each other. "I'm not trying to con you. You've been too good to me for that, and it's not my game anyhow. Sure I want my money back, and I'll get it, if I can. And I'll also do whatever it's gonna take to get the *sicarias* off my back.

"But afterward, I'm history. I'm out of the trade for good. This"—he pointed to his side and the drain that Eva now saw needed changing—"hurt too much, and how good is a fast buck if you never get a chance to enjoy it? Truth is, I didn't want this deal from the start."

Eva looked away. It was what her husband had told her right before things had come apart.

"Well, don't believe me, if you don't want to. But I'll tell you one thing, I know the rules, the first of which is only the *real* quick survive. Early on I did some business with the Ochoas, and they owe me at least one *big* favor. Maybe I can swing it. But until I can reach them, or until I'm able to move . . ." Again he glanced down at his side.

"So, what am I telling you? Any skilled *sicaria* is going to come up with this stuff." He meant the information and the leads.

"And I don't care who your friends are or how they managed it with Monroe—they'll have more trouble than they'll want. Guaranteed. Even in New York. *Especially* in New York, which is the single biggest market. There people—bad people—will owe the Cartel, and they'll kill for coke or the promise of it. It won't matter who."

When still she said nothing, Nathanson again shook his leonine head. "I understand loyalty. Usually it's good, it's laudable, but in this case it's dumb. These are South Americans your friends got themselves balled up with, not the Mafia. A life—their own, somebody else's—doesn't mean the same thing. It's cheap, or at least cheaper than salvage.

"Way I see it, the only chance your friends got—which *you* can give them—is me, if you act fast."

Eva glanced up at Nathanson.

He nodded. "Me—all I want back is my money. If they give me my money *and* they still got the dope, maybe I can arrange something through Ochoa. A give-back, and an apology. I'm not promising anything, but it's a possibility. The guy I dealt with, the source, is strictly small stuff; he'll take orders or else. But the question is the *sicaria*, who will have to be satisfied in some way. *Can* they call him back."

Eva thought about Bill Cicciolino, how he had acted and what he had said on the boat. Would he actually give back both the money and the drugs? Then apologize and make some sort of peace payment to this assassin, which is what Nathanson was suggesting? She didn't think so. Especially not in New York, where he had a certain amount of power.

And then, she herself had chosen to get off *Whistler* because she did *not want* to get involved in any part of what Cicciolino had proposed. The others obviously did. Could she now stand by, knowing that they could possibly be murdered for what they had done?

Or could all his talk about *sicarias* be merely a ruse to get her to confirm the little he had learned about Cicciolino, Tug, and Jay Gelb? To get her to reveal their identities and make his own salvage effort easier? She studied Nathanson's green eyes, his oddly handsome face, his large shoulders, which were uniformly muscled, like those of a swimmer. She didn't know. And what she knew about him wasn't the best.

"I can see you want to think about it," he said. "Just don't take too long. But while you do, let me add this"—he peeled another bill into the stack on the night stand—"which is for yesterday. This"—he added another—"is for today, and you'll get one every day you stay with us. We gotta move now, and I don't want anybody traceable, like Southworth, coming and going from the place we'll be at. From what I can see"—his eyes again flickered toward Creach—"we still need your help. And maybe you need ours.

"New York? Unless you got family or something, I wouldn't plan on going back there, not on a bet. I don't know how you got separated from the boat, but I'd guess it had something to do with the plane and the dope, right?" Nathanson waited, but Eva maintained her silence.

"Monroe had to have some sort of passenger list for that charter. Just one name is all the *sicaria* will need. He'll go from one to the other to the next. Don't think he won't. Your friends won't want to give you up, but they will.

"Can I prove it to you? Do you have a few days?"

It wasn't quite a blink, but he assumed she meant she did.

"You help us move and get patched up, I load a few more of these on you"—he meant the thousand-dollar bills—"and I prove it to you . . . what I said about the *sicaria*. Then you decide what you do from there. We agreed?"

Eva thought for a moment. If he was right, she certainly did not want to go back to New York, and money would be essential. Eva had been careful, but Thermidor, for all its critical success, was a tiny restaurant with only thirty covers counting a four-stool bar. Also, the overhead of running a restaurant in New York was outrageous with all the payoffs and bribes that were expected: sanitation, health, building, and fire inspectors, all of whom could shut her down. Then there was the police. Once they discovered a woman was running Thermidor, she had to pay the ward boss to pay a captain to keep the beat cops out of her kitchen. They were eating and stealing everything in sight.

As for cash, she probably couldn't put her hands on more than $30,000 or $40,000, which wouldn't last long on the road with a small child.

If Nathanson was wrong, Eva could poke around Nassau and see if she could come up with some novel Bahamian recipes for

Thermidor. From the spices that she had seen in the kitchen down-stairs, Denny had to know something about Carib cooking. "When?"

"Do we move?" Nathanson glanced at the clock on the stand. "In about ten minutes."

Eva was surprised.

"Think you can handle it?"

"Not without some food." She turned to leave the room.

"Hey—what's your name again? I was a little out of it when—"

"Eva," she said over a shoulder.

"Eva, you forgot your money."

She stopped and walked back. A deal was a deal, and money money, as long as she wasn't being asked to do anything wrong.

"You see any clothes you like in the room you're staying, tell Jared or Deke to take them along."

The two young black men now appeared in the door, carrying a wheeled stretcher. "You ready, Brian?" the first one, Jared, now asked, smiling. "Got the bus just down stairs in the side yard, like you said."

"We are if Eva is. But Creach is first." Nathanson looked toward Eva, as though for her okay.

"Could I get something to eat first?" And make a phone call, she thought.

In the den at the bottom of the stairs, she put through a call to California and charged it to her number in New York. She told her mother that she might be coming out to see her instead of returning to New York. "What about school for Sandy?"

"Well—there're schools there. Good ones, as I remember."

"What's wrong?"

"I'll explain when I get there, but it's nothing to worry about. Just a little glitch."

"With the restaurant? I thought everything was going well, and you were looking for a bigger location?"

"Ma—this call is costing a fortune. I'll tell you when I see you."

After speaking for a while with her daughter, who seemed to be enjoying her stay with her grandmother, Eva hung up. She thought about calling her chef at Thermidor, but why? She wasn't due back for two weeks.

When she hung up, she turned to find Denny watching her from the doorway.

"You didn't need to do that."

"Do what?" Call my daughter? she thought. Of course she did.

"Charge it to your phone. Around here, you on our side, you on our side. Simple as that. You just call when you need."

Eva did not step away from the phone. "What side are we talking about, Denny? Can you tell me that?"

He smiled. "Why, nature's side, of course. It's what Mr. Brian always say, which reminds me. I got the eats you been waiting on. This way, please."

Following the older black man down the dark hall toward the dining room, Eva was curious about two matters: One, how he had come to know she was hungry? Could there be a monitor in the sickroom? It would explain why Nathanson and Creach had been left alone. And, two, how could running cocaine ever be thought of as an activity that was on nature's side?

Another thing was clear, however. They were also skilled in the second technique of survival—flight. In less time than it took Eva to devour a platter of stone-crab claws, the "bus," as they called a large cargo van, was loaded with Nathanson and Creach in litters, the medical equipment that Southworth had found them, and many of the valuables that Eva had seen on the night before. Rugs, tapestries, paintings, and books were packed into every available space, along with Nathanson's wardrobe and all the clothes from Miss Nattie's room.

It was dark in the alley where they had parked, and darker inside the back of the van. "Jump in," said Nathanson, and the accordion door was pulled down. He snapped on a dim battery light. "Don't worry, it's not far."

It wasn't—just over the bridge and across the harbor to Paradise Island, Nathanson said when they got out. "About a mile as a gull flies. Creach owns the penthouse in this building. Some will tell you he owns the building too," he added, "though I think it's a lie." He glanced over to see how Creach took that, but the eyes of the short, wide black man were only partially open and cast with pain.

From four directions of the compass, the windows of the apartment surveyed Paradise Island, the harbor, Nassau, and

Nathanson's house. On his orders, the two young men drove away with his possessions, headed for "the boathouse. And be careful now in the loft. We've got all that other stuff there."

Days went by, and with the exception of Creach's throat, both men began recovering nicely. Creach spent his time watching the house across the bay through binoculars and writing long, detailed reports to Nathanson, who remained in a bedroom with a phone, trying to reach his contact in Colombia.

On the sixth day they all agreed it was safe enough for Eva to go to a drugstore for prescriptions for Nathanson and Creach. She took a taxi over the bridge into Nassau proper, but she decided to walk back. It was cool and breezy, and she thought she would stretch her legs and try to think about something other than having to return to New York soon. Across the water on the other side of the harbor, she could see the high rise that Denny had told her Creach definitely owned. It was the most prominent of a number of luxury condominiums that were clustered near the water in that direction.

Nathanson's house was no more than a block or two distant, and she wondered if the package with her things had arrived. How long could it take from Bimini, which was only ninety or so miles away? If nothing else, she would need her driver's license, which was a hassle to replace, and her credit cards. Denny had said he would fetch the package for her when it came, but maybe she could save him a trip. Used to a daily jog, which had been impossible for days now, she really hadn't walked far enough to satisfy her.

And there it was, tucked into the side of the alcove of cut pink stone that framed the front door. *"Ms. Eva Burden,"* it said in a scriptlike letter that Eva guessed had been written by Arlene Gelb, who was an artist. *"C/o Nathanson, Water Street, Nassau."* But the box was large, and packed, Eva could feel, with newspapers to prevent damage.

Better to open it and take the bag itself, which had a shoulder strap. Nathanson had given her a ring of keys, one of which would let her into the high rise, and she wondered if his house keys might be on it too. The largest key fit the old, round lock, and the heavy door swung open. But she had only opened the box when the doorbells chimed.

Eva jumped and was momentarily frightened, until she parted

the curtains in the sitting room and looked out. Standing in the marble alcove was a tall, striking-looking woman, who had obviously arrived in the black limousine that was parked in the street. A squat chauffeur in uniform and cap was waiting on the sidewalk by the gate, his hands clasped before him. Eva guessed the woman was some friend of Nathanson who had been driving by and decided to stop.

She was tall and angular, dressed in an exquisite emerald-green satin suit. Her hair, which had been gathered into a bun, was an unusual auburn color that looked natural, but when Eva opened the door, she was surprised by the woman's skin. It was golden in hue, and her features were obviously of mixed race. She had a high forehead, prominent cheekbones, and hazel eyes that were slightly slanted. And yet her nose, which was long, sloped, and definitely Indian, was thin. Her mouth was wide, and her lips full and somewhat Negroid.

She smiled, and Eva thought that she had never seen a more striking and exotic-looking person. "Please pardon the intrusion," she said in halting but precise English, handing Eva a small card between fingers that were gloved in the same material as the dress. "Would Mr. Nathanson be at home? He is the man who deals in antiques and . . . collectibles, is he not?"

Eva glanced down at the card that said, "Please speak slowly. I am deaf and must read your lips." Below were lines in Spanish and French. In handing the card back, Eva glanced up over the woman's shoulder and caught the rainbow flash of binoculars on the balcony of Creach's penthouse apartment across the bay. Her eyes moved to the chauffeur on the sidewalk. His face looked almost Oriental, but his body was strange—a powerful upper body with an enormous chest, yet short, bandy legs. "No, I'm sorry, he's not here at the moment."

"When do you expect him?" The woman's eyes flickered down on Eva's lips.

Eva did not know what to say or who the woman could be, but the Spanish on the card and the slight Spanish inflection in her voice now made her wary. "I don't. Not for a while, at least."

"What would that mean? Days, weeks?"

Eva shook her head. "I have no idea. I only know that he is away."

"May I ask since when? Has he been here recently?" The woman's eyes moved beyond Eva, scanning the hallway. Another car now eased into the curb near the corner, and with the finger of one hand the chauffeur gestured to the driver, pointing as though to direct the car down the side street.

"I don't know that either. I'm . . . only a friend. I came here to pick up some mail." Eva tilted her head toward the box on the floor.

"And you are Miss Eva Burden?"

Now Eva was alarmed. Nobody in Nassau but Nathanson and his retainers and Southworth knew her name. Obviously the woman had approached the door sometime earlier and had read her name on the package.

It was then that the phone began ringing in the study just off the hall. "You'll have to excuse me now—the phone. Who shall I say was asking for him?"

The woman paused, as though deciding whether to step in or not. She was tall and looked strong. But she only said, "There will be no need for that."

Eva now had both hands on the door, which she began closing. "Sorry—the phone."

Once it was shut, she threw the bolt and moved quickly into the study, where she picked up the phone.

"Eva?" It was Nathanson. "Get out of there quick. Don't use the side gate, they've already got that covered. Go out through the doors in the dining room and cut across the garden, around the maze to the far corner. There's a gate. Climb over it, otherwise you'll set off an alarm. Go *now*!"

"But my things?"

"Forget your things, just *go*!"

Out in the hall, Eva paused at the box. Her passport and wallet and money were in there, and, if Nathanson was right about those people, once they had her name and address. . . .

She threw open the lid and began searching madly through the contents, tossing her clothes out onto the tiles of the hall: her bathing suits, tennis shoes, a dress, heels. For safety's sake, she assumed, Arlene or Gerri had packed her passport and wallet in her purse in the middle of the package.

Once she had it, she ran straight down the hall toward the back of the house. There, an intersecting hall led to the kitchen, the butler's pantry, and the dining room in one direction and to the long living room in the other.

But she heard a sound, like somebody approaching the swinging door into the kitchen, and other sounds—voices—coming from the dining room. The door was partly ajar.

She chose the butler's pantry and, stepping in, she eased the door to. The pantry had two other doors, if she remembered correctly: one leading directly into the kitchen and another into the dining room. She moved in that direction.

"You sure?" she heard.

"Sure I'm sure. He can't go to no banks here in Nassau. Would you? The Defence Force watch Brian like a hawk—his comin's and goin's. What he buy and sell, how much, from who. Why you think he in antiques and stuff? Cash business, he tol' me hisself. No way to check what-all he makes or what things worth."

Eva recognized that voice. It was Deke of Jared and Deke, and Jared now answered, "Well—I don't like it. The man'll know, and you know it."

"Not if you don't tell him. Put that thing away. Who you afraid of anyhow? They all across the water at Creach's."

"The man *sees,* I tell you." There was a pause. "And then there's Denny. And Creach."

Deke scoffed, "Creach?" Eva guessed they were at the door that led into the hall. "He half-missing. No voice. You see his han'?"

When she heard their feet in the hall, she slowly pushed back the door to the dining room. The room was empty, but one of the French doors was open, and she made directly for it.

Eva had to wait before stepping out. First one, then another, and finally a third small, squat man moved through the arched gate from the side street and scuttled quickly toward the kitchen. They were wearing white, open-neck shirts and what looked like white service trousers. In all, they looked like a catering crew, each carrying something shiny in his hand.

Eva stuffed her purse under the belt of her Bermuda shorts and bolted. She had just bought herself a new pair of jogging shoes, and she ran as fast as she could out around the maze, as Nathanson had told her, and then straight toward the gate, which was also arched and was maybe fifty yards away.

But the lawn was well-watered and the sod deep and spongy.

It slowed her pace, and she heard something behind her. Turning, she saw one of the little men set out from the end of the maze after her with something like a short sword with a wide blade in his hand.

She considered stopping. She'd never make the gate before he got to her. She could explain, she never really had anything to do with their money or their dope, that she was against it from the start.

But then she thought of what Nathanson had said about who they were and what they were after—salvage, anything they could glom—and how it didn't matter who you were. Anybody who got in their way would be dead.

She sprinted. Summoning every bit of thrust she could, she hurled herself at the gate, which she saw was locked with a long through-bolt. She hit it with her right foot midstride and pushed herself off the bolt post in a leap toward the top of the arch. There she came down hard on her stomach, the envelope purse cushioning the blow, and she tried to roll over, off into the alley that she could see below her.

But the man jumped for her ankle and caught her. She kicked out at him again and again, but he began dragging her back. Another of them appeared and reached for her left leg.

That was when the new shoe slipped off, and she toppled over the gate onto her back. She tried to pick herself up, but the wind had been knocked out of her and she was dizzy. She could hear them sliding back the bolt to open the gate.

When they did, a deafening alarm went off, and she looked up to see the flash of their knives, as they reached for her.

But suddenly they stopped and moved back, then closed the gate. The ringing ceased.

Eva felt a hand on her arm and was helped to her feet. "C'mon, quick. The car's this way. What you come back here for? I told you I'd get the packet for you." It was Denny, who had a short-barrel automatic weapon in his other hand.

But her fear now turned to anger: at the two Indians—were they?—on the other side of the gate and at the woman, the *sicaria,* who would have killed her because some drug baron had arbitrarily given her the license to recover his property and mete out punishment to anybody who got in her way, anyplace in the world.

"Wait!" Eva snatched the subgun from Denny's hands. "I

want my other sneaker." Raising a foot, Eva kicked open the door, and with the gun at the ready scanned the yard. She had fired automatic weapons before as part of her navy training, and she was fully prepared to take out anybody who got in her way.

Or was she? The deafening ringing had begun again, and it was like an alarm in her brain. What was happening to her?

There was nobody in sight, only the lawn, the maze, and the garden with the house beyond. She snatched up her other new running shoe and backed out of the gate. Denny closed it, and the ringing stopped.

That was when they heard a shot, a scream, and another shot.

Eva snapped her head to Denny. "Jared and Deke—when I was in the house I heard them—"

The old man nodded, then shook his head. "I'm sick-disappointed with them two. We all are, Mr. Brian and Creach too. We trusted them boys, and there we saw them sneaking in here, trying to rip us off. *But,* it wasn't like anybody put a gun to their heads." He sighed. "They chose."

Trembling, Eva handed Denny the gun. He took her arm and directed them up the alley toward the car.

CHAPTER 16

STREET LEVEL

◆

FROM THE DOSSIERS of major street-level drug dealers, Assistant Chief Bill Cicciolino chose one Hector ("Chino") Santos Cabrón as his pigeon. There were five excellent reasons.

One, Santos plied his trade in a section of East Harlem called "El Barrio" that wasn't all that far from Cicciolino's co-op on Ninety-fifth Street. It would make the going and coming more convenient.

Two, El Barrio was presently a mixed neighborhood. As the name suggested, it was largely Spanish, but it was also Harlem, and therefore situated in an area that was overwhelmingly black. Also, yuppies had begun to gentrify a section to the south, and a couple of older, well-fed white men would not draw a second glance.

Three, Santos had been sat on—not too hard—three-and-a-half years earlier when a drug task force netted an even half-dozen of his runners while conducting a highly publicized and consequently ineffective sweep of the area. That meant Santos would be cocky and flush with the profits from three years of uninterrupted operations.

Four, Santos had begun his career as a chili pimp and heroin pusher—two activities that he still practiced, "somewhat like a hobby," the report said—and was generally loathed in the Barrio community. Second-generation Puerto Ricans now had a stake in East Harlem, courtesy of the Urban Homesteading Program, which had virtually given them fat chunks of New York real estate, and it was their kids Santos was preying on. His death at the hands of New York's most visible (if not its top) cop would be cheered.

And five, El Barrio was in Precinct 25, where the type of squeeze Cicciolino had in mind would be possible, especially when conducted by Clifton Banks. Banks was a forty-four-year-old black former linebacker for the Jets who had worked under Cicciolino in Manhattan South and who owed him his appointment to deputy inspector. More, Banks was ambitious, and he knew Cicciolino had the ear of the first dep, and therefore the commissioner and the mayor, from whom any higher appointment would flow.

Banks was presently riding shotgun in an unmarked car driven by Police Officer Aceveda, a woman, who could act as translator if needed. Cicciolino was sitting in back. All three of them were out of uniform, dressed in loose-fitting, casual clothes.

It was a warm spring night, and they were up in the low 120s, working their way east. Building abandonments and demolition had ravaged the street they were on, such that the solitary structures that remained stood out like mesas or buttes, forlorn amid a rubble desert. And yet turning onto a cross-street that was still virtually intact, they got dead-stopped in traffic. It was the kind of weekend gridlock that struck barrios and ghettos citywide.

Cicciolino eased his back into the cushions of the seat and relaxed. The shit was out there, he thought, and the scuzz, who cooped in these mean streets, would do it no matter what. Especially on a Saturday night when the only police call worth answering was a DOA.

Up ahead there was an obstacle course of cars double- and triple-parked through which traffic had to snake. The drivers were in the buildings sleeping, fucking, eating, or more probably copping something illegal. Cicciolino turned his head and looked out the side window, which was rolled up.

The sidewalk was packed maybe three deep with a few niggers but mainly spics, kids, and dogs who were merging, breaking, and forming little volatile, unpredictable groups. Cicciolino wouldn't foot-patrol that block for all the cocaine in Colombia.

The car drifted on a few more feet, the police radio rattled then squawked, PO Aceveda turned it off without bothering to ask.

In the other direction, two kids in Yankee hats were slamming a hard-rubber baseball against a graffiti-scourged wall. Ghetto blasters bristled on stoops, and there was a face in nearly every window. Inside one of the junker cars that dotted the area like mechanical turds, a pair of haunted eyes, lit by a street lamp, looked out at them. In a kind of salute, a bottle in a brown bag was raised until a mouth clamped down on its slippery green neck.

"I feel like a character out of *Bonfire of the Vanities*," said Cicciolino, just to make conversation.

"Yeah?" Banks replied. "Somehow you never reminded me of a Social X ray. Maybe you're more a Lemon Tart."

Cicciolino laughed. A very dark-skinned man, Banks had a square face and square body, as if he'd been chipped from two blocks of black stone, and the impression of strength, determination, and truculence was not deceiving. If anything, Banks was too tough—on perps, on the public, on his men, and on himself.

But he had struck just the right mood tonight, Cicciolino thought. Here they were, out in the field having fun. No police business, they were just observing. It was like a little sociological experiment they were conducting. For the first dep, who—*everybody* knew—was a closet intellectual.

Also, it made the point that Banks had read the book, which made Banks feel good. Cicciolino wondered if Banks had ever met Brant informally over, say, lunch or a few drinks. The chance for imminent promotion would keep Banks so preoccupied he'd probably forget about Cicciolino entirely, and he made a mental note to set something up when Brant got back in three weeks. The first dep had flown to Miami and then on to Nassau the night before, leaving Cicciolino in effective control of what Cicciolino was touting as Brant's "pet project."

"Here we go," said Banks, tilting his square head toward the *farmacia* they were now rolling past, knowing he did not have to explain to Cicciolino.

In the storefront next to the pharmacy was a cracked, palm-greasy glass door. Behind it Cicciolino could see a dot-head receptionist in elegant silks sitting at a desk where she could control the flow in and out. On the sidewalk stood a line of nervous, sick-looking people, each doing a little smack dance while waiting on

Dr. Bhenge Maduli. So said a sign above the door. Maduli was obviously the local pill-palace pasha with a medical degree from some Third World university who was mining his fortune from U.S. taxpayers.

To Maduli you took your nervous condition and Medicaid card. He charged the government a full office visit plus a series of tests that never got performed. You brought his prescription next door to the *farmacia* and got a nice supply of Valium or Dilaudid, which you sold on the street for your P.M. fix. Cicciolino would bet his pension that Maduli had a piece of the *farmacia* too. But all he could see there was a busted accordion Beirut blind with a six-by-three foot slot torched out of one side. It was filled with brilliant white light on which was silhouetted the figure of a skinny, trigger-happy-looking rent-a-cop. He had a hand on his hip, inches from the carved, holstered butt of a .44 magnum.

The good drugs you got on the corner. There three young jive-ass bloods, were flogging crack by the vial or the clip of ten—three sales so far—with another bigger, older nigger, whom Cicciolino thought he recognized, standing well back in the shadows selling smack. No frenzy there. His trade was paced. He took time to talk and even joke with his customers. Cicciolino now placed his gap-toothed grin, having busted the sucker years ago.

Unlike crack, which was explosive on every level (hadn't Cicciolino just seen it himself down in the Islands?), heroin was an established, orderly, even civilized business, as civilization went hereabouts. Cicciolino would also bet Boomer, which he now remembered was the nigger's name, extended limited credit to his best customers when they were hurting. Cicciolino wished they had happened upon a boatload of heroin, not cocaine. At least with heroin he'd have better people to deal with.

The reason for the traffic jam was on the other corner. Gathered there was a group of what looked like fifties junior high school girls complete with tight skirts, ponytails, and bobby socks, until you looked close at their faces. They were black, tawny, and brown girls but their makeup made their eyes big as lurid saucers, their lips wide and ductile, as if extruded from bright, red rubber. They were the reason for the immediate traffic snarl. Chicken hawks with license plates from as far away as Delaware were cruising the block, looking for a little lap dance or something more exotic. Cicciolino imagined they hadn't been there long. Sex with kids was a trade that wasn't much tolerated even by dopers. It had to move around.

"You know the question, what's wrong with this scene?" Banks asked. "You'd think—here we got two separate, complimentary operations. You know, drugs on this corner. Kiddy sex on that. Wrong. It's all part of one scheme hatched by that little hotshot over there, who *be*—" Banks paused dramatically, "our man."

He pointed to the chili-pimp Rican with the gold chains and lipstache who was sashaying out to work a deal with the driver of the car in front of them. He wasn't young but he was fashionable, Cicciolino could see. He had big, wide zoot-suit pants with pleats down to his knees. "Santos?"

"None other. And think of the beauty and the—" Banks searched for a term, "impunity of that little asshole. Stopping traffic to sell his pigmeat, while his real action is happening across the street. The more traffic he stops, the less chance there is of a bust. But if it happens, hey, he don't go down, only the Yo-bros there on the corner. Or if there's a raid, he sees who done it. Meanwhile, he keeps an eye on the store, moves it around at least once a week, from what we know.

"Then, what we see here is just the tip of his iceberg, what he does for fun. To look at him standing there in his diffy rags, you'd think there ain't no way that little chump-change son of a bitch is worth more than what he got in his back pocket. But, as the bard says, appearances are only appearances, and that little lump of slime, he works hard on his. Truth is, he got people legging for him all over Harlem, Spanish Harlem, and—they tell me—all the way up into the Bronx as far as Tremont Avenue.

"He's got to have millions by now, and a good man with a buck, I hear. You know, investments out-of-town, out-of-state, out-of-country. All sorts of money. Still, he lives in a fifth-floor walk-up, you know, one building standing out in the rubble with four layers of protection each floor down.

"You got his sheet?"

Cicciolino nodded. Better, he had a folder about three inches thick on Hector ("Chino") Santos Cabrón. He knew everything official there was to know and a whole bunch more from the paid informers and stoolies who had plea-bargained to bag him over the years without proof. "Chino" had been arrested, charged, indicted, even convicted, numerous times, but he had never spent more than five months at one sitting in the can. "What's his specialty?"

"Whatever's hot. A few years ago it was heroin, then blow, now crystal. The girls are just a little, you know, *kink* in his personality. Rumor is the new girl's always his favorite. She gets to visit his fifth-floor boom-boom room until she ages a few months and a newer, younger girl comes along. Wasn't there a song about that?"

Police Officer Aceveda mumbled something, and Banks asked, "Say what?"

She turned her head to him, and her eyes flashed. "I said, he's a mothah-fucking, cock-sucking viper, and somebody should blow him away. *Sir.*"

She was a good-looking, sharp-featured young Hispanic woman with a yellow complexion and fiery eyes. Cicciolino wondered what was going on between her and Banks. In his experience nobody—man, woman, or child—*ever* spoke to Clifton Banks like that.

Banks only looked away. "Long as that somebody ain't Aceveda. Or Banks." Banks paused, then went on. "We could get him on a gun charge, like you can see, or maybe on the girls, could we set him up. But there, he probably knows who he's dealing with, creeps bein' creeps, and the gun?" He shook his head, and Cicciolino knew what he meant. The courts were so clogged already that with a good lawyer, which Santos undoubtedly could afford, he'd walk.

"He got a lab?" Cicciolino asked.

Banks inclined his head. "They say. He's Mr. Reliable, always got shit to sell. But where? Wouldn't I like to know."

Santos probably moved that around too, Cicciolino decided. All you needed was a kitchen stove and some pots and pans. There were abandoned buildings all over the area where you could turn on the gas with a pipe wrench and a length of flexible tubing.

Suddenly the front door popped open, and Banks was out of the car, his right hand reaching up under his windbreaker for the holster at the small of his back. Cicciolino watched his tan hand wrap the grip of a sub-nosed .38. "Hey, you—asshole."

Santos glanced at Banks and was about to turn back to the john when he realized who and what he had seen. As did the john in his rearview mirror. The brake lights went off, and the car shot forward.

Me? Santos asked with a hand to his chest. It was a delicate gesture, and a pleasant smile appeared on his face.

"You. Asshole. C'mere."

Santos looked around, as if for help, but there was nobody: not his girls, who had bunched together, one of them giggling. Not from any of his fellow *calabozos* who were hanging out nearby. Not from any of the young felons in his employ across the street. Suddenly sidewalks on both corners were empty, which said something for how visible Banks's presence was in his—only one of his three—precincts.

Cicciolino lowered himself down in the backseat and quietly cracked the back door. He now had his own weapon resting in his lap, so he could cover Banks just in case. He never wanted it said he was taken by surprise or was afraid to go at somebody when he had to. And also because he didn't care for Ricans.

Like niggers had been four, five hundred years earlier, they were a mistake. People made mistakes, why couldn't governments? And the idea of granting U.S. citizenship to a bunch of ignorant, shit-poor greasers from an overpopulated Caribbean island a thousand miles from the American mainland had been a categorical error, no two ways about it. Given the way they bred, there was no end in sight, except for what was happening now. Maybe the best thing was for the spics and niggers to go out in a big flash of white, blinding powder. Far as he could see, it was killing mostly them, and some others that didn't deserve to live either.

And maybe—who knew?—the entire country was a mistake: mixing everybody up so you got a bunch of bastards who created trouble and crime and some new generations that repeated the process on a grander scale. Far as Cicciolino was concerned, the only place in town he felt really at home was in Little Italy among his kind.

Maybe he chose wrong, becoming a cop. But in his time the ranks of the Mob had been filled out with so many ignorant assholes with their dumb tribal shit and rituals that it hadn't been a viable option for a college grad. Who was also a lawyer. Cicciolino understood things had changed somewhat, but too late for him.

Which was the way of things. Wasn't there waste in nature? You had only to walk into a forest to see it—all the trees and dead shit on the ground. It was messy and chaotic. Here in the city there were whole boroughs dedicated to nothing else. Only the strong, who lived mostly in Manhattan or the suburbs, survived, and often on the humus or carcasses of the dead. What he had here in front of him was human waste, no two ways about it. Garbage. Forty-nine years of experience couldn't be wrong.

"*Now!*" Banks roared.

Santos took a tentative step forward. And another. "*¿Por qué, señor?*"

"*Por qué* you," Banks muttered to himself. Then, "Drop your pants!"

"*¿Qué?*"

"I said drop your pants and turn around. The lady wants to see your ass."

Again Santos smiled, glancing at the corner to make sure his operations had split, and then up at the sky as though unbelieving. He had large, expressive eyes, and his lipstache looked as if it had been trimmed to a fault with a barber's straight razor. He tried to peer through the darkened windows into the car.

"You heard me. Your fuckin' pants, asshole. Drop 'em!"

He hunched his shoulders resignedly. "That all you want, man, you got it. You' the hero. It you' turf. NYPD."

When his hands moved toward the belt, Banks added, "Slowly. And, asshole—?" He waited until Santos raised his head. "You touch your left pocket and you' be one fuckin' dead little mothah-fuckah. *¿Comprendes?*"

The belt opened, the fly went down, the pants fell into a pool around his ankles. He looked up at Banks and the car, as though to say, Like what you see?

His underwear was something meant for a woman or a queer. It was skimpy, netted with what looked like lace, and so tight it made the skin of his thighs and belly lump over the band.

One of the girls laughed, another called out something in Spanish.

"Now turn around and drop your shorts."

Santos sighed and look dejected. "Aw—*man?* You dissin' me? What you want next, suck my dick?"

"Do it."

Santos shuffled around and bared his hairy crack.

The girls were laughing now. Somebody from across the street shouted, "Faggot!," and a car passing in the other direction blew its horn.

"You wan' me to bend over now?"

"No—you just stay like that for a while. Lady's seen enough. Says she'll pass." Banks slipped back into the car, and Officer Acevedo slipped the car into gear, so that they rolled past Santos. In spite of the *macho* act, he was scared. His cock and balls had almost disappeared.

Banks reached over and hit the horn twice, and when Santos's hand jumped for his pants, Cicciolino swung the rear door open and pointed his weapon at Santos's head. "Try it, cock bite. Hard to miss from here."

Anger now replaced Santos's fear. He was caught, frozen, bending over like that, and one of his stable gave out a long, high-pitched squeal of pure joy.

But they were soon beyond him, and Banks threw an arm over the seat and turned to Cicciolino. "My kind of lineup," he said through a smile, partly in explanation, partly in apology. It had been enough to get all three of them flopped, but with Santos's gun, the girls, and the dope there would be no complaint.

It cemented the idea that Banks and Cicciolino were street cops from the old pre-Serpico days, which would be helpful for what Cicciolino had in mind. He raised one dark eyebrow. "Don't often see a man baring his soul like that anymore. Takes courage and guts."

Police Officer Acevedo began laughing. "You two do this sort of thing often?" she asked.

Banks would not have had her drive if he weren't sure of her confidentiality, and Cicciolino said, "Couldn't be often enough for me, which is why it was so nice. For starters."

Banks's head swung back to him. His smile fell. A question appeared in furrows on his dark brow.

"Starting tomorrow, Cliff, I want you to squeeze Santos. I want you to put the word out on the street that he's hot, and anybody supplying him product'll get his ass tacked to the wall.

"To back it up, I'll give you forty extra men. The first dep wants you to stop his flow of coke cold, if you can. We want to see what he'll do then—who he'll go to, how he'll make up the loss, what sort of dent it'll put in his operation.

"The second object is—how did Brant phrase it?" Cicciolino

asked, looking out the window as if trying to recall. "A kind of experiment in supply and demand, I think he called it. The idea is to see once and for all if drying up supply on the street level is a viable option. You know, how practical is it? How much manpower is needed, how many hours, what it'll cost?

"Me? I don't think it's doable, but I don't call the shots. And then there's the difference between *thinking* it ain't doable and *knowing* it ain't doable. And—hey"—Cicciolino reached out and slapped Banks's shoulder— "we might get lucky and make the little asshole do something rash that might even be fatal."

"All *right!*" seconded Police Officer Acevedo.

Banks merely turned back to the windshield. Several blocks later he asked, "*Forty* extra men?"

"Don't ask me, but it sounds like he's serious. If it's too many, we can always pull some in. They're mostly my staff, and they'll be glad for the break from downtown," by which he meant headquarters. "I'm sure you'll find something for them to do.

"You know him?" Cicciolino asked.

"Santos?"

"No, no—Jesus—stay with me here, Cliff. We don't have to think Santos till tomorrow. *Brant* I'm talkin'."

"Shook his hand once."

"You wanna?"

Yet again the block of Banks's head swung to Cicciolino. Their eyes met. Of course he wanted to meet Brant, if that was what Cicciolino had in mind. Brant could bust Banks's career wide open.

"When he gets back—two, three weeks—I'll set something up. You eat Italian?"

Banks looked away and through a smile shook his head. "You think I'm gonna say no?"

And all three of them laughed.

Banks then asked Cicciolino if he wanted them to take him home. "Nah—I'll walk from here. Nice night. I like to window-shop." Especially in a certain photo gallery near Madison.

CHAPTER 17

NATURE'S SIDE

"I STILL CAN'T believe it's a woman," Eva Burden said, lowering a pair of binoculars. She was standing on the deck of Creach's apartment across Nassau Harbor from Nathanson's house. Nathanson was by her side, leaning against an end wall. Creach, who was now able to get around with the help of a cane, was sitting in front of an antique brass telescope on a gleaming, wooden tripod. "And she's so beautiful and so . . . chic."

Not so the entourage that the woman had brought with her, Nathanson thought. He had never seen uglier men. They had high, wide cheekbones and pronounced supraorbital tori, like some throwback to Neanderthal man. And they were squat but out-sized, with wide shoulders and barrel chests. Although their legs were bowed, their gait was pigeon-toed, which made them roll when they moved. Yet they were nonetheless quick and could bear great weight. Only three of them were now carrying Nathanson's mother's Bechstein concert grand toward a moving truck that they had pulled up on the sidewalk by the back gate.

"But why food?" Eva asked. It had been the first item that had been carried out, a good month's supply of frozen meat that

Nathanson had recognized as coming from the two large freezers in the cellar: roasts of beef, legs of lamb, and a side of veal, which was always difficult to come by in Nassau. Two Indians had filled a small van and driven off.

Creach thought he knew why, which only added to his shame. The entire project had been a disaster from the moment they saw the plane in the cove. And the loss? So far they had blown the money, the dope, their buy boat, nearly their lives, and for sure Jared's and Deke's who had been just a couple of dumb kids looking for a quick score. Now Nathanson would lose everything of value that they hadn't got out of the house, all because of Creach's temper and his mouth.

Well, he didn't have to worry about that anymore, did he? The little broad, Eva, had only looked away when he had pointed to his throat and raised his eyebrows in question. And then Southworth, who wasn't much of a doctor but at least was honest, had said, "Maybe you might get an amplifier. *If* you can whisper, after you heal. But to speak again? I don't know. You'll have to see a specialist. There's nothing *I* can do."

Nor for the fingers of his left hand that hurt as though they were still there and being dunked in hot oil. Sometimes Creach thought he could even wiggle them.

He leaned forward and focused on the shadows of the grapevine trellis where from time to time he caught a glimpse through the leaves of the *sicaria*'s red hair. There had to be some way even in his condition he could get down there and put her out. It was the only way he could see of buying them time.

Later, when he and Nathanson had healed completely, they could sail over to Bimini and poke around. Monroe might be dead and *Whistler* sunk, but there was no way Creach could have another peaceful moment knowing how they got done by five middle-aged white assholes who were probably from New York. Far as he was concerned, it wasn't over. Not by a long shot.

Said Eva to Nathanson, "Doesn't it bother you that they're taking your things?"

He hunched his shoulders and looked away at a plane that was circling the harbor. "It might, if I could so something about it." To conceal his bandages, he was wearing a Hawaiian-style shirt that had been given him by a former girlfriend as a kind of joke. It was white and printed with bright green leaves and big orange papayas. Denim cutoffs completed his garb for the late afternoon. Nathanson hadn't worn shoes for a week.

"But the loss itself—what about that?"

Nathanson turned his head to her. He hadn't known why he had liked looking into her eyes until Denny pointed it out one morning, bringing him a cup of coffee. "That little girl, the doctor lady—ain't it something? She got your eyes exactly." In the hall he had added, "And that ain't all."

Nathanson agreed. He supposed it was egocentric, liking your own eyes. But you liked what you liked, and Nathanson liked looking at Eva Burden.

"I mean, most of the things I saw in your house aren't easily replaceable."

"More easily than our lives. Yours, mine, his." Nathanson moved his chin toward Creach. He twirled a blonding end of his mustache. He needed a trim and a haircut, and wondered if he could ask her to give it a try. She was so good with her hands.

"C'mon," she said, "you're being evasive here. Why not try candor for once. Maybe we can be friends." She smiled.

That was it, Nathanson decided. It wasn't so much her eyes after all as her smile, which was a bit off-center and exposed the interesting space between her otherwise even teeth. She wasn't exactly pretty, but the way she raised one eyebrow and turned her head to the side, as though assessing him down the length of her slightly curved nose, was provoking. It seemed to say, I know your secret. You're better than you pretend to be. Admit it, and—as she had just said—maybe we can be friends.

It posed a dilemma for Nathanson. First off, he wouldn't admit to being better than he was, even if he was, which he wasn't. Nathanson was who he was, good, bad, or more often than not just another creature who was now especially thankful to be alive. And second, with a body like hers, there was no way friends could happen with him until maybe *after*. He'd always be thinking about her in unfriendly ways. He let his eyes slip farther.

It was hot and she was wearing a floral-print bandeau that Nathanson didn't think he had seen before and a pair of white linen shorts that his mother had worn but never like that. The bandeau was mainly blue with big red roses, and the relationship between her tanned shoulders, narrow waist, and the flare of her hips was something Nathanson could not look at too long without thinking he should go do something else.

The first couple of days that he was feeling better, he told himself he was just horny. He had nearly lost his life. Now that he was alive, he should celebrate. But then he got to noticing her crisp step and the taut tendon at the back of her shapely legs, as she moved between Creach's and his beds. Also there was the way she filled out anything she wore, like the bandeau with the bursting roses or the linen shorts that were stretched smooth across the base of her spine. Finally, there was the balance between the length of her legs and the size of her torso. Nathanson was into structure, and Eva Burden looked like a member of a smaller, more finely formed race of people. One that he would like to get to know. In the particular.

"Are you with me?" she asked.

"Pain," he said, flicking a hand to indicate the wound in his side. "What was the question?"

"Is there anything I can do?"

Nathanson traced the fine blond hairs, like a kind of down, on her high forehead, and pulled in some air, which he let out slowly. He had some ideas, but he didn't think she'd go for the direct approach. Better she should get to know the *good* side of him, and maybe then. . . . He shook his head.

"Your things."

"They're just things."

"And things aren't important?"

Again he hunched a shoulder, making sure their eyes met before his moved off.

She waited.

After a while, he said, "I s'poze, but we got most of the good stuff out."

"So, *good* things are important?"

"Maybe."

"As important as nature?"

His eyes flashed at her. "You been talking to Denny?" Denny could be devious, and Nathanson was getting an idea of what the old man had in mind. A couple of months ago he had said, "All's you bring into this house is women. Ain't it time you got yourself a *lady*?"

"Denny said you were on nature's side," Eva went on. "He

said it . . . proudly, and I'm just interested in what it means. So far we've got you on nature's side along with *good* things, like old, well-made furniture, Oriental rugs, some paintings, and some books. It's nice, but not like any nature I know."

Nathanson wondered what she wanted, questions never being *just* questions. To get to know him? In what way? He himself preferred the *womanly* approach. "Maybe you don't know nature."

Eva waited.

"You mentioned things. The way it is we need things—roof over your head, something to eat and drink, other things to entertain you and occupy your mind. Good things are better than bad things, or no things at all."

When it appeared he would not say more, she asked, "And that's your argument for nature?"

"*Human* nature."

"To surround yourself with *good* things?" She laughed and looked away. "You're the strangest yuppie I've ever met."

Nathanson laughed too. "You could get into a lot of trouble hereabouts calling people yuppies."

"Well"—she returned her smile to him, canting her head to regard him assessingly again— "at least you seem to have a sense of humor."

He touched his side. "Don't I need it?" He smiled himself, which puckered a dimple in his right cheek and exposed his own even white teeth. But for the wound, Nathanson was in splendid condition.

"Your nature seems pretty bare bones to me, pretty grim. Isn't there an upside?"

"You heard it."

She tried to look away, but their eyes were now locked.

"And maybe the idea that the whole point of owning things is to give you a chance to be out in nature. On your own terms. Whenever you want."

"You mean, *nature* nature?"

Again Nathanson smiled and gestured his hand at the sky. "I won't feed you any New Age bullshit. We were into nature years ago. You know, when it was lost, before it was rediscovered by the people who jog in Central Park. Or belong to the Sierra Club."

"*We?*"

"Creach and me."

Again Eva's brow glowered, and her eyes flickered toward Creach, who had not taken his eye from the antique telescope.

Nathanson watched her look down at her small, capable hands before glancing up at him again. "Tell me something. When you're out trafficking in cocaine, are you with nature then or on some other side?"

Nathanson tried not to alter his smile. To her other qualities he now added a certain mental toughness, which he also admired. "I do more than traffic in cocaine."

"Now that it has made you rich."

There was a certain amount of truth in that too. "Wealthy."

"Now that it has made you wealthy." There was now an edge to her voice, and Nathanson wondered why.

"I'm not perfect. I've made mistakes."

"You mean with the men on the plane. The Bolivian transporters."

Nathanson shook his head. "I don't mean that. You know what I mean."

She looked away, as though to say she wished she did. And suddenly, in that simple gesture, Nathanson felt different about Eva Burden. It was no big change, nothing radical. He would try to get to know her now, if she would give him the chance.

But he said nothing. It was not his way, and maybe the feeling would pass. Usually it did.

She had raised her binoculars. It was nearly dark now. "But isn't there something you can do about your house? I'm no fan of the police, but the idea that some people—a bunch of obvious foreigners—can break into a house in broad daylight and . . . *rape* it, is contrary to everything that any established country with laws is about."

Nathanson was tempted to say, Not in nature, but you couldn't take it too far. "The government and police here are on the pad, starting from their president, a guy named Pindling, right down the line. And somebody like her"—with his own binoculars Nathanson followed the red hair from the trellis to the light over the back door and into the kitchen—" wouldn't attempt this without permission from the top, which is Medellín."

They now saw a single light appear in the small study off the library in the house. The red hair passed by the window, and then the dark face of an Indian appeared at that window and seemed to look directly up at them, as though he knew they were there, before drawing the curtains.

"And with the money they're throwing around," Nathanson went on, "people can forget they're Colombian or Bahamian or American for a while."

Or human, Eva thought.

"Or human," he added, as though reading her thoughts. When she turned to him, he smiled. "And then I'm not sure I'd want the police messing around in my house."

With her eyes on him like that, she waited.

"Might give them an excuse to mess around in my life." A big man, Nathanson had a deep, easy voice. "And who knows—I might get some of it back someday. See a piece at an auction or in a shop. What's happening down there," he continued, mainly to cheer up Creach, "is just a collection action, Colombian style. The cartels are just like Chrysler or Boeing in the States, they just don't lose. If they do, your money and your things become *their* money and *their* things for the best reason in the world. Power. Why have it, if you can't use it to your advantage?"

Now another Indian appeared on the street in front of the house. He waited for a break in the traffic, then crossed to the entrance gate of the dock, which he opened and stepped in. He was wearing a dark Andean fedora and a dark poncho. In the deepest shadows of the corner of the lawn he sat and drew the material around him. From a distance he looked like a cone-shaped rock or monument.

Nathanson eased himself off the wall. A phone was ringing behind them in the penthouse. "A picket," he said. "Because of what happened with you, she knows we're watching her from someplace. She's betting we'll make a play. That's why it's been taking her so long"—to clean out the house, he meant.

Denny now appeared in the darkness behind them. "Phone's for you, Brian. The call you been waiting on."

Nathanson's first steps were careful, but by the time he reached the sliding screen doors, he was moving quickly.

Before Denny could close the screen, Creach was on his feet, swinging his injured leg around the chair. He handed Eva a note, then held out his good hand and shook hers firmly. "Thanks," she thought she heard him whisper. "You're the best."

When five or so minutes later Eva entered the kitchen, which was lighted, she opened the note. In neat script it said, *Think I'll stretch out my leg, like you told me. Without you, Brian and me would be dead now. Don't think I'll ever forget.* It was signed, *Creach.*

Eva returned to the deck and trained her glasses on the house. She assumed it was her watch.

"Brian?" the voice on the other end asked. "This is Jorge Luis Ochoa. I understand you've been trying to get in touch with me. How are you?"

"*No estoy bueno,*" Nathanson said, and he explained why—the busted deal with the Bolivian *transportadores* who had stepped on the delivery. "They tested ten percent light, which we would have gone along with had they not stolen an entire shipment from us before. They're Bolivians, three brothers name of—"

"Romero," Ochoa said.

"Then we got pretty banged up, and the source, a guy I dealt with before, didn't wait for me to get back to him. He went out and hired a *sicaria.*"

"Londoño," said Ochoa. "So, it was you on the other end of his deal. I wish I had known." He could have assured the others that it was just a mix-up and something would be worked out. It would have obviated the need for a *sicaria.*

"What can I do for you, Brian?" Now that it was too late and the *sicaria* had been dispatched.

Nathanson didn't know how much he could ask. They had met in the old days of the Colombian coke trade when Ochoa was running the Sea-8 Trading Corporation for his uncle, Fabio Restrepo Ochoa, and Nathanson was a grad student in oceanography at the University of Miami. One day a drug task force made a grab for Jorge Luis in the parking lot of a Coral Gables shopping mall. Nathanson lived around the corner, and when Ochoa arrived at his door needing help, he got it with no questions, no demand of cash, and he soon found himself back in Colombia. For years they dealt with each other agreeably, until the Cartel became a formality, the bounds of which could not be breached.

"The *sicaria,*" Nathanson now said. "*She's* a redhead. Seems to have a small army of squat, ugly Indians."

"Boyacas."

"You know her?"

"Of course."

"What can you tell me? I need a . . . *handle*," he said in English. "Some way of approaching her. I got a hole in my side, and my house is being looted. Tell you the truth, Jorge, I'm too old for this shit. Is there a chance she could be bought off?"

Probably not after having seen your house, thought Ochoa, who on several occasions had been Nathanson's guest. But he paused before answering.

Like Nathanson, Ochoa was sitting in a penthouse. His was situated on a bluff in the El Poblado section of Medellín, where he could look out his study window toward the Cordillera Central of the Andes. It had just become dark, and lights had appeared everywhere, it seemed, along the lower flanks of the mountain range except for one large patch. There, only a small group of lights were clustered in the middle. It was Finca Los Llanos, the Londoño family estate that Ochoa would not mind owning himself. An idea began to develop.

What . . . *what if* by some twist of fate, the sins of the father— the old reprobate, "Don" Pacho Londoño, who held title to the property—came back to haunt him, and somebody other than Ochoa himself, somebody entirely justified in her actions, made Finca Los Llanos available. Justifiable homicide, Ochoa was thinking. He himself already held much of the Londoños' debt. Sure, he would have to pay more and perhaps even a premium, but in the entire country there was no finer property, the fields and barns and houses of which had been perfected for over three hundred years and had Old World charm.

Pachito, the son, would be satisfied. He'd complain and appear sorrowful in public at having to yield his family seat, but in private he'd be overjoyed to be out from under the old man and his debt. Also, he could save face by saying that at least the property had remained in the family. Ochoa was a cousin. In such a way he might even be made to seem like he *saved* the estate.

"Her name is Solange Mercier La Guatavita, but she's known in the trade as *la Sorda Roja.*"

"She's actually *deaf*?" Nathanson asked. Eva had told him about the card she had shown, but he thought it had been a ruse of some sort—to distract and thereby disarm her prey.

Ochoa then related her story, but in greater detail than he had to his two Cartel compeers. As he spoke, he also opened a bottom drawer of his desk, which contained a small safe, and plied the combination lock until it opened.

He mentioned that her mother, as the name suggested, was some mix of Indian, and her father a French mining engineer who made an emerald strike in the Montserrate of the Andes. He ran out of working capital, however, and needed a partner.

Enter "Don Pacho" Londoño, who had never been one to work for his money, and, like so many Antioqueños, believed he could do whatever he pleased, once out of Antioquia, "Stories came back about him—murder, rape." The Indians who were employed at the mine went on strike, and Londoño over Mercier's objections put them down with *pistoleros*. "You know how things can go in isolated places like that. He had money and power. He was white and Antioqueño. His word was law."

Then, one night, after it was rumored his money had run out, Londoño arrived back at Finca Los Llanos. He was badly cut and near death, with a young Creole girl tied across his saddle. She had been raped and struck on the head so hard that for a while, after she recovered physically, she couldn't speak. When finally she managed that, they discovered she was stone deaf and had blacked out the entire incident.

"Londoño told the family that his partner and he had been set upon by thieves. The partner and his wife had been killed, their child beaten over the head and raped, and the take from their best year at the mine stolen. The loss included the huge, unflawed emerald—a single stone—that Mercier had used as proof that he had discovered gems where he had. It's a marvelous thing and absolutely unique. So big it almost doesn't fit in the palm of your hand."

An official inquiry was mounted, but without witnesses or corpses, nothing was done. There was a flooded fissure at one of the mining sites so deep that the bottom had never been sounded. "Don Pacho suggested that the thieves must have dumped the bodies there. The authorities monitored gem markets the world over, but nothing like the Mercier brooch stone, which is what it's called, was ever offered for sale. They speculated it had been cut into several smaller stones and disposed of that way."

The mine reverted to Londoño's creditors, and he made his partner's daughter, the deaf girl, a *doméstica* or servant in his house. "As she grew into the woman that I guess you've seen, what more could a lecherous old drunk want but dumb? But she wasn't. One day when she was around fifteen, she got hold of a gun and fired it at his head. It's maybe the only time she's missed. She's had a lot of practice since."

The girl fled to Medellín and the Barrio Antioquia, where she hired herself out and at least got money for what Don Pacho was making her do for the honor of living among the Londoños. "And good at it. I don't think she was nineteen or twenty before she had her own string of women working for her. She even sent herself to university, but she still lives there."

"In the Barrio?" Nathanson had been to Medellín often enough to know what it was.

"Surrounded by some of the Boyacas who had worked for her father. In a kind of compound of maybe two, three hundred people, like her own small army. Nobody gets in without her permission. Those who try—"

Don't get out, Nathanson concluded, wondering why Ochoa was telling him all of this. "But why her?"

"You mean, why did Pachito hire her as a *sicaria*? Or why did she consent to be hired by him after Don Pacho?"

"Both."

Ochoa thought for a moment. He had found what he had been searching for in the desk safe. He placed it on the blotter of his desk and then closed the heavy, armored door, spinning its lock. "Well, she's the *complete* professional, and takes pride in her reputation. And they're about the same age, Pachito and she. They grew up together, and, you know, they both had to live with Don Pacho. At least she got out. Pachito still has Don Pacho around his neck.

"They tell me the old man still has 'good' days when he comes into town here and has a fling. Runs up a lot of bills. He even once tried to go see Solange. She had to stop her Boyacas from cutting him to pieces. I heard she said she was glad he'd stopped by, since it gave her a chance to thank him for her education." Ochoa paused. "I don't think she meant university."

It was Nathanson's turn to think, and both men listened to static crackle over the international wire. "The emerald—it sounds magnificent. I assume you've seen it yourself."

"I'm looking at it now, or at least a fairly recent photo."

"How recent?"

"Two, three years at the most." Ochoa explained that he had run into the elder Londoños when he was on holiday in Spain. They had agreed to meet that night for dinner, and Don Pacho had made his wife wear it.

Mortified, flushed with shame, she had tried to cover it up, but Londoño had pulled open the material of the bodice, making a scene. "What—you afraid people might find out your husband wasn't a fool after all?" It ruined the meal. Nobody could take his eyes off it. Ochoa assumed Don Pacho was just a little too drunk to be cautious, or else he had wanted to brag in front of his wife's side of the family.

Said Nathanson, "She, the woman, the *sicaria*—she's never seen the emerald?"

"Obviously not, which is the reason I troubled you with the story. If she had and knew who now had it, well—any question in her mind about who killed her parents would be over, along with Pachito Londoño's problems with the old man."

"Then you're saying she's never seen your photo."

"Exactly."

"And the photo—what does it show?"

Smiling now, Ochoa leaned back in his desk chair so he could both view the photograph and see the dark expanse of Finca Los Llanos in the distance. In that way it was like sighting in a target with a gun. "Don Pacho and his wife, Doña Dolores, are sitting in the window seat of a restaurant. They are obviously advanced in age. Beyond them, out in the street, one can see an F series Mercedes. Around her neck swings the Mercier brooch stone—it could be none other—glinting on her bony chest like a fiery green tiger's eye."

Again they listened to the stratosphere, before Nathanson asked, "I wonder, Jorge, if you might spare me that photo."

"A copy, of course. In memory of 1975 and Coral Gables. Where shall I have it sent?"

Nathanson gave him Creach's address, then asked, "How long do you think it'll take?"

"I'll have a copy tomorrow on the first plane to Miami. My people will forward it from there."

"Thank you, Jorge."

"Not necessary. If I could call her off, I would. Good luck, Brian."

When Nathanson turned around, Eva Burden was standing in the door with binoculars in her hands. "You better take a look at this. I think Creach has gone over to your house."

As Nathanson moved toward the deck, she explained, "I thought I saw some activity by the dock. Something like a small boat. But as you can see, it's so dark there." She handed him the glasses. "Then, maybe four, five minutes later, I saw a small light under the dock flash once, and then the Indian, the one who positioned himself on the lawn above the dock got up. He drew his knife, the big one, the—"

"*Penilla*," Nathanson supplied.

"—and he made his way down to the dock where you see him now."

The Indian was peering down into a small red pulling boat, which with low tide was five or six feet below him. It had been tied under the dock. Creach owned such a boat and, as Nathanson now explained to Eva, there was, ". . . a passageway, there under the pilings. It's concealed behind what looks like bank battens. From there it leads under the road, directly into the house. Only Creach and I and Denny"—who now appeared in the open door— "know about it. It's something from the eighteenth century. The man who built the house was a privateer. He didn't want everybody knowing what he brought home."

"Why didn't we use it the night I brought you back?"

"Denny didn't know who you were."

Eva glanced at Denny, who tilted his head in apology.

"But Creach—" she went on, now genuinely worried about him, "What can he want? Did he forget something? Surely he doesn't think that alone he can stage an assault on them."

Nathanson lowered the glasses and traded a glance with Denny, who reentered the penthouse. A minute or so later he returned with a shirt, jacket, and tennis shoes for Nathanson, and two large handguns.

Eva debated whether she should say anything. Finally she couldn't help herself and blurted out, "Is that what you call being on nature's side?"

Nathanson lowered the glasses and turned to her. His initial urge was to say, Definitely. Think of it as survival. Denny tells me you weren't above it yourself the other day, with a MAC-10. But he was just worried about Creach and angry that he had taken off without any discussion or planning. A raid on the house was something that Nathanson had been mulling over himself. But there was no sense in taking it out on somebody else, especially Eva.

"You've got a point," he said. "But consider this. Creach is my partner and friend, has been for the last sixteen years. They probably killed Jared and Deke, and they're here for murder."

Eva looked away.

Creach was standing in the open doorway of the tunnel beneath the dock, waiting to see if the Indian would get down on his hands and knees and discover him. He could see his sandals through the dock slats; the shadow of his fedora and poncho was cast across the water.

It had been the squeaking of the rusty hinges of the bulkhead that had brought him. Creach didn't plan to close the door. If he was unsuccessful in the house, it might be his avenue of escape. After a four-minute eternity, the Indian moved away.

The tunnel was made of granite block that was covered with slick green moss. Creach had abandoned the cane in the pulling boat, and, having planned the raid for days as he watched the *sicaria* plunder the house, he wore a stiff oystering mitten over his injured hand. A leather glove covered his right. Under his belt he had tucked a Saturn 2-22.

Without a clip it was about the size of a Colt .45 Government Model and looked like a conventional machine pistol, until you examined it closely. Instead of one barrel, the Saturn had two. In its semiautomatic mode, it fired two .22 LR rimfire rounds with little detectable muzzle jump, especially when equipped with the extra weight of a sixty-round magazine. Unlike larger-caliber weapons, its report was muted.

Firing the Saturn at full automatic, however, was an experience in and of itself. The weapon disgorged its clip at an incredible three thousand rounds per minute. Each footlong clip could be spent in two seconds flat, and the damage inflicted—especially with CCI Stingers, a high-velocity ammunition—was truly horrendous. In other words, it was a rare but ideal close-action, antiterrorist weapon.

Like a system of steel buttresses around his belt, Creach had fitted clips for the Saturn. Beneath his shirt and again as much for support as protection, he wore Kevlar, upper-body armor. After duty in Vietnam, U.S. Army warrant officer David Creach had spent another hitch as a weapons-procurement specialist. The training had proved helpful in civilian life.

In a holster by his right side was a silenced Ruger Mark II, an assassination weapon. At the small of his back he also carried three fragmentation grenades. If he did not leave Nathanson's house alive, the *sicaria* and her Indians wouldn't either.

As on a ship, the door at the other end of the tunnel was sealed with a wheel-lock bulkhead that Nathanson had installed to keep the dampness of the tide-wet tunnel out of the cellar. It opened into a wall of hinged cabinets that lined a small storeroom there. The cabinets had to be pushed open, and only then could the bulkhead be secured from the inside.

Creach was hoping that nothing had been placed in front of the cabinets, but he imagined that the *sicaria*'s purpose had been removal not rearrangement, and for sure they did not know about the tunnel. Otherwise they would have posted a sentry and taken him. He found the cabinets unobstructed, and eased himself into the pitch-dark storeroom.

Slowly. Counting to five before every new movement. Time was on his side. After all, the *sicaria* was waiting for him, although another way to look at it was as an unparalleled opportunity. It beat tracking her down in Colombia, especially with a gone left hand, a shot-up leg, and a ruined throat.

Creach closed his eyes and counted to sixty, which seemed like an interminable amount of time there alone in the darkness. Then he eased the bulkhead nearly closed and pushed the cabinet in front of it. He moved first to the cellar steps. After listening again for a good while, he flashed the penlight up at the door, which was closed. There were no windows in the cellar, and with the penlight still on he made his way to the two large freezers, the red operating lights of which he could see on two sides of a corner wall.

If they had already taken all the frozen meat, why leave the freezers on? Carelessness? Unconcern? They weren't paying the electric bill.

Creach had another thought, and he paused to gather himself. Even so, when he raised the lid of the first freezer and the interior light clicked on, he flinched. He had learned in Vietnam you were never prepared to look at death. It always struck you different—stupid, tragic, pointless, cruel—and made you wonder if anything was worth dying over.

There was Jared, or at least Jared's head, in a corner, staring up at him, his eyes popped with white frost and his skin a strange, shiny gray color. His torso, Creach imagined, was somewhere at the bottom of the box, since three arms and four legs that had also been cut off cleanly like butchered meat were stacked neatly, log style, in the middle. Kitty-corner was another head that looked to Creach like a Halloween mask with the coarse, lank hair frozen askew, the eyes crossed and the tongue lolling out. It was one of the Indians. At least they hadn't gone down alone, Creach thought, and he closed the lid and raised the second to find Deke, who had been the larger of the two little boys whom Creach first met when he teamed up with Nathanson fourteen years earlier.

Deke had been wide, athletic, and almost puppyish, always wanting to run and jump and tumble. And fast, with good hands, quick speed, and a nimble mind. Creach had tried to convince him to learn how to play American football and to pay attention to his studies in school. Creach had thought he would send him to college somewhere in the States. But Deke's blood was just a little too hot and pressurized, Creach guessed. He had trouble doing anything that wasn't active in a strict sense. As he grew older, that meant chasing women, which required money.

Creach reached out and touched his forehead, which felt slick, as if it were running with sweat. It seemed almost as if he were still smiling. His mouth was open a bit, and Creach could see his teeth. Well, Deke, he thought, closing the lid—you tried to rip us off, and young man, oh man, how you paid. It would have been far better for you had you never known us. Or known me.

Once again in the darkness at the bottom of the cellar stairs Creach continued on with his sixty-second pauses, leaning into the main beams and pressing his ear against the wood or the cold plaster of the wall of the stairs that led up into a hall closet. It would be there, he guessed, that he'd be most vulnerable. The floor was cypress and creaked.

The *sicaria* had arrived with nine Indians, but he had only been able to count seven from the penthouse. And if she had picketed one at each corner of the property, a fifth across the street, and one was dead, that left just the woman and two others in the house. How would she have positioned them? Near her, someplace where an "intruder" would have to come through them to get to her, *if* she was good, which Creach wasn't sure of. Again, if she *was* good, why the wait? Why hadn't she moved off the dime, as he used to say back in Newark when dealing bags of boo?

Newark—had it prepared him for something like this, he thought, easing open the hall door the slightest amount and scanning the little he could see in the dark hallway. Definitely. He didn't know how many old empty mansions he had snuck into, like this, deserted when, after the '68 riots, old white money began abandoning the city. Certainly it had prepared him for violence. People talked about the South Bronx and Southeast Queens being bad, but when Creach had been growing up, Newark had been the baddest motherfucking hole he'd been to yet—including Saigon and Medellín. The shit and abuse he'd seen and gone through! Far from caring if you lived or died, the power structure, white *and* black, *hoped* you'd die and relieve them of your problems. But after his mother did, Newark made Creach strong and quick. And he made sure he, his two brothers, and four sisters survived.

He would need that quickness now, and he thought: Two toots would get him up for what lay ahead. Fifteen minutes of *fly* or die. But Creach killed the thought. What was needed was calm, clear thinking, step by step, since with the bad leg he couldn't *fly.* If everything worked right, he wouldn't have to.

There was nobody in the hall, just the light on in the small study at the front of the house. There, night after night, they had seen her red head bent over Nathanson's desk before one of the Indians closed the drapes. Where were her guards? With the Ruger out and pointed at the lighted, open doorway, Creach moved down the long hallway slowly, hugging the walls where the boards would be less likely to give him away. When he stopped, which was often, he pressed an ear to the plaster and listened for any movement and even breathing that he knew could often be detectable in a quiet house if you concentrated your senses on that one ear.

Still nothing, and nothing again when, checking the sitting room, which would be behind him as he entered the study, he found it close and stuffy, as though nobody had been in it for days.

And there she was, sitting at Nathanson's desk with her back to him—the long red hair, the black dress. She was on the telephone speaking softly, whispering, in some language Creach had never heard before. She seemed smaller and wider than she had appeared through the binoculars from the deck of his penthouse across the bay.

Creach stepped into the room, the Ruger raised, and moved as quietly as he could toward her to a distance of ten feet where he would not miss.

He cleared his throat, but she did not turn around. He cleared his throat louder, but still she did not respond. Creach was not very mobile, but there was no pain in his left thigh and his left hand. Not now. Loading all his weight on that side to protect the long barrel of the silencer, he reached out to touch her.

It was then that the woman spun around. But it was not the woman. It was one of the Indians wearing a red wig and a black dress. His face looked so much like the decapitated head in the freezer that Creach was momentarily disconcerted. He paused, which saved his life.

For he saw the eyes of the Indian at the desk glance over his shoulder. Creach fell away to the left, and a large, shiny blade flashed by his right ear and chunked into the Indian's neck. He screamed. Blood spurted across the blotter.

Creach wheeled and fired at the Indian behind him. He fired again and again, but still he kept coming, his arm cocked, the blade flashing. Creach rolled away, and the blade sliced into the carpet as the Indian fell.

But the first Indian, the one in the wig and dress at the desk was now up and running past him toward the door, blood still pouring from his neck and a hand squeezing a beeper on his hip. The Ruger held ten rounds, and Creach put four into his back before the Indian turned the corner and, screaming now, thrashed down the hall.

Creach dropped the Ruger and pulled the Saturn from under his belt, jamming a clip of sixty into the mag well. Holding the weapon against his body with the oystering mitten on his left hand, he tugged back the cocking handle until the bolt step merged with the sear nose. In such a mode the Saturn was in ready-to-fire position, and Creach had to take care to keep the fingers of his good hand away from the trigger as he pushed himself off the carpet.

Using the desk for support, he got to his feet and wished for the second time that he had brought along enough coke to keep him moving and fearless until . . . which was the nature of the shit, he knew. He'd been doing too much since he'd got banged up, and it could get you killed. At the same time, it could save you too, and he suddenly felt drained and hurting from just one little tumble on the carpet.

The stairs, he thought. The Indians would be coming up the hall or through the library or living room for him. There were six of them left. Could he just get himself to the second floor, he could take the back steps down or the grapevine that grew up the side of the building. It had thick, ropy main creepers that years ago Jared and Deke had used to race each other to the main stairway windows for the two dollars that Creach and Nathanson would place on the sill. Even with his one hand and his legs, Creach would be able to let himself down, and if not, he'd just jump partway. It wasn't that far, and there was an area with grass below.

He had come for the woman, the *sicaria*, but she was smarter than he'd given her credit for and was probably long gone now—in Bimini or New York—having taken quickly what she could and left the Indians behind for the punishment part of her assignment. Because of what had happened with Eva and the warning telephone call, she had to have known that they were someplace close by, watching her, and might be tempted to reclaim what was theirs.

Now Creach wanted only to get out. As Nathanson had said, "Let them sit. The house has been there for three hundred years. There's nothing valuable to them in it, and they won't last two months. Watch."

Creach hadn't, and he was sorry now. And sorrier when two Indians appeared below him in the wedge of light from the study door, and he had to give away his position. He spun and, touching the trigger of the Saturn, fired the entire clip in a two-second burst. Creach had never used the gun, which had been developed in the seventies as a prototype machine pistol, to defend himself. Creach was a gun collector, and he had bought as an investment what he had been led to believe were the last two Saturns not already in the armories of major weapons-museum collections. He *had* fired it, however—at ten rows of two-inch pine boards with the slugs piercing to the sixth board and the pattern so closely grouped that it was hard to determine from the spot holes how many bullets had passed through.

But what it did to human bodies was horrific, blowing the two squat men across the wide foyer of the hall, nailing their ruined, ripped-up bodies to the wall. Four down and four to go.

Creach fled up the stairs as well as he was able, heedless of the pain. In a way the damage that the gun had inflicted scared him. What *if?* he thought to himself. At the top of the stairs he ejected the spent clip and inserted another. He had four left, plenty if you thought one for each Indian. Not enough if he wasted any, and, cradling the Saturn in the oystering mitten, he reached to the back of his belt to make sure his frag grenades were still there.

The rear stairs. If they were smart, they would have already sent somebody around. Several somebodies, who, finding the staircase undefended, would have already begun an assault.

Creach snatched a grenade off the belt and, in passing the main stairway, checked to see if the windows there were open. They were, but they were also covered with screens that Creach knew how to open. With two hands.

Even before he got to the door, he heard them on the long, cornered flight of back stairs, incautious now that they had found it empty and were making a rush.

Creach pulled the pin on the six-second charge. One thousand one, he said to himself, placing the grenade in the mitten and stepping beyond the door where a burst through the panels would not catch him. One thousand two—he reached for the knob with his good hand. One thousand three—he turned the knob and heard their footsteps plain now, no more than the short flight of steps after the corner away from him. One thousand four—he pulled open the door and off the mitten bounced the grenade down the bare wooden stairs, and with the other hand craned only the Saturn into the stairwell and squeezed.

The burst forced the gun up. It struck the ceiling and was knocked from his hand. He could hear high-pitched howling, like from dogs or wolves, and bullets splintered the closing door, shattering the plaster of the ceiling and wall.

Creach threw himself to one side, and the blast from the grenade blew the door from its hinges and brought down the ceiling of the hall he was in.

Two more gone. Creach shoved the plaster and lathing away and crawled to the stairwell to make sure and see if there was any sign of the Saturn. None. Below him was a gaping, empty hole

through which billows of thick plaster dust were sifting. Somewhere in the darkness wires were sparking.

Would the quick loss of six make them cautious? Creach
didn't think so, or at least he couldn't know, considering how they
were coming at him. Frontal assaults, as if they had a small army.
Maybe he was wrong about how many he had seen.

Pulling himself up, he staggered through the rubble in the hall,
debated a moment since it was, after all, Nathanson's house, and
decided he could always make it up to him later, *if* he survived.
Creach wrenched another grenade from his belt, pulled the pin,
waited three seconds, and bounced it down the curved main staircase into the darkness there.

It was then that he began to smell smoke. He rushed toward
the main stairway windows and was blown into a wall by the force
of the blast on the stairs below him. Again he picked himself up,
and with the fist of his good hand punched out and then ripped
from its frame the screen of a window, hoping none of the remaining Indians had the cool and the tactical savvy to have waited in
the back garden. *Why*, when they had to know by now that he had
got into the house by some other route? And then they seemed
leaderless, as if they were reacting viscerally, as they would to an
attack in the woods or the jungles or the mountains of wherever it
was they came from.

Propping his butt on the ledge, Creach fit his head and body
through the open window and groped blindly in the darkness for
a main cord of the grapevine, which he found. He let himself out
slowly until he could grasp it with his legs, then slipped down
through the wide green leaves until he got to the arched windows
of the kitchen. All three were lit with flames that an Indian in the
kitchen was feeding with some fluid from a large plastic jerry can.

Reaching out, Creach grabbed onto another cord and swung
himself between the windows, but his hand kept slipping, and he
fell slowly down past the windows onto grass. There, he debated
tossing his final grenade, which would leave him defenseless. There
were two Indians left. Was his mission accomplished? Creach-
style, it was, he decided ruefully. He had killed a few Indians,
discovered that the *sicaria* was no longer there, and destroyed
Nathanson's house.

Creach pulled the pin, waited two seconds, then hurled the

grenade through the window so that it would carry into the kitchen and reach the flames. He turned and fled toward the garage where Nathanson kept his car, a battered MG T-C that could be—usually *had* to be—started with a push down the hill of the side street. They would not have taken that.

Glancing over his shoulder, Creach saw the Indian try to reach into the fire to snatch up the grenade. When he jumped back, his hand was in flames from whatever accelerant he had poured on the blaze. He looked from it to the windows. Too late.

The blast spewed flames through the grape trellis and showered Creach with hot shattered glass.

In the garage Creach found the key where it always was—in a rust hole near the right running board—but he did not try to start the car. Instead he opened the accordion garage doors and gave the T-C a push that, he knew from experience, would be enough to let him coast down the hill. Only when he had nearly reached Water Street at the end of the property would he turn the key and pop the clutch. The muffler was shot, and the car was loud.

The car jounced over the deep gutter. Creach twisted the large wooden wheel and directed the low wreck of a sports car down the street.

Now the entire rear of Nathanson's house was in flames, and Creach felt lower than he had at any time in his life. Everything he touched, it seemed, turned out bad. *Worse* than bad. Deadly or destructive.

Near the corner Creach twisted the key, double-clutched to force the gears into third, then popped it. Nothing. Again. Nothing still. He had nearly rolled to a stop out into Water Street with traffic now bearing down on him in both directions when he looked up to see the Indian—the one who had positioned himself on the lawn of the dock overlook—on the sidewalk, facing him. Creach had forgotten about him.

He reached for the key, which he twisted, and plunged his foot into the starter pedal on the floor. With a backfire and a burst of smoke the car caught. On two cylinders.

Creach spun the wheel and started up Water Street toward Nassau city center and the bridge that would take him to Paradise Island. But slowly.

*   *   *

From the deck of the penthouse, Nathanson and Eva watched the Indian jog after Creach. It was early evening, just the time in high season when vacationers were leaving their hotels and boats to dine, and the streets were crowded with cabs and chauffered cars. Under every streetlight at every corner, it seemed, there were groups of women in brightly colored dresses and men in tropical evening clothes waiting to cross. Now, with fire engines moving toward Nathanson's house, traffic ground to a halt. The Indian gained on Creach.

"Why doesn't he turn around and run with the trucks?" Eva asked. "He's going to get caught like that. Look at the bridge," which they could see from their vantage. It was jammed solid for perhaps a quarter-mile leading into Nassau, and traffic was building up leading out in the direction Creach would follow.

Suddenly, when the Indian was nearly upon him, Creach reversed, and out of a cloud of blue smoke pulled around the car in front of him and mounted the curb. There, on the verge of the esplanade that traced the harbor, he began working his way toward the bridge, dodging trees, hydrants, and culverts, spurting forward whenever the Indian, who was quick and did not flag, approached.

"He must not have a weapon," Nathanson said, lowering the glasses and turning to Denny, who merely scooped up the two handguns he had been loading and made for the door.

Nathanson followed him but soon returned with a long bolt-action rifle with a telescopic sight, a box of cartridges, a silencer, and a tripod.

Eva looked away.

Nathanson fitted on the silencer and tripod and propped the rifle on the low wall of the deck. He opened the bolt of the rifle and chambered a cartridge. Glancing at Eva before ramming it home, he said, "Call it Darwin. If you think he's not relevant, check the house, check the Indian, check Creach."

"You just happened to have those gadgets hanging around?" She flicked her hand at the silencer and tripod. It was an assassination weapon pure and simple.

Nathanson shrugged. "Creach collects guns."

"For survival."

"I have an idea that's just how it'll be used." He touched his eyes to the scope and wondered if she would be content simply to stand there and watch Creach get butchered by the Indian, who now had a *penilla* in his hands. Creach in the TC had mounted the sidewalk of the bridge and was attempting to inch the old, open car around a bus that was stalled in traffic there. People on the sidewalks, having seen the long, shiny blade of the knife, were scattering; some had even abandoned their cars. The Indian was maybe fifty yards away, but Denny now appeared on the other end of the bridge, half-running, half-walking as fast as he could at seventy-one years of age, his left hand stuck in what looked like a Wheaties box.

"Or would you prefer I observe the Fifth Commandment and watch him go down?" he said, trying to sight in the Indian, who was still running along the line of cars and past clutches of horrified tourists. Flicking off the safety, Nathanson glanced behind him, but she was gone.

Creach didn't know what to do: stick the old car in reverse and attempt to run the Indian down or to try to get out and hoof it. He was so jammed in between the bus and the railing of the bridge he couldn't open the door, and his left leg was numb from his earlier exertions and would not respond. He pushed down on his thigh, and pushed on it again, but it just would not move.

Luckily he turned in time to see the Indian sprint the final few feet before vaulting the square boot of the car, the *penilla* cocked and his face contorted in an ugly smile. Creach threw open the door the three or four inches it would move and flattened himself against the hot side of the bus. The blade whistled past his nose and split the wooden steering wheel.

Shrieking now, the Indian was on top of him. The Indian pulled out the knife, and Creach only managed to raise the oystering glove to deflect the blow that sank deep into his biceps. Creach howled. With his other hand he pulled one of the Saturn cartridge clips from under his belt and took a swipe at the Indian's head. He missed, and the Indian cut at him backhand, so that Creach had to throw himself forward into the wheel. The blade sliced across his back.

Something heavy then slammed into the side of the bus, and a corrugated metal panel clattered to the pavement. The Indian snapped his head to it and saw—as did Creach for the first time—

Denny running toward them with some kind of a box raised in front of him. Roaring now, the Indian yet again cocked his arm.

Creach tried to raise himself up and hurl his body at the Indian to hold him off until Denny could arrive. But the boating shoe of his good leg slipped on the rubber mats that Nathanson had scattered on the floor of the car to cover a rust hole, and he knew it was over, he'd had it. He twisted his head aside so at least he wouldn't take the blow in the face.

It was then that the Indian's head exploded. Like some sort of fruit or vegetable—a pumpkin, that was it—the back of his head spewed blood and orangy-looking bone over the side of the bus, over the car, and over Creach, who was writhing now with the pain in his hand, his biceps, and back.

People somewhere—inside the bus, he guessed—were screaming. Off in the distance he could hear the singsong claxon of a police car. He turned his head to see Denny reach his hand over the railing bridge and drop the box into the water below. Creach had something wet on his lower lip, and he raised his right arm and wiped it away.

The Indian's body slumped off the car and fell beneath the rear tires of the bus, which now tried to move forward, out of harm's way. It rocked on the lifeless form—over and back, over and back—until, gushing a cloud of diesel fumes, it powered up the rise of the bridge.

Said Denny, "This time I'm taking you to the hospital. Maybe there you'll stay put."

Creach wanted to say, They were gonna burn the house anyway. They had a big gas can and everything, all ready to go. Instead he spat and spat again; whatever had been on his lips had the texture of slime. And you could think of it another way; at least now there was a chance of an insurance claim.

The police were getting closer now. Denny said, "David—it's time to finish this part of your life and close the door. I won't say it again, but you gotta quit. I don't know what it's gonna take for you to do it, but, if you need help, I'm here. Lord knows you been lucky." The old man reached into the car and collected the spare Saturn clips from under Creach's belt. The less physical evidence, the better.

At the rail of the bridge he let them fall into the darkness and the water below.

*   *   *

Up in the penthouse Nathanson raised his eye from the scope of the rifle and considered where and how he would get rid of it too. There would be an inquiry about Creach, the fire at the house, and whatever was found in its ashes. How many days would that take, or, rather, weeks?

Creach had a good lawyer, bribes would be paid, but it would still take too long to wait.

Nathanson turned toward the open sliding doors and his bedroom, where he would pack. He would take the ferry into Nassau and drop the weapon over the side. He'd catch a cab to the airport.

When he looked into Eva's bedroom, he saw that she too had fled. The drawers to a bureau and the closet door were still open, some of her clothes gone.

A pile of rumpled thousand-dollar bills was on the bed. Under it was a note.

> This money was washed in water and purged by the sea but it wasn't enough. It's drug money, and I was wrong to take it even as a fee. My advice—for what it's worth—is to give it to charity and forget the rest. Hasn't it already killed enough?

PART IV
EAST SIDE, WEST SIDE

CHAPTER 18

POSITIONING

Soho, Lower Manhattan
New York, New York

WITH A PASSKEY Solange Mercier, *La Guatavita*, let herself into
Eva Burden's loft apartment on the sixth and top floor of a former
commercial building off Broome Street. Maluko, her retainer, had
obtained the key from the building superintendent for a decagram
of cocaine so pure the man could scarcely believe his luck.

Stepped on twice, he had twenty-five hits of sniff at twenty
dollars apiece, which was five hundred dollars, less a C for his own
sinuses. Cooked slow and allowed to cool into crystal, it was two
thousand dollars over and above the C up his snout. Not bad to let
a chink or whatever check out the little blond broad's pad. "I'll be
watching you," the super had said. "Nothing out. Not a lamp-
shade, not a chair. Not nothing."

Better when he laid another dec on him for the privilege of
hanging out in the empty loft on the fifth floor.

La Sorda Roja, who had taken the elevator to make sure she
was not seen, closed the door to Eva Burden's apartment and

looked around. In Nassau for the three days that she was there she had discovered little about who had stolen the shipment but names. There was, of course, the name of the woman, Eva Burden, on the box on the doorstep of the house in Nassau. She assumed it was that of the person who had retrieved and opened it.

Then there was the name A. Gelb, who had mailed the box from Bimini. It was the same surname as one of the three names on the message that appeared to be a kind of rough draft for a telegram she had found in the kitchen trash of the Nassau house. The note had read,

> Here in Nassau. Sorry overreacted. Met some friends and will get in touch back in NYC. Can you send my bag and effects via inter-island flight C/o B. Nathanson, Water Street, Nassau? Explain all Tug when back.

It had been sent to Messrs. Tug McCann, Bill Cicciolino, and Jay Gelb, care of Bimini Police Constabulary. At first Solange Mercier had thought one or all three of the men might be police, until it occurred to her that none of the names was identifiably Bahamian. Also, the police constabulary would be exactly where one would send such a message, had one been on holiday and become separated from one's party. Say, because of a firefight about which one might "overreact."

And then that term alone was conspicuously American, like the references to New York and the names of the other three. *Bill* Cicciolino. Why not Guglielmo, with a name like that? And *Jay* Gelb? It was close to Jay Gould, a name she knew from her reading of U.S. history. But Tug? It was a name she had never seen before, and she assumed it was an American, or perhaps, given his surname, an Irish corruption of some more formal name.

Finally there had been the telephone record. Mercier had had Maluko phone the Nassau office of the telephone company to say that he was Brian Nathanson's houseboy and that Mr. Nathanson was planning an immediate, extended absence from Nassau. Would it be possible to have a phone bill made up and sent to them posthaste? They would be happy to pay any added expense.

The bill had arrived on Mercier's final day in Nassau and had contained, as she had expected, the record of several short calls to Colombia, which, she assumed, had been followed by longer con-

versations from pay phones, as was the procedure for setting up a
deal like the one that had eventually soured off the Berry Islands.
All other calls were local, but for one that had been placed to a
number in California and had been billed to another number in
Manhattan.

The California number was registered to one Margaret Pease
in Long Beach. When Maluko phoned and asked for Eva Burden,
the woman on the other end had said she was not expected for
another week, could she take a message? The second number—a
contact in the Colombian consulate in New York discovered—was
owned by Eva Burden. A Broome Street address in Lower Manhattan was given.

In Bimini, where Mercier and Maluko traveled next, a man
named Sidney F. O. Thomson, who said he was the "inheritor" of
Monroe Yacht Holiday Enterprises, Ltd., seemed to understand
immediately who they were. Solicitously and with every courtesy
he showed them the newspaper reports of Monroe's death and
allowed her to spend an afternoon with Monroe's records. Year
after year for six years, a Mr. Gelb had chartered *Whistler*. In the
third year a Mr. Cicciolino had paid by check #1334 Chem. Bank,
a note said, but unfortunately she could not find the item itself,
which might have contained an address. "Cash," Thomson explained. "Mr. Monroe always insisted on being paid cash. He had
a certain predisposition to *liquid* capital," the yen for which, she
decided, had also probably passed to Thomson from the gleam in
his eye. "His paper records are virtually nonexistent."

Closing the door of the loft, Mercier now looked around. It
was one big former commercial room on the top floor of the
building, the roof of which was supported by ornate cast-iron
columns in the Ionic mode. Some had been painted white. Others
were striped with red. Still others had black capitals with golden
volutes. There were tall four-pane windows along two walls, and
the view—Mercier saw at a glance—was superb.

She turned and gathered up the mail that had been pushed
through a slot in the door and held in a wide catch bin. Among
bills and fliers and unsolicited mail, there appeared to be only one
personal letter from a "Jack Pease, Soledad Prison, Soledad, California," which she slipped into a pocket of her slacks to open
later.

Grouped near the north-facing windows were several paintings in progress on easels and two large drawing desks. There were
also children's toys—a tricycle, roller skates with rubber wheels,
trucks, balls, and a Hula-Hoop—gathered in a corner. That end of
the loft had been sectioned into a living area, and at the telephone
table there Mercier searched the drawer and discovered a personal
telephone directory that contained no listing for Cicciolino, Gelb,
or McCann.

She was about to replace it, when she decided to scan all
listings and found three—work, home, "O'Casey's"—under Tug.
It was a simple matter to cross-check the numbers with the Mc-
Cann listings in the Manhattan telephone directory, and she soon
found a match for work—the McCann Group, Paper Brokers
Unlimited—and a listing for O'Casey's, which appeared to be a
restaurant, but none for "home."

Touching the button of the pager on her belt, Mercier signaled
Maluko, who was waiting in the apartment below with two of the
other nine Boyacas she had sent for from Medellín. They were
monitoring the elevator and stairs. Maluko was her ears. Unfortunately his English was not entirely fluent, which was a weakness,
but in all else he was a skilled assistant. He was honest, dedicated
to her, courageous, and he controlled his other tribesmen with an
iron hand, which more than made up for the lack. While he began
making the phone calls that she required, she continued her search
of the apartment.

The woman, Eva Burden, was petite—as Mercier had noticed
the day they had met in Nassau—and she was tasteful, if conser-
vative, in her dress. Mercier admired a rather full collection of
evening dresses and smart suits that, she imagined, were worn in
the restaurant she either owned or managed. Among other framed
photographs on a large antique sideboard were several group por-
traits of restaurant crews with Eva Burden standing in the middle
and obviously in charge. There was a small brilliant red lobster in
the lower right-hand corner of the place mats on a kitchen table.
Shadowed print said, THERMIDOR. The phone number matched
one of those listed under "work" in her directory. They were
among the numbers that Maluko was now calling.

At one time work had been medical, Mercier gathered from
many of the books on the shelves of a reading area—two chairs
and a rug that were gathered near the windows—and Eva Burden

had been some type of officer in the U.S. Navy. There were other, dated photographs of her in various uniforms. She had also been married not many years earlier to a tall, handsome man, although there were no signs of a man's personal belongings in the loft. Her child from that marriage was no more than three or four years old.

Maluko, she could see, had begun speaking into the telephone, and Mercier undid a system of locks and clasps on a window, which she opened, stepping out onto a flat roof that functioned as a type of porch or patio for the apartment. On it was a hibachi, a group of wrought-iron chairs around a table, and two chaise longues.

It was a clear spring day with a warm wind sweeping up from the streets below. Mercier lit a cigarette and turned to the view of what she considered the richest and most accessible killing ground in the world: Lower Manhattan and the financial district to the south; the Hudson and the wharves and cities of New Jersey to the west. Behind her was the rest of Manhattan and an urban sprawl that extended all the way to Boston and beyond. Across the East River she could see the Brooklyn, Queens, and Long Island sections of the megalopolis.

There was so much going on, so much money, so many people and laws, regulations, do's and don'ts—all written down the way Americans preferred—that the area was impossible to police. And once one set of laws could be broken with impunity (she knew from the history of violence of her own country), others followed quickly. Getting caught then became an inequity to be fought by every means in a court of law or, if lost there too, otherwise rectified, which was where people such as she came in. It was only a matter of time, she imagined, before *sicarias* of some kind were employed by the central sources of power here, and not just by traditional criminal elements.

Mercier had a little theory that the major parts of the world cycled between order and chaos but neither contemporaneously nor coequally. Presently the pendulum was swinging in the direction of chaos, and those who were more experienced in its potentialities were definitely at an advantage, especially in another part of the world, like this, which was still clinging to its illusion of order. And without a doubt South American chaos *was* superior chaos. That too she knew firsthand.

She also believed that what she was now seeing before her—

the towering buildings, the busy streets, the jets stacked up over Kennedy, waiting to land—was an illusion that could be fatal to credit. It *looked* like a civilization that was based upon a sophisticated, complex, and perhaps even nurturing culture, but in reality little had changed in South *or* North America since the coming of the white man. As then, the central impetus was to dominate and enslave. In order to survive, one had to be ruthless with those who would be ruthless with you and suspicious of those who claimed otherwise. And if, like she herself, you were not white or were at all disabled, you had to be doubly vigilant. Or doubly quick.

Mercier reached for her back pocket and pulled out the letter from J. Pease, prison inmate, to Eva Burden, who was obviously his daughter. Other than his description of some problem in what seemed to be mechanics, it was a long apologia for the event that had arrived him in prison, followed by an exhortation to Eva to beware of:

> . . . men. Baby, trust me—you're better off on your own. Don was typical. I hear these guys talking about their relationships, and there isn't any love anywhere, even when they say there is. They're all hustlers, out after something. Every last one of them has some sort of hidden agenda.

Good advice, even though it would not help his daughter survive, Mercier thought. Now, seeing Maluko in the window, she stubbed out the cigarette, flicked it over the edge of the roof, and returned to the window.

"Work" was indeed the restaurant, Thermidor, and what Maluko described as a young woman answered, saying they were open. Could Eva Burden have returned to New York but not to her apartment? Why? Because she had been frightened by what had happened in Nassau and she was guilty and had something to hide? It was a possibility that they would have to investigate.

A telephone message at the McCann Group advised Maluko to leave a number so his call could be returned on Monday. O'Casey's was a restaurant on Forty-first Street between Madison and Fifth that Maluko said was loud and seemed very busy on a Friday afternoon.

*　　*　　*

Two hours later Maluko—dressed in a chauffeur's uniform—pulled back a barstool for Mercier, who sat. He then returned to the limousine that was double-parked outside.

Tony, the head bartender, glanced at Kevin, his associate, before moving toward her with a smile and a bar napkin. " 'ello, luv. What's your pleasure?" He was a natty, affable Brit, who had been a fixture at O'Casey's for a decade. He looked down into her limped green eyes and then traced the line of her high, wide cheekbones, her long, graceful brow, her full lips. She was wearing an opal satin suit that had been designed by Givenchy and was cinched tightly at the waist with a gold belt that emphasized her hourglass shape. When she had entered the bar, most conversations had halted for a moment.

Her smile was pleasant but muted. She raised an unlit cigarette, and, when Tony struck a match and held the flame to its end, their eyes met with a force that made his nostrils flare. "I'm looking for Tug McCann," she confided, so that he had to move closer to hear. "I've been told I can find him here. Do you know Tug?" She arched one eyebrow, as though to suggest that she did and the association had proved agreeable.

Tony could not help himself. He was a man who appreciated women, and he knew for fact that she could make him happy. "Tug McCann? We haven't seen Tug for . . . how long has the Tugger been away?" he asked a well-dressed man sitting an empty stool away from her.

With a large cigar positioned in the middle of his mouth, the man had been admiring the sheen of her satin thigh and the line of her legs, which were turned toward him. He removed the cigar. "Who?"

"Tug McCann."

"Gotta be two, three weeks now. Let's see, I have it here somewhere." A large, prematurely gray man, he reached into his suit coat for his pocket secretary.

"Good friend of Tug's," Tony explained. "So tell me, what's a beautiful—no, a *gorgeous*—woman like you want with a rapscallion like Tug?" He liked the way she followed his lips when he spoke. It was like the first movement of a kiss, and Tony decided at that moment that a kiss from her would be step one in making his day. Or his week. Or his month.

"Business," she said in such a warm, confiding manner that Tony had to remind himself that he actually worked there.

"Something to drink?"

She cupped one broad shoulder so that the placket of her suit jacket opened and her body exuded some priceless exotic perfume that cut through the cigar smoke. "I'll leave that up to you. Something dry with wine."

The scent made Tony think of satin sheets, caviar, and champagne, and he turned for a bottle of Dom Pérignon. Kevin met him at the wine rack. "What she want?"

"Tug."

Kevin smiled and shook his head. "I should have guessed Tug. What's his secret?"

Money, thought Tony. And blarney. Tug had a way of making everybody believe he thought they were special.

Placing the glass before her, Tony said, "This is with George." He indicated the gray-haired man with the cigar, who had signaled him.

"Do you know Tug?" she asked, turning from Tony to the other man a smile that neither would have described as predatory.

The man nodded. "Would you mind if I moved over?" He pointed to the seat between them.

"If you prefer."

The man opened his palms and looked up, as though thanking heaven.

After she had tasted the champagne, she turned to him. "Tell me about Tug. How long have you known him? Are you in the paper business too?"

CHAPTER 19

SABUESOS

◆

BILL CICCIOLINO WAS sitting in the den of his East Side apartment when the ship-to-shore call from Gelb came through. He'd been expecting it, but before he could boost his bulk out of his easy chair and walk across the small room, Gerri picked it up.

"Wait!" she said, "I don't want to hear. You want to talk that stuff, you talk to him. Here—" she went on without her hand over the phone, "one of your partners in crime."

Gelb sounded almost joyous, even though Cicciolino could hear the wind howling and the water roaring over the boat. He said they were a hundred or so miles offshore and would head in whenever the storm broke. "We'll make Barnegat Light by Friday afternoon. Maybe a little earlier, a little later. Depends on the wind, but the way it is now, we could *surf* there. You get the other boat?"

Cicciolino pincered his temples. If some DEA prick was monitoring the call, that was it—he was in the shitter. "Jay?" he said as gently as he could. "You think we should talk about this now?" There was a static-filled pause. The whole conversation sounded like sandpaper being dragged across the mouth of a microphone. " 'Course I got the other boats. The tank, the suit, your other clothes. Everything's in place here, but, you know, I had it in the back of my mind that we were going to do this on the weekend," when there'd be plenty of other pleasure boats in and around Barnegat Bay.

"I scrapped that plan. Bookshelf aboard ship is *mucho informativo*. There's probably been a tracker on *Trekker* since Grand Bahaman or Bermuda. Sounds like a lyric from a song, don't it?"

Don't it, from Gelb?

"Anyways, it don't matter now."

Why not? Cicciolino asked himself. It could only mean they had to dump the dope and there Cicciolino had gone out and bought out of his own pocket a used Bayliner 23 for thirteen thousand dollars cash—no checks, no papers signed, no paper trail. It was staked out on moorings in Barnegat Bay, like a decoy at a duck hunt.

"Us being clean to the sniff, as it were."

Said Cicciolino, "Put Tug on."

McCann didn't sound right either, as if he'd been into the sauce or had cabin fever or something. "Weather is just incredible. Thirty-, forty-foot waves, I swear. Nearly pitchpoled once, but Jay really knows what he's doing. And this boat! Jesus, what a *find*. I gotta get me one."

Cicciolino kept saying to himself, You'd think they'd be shit-scared of the storm, the sea, even the phone call and whatever might happen when they put in. Like jail for a long, long time. He wondered how well Jay Gelb would weather hard time in some major federal stir.

But Cicciolino tried to think positive and figured he didn't know what it was like—the rush, the exhilaration of facing a storm like that and surviving. And then McCann would not have let Gelb talk so openly without their having done something smart with the load.

Still, he took precautions. There was no sense in all of them getting busted. With a fishing pole and tackle box, he trudged a half-mile from the last parking lot in Island Beach State Park to the Barnegat breakwater, which *Trekker* would have to pass. It didn't ease Cicciolino's mind any when he got there.

In contrast to the day, which was mild with high fish-back clouds and virtually no wind, the shore was besieged by towering rollers, remnants of the two-day storm out to sea. Waves thundered into the granite blocks of the breakwater, sending spumes of briny foam into the evening sky. And Cicciolino no sooner cast a lure into the water than a Coast Guard patrol boat corked out through the waves, the crew in the lee of the doghouse buttoning on life jackets and brilliant orange sou'westers, as if they'd just been called to a scramble. From a locker one of the guardsmen pulled an automatic weapon and checked its clip. Another had a long flashlight in his hand, and a third had some sort of a hound—something like a Chesapeake—on a leash.

Cicciolino despaired. What to do? Take his part of the $2.4 mil, which was $800,000—*if* he could get it out of McCann's business without McCann—and split? He liked Arlene, or, rather, his cock *loved* Arlene—and with her $800,000 and whatever else they had, they could live all right, if they could find someplace acceptable. He didn't care whose kid it was—Cal's, Schmal's—he liked kids who weren't fucking retarded, and Gerri and him were splits, no two ways about it. Nobody in his family either side was retarded, *ever* as far as he knew, and he'd checked.

For thirty-four minutes Cicciolino sweated it out when, like a submarine suddenly rising from a wall of waves, *Trekker* appeared. It was nearly right on the mossy blocks of the breakwater with the Coast Guard patrol boat a couple hundred yards behind. Cicciolino had forgotten how big the boat was or remembered it only alongside other large vessels, but she seemed almost to fill the narrow inlet. He didn't know how in the boiling surf Gelb was keeping the yawl from broaching on the inlet rocks.

But there he was at the wheel wearing a Day-Glo yellow sou'wester and looking like Salty fucking Brine, hairy face and all. His Trotsky glasses flashed in the thin light from the west as he turned to Cicciolino and waved, his smile full. He said something to McCann, who was standing in the companionway, and Tug turned and raised a fucking rocks glass, for crissake, of Cicciolino knew what. He too had a goddamn beard that shrieked ocean voyage, and the boat was covered with dried salt sea spray.

Cicciolino reeled in the lure, picked up the tackle box, and turned toward the parking lot. When the Coast Guard boat had passed beyond him, he tried to sprint through the soft sand. He staggered, nearly fell, then flung away the two objects he'd had since he was a kid.

In the car Cicciolino flicked on his blinkers and brights. He pulled out his shield, which he would flash at any cruiser that tried to pull him over.

At the helm of *Trekker* Gelb was elated. He felt like Mighty Joe Young. In a kind of vivid flashback—a brilliant shard of memory so real he almost forgot he was docking nearly sixty feet of yacht—he remembered evenings when a magenta twilight had cast a pinky glow over the neighborhood where he, Tug, and Chick had grown up. Just such a tone now pervaded the contained, quiet waters of Barnegat Bay.

Suddenly Gelb yearned for those evenings when radio shows—*Flash Gordon, Sky King, The Lone Ranger*—came wafting out open kitchen windows along with the aromas of suppers being cooked. In one sprint after a fly ball, Gelb had once counted seven different, distinct meals, and he tried to recall them now, but failed.

He would give anything, even *Trekker* that he so much loved, for just an hour back there on that street. Why? Because he was a man . . . poised on a mountain of offal. Cocaine was not supposed to give you hallucinations, but he could see it: all guts and pinky entrails. One misstep, and he'd come caterwauling down into the corruption, and nothing that he was or had been or could be would be his ever again.

He thought of Arlene and her baby. Why hadn't she told him about that in some other, less impersonal, less public way? It would have made all the difference. He wouldn't feel so desperate, so wild.

But Tug, who was standing in the bow with a boat hook, now shouted and pointed starboard at the dock. Throwing the engine into reverse and goosing the throttle, Gelb caught sight of an apparition in the binnacle lens that startled him, until he realized that the scruffy beard and windburned face was his own. It had to be. There were his glasses.

Compose yourself, his third-party self advised. Gelb had stoked his nose deep maybe a half-hour ago and wouldn't require more mind fuel, as he now thought of cocaine, for a good hour or two, if the curve of the burn ran true to form. Tug had said, "Aren't you supposed to cut that stuff with baking soda or something?"

Gelb didn't know. Or care. It made him feel alive, strong, and vigorous when he was with it, like home-made shit when he wasn't. He panicked to think a day might come when he would be without it, but that was the beauty of cocaine too. It gave you a kind of immediate tunnel vision in which the past was conspicuous only by its marked, improbable absence. While the future seemed limited only by the bounds of his underexercised, middle-aged imagination. If in the future he needed cocaine, he would *get* cocaine. Simple as that.

He looked up. The stuff was marvelous. There he had docked the boat perfectly, with hardly a conscious thought about what he was doing.

A Coast Guard lieutenant was standing on the edge of the dock. They were nearly nose to nose.

"Hi—Derek Pape here. Rough passage?"

"Might say that," Gelb fairly chortled. "Forty-foot waves at one point."

Pape's eyes roamed *Trekker*. He was a small, vulpine-looking young man with a pale, sharp-featured face and quick, dark eyes. Everything that he was wearing looked brand new and too big for him: safety vest, deck jacket, even his legal-size clipboard and service cap that seemed to be balanced on the points of his ears.

"May I come aboard?"

The sweep of Gelb's hand was elaborate and seemed to include the masts themselves. "Be my guest."

Pape sidelonged McCann, who was moving toward him, then checked his crew. They were armed and positioned at three points on the dock. Only then did he climb aboard. "Anybody else below?"

"Not a soul." Gelb moved as though he would follow Pape down the ladder.

"I'd appreciate your remaining on deck while I make my initial inspection, sir."

Gelb could not be sure; the glance was so quick. But in the twilight Pape's eyes looked incandescent and pupilless, as though they were flaring with pale fire. Gelb thought of Dante, Conrad, Nabokov, and Stephen King. Life was bizarre. Gelb imagined that the kid was midwestern, maybe from one of those Viking colleges like St. Olaf's or Macalester. Gelb had once lectured there to a roomful of blonds. Later, at a reception, a grad student who looked like Ingrid Bergman's better-looking younger sister asked Gelb where he was staying. He said the Holiday Inn. "My place is nicer," she replied, but Gelb had begged off, mentioning that he was married. "To a cheat," he now said.

"Say what?" asked McCann, who looked into Gelb's face. "You all right? Jay—I'm gonna get you a drink. It'll loosen you up. Bill ought to be by in no time. How long you think it'll take him to get here from the breakwater?"

"Lieutenant said nobody below while he's inspecting," Gelb announced.

"It's all right," Pape's voice came to them from below. "You got documents for this boat, Mr.—"

"Gelb. *Professor* Gelb," Gelb supplied.

McCann moved down the companionway to the bar.

"Of course I've got documents. Got them right here for you." Gelb pulled open his sou'wester and began searching under his sweater. "Wanted to keep them handy. And dry."

Moving past the lieutenant, McCann ventured a thin smile that foundered on the young officer's stony boyish face. "I wouldn't do that, were I you."

"Why not?"

"We might have a few questions for you."

McCann opened the hinged bar and thought, Fuck you, Ulysses, and the nymph you rode in on. But he said nothing, only poured two strong drinks. If he was going to be busted, better high than low.

Also, he had something to celebrate—life. Out there on the truly *high* seas, with Gelb playing his Colombian rendition of *Lord Jim*, McCann thought for sure they would purchase their spectacular discovery with their lives. It had been like being on the Cyclone at Coney Island but not being able to get off, and his father's pithy deathbed soliloquy had come back to him with every mountain of wave *Trekker* had climbed. "Nothing's free. You pay for everything you do, one way or another." A pub owner, he himself had died banally from booze and cigarettes.

And finally McCann understood that the boy wonder in the campaign cap could put them away, if he chose to *really* search the boat. With scuba gear and nylon line, Gelb had lashed the boxes to the *Trekker*'s fin keel, and they would only have to pull the boat to find it.

Pape glanced up from the documents. "This a drug boat?"

Gelb blinked. "Not *now*. I think maybe it was at one time. Certainly the price was right."

"What price was that?"

McCann handed Gelb his drink. "You planning on buying a boat, Lieutenant?" He didn't want Pape to think they were guilty about anything.

Pape's eyes fell to the tumblers with obvious distaste.

"Place to do it is the Bahamas," McCann rolled on in a fatuous tone of voice.

"How d'you get it out?"

That too was none of his business, and McCann winked. Pape turned to Gelb, who had recovered himself enough at least to say nothing. McCann raised his glass. "To a successful passage. Pity you're on duty, Lieutenant."

Pape glanced down at his clipboard. "Any alcohol, tobacco, firearms on board?"

Said McCann, "Bottles of booze have all got American tax stamps. When we bought the boat, it was already here. The cigars I got in Bimini. Two left. No guns."

Pape's eyes flicked up at him. "Not even a shark gun?"

McCann shook his head. They had dropped the guns over the side along with all the scuba gear so no suspicions would be raised. McCann only hoped Gelb had distributed the load evenly, and *Trekker* was not listing to one side or the other. "Neither of us would know which end to shoot."

"I'll ask again. Any illegal drugs aboard?"

Said Gelb, "You mean you'll go easier on us if we admit it now?"

Drink your drink, thought McCann. Cocaine was dangerous shit. It made everybody into a hero, which was another way of saying asshole.

"Mind if we conduct a search?"

"Gee—I thought you already had."

"Not by half."

McCann widened his eyes so that his forehead wrinkled. "We can stand it, if you can."

"You captain here?"

McCann pointed to Gelb.

"You mind, ah . . . *Mr.* Gelb?"

"Who's he remind you of?" Gelb asked McCann. "Captain Queeg or Mr. Roberts?"

Pape pursed his lips and let out an earsplitting whistle.

Startled, Gelb sloshed some of the drink out of his tumbler. They then heard a scratching noise on deck.

"Search team," Pape explained.

The muzzle of a large dog appeared in the open companionway.

"What's that?" Gelb's hand jumped to his eyeglasses.

"What's it look like?"

"A *sneef* dog!" Gelb nearly shouted. "A *sabueso.*"

"You got it, and in Spanish too." Pape turned to Gelb with interest.

Snagging a paw on its long leash, the dog tumbled down the ladder and turned directly to Gelb, who said, "Well, keep him the fuck away from me! I hate dogs. I *despise* them." His paranoia was now jacked sky-high. After his last hit, he had tossed everything that had touched cocaine overboard—a slicker, a Patagonia jacket, three pairs of L. L. Bean dungarees. He had then scrubbed the head, where he'd been snorting, for an entire hour with a heavy-scented pine cleanser. After that, he had taken a long, thorough shower. The only cocaine on board was up his nose.

But the dog kept advancing, his wet nose working.

"And I'm a Jew. You know about that, don't you, Lieutenant?"

Pape only regarded him curiously, while the dog worked closer, his nose now only inches from Gelb's oilskin coveralls.

"Jews, like blacks, don't care for dogs. Dogs were used on us too. By the *Nazis!*"

The dog's handler was black, and his eyes met Gelb's.

"Strip me, search me—but get that fuckin' *sabueso* away from me! *Now!*"

"The fuck's going on here?" Cicciolino demanded from the top of the companionway ladder.

"I don't know, Bill," said McCann. "Ask him. You know about Jay and dogs."

Cicciolino pounded down the ladder and seemed to fill the companionway with his girth. He flashed Pape his shield. "Assistant Chief Bill Cicciolino, NYPD."

Pape tilted his head. "The guy from the television?"

"That's right. The chief. What about these two guys"—Cicciolino's eyes flashed over Pape's epaulets—"Lieutenant? They got any booze or broads aboard? If so, let's share 'em."

And to McCann and Gelb, "What took you so long? I expected you yesterday." Cicciolino then confided to Pape the details of their vacation in the Islands, their finding the boat on their last day in Bimini, and Gelb's plunging. "Didn't talk price or nothing. Ain't it something? That's butternut and rosewood." Cicciolino pointed to the cabin trim. "Hull's *aluminum*! Never rust, never rot. Shee-it, ain't it nice."

"Do you know *Professor* Gelb and Mr. McCann broke the laws of the Bahamas?"

"Yeah? How?"

"By sailing this boat in their waters. A marked boat should be transported *out* of Bahamian waters and only *then* sailed under its own power."

"Which is the reason there's so many of 'em so cheap down there."

Pape nodded.

"See?" Cicciolino said to Gelb. "I told you there's gotta be a catch somewheres. Well—can he register it here?"

"Yes, after he pays the duty. But had they been boarded—"

"Then all's well that ends well. I'm glad it's not in my jurisdiction." Or yours, Cicciolino thought. He'd seen those eyes before; the kid lieutenant was a cop hungry for a collar. "What happens next here? I got reservations for three at the Top o' the Mast in Seaside Heights. You go there much? How's the chow?"

He didn't give the little prick with the stone face a chance to answer. "Jay—way that dog is acting, he's got a problem with your clothes. You find that rain slicker here on this boat?"

Gelb nodded, as he knew he should.

"Maybe it's that, but we want everybody happy. Right, Lieutenant?"

Asshole didn't even blink.

"Ho-kay. Jay, you strip down so the authorities don't have no questions about what's in your shorts. Tug, at least show me the courtesy of a fuckin' drink." Cicciolino arced McCann his right hand. "Good to get you guys back." They shook. "And Jay." Cicciolino put a little extra into Gelb's to reassure him. He liked

Gelb. True, he was fucking his wife, but from the hints she had given him, so had half the fine-arts photographers in New York.

The dog and its handler proceeded forward. Cicciolino clinked glasses with McCann, while Gelb, half-concealed behind a galley countertop, stripped down to his briefs.

"Jesus Christ, Jay," said Cicciolino. "I know the trim look is in. It's good for the heart and everything. But don't you feel . . . you know, *naked*, walking around in all them bones?"

Gelb didn't know what it was, but something about the statement struck him as sublimely comical, and he began to laugh uncontrollably. He tried to stifle it with a gulp of scotch and had to lower his head and splutter it into the sink. When he straightened up, he saw Pape eyeing him suspiciously, and laughed even harder.

By that time the dog and its handler were returning to the aft end of the yacht, and again the dog made straight for Gelb.

Cicciolino said, "If this is a strip search, bend over, Jay, and let Fido sniff your ass. It'll save Mr. Roberts here from committing official misconduct with a rubber glove." When Pape's head swung to him, he added, "I'm a killjoy, really. Were you saving the best part for last?"

It was the rain slicker, they decided. Pape and his crew took it out on the dock and worked it over with a searchlight and dusting tape but found nothing. When they straightened up to confer, the dog—unattended—pissed on it.

Said McCann, "Must have been that barmaid I saw you with in Bimini, Jay." And the three of them roared. They laughed, and Gelb felt just the way he had when a kid on the streets of the Lower East Side. Part of the gang. Needed, wanted. *Integrated.*

Much later that night after dinner, drinks, and bullshit about everything except what concerned them most, Gelb donned the wet suit, tank, and fins that Cicciolino had brought him. Both Cicciolino and McCann, equipped with flashlights to signal Gelb, then strolled up the dock and, splitting up, patrolled the shadowed buildings of the marina. They stood for whole minutes watching sectors of the harbor and the feeder roads to the docks for any sign of moving or occupied cars.

Finally each flashed Gelb a single signal, and he slipped into the still-frigid waters of Barnegat Bay. Working without light himself, he felt his way down the graceful hull of his now-beloved *Trekker* until he felt the blade edge of her modern-design fin keel. There too his hand fell on the multiple coils of line with which he had snugged the bulky waterproof flotation cartons up on the stem of the keel.

Gelb did not simply cut the line and let the cartons float to the surface. Instead, untying one at a time, he kept them linked and submerged until he swam up to the transom of *Trekker* and waited for the single flash from each of their lights. Only then did he release the load and allow it to rise slowly, holding it back so that the cartons would hardly create a ripple breaking the surface of the tranquil bay.

Keeping in shadow until the last leg of the transfer, Gelb swam the train of cartons to the Bayliner. Although a tacky, sport-fishing boat, it was ideal for moving inconspicuously through local waters. After all, they were in New Jersey.

Once aboard, Gelb removed his tank, flippers, and wet suit, then dried and dressed himself in the warm clothes he found on a rack near a heater. The point was not to look as if he had just emerged from the water, but rather like a boater who was pulling something from the dinghy that was tied off the ladder.

One at a time, he pulled each up on the deck and stored them in various parts of the boat to maintain trim—three in the bow, three in the main cabin, and three and the partial carton in the stern. Fixed to its side was another, small package about the size of a shoe box. Gelb brought that with him when he returned to the cabin, and closed the sliding glass door of the Bayliner.

As his final, coordinated act, Gelb struck a match and lit one of the cigarettes that he found on the salon table, signaling that all was completed. He stubbed it right out. The hot smoke burned down his throat and scorched his raw nasal passages.

The further plan was for Gelb to bunk in the Bayliner until first light, when he would weigh anchor and head north, hugging the coast until he reached a pier in Hoboken that had twenty-four-hour armed security. It was the weekend, and he would hardly be noticed among the flotillas of other boats.

A day later Gelb alone would return to Barnegat and take *Trekker* north to a dockside berth that Cicciolino had secured for him at the City Island Yacht Club.

But Gelb could not sleep. Instead he reached for the shoe box.

Not for the first time he wondered if he had taken enough for himself. One little voice said certainly it was enough: You're no fucking addict. Go slow, shorten the lines, wean yourself off the shit, quit, and never look back. If you can't, there's always detox and some private rehab center. With all your money, you'll be able to afford the best.

The other little voice said, What do you need all that money for? Millions, tax free. Take part of your profits in powder. How'd you like to be buying the shit on the streets?

Gelb didn't care much for the second voice, but it had a point.

CHAPTER 20

CITY MOVES

LOOKING OUT FROM the fifth-floor windows of his apartment in his building on the vacant lot in East Harlem, Hector ("Chino") Santos felt violated. Gored. It was, "Like . . . like"—he was so mad, so furious he couldn't think—"they surround' me. Get me alone. And now they doin' turns!"

Somewhere off in the large apartment he could hear one of his bitches giggling, but not Martita, not her. She was *bad*/dirty but smart, which was the reason she had stayed so long, and now her large dark eyes followed him to the other window, where he could see three whole blocks without another building.

There they were, just as they'd been for the last three weeks, in the unmarked cars, in street clothes on corners, all over East Harlem. One cop, dressed as a fuckin' bum, slept overnight in a sleeping bag on the stoop, and then in the morning Santos caught him pissing on the Honduran mahogany door with the hammered iron grill, the polished brass, the locks, bolts, chains, and shit that would've cost him five thousand dollars if he bought it in a store.

When Santos had roared and reached for his piece, the bum had pointed to the other cops who had moved in. "Nah, Chino— don't do it. That's the easy way, man. You don't want it, we don't want it. We' gonna get you, but we like it slow. You know?" He then rolled his hips. "Me? Just gettin' in line. Firsts is what I want. You' *cherry*, Chino. Put some lice up you' ass, know what I'm sayin'? And then, you know, we take the *whole* works." He had waved his hand to mean the building and everything.

Cop talk, and cheap. Santos had heard it maybe all his life. He had lived in the building since he was six, when his mother had brought them to the mainland and New York. When he got bigger, he had singlehandedly run one landlord after another out until he was able to buy it himself for a dollar from the city under the Urban Homesteading Program. Santos then got himself a one percent federal loan to "retrofit," papers said, the place with new everything, basement to roof.

He was supposed to make ten apartments, two on each floor, and rent the others to the working poor. Instead he made eight for his main runners and customized the fifth floor with a Jacuzzi, sauna, weight room, even a fuckin' boom-boom room for the *putitas* and himself. In the basement he built a bar and clubhouse with a shooting range to stay sharp. But he also warned them all: Nobody stashed no, did no, or let nobody with no dope in. If they did, they were *gone*, and he meant it. "Question the fuckers. Make sure. Rip off their clothes, you have to. You find something, don't wait. Flush it." Santos would kill, and had, to keep his building from getting grabbed under the law about dope dealers that had to be unconstitutional.

"Like, like . . . the way they let them niggers in here," he now announced to the window.

"Ah, *sí*, Chino. *Sí, sí.*"

They had singled out Santos, laid the heat on only him. Other dealers—competitors, black dudes he never saw from Harlem—had pushed right into his territory like by fuckin' invitation. "What?—they print cards?" He could see two now, doing business openly in what used to be his spots: one under the awning of a bodega, the other out of a parked car in the shadow of a news stand. Chino had half a mind to call *La Prensa*, his congressman, or some fuckin' thing. "Is discrimination, is what." Somebody *got* to the cops, made some kind of *deal* to push him out, and that was it. Like the bum cop said, his ass was *marked*.

It had all begun with Banks, the precinct commander, and the other cop, the night they'd tossed him on the corner. Then he seen the other cop—the one from the tube who held the gun on him from the back of the car—a second time, day ago when he bumped into him on the street. Guy was big and walking right at him. Then he stopped suddenly, like changing his mind. When Santos was just about even with him, he spun around and stepped into him. Santos went flat on his ass.

"The luck of it. We meet again." The cop helped Santos to his feet and, brushing him off, patted him down. "Still carrying a fuzz buster?" He meant Santos's piece. "In your present state of affairs, Chino, I wouldn't, was I you. We get hard up—hey—there's always that. How you doin' otherwise? Getting much statutory ass?"

Then came the funny part, the part the cop had set up. "Oh, look—" he said like somebody reciting lines, and wanting Santos to know he knew it too, "you *dropped* something, sir." He pointed down at the sidewalk, and there was a beeper, one of the expensive kind with the digital display that worked off a satellite and could reach you anywhere in the world.

"Ain't mine."

"Gottabe, 'cause it ain't mine either, and it wasn't here a minute ago. Habit of mine—watching my step." He winked at Santos. "You take it. Last I heard, it ain't illegal, having one of these. Put it in your apartment. Watch it at night before you take your children in your bed, say, Monday or Tuesday night. You'll like how it works, I promise you. Thing like that could put you back in business."

Santos had backed away; he was sure it was some sort of setup. "I don't want it, cop. Not from you, not from nobody."

"Sure you do. Take it. I don't want to say trust me, because you won't, but maybe, if you're good and do like you're told, I can make all the shit in your life go away." He slipped it in Santos's jacket pocket, then stepped by him and walked into the cigar store they were standing in front of.

Santos had looked around but could see nobody else, like the guy had picked the place and time with care. He thought, Throw the fuckin' thing away. It had to be a homing device or eavesdropping or something. But once back on the fifth floor, he took off the back and checked it out. Santos was good at electronics—in his line it was necessary—and the thing was nothing more or less than what it was: an expensive, high-tech pager.

But it bothered him. All Monday night he had not gone out.

Why? He had nobody on the streets, not even his girls. He had seven of his best people on Riker's Island awaiting arraignment. Anyways, he had no nothing he could sell, and the word on the street was he was dying. "They say you got somethin' like AIDS and you as good as dead," was how he heard it.

But nothing. Not a fuckin' beep from the thing, and the display board was a strip of gray cloud.

"You need me, baby?" Martita now asked. She was curled up on his purple velvet sectional, which nearly bordered three walls of the large room. It made her look tiny, which she was. Santos did not know how old she was, because she would not tell him, but right from the start when she came here, maybe five, six years ago, he had liked her because she wasn't like the other girls who were dirty to get drugs or money. She liked it, especially moving around and performing for him, doing sexy little dances and teasing him with her mouth and body until, like a chicken, he ran her down and did her there and then.

Now she had on only ankle socks and high heels, the way he liked, and a kind of sequin tank top and panties to match. She was a dark girl with big red lips that she pouted before showing him her tongue. "Suck you off, you say *please*. Suck you off, you *beg*."

Santos spun and pointed a finger at her.

"I know, I *know*." She straightened her little, birdie legs, and looked down at them. "You' big man. You no beg nobody." Reaching forward, she grabbed her ankles and pulled them back, spreading her thighs so the strip covering her crotch sparkled. "But you beg Martita. You beg her good. You no beg, no—" She flexed her ass, which had shape, like chipped from something hard, and he loved.

The patch winked at him, and he decided he'd give it to her the way the bum cop said they'd give to him and she liked. Maybe it'd give him AIDS, the way he'd heard it did, and then what was said on the street would be right.

But he only got her bent over the edge of the bed, when the beeper—the one the cop gave him—went off. He moved toward the bureau, and there it was, a number to call. He pulled up his pants. He reached for his jacket and slipped the beeper into a pocket.

"Aw, man—you gonna fuck me, or what?"

He headed to the door. For twenty-five cents he could find out what this was all about. No crime in using the phone. He'd wait, he'd listen.

"You don't, maybe Justino will."

Santos spun around and moved in on her. All his rage of the last three weeks rose up in his throat; it made his eyes roll and his head spin.

She tried to scramble across the bed, but he grabbed an ankle, pulled her back, and began beating her face with his open hand. Backhand, forehand, backhand, forehand, each smack echoing off the walls until she was bleeding from her nose and mouth.

With the hand raised, he looked down at her. She hadn't even put up her hands, and was just down there on the bed with tears in her eyes, smiling through the blood. "Now when you out there, maybe you not so pissed off. And when you come back, you gonna *have* to beg."

He couldn't hit her again. Man, she was just trying to cheer him up. Maybe she knew him too good.

When Eva Burden arrived at her apartment on Broome Street in Soho shortly after noon the next day, her plan was simple and straightforward. She would put her affairs in order, try to get in touch with the people who had been on *Whistler* with her, and leave New York.

There had been enough killing, and at least four of them could not know what they had got into. Bill Cicciolino? At the very least he was not their good friend.

"You want everything but food should go?" asked one of the three men whom Eva had arranged to meet her there. They were wearing the brown coveralls of a moving-and-storage chain. Two were white, one was black.

"Yes. Just box and send it to your warehouse in San Diego," which Eva judged far enough from San Bernardino, where a friend of hers lived, to at least throw off a trace for a time.

"All paid?" It was New York, and the man was angling for a tip.

Eva suspected she would need all the money she had. "You'll find plenty of canned goods and frozen food. There's liquor in the corner cabinet. Take it home or whatever."

"No cash, no tip?" Another mumbled.

"Before you even *start* to work?" Eva hadn't lived in the city without learning something; she opened her purse. "Let's see, I think I have the number of your office here somewhere. They didn't mention hidden charges." She glanced up at them. "Is there a specific dollar amount you have in mind? Or do you work on percentage?"

The first man, who was small and white, raised a hand in a gesture of peace. "No need for that, just point the way. We pack. We ship."

Said the man who had asked for a tip, moving by her, "We see you before we leave."

"Count on it. I'll try to have somebody from your office here too."

He was a tall black man with a shuffle and a glassy-eyed sneer. Once in the door, he scanned the kitchen area disdainfully. "Where be the cabinet?"

The first man spun around on him. "You go near the booze and you're gone, un'erstan' me, pal?" and when he didn't answer, "Are we understood? I hope we are, 'cause I'll blow the whistle on you soon as you look in that direction."

Eva began walking toward the section of the loft that functioned as her bedroom.

"You get paid just like the rest of us, and you work." The third man said something, but the complaint continued. "Nah, nah, nah—I'm sick of carrying that lazy hump and his attitude. We get more done without him. The only reason he's here is minority hiring."

"Who you callin' lazy hump? You can't boost half the shit in this place."

"You. Lazy. Hump."

Eva appeared in the doorway, a phone in her hands. In the navy, at L.A. General, and later in her two restaurants, she had supervised staffs of squabbling nurses and waitresses; three movers were child's play. "Excuse me—I'd like to make a few phone calls. I could begin with your office."

The men regarded her balefully, but with their anger deflected, they split up to do their work.

Back near the bed, Eva punched the playback button on her answering machine, which was blinking, and listened to a clerk in a jewelry store say her watch was ready. There followed calls from Kitty, her chef, who was also managing Thermidor in her absence, asking if she would get in touch with her as soon as she returned. "I keep getting calls with some foreign man asking if I'm you. He seems very *interested*, if you know what I mean."

Eva couldn't imagine who that could be, although many of her patrons were foreign businessmen and staff from the UN and foreign consulates. Thermidor had the best kind of "by reservation only" custom, and it would be difficult to leave it. Eva planned to make Kitty an offer she couldn't refuse.

And finally there were three recent calls from Tug McCann.

"Hi, Eva. It's me, Tug. Just checking in to hear if you're okay. Why don't we have lunch and talk? You know my numbers."

Then, "Eva, Tug again. Look, if you're there, please give me a buzz. I'm worried about you." In the background she could hear voices, laughter, and glasses. Somebody said, "Tony—give us another here when you get a chance." He had been using the bar phone at O'Casey's.

And finally, "Eva. Tug here. Get in touch, please. We really should talk."

She could not agree more, if only for his sake. She dialed his office.

"Eva—I'm so glad you called," said his secretary. "Tug's desperate to see you, but he's just gone to lunch."

"O'Casey's?" she asked.

"Where else? He's meeting a supplier and a client there, but I'm sure he'd like to see you."

It would be better there among a crowd; with the hubbub and the distraction of his other business, she could leave more easily. She could tell him what she had learned in Nassau and witnessed firsthand. And how much trouble he was in. Up until the morning in the cove they had been good together, and she owed him at least a warning.

The Gelbs and Gerri Cicciolino? They had made a mistake, but they didn't deserve to die for it. And there might still be time for them to bail out.

Eva packed a suitcase with only the clothes she would need for traveling. She thought about her car, an older BMW that was in "Bristol" condition; Tug had found it for her through one of his innumerable "friends." Because she used it so seldom in the city, she had parked it in Queens, again through a connection of McCann.

The car would be the safest way to leave with no ticket trail, as on a bus, train, or plane. But then she'd have to face the long drive to California. There, however, it would be essential.

She had gathered her mail coming in the door and was surprised there was no letter from her father, who had written to her every month that he had been in prison. She wondered if there could be anything wrong. The rest was junk mail, which she threw away, and bills, which she would pay later.

Out in the hall the movers were already loading furniture on the elevator. Eva took the stairs, carrying the heavy suitcase like a bundle in her arms, so the corner wouldn't bump off the stairs. On the landing of the loft below, she saw the building super talking to somebody in the doorway, who then ducked back. Eva did the same behind the edge of the suitcase. The super was a busybody and a boor, and she had no time for him. Her final month's rent would be paid by her deposit.

"Eva—you back for good? What's going on?" he called down the stairwell, but she just kept moving.

Out on the street, luck was with her. She started walking quickly toward Broadway when she saw a vacant cab and raised her hand.

Brian Nathanson watched Eva open the door and push the bulky suitcase into the cab. She then walked around to get in the other side.

Nathanson smiled. It was a cool spring morning in New York, and she was wearing what looked like a short ribbed-cotton dress and a cropped cable cardigan that he recognized as having been his mother's. It ended exactly at her narrow waist and made the skirt look as though it had been molded to her, especially because of how she walked—quickly, almost adventurously, on her tight, well-formed tanned legs.

Which nearly made Nathanson miss the two Boyacas, who now also left the building. Both were dressed in white coveralls. Here in New York they looked like kitchen help or wombats from a cleaning service. They got into a white van.

"How much money you make in a day?" he asked the driver of his cab.

Their eyes met in the rearview mirror. The driver shrugged. "Three hundred on a good day."

The best, Nathanson thought, but this was the Apple with the greed worm in its core. He placed two crisp notes in the fare slot. "You get another when we're through."

The cabbie put his fingers on the bills, but he did not pull them away. "What I have to do?"

"Follow that van and the taxi in front of it."

"Anything else?"

"Not a thing except maybe wait for me now and then."

"This a dope run?"

Nathanson looked away; the cabbie would not believe him if he told the truth. "Do I look it?" Nathanson had shaved off his Vandyke and had had his hair cut short. He was dressed in a dark Chesterfield coat and a brown soft hat. Anonymity was the best disguise, especially in New York, and after all, here he was a native.

The money vanished. "The car or the van? There's only one of us."

Nathanson thought for a moment, as the other taxi and the van moved off. He had come to New York for a number of reasons, the most pressing of which was to put an end to the project that he had begun with Creach nearly a month before. He had lost much: $1.25 mil, a good boat, a better house, some of its belongings, and nearly his life. Creach himself was maimed and would never be the same, and there was the $1.25 mil that he had put in too.

More to the point—he did not want to have to live with the insecurity that they might come back for him. He would rebuild his house in Nassau and spend the rest of his life there, and he flushed with shame every time he thought of how he had watched the woman and her Indians sack, then burn, the house, the one place on earth that his stepfather and mother had decided to own for keeps and pass on to him. According to their request, he had sprinkled their ashes on the back garden there.

Creach had been right. Injuries or no, they should have taken it to the *sicaria* there, where he could have called on people to help. He had thought they would take what they could find, be satisfied with that, and split. It had never occurred to him that they would burn down his house, and he wondered what her orders were? What went around could go around. Colombia wasn't all that far or Medellín so remote that Pachito Londoño was untouchable. In his pocket Nathanson had a single photograph that showed a dark, older man with an even older-looking woman who were seated before a window in a restaurant. They were dressed in evening clothes, and beyond them in the street was a new-model Mercedes. Around the woman's neck hung an enormous, clear, and sparkling green stone. The note said:

> From the desk of Jorge Luis Ochoa:
> One life insurance policy guaranteed to make Brian Nathanson *sicaria*-proof, at least in his present situation.
> For Miami,
Jorge Ochoa

Nathanson imagined that he could call on Ochoa's help again, if need be. "It's the cab we want, don't let the van see us. Let's go."

CHAPTER 21

LUNCH/POWER

THE DAY BEFORE at lunch Tug McCann had thought, Jesus—somewhere, sometime I must have done something mighty good. The hits just keep rolling in.

Sitting to his immediate right at the bar was a tall, beautiful, intriguing woman, dressed to the nines, who had handed him a card that read:

Mlle. Solange de los Páramos
Directrice
Opération Atlantique du Nord
PAPEL PORTEÑOS, S.A.
Buenos Aires

She had just finished telling him that in anticipation of a strike in Argentina, Papel Porteños—a large South American wholesaler—had sent her from Paris to New York to purchase all the newsprint she could buy at or around $685 per metric ton. Since Papel Porteños had no North American buyer, would he be interested in fronting the deal? If all went well—who knew?—his brokerage might establish an ongoing relationship with Papel Porteños that would be beneficial to both parties.

Would he be interested? She had to be kidding. Buying volume he could wangle a discount of between thirteen and eighteen percent. Say it came in at fifteen, he would make a little over two hundred thousand dollars on a two-thousand-ton order. "What kind of volume are you talking?"

"We require thirty-five hundred tons immediately. After that, we'll just have to see. But I think you can count on at least that much until the strike is over. Right now, it doesn't look good."

McCann smiled. From his perspective it looked wonderful. Clinking his raised glass against hers, he speculated on the wisdom of allowing women to conduct negotiations in business. Mademoiselle Solange de los Páramos had probably been out being fitted for the exquisite turquoise-colored silk dress she was wearing when she should have been learning the intricacies of the U.S. paper market. How could she not be aware of the fact that with volume like that she could have gone directly to paper producers and saved a bundle.

Until she added, "It's something that Papel Porteños would like to keep quiet. As far as you're concerned, you don't know who in South America is buying it. We'll give you a shipping address when the time comes."

So other producers didn't get wind of it and jump in, he concluded. He wondered what Papel Porteños would charge on the other end.

"I'm to remain here in New York at least until we have some idea that you can fulfill our needs."

Tug had smiled, regarding the long, gentle slope of her forehead, which was fringed with blonde hair, her high cheekbones, and her eyes that were shaped like almonds but such a deep green color they made him think of a tigress. "How did you get my name?"

"Mr. Charles W. Richards of Repap Enterprises."

"Bozo?" Which had been the man's nickname.

She handed him Richards's business card. On the back in pen and ink was McCann's name and business phone number.

"But Bozo died—"

"Last March. Worked himself to death, I should imagine. He was a dedicated man in every way. Tireless." She smiled.

"You knew Bozo?" He had been one of McCann's good friends in the industry.

"Well enough to know his strengths."

And his weaknesses, McCann concluded, his eyes sliding over the rake of her shoulders, the flare of her golden chest. "You did business with him?"

"In a roundabout fashion." In fact, she had never met the man, whose name and other information about international paper trading she had gotten from the Papel Porteños representative in Bogotá. Only her letter of initial credit was at all genuine. It would cash. She now slid the bank draft to McCann. "He spoke of you highly. Said you were nothing if not discreet and all our dealings would be kept strictly private."

McCann gazed down on the check for $100,000, and all his worries vanished. For him six-figure sums were imbued with a legitimacy that was difficult to question. In four short days, if all went well, he would upgrade his mark to seven-figure sums.

"You have a lovely tan," she went on. "I understand you've been away on holiday."

McCann's brow glowered, and he studied her strange features. Her nose was long and straight but somewhat flat, her mouth wide and lips full. Her skin was an olive color. She reminded him of a taller, younger, somewhat darker Sophia Loren except for the hair. Her hair was like a . . . revelation, it was so brilliantly red. Piled on top of her head in lustrous waves, it looked at once prim but casual and very, very fetching. An Elizabeth Arden masterpiece, he thought. The salon was just up Fifth Avenue.

He lowered his eyes to hers. "I was in the Bahamas. Ever been there?"

She shook her head. "I'm French. For sun I go to the Midi. Or Tunisia."

McCann spoke glowingly of the Islands, mentioning several—but not all—of the advantages of a bare-boat charter. He discussed the climate, the food, and the conviviality of the people, but she seemed distracted. When she rose to leave, he suggested dinner and a show. "Or maybe you'd prefer the Met. I have tickets." Nothing bruised McCann's manly pride more than to have a beautiful woman walk away, especially in front of the group of men.

Her hand, two fingers of which glowed with gold and—was it?—emerald, touched the back of his hand. Her smile was tinged with subtle promise. "We'll have plenty of time for that. Unfortunately I have another engagement. More business."

And nothing turned him on more than when a beautiful woman did. McCann reached out and touched her elbow. "What about tomorrow?" he called after her. "How 'bout lunch?" Actually Cicciolino and he had scheduled probably the most important meeting of their lives for lunch tomorrow, but Tug had made a career of juggling people, money, and deals, and it excited him. The action.

Also, the way she turned to him—swinging her shoulders and head; one long, svelte leg moving behind the other, like in a kind of dance—was enough to stop his heart. His eyes slid down the angles of her body, which he had missed while she was sitting beside him.

"*Je vous demande pardon?*" A tall woman, she had to bend to peer at his lips.

"Lunch? Tomorrow?" he repeated loud enough for several of his friends to hear.

"Same time, same place?" she asked.

"You don't mind it here?" O'Casey's, while upscale, was mainly a place to do business: big drinks, good steaks, a broiled fish entrée for the weight-conscious.

"I love it here. Ask Tony. I've been trying to contact you for days."

McCann beamed with pleasure. He glowed.

"I was about to give up."

Thank God and Gelb, who over McCann's objections had turned *Trekker* to run wildly with the breeze toward the coast and Barnegat. He'd got them home early.

And watching her silken glide toward the door, McCann's ambition—fired with several tumblers of Absolut—blazed with thoughts of how it might be to control North American access to the South American market. Did Solange de los Páramos, who was French, also speak Spanish? Of course. Porteños was an Argentinian firm, and de los Páramos sounded Spanish. Races and nationalities in Argentina, as he remembered, were all mixed up.

But it was her method of communicating that appealed to him most, how she stared at his lips, as if she wanted to bite them or something, when he spoke.

"See—what did I tell you?" Tony had said, when topping up his glass. "George tells me that after five minutes of conversation last Friday, he had to send Kevin out for Chap Stick."

It was not actually funny, but Tug began to laugh. During the course of almost any day he smiled almost constantly, chuckled often, but seldom did he vent his mirth; and he had a delightful, raspy, cackling, infectious laugh that caused others at the bar to smile and then look at each other and finally to laugh at the sheer unbridled joy he was experiencing.

Tears formed in the corners of McCann's eyes, and his face assumed an alarming shade. He pulled in a breath, tried to contain himself, and then burst forth anew, turning with popped eyes to the man beside him, as though for aid, and finding only another smile that drove him to new heights.

He thought of the money, all that cash on the boat, and how easily they had banged it into a bank and then concealed it in his business. He thought of the skirmish with the plane and Eva getting lost and the shake-and-bake routine with the old pirate, Monroe, in the bar. Then Eva's telegram, and Gelb finding *Trekker*, and the way they had dealt with the schooner, *Whistler*, and Monroe. God rot his lying, thieving, miserable soul.

And finally the long passage north with the storm and Gelb picking up—of all the books and magazines on the boat—the one about the computerized radar-tracking system that had probably monitored their progress from the moment they passed Grand Bahaman Island. Then, Gelb's idea of lashing the dope to the keel and how they had handled Lieutenant Boy Wonder, who so much wanted to swing their asses from a yardarm.

It had been a major, dangerous, physical adventure in the middle of his life that he had not sought, would never have thought of getting involved in, but was *working out*. Throughout it all—he only now realized—he had been strung tighter than piano wire. His apparent calm had been only face, the one he put on, like an armored mask, for deals.

Speaking of which, he had a backlog of over a month's business, Papel Porteños, and tomorrow one Hector ("Chino") Santos Cabrón to deal with. McCann dried his eyes and asked Tony for a glass of water.

McCann looked down at her card, then raised it to his nose and breathed in her perfume. Solange de los Páramos. He knew that *de los* probably meant, "from the." But he wondered what *páramos* meant. He would have to ask her.

That was Monday.

*   *   *

Tuesday morning Hector ("Chino") Santos Cabrón got up earlier than he could remember. In fact, he hardly slept at all and kept shouting for Martita to come in and "Do som'sin'—make me sleep!" Santos himself did no dope, which was for losers, so pills were out, and he would not even take a beer to make him drowsy. He either conked right out or he fucked something until he could; but he could not help Martita do what she wanted to do to him, which made things worse.

"Don' laugh," he whispered over her shoulder. "Jus' don' laugh, I warn you."

"Me laugh at *you*, baby? You jus' non eat, ees all," she said, turning over. "Like Mama tell you, non eat, you die." She spread her legs.

Martita had what Santos thought of as a bad/dirty twat, the kind he liked. He was a diver and spent most of his sack time below Fourteenth Street, like they say, which was why pigmeat got him off. And he knew from experience there was all sorts of cunt out there, but none like Martita's. Or at least none he'd gone eye to eye.

There were red furry twats, big like a Viking's beard with hair running up the stomach, and fine, wispy blond twats that tickled your nose when you sucked in, then the curly brown kinky kind so rough, man, they made your tongue tingle. Martita, though, had come to Santos young—maybe eleven or twelve—through a cousin in San Juan who helped her split from an orphanage where two butch supervisors had been trading off on her. She wasn't cherry *veramente*, since them dikes had stuck everything in her but their elbows, but she hadn't learned much sweet dick neither, which made her like it more.

Santos could hardly believe it when he got her pants off. Here she was this tiny, *fine*, little-doll girl type with east-west tits, perky, knobby kid nipples, and a blocked-out, tight tan ass. But when he turned her around, she didn't have some kid's cunt. No. She had this woman's big black bush that was dense, man, and a hanging, droppy-lip gash—the kind that made you think you frenching a platypus. Santos had seen one at the zoo.

He couldn't help himself. His cousin had hardly left the room when he'd rolled her around, tickling and licking and biting—all the sister shit you got into when the lights were out—and then he went downtown on the bitch, and there it was. This little sticky-up thing with a head and all where her clit shoulda been or *was*, she later told him. His face came up.

"Wha's zis?" he asked. "Wha's what? You no like me?" She was about to cry. "This thing?" It was so big he could grab it between his fingers. He gave it a squeeze. "Don' do that, man," she giggled. "I come." Santos didn't let go, he couldn't. He felt like a fucking doctor or scientist who had made a, you know, discovery. She then kind of blushed and said at the orphanage they called it her *macho*, which Santos learned from the real doctor, who checked his foxes for clap and shit, wasn't so wrong. He said it was a genetic animally or something that only a few women had, and he offered to cut it off on the house.

Santas got her out of there fast. Here he had on his hands this little girl who was also a boy, who had this big woman's twat and a fuckin' *dick*, and who could come more than any girl he'd ever been with, which made him feel good. "Don' you tell nobody about this. *Nobody*," he warned her. "And you live here. I don' wan' you out on no streets in your condition. Uner'stan'?" She wasn't dumb, and she didn't say no. That was five years ago. No, six.

"Don' pick at me," Santos said, trying to tie the tie that went with the fuckin' three-piece suit the guy said to get. Santos kept thinking it must be the cop, but it wasn't his big, tough voice.

"Who' pickin'? I jus' wan' you look good. Han'some, like you is. You could be down on Wall Street."

"Where you get Wall Street? And how you know to tie a tie?" which she did without answering him. Looking over her shoulder at himself in the mirror, Santos thought, Man, don' you look dumb. That suit—it somethin' to get buried in.

At the door with the trench coat over his arm and the fucking umbrella, the way he'd also been told, he pointed a finger. "When I get back, you better say who."

She shook her head. *"Nunca."*

"Why not?"

"I be scare' what he do to you."

Santos went for her, but he was already late for how long it would take him. He'd get her when he got back. Then, to make it worse, she yell down the stairs at him, "They ask you, you wan' a *real* job? Take it."

A real job, Santos kept saying to himself on the subway that was packed with working stiffs headed south into Manhattan. Santos was proud he never had a real job in his life, and at thirty-seven, after twenty years running the streets, he could probably buy and sell half the humps he could see. *Together.* And still have enough left over to buy the fucking subway car, that's how much he had, not counting what he set aside for business.

Business. He shook his head. They could nail him good, take everything he owned, everything else they could find or steal, and ram him in the slam for the rest of his life. And then where'd he be? Worse off than the suckers around him, rocking and nodding, half-asleep, their eyes he could see bored and dead.

Maybe he worked too hard. Maybe he was always at it. Santos didn't have to do girls. Fuck he do girls for?, which made other people, like cops, hate his ass. Fuck he do anything for? He do it, was all. Maybe it was time to get out. Maybe the cop was trying to tell him something, like, You don't know it, you' dead too.

Not yet, baby, he said to himself while the car slowed down, pulling into the Forty-second Street station where he got out. Sure, they could plant something on him, which his lawyer could beat with enough money and a fink. Otherwise he was clean and had been smart and put what he saved deep. One thing was sure: He might do time, but he would never again be poor. *Ever.*

Thus Santos was feeling better about himself by the time he shuffled out onto the platform among the empty suits and office lifers. Except for shaking the cop tail that was still on him, he had the day to himself. He would have lunch at some nice place, like the voice on the phone promise. He didn't have to say yes or no. Just listen. And that wasn't half-bad. Or half-poor.

Santos liked the look of O'Casey's. It had a big green flag outside and lots of blond, paneled oak with frosted-glass windows. Like with velour and leather, Santos was into wood, and, when he found it repeated in the little foyer with a pay phone that his eye snagged on and throughout the bar, which was in back of a frosted-glass door, he sort of relaxed. If it came to nothing, at least he wouldn't waste no time in no dingy joint.

Place was bright and packed both at the bar and all the little drinks tables along the wall. The dining room was deeper in with an oak staircase leading up. Another door closer to the bar went down, most likely to the toilets and more phones, he hoped. It made him nervous to be too far from a pay phone. Santos could barely read, he could write only his name and address and a few words in Spanish, but he could repeat the numbers of every pay phone that worked in East Harlem.

Now in the door with his trench coat over one arm, the way he'd been told, and the umbrella Martita had paid seventy dumb bucks for when he could have had one of his runners snatch one on a subway, Santos looked around. The phone number of his high-price lawyer jumped to the front of his mind.

No Irish bums or hard hats here. Guys were mainly white, with one Cuban by the cut of his mustache, all dressed in expensive suits, like him. They were talking loud, smoking cigars, eating lunch right at the bar, laughing, drinking.

The four or five women he could see were business chicks. There was a big blond with tits, lots of lipstick, and glittering eyes. He heard her say, "Hi, Ollie, nice to see you again. I'm Mary Lee, remember?" Ollie didn't want to, and when she turned her head in disgust, her eyes flicked over Santos and back at her drink. He guessed he'd passed the test and at least *looked* like he belonged. There was a gray-hair woman with nice legs, and some tall, like-mulatto lady who just sat down. She had red hair and was wearing a shimmering dress and gold shoes that made her body look like two wedges of pure ingot.

People coming in kept pushing by Santos, and he stepped forward like he been told, toward the coat-check girl, who smiled and took his things. When he turned around, he thought he saw some man near the redhead signal to one of the bartenders, who caught Santos's eye and pointed to the only empty barstool. In front of it was an iced glass on a napkin.

Me? Santos asked, pointing at his chest. "But ain't there somebody . . . ?"

"You." The bartender pulled the glass away and dumped its contents in a sink below the bar. "What can I get you, sir?"

"To drink?"

The bartender looked away toward his other customers.

"Wha' was zat?" Santos was suddenly aware of his English, which, like the Spanish he had almost forgot, was bad.

The bartender leaned closer, not understanding him.

Santos pointed to all the glasses on the back of the bar. "Wha' was *zat*? In the glass?"

"Water. It was there to reserve you your seat, sir," Tony said in precise British English. "Now, what's your pleasure?"

"One a' them." At least Santos would pretend to be cool. He reached for his fourteen-karat gold case that held small dark cigars that he smoked sparingly. He glanced at his gold Rolex oyster-shell watch he got for some dope from a junkie too sick to say no.

"Water?"

"I don' care what it cos'. Iz what I wan'."

"It's taken care of."

"It is?" Santos looked around the bar, but he couldn't see anybody looking his way.

The bartender returned with another iced glass and a small green bottle. Perrier. Santos had seen the stuff in a bodega where he had a spot, but he never tasted it. The bubbles tickled his mustache. He drew on his cigar and again tried to catch somebody looking at him, but everybody seemed deep into their own shit, and Santos decided he should start hanging out in a place like this. Better class of people.

All the joints he went in East Harlem somebody was either trying to hit him up for something or rip him off. Some spots he had to bring five, six guards, all of them wearing Kevlar body armor with every kind of blaster they could carry, and still he felt like a fucking target. Even sometimes with his own runners. Every once in a while he done one, some fuck-up, just to keep the others in line, but he knew he couldn't go on with that shit. Not with the heat on him the way it was. Sooner or later he'd get careless and caught out. Then he'd be lucky if he was still free. Or alive.

Somehow he had to quit, but not with his tail between his legs. They'd never let him keep what he got: not the cops, not his competition, not the fucks who ran for him. He'd have to move quiet, then sell his property cheap. But to where? Back to Puerto Rico? Santos hated the place and thought of himself as a New Yorker. Maybe he'd move downtown here, now that he could afford it.

"Mr. Santos?" somebody said in his ear, and he jumped, his hand jerking to his belt, where he'd slid a small-caliber piece into a belly holster. "Your table is ready."

"It is?"

"This way please. We have a window for you. Upstairs."

Santos glanced at his drink, then decided, Fuck it—they could buy him another upstairs; and he followed the hostess out of the bar, through a small dining area, to the oak stairs that led up into another dining room. He looked right and left, trying to read the face of anybody who was watching him, but nobody did more than glance at the hostess, who was young and pretty. Except the redhead, who—it was strange—was a little, you know, black. Like Santos himself, though he'd never admit it.

The table for two was right in front of an arched window that looked down on Forty-first Street, and all the people and traffic passing there. Santos didn't know if he should tip the hostess, and by the time he decided why not, she said, "Enjoy your lunch," and split.

Next came a waitress who was some kind of Spanish and had a young Madonna face but a big, sexy body that in a couple years would run to fat. Now, though, she was *simpática*, and Santos wondered how much she was pulling down with her tray in a joint like this. "Would you like to order?" Her eyes fell on the menu, like he should pick it up and say.

"Nah—I think I got somebody come see me."

"You're not going to eat?" It was like he broke her heart.

"Like I say, I—"

She turned to move off toward another table that was calling her, and Santos's hand jumped for her wrist. "Wai', wai'—"

She stared at his hand until he let her go.

"Sorry, I"—"used to my bitches," he nearly said—"eat. Bring me"—he opened the menu like he could read it, then handed it to her—"bring me the biggest steak you got. And"—he got an idea—"a bottle of wine. I don' drink it, can you take it home?"

She looked away, like it didn't happen much, and nodded. "I guess."

"Then bring me your best wine."

She paused for a moment, and her eyes seemed to clear. She then nodded once and left.

Yeah, Santos thought. That wasn't hard. Maybe he'd bring Martita down here. She'd like the window and the whole nice scene inside and out on the street.

Reaching into a pocket to light another cigar, he moved his

head toward the glass and tried to check out the limousine that was parked right in front of the joint. It was one of them stretch Mercedes you only saw on Park Avenue or the tube when the German president or some Arab was going somewhere. There was a kind of Indian in a monkey suit and cap leaning against the fender, his arms folded across his chest. Santos had seen guys like him before—mules running blow for the Cali cartel. They got caught, so what?, he been told. Stir here was better than what they left.

The redhead, the one with the gold everything and the dynamite body, now came out of the bar and said something quick to the chauffeur, then returned to the bar.

Santos hefted his own gold lighter and was about to light his cigar when somebody said, "Try one of mine. I think you'll like it."

Santos looked up: red face, white hair, good suit, cigar. Irish. He'd seen the guy with the redhead in the bar, and he put together it was him who set things up. He could remember now the bartender looking his way before the routine with the bar glass. And the redhead watching the hostess lead him away. The only eyes in the bar.

Suddenly Santos was on his guard. He lowered the lighter into his lap, where he could drop it and move toward his belt if he had to. "Yeah? What kind you got?"

"Upmann's. Seldom smoke anything else. May I sit down?"

Santos took the cigar and waved it at the seat. "You' table." You' deal, he thought.

For McCann it was a moment of truth. He looked down on the sallow little man with the trim mustache and the solid-gold lighter who was packed into his expensive, tasteless suit like a rat in a bright box, and he nearly bolted. He tried to remind himself of all the scuzzy things Chick had said about Santos—kids, murder, heroin, etc.—but nothing helped.

It was one thing to react to a firefight with an incoming plane or to respond to a maneuver by somebody like T. J. Monroe. But it was quite another to look into the nervous eyes of a person whom you were plotting to murder, to share a drink, and to part with an understanding. It was something outside of McCann's experience or expectations of himself.

Chick had said, "Don't matter what you tell him—your name, your bank balance. I'll bet my share he don't keep no records.

Fuck, he don't even fucking read or write, from what we know. He's just one lucky death-and-sleaze dealer who got ignored, far as I can tell. Or—"

"—*formerly* lucky death-and-sleaze dealer," all three of them had chorused. Gelb had been with them in McCann's apartment.

After a while Gelb had asked, "But, you know, Chick—what does that make *us*?"

"Gee, I don't know, Jay. Maybe we should examine the question so we have at least a working idea," Cicciolino had responded, as though speaking to a child. "Later—after it's over—I'm all for a healthy round of self-loathing and recrimination, but right now we can say we're not sleaze merchants. You sell little girls on street corners? When was the last time a child sucked your cock?

"Then, our pigeon has been dealing drugs, starting with marijuana and running through speed, acid, angel dust, PCP, heroin, coke, crack, designer drugs, and now the new wonder substances ecstasy and crank. You try any of that, Jay? I hear it's dyn-o-mite. But not just himself. No, not Hector—"Chino"—Santos Cabrón. He's got himself a small army. He's Little Big Time in East Harlem, and has been for ten fucking years.

"So we find him dead in possession of a half-ton of pure product that would translate into a couple hundred million bucks of crack. In exchange for that public service we find ourselves suddenly compensated, regrettably at a much lower figure. If you want to give your three-point-three or whatever it'll be to charity, you should contact my wife. I'm sure she's got a list longer than my dick."

But—Tug now thought, sliding into the seat opposite Santos—dead was dead and murder, murder, though he wasn't the one who would do him.

Santos looked down at the long moist cigar that felt almost spongy between his fingers. It was one of those with no hole in the end that he'd seen guys lick, suck, roll on their tongues and, you know, bite before lighting, and he didn't want to get into that.

McCann reached for it. "Let me help you." He clipped it with a cigar tool, then pierced the cut and handed it back.

Santos looked around. "This a smoking section?"

Tug chuckled. Him of all people. "You got to be kidding. It's a *paying* section, if you know what I mean."

Santos lit the cigar, which tasted about as good as he ever had, and it occurred to him that just *making* money wasn't all of it.

The wine arrived, and McCann picked up the bottle. "Château Margaux. Good selection. What are you having to eat?"

"Steak."

"Steaks here are good. You put the order in yet, Camilla?" he asked the waitress.

She shook her head.

"Make it the special. How you like your steak done, Hector?"

"I tol' her burnt." Santos didn't trust meat that wasn't done good. "You got a name?" he asked, when the waitress had left.

McCann, who was naturally cautious, looked away.

"Jyou know mine."

It was a matter of public record, McCann thought, his opinion of Santos hardening now that they were coming down to the deal. But he made it a point never to insult the other party in any negotiation. "Does it matter?"

" 'Pends on wha' you got."

McCann reached for the wineglass. He raised and breathed in the full, rich bouquet of the newly disembogued wine that was still lightly scented by the tang of the cork. "I've got a half ton of the purest cocaine that you have ever buried a nostril in." His eyes jumped to Santos's. "I also have a big block of ice that I can drop on your present problem. Interested now?"

Santos was, and while he listened to the details of the guy's proposition, he stared down at the ruby-red wine in the glass that a shaft of reflected sunlight made bright as a stoplight. He wondered for a moment if this was the end of things for him. You know, the suit, the last mile he walked earlier, the last meal, the works.

"Where zis happen?" he asked, when the guy had finished. "An' when?"

"Somewhere here in the city. I think you can appreciate why I don't want to be more precise. We'll pick you up, take you there. We'll let your guys check the product. Only when you're satisfied it's what we say it is do you tell us about the payment. You know—where it is. We check that out, and, when we find it's all there, we shake and you split. That way nothing can go . . . you know, sour.

"When? The sooner the better. We're ready to roll."

"Wha' happen if I get the stuff, and you no get you' money."

As though aghast, McCann said, "But—you wouldn't do that, I hope?"

Santos looked away. He wasn't thinking of himself, he was thinking of Justino, who'd be the one to check the dope. *If* Santos went through with the thing, and he was a long way from that. If he did, though, sooner would be better. Guy like Justino would need time to set something up, a place to store it, people willing to buy. He wouldn't hold on to the stash and let it out slow the way he should. He'd sell it and blow it. "Maybe non me, but—"

"You mean, you don't have control of your—" Henchmen? McCann did not know the proper term, and he waved a hand.

Santos tilted his head. "Is a lot of volume. Score like that, one guy could get rich."

"What I want to know—*could* you do it?"

"Could." Santos nodded. Can and will was another thing. Not to McCann. He was a natural salesman, and he knew once you got a prospect to say he *could*, it was just a matter of talent to make him say he *would*, and McCann possessed every necessary skill. He raised the wineglass and let the nectar creep into his mouth, tasting all those warm, rich Bordeaux sunny days and the respect with which they had been preserved in dark, careful cellars. He decided he would order Solange a bottle when he got back to the bar. It was his cocaine. It freshened his palate, warmed his throat, and filled him with a sense of well-being. Immediately.

"Price?" Santos asked.

Now they were down to it. "Twenty-five thousand a kilo."

Santos shook his head and looked away. He raised the glass and touched the wine to his lips. It tasted bitter or sour or something. He took another sip—why not?—the guy wasn't real. He could get acceptable cocaine for fifteen thousand dollars a kilo, sometimes less, depending on supply. Or, he *used to* get acceptable cocaine.

"Think about it," McCann went on, wrapping him up, drawing him to the close. "No more hassles. You'll own the streets again. Guaranteed. Why fuck around with Cali or Medellín and the possibility of getting busted? Here you get product *and* safety. You'll sleep nights."

It was the second time the guy seemed to know where he was at. But was it worth paying ten thousand dollars a kilo more than the going price for a guarantee they couldn't really guarantee? Santos wasn't stupid. If they had cops, they only had certain cops. Thing like this you couldn't spread around.

"Think about it," the guy repeated, reaching for the bottle.

"Is this why the heat?"

The guy tilted his head and poured them both more wine. "Did I, or did I not, mention a big block of ice?"

Santos shook his head again. He shook it some more. "Know wha' I think?"

"I'm all ears."

"I think we got a shakedown here."

McCann touched fingers to his chest. He shook his head. "A shakedown is something else. In a shakedown there's no exchange, no sharing of confidences. No mutuality. No respect."

Confidence? Santos raised the corner of his mouth in a kind of smile. "You a cop?"

Guy shook his head.

"You talk like a cop."

"I hope you mean that as a compliment."

"Bagman?"

"Hector—that's a tad blunt. Call me a . . . sales engineer. I'm here to see that the deal goes through and everybody's happy."

"What about the cop? Chick—?"

"—o-lee-no," McCann supplied, just as if he were back at elementary school. "What about him?"

"He in on this?"

"Gee—I wouldn't know. Or say, if I did. You wearing a wire?"

Santos had thought of it, but he knew guys got dead for less. And who would he go to with evidence? Him against a fucking chief. He shook his head again. "Too big." He meant the deal. "Too much. I got no money like that."

"Sure you do, and don't shit me. More to the point, you can get your hands on it quick. You do much banking? I bet you do. Someplace close, like your basement, where you can make quick withdrawals, right?"

Santos only eyed the bastard. What was his was his, and he didn't like nobody even talking about his money.

"And look at the bright side. With that much raw material, you'll be independent for the next ten years. Who knows what'll happen? Bunch of new politicians here and in Washington might make things tight, and there you are up in East Harlem with no heat, sitting on a mountain of shit."

Santos shook his head and tried the wine again, which was growing on him. "Jyou talkin' eight, nine million bucks. Nobody got money like that. Cash."

"Bullshit. You do. And I'm talking twelve-point-two-five."

"Point-two-one-five," Santos corrected. Maybe he couldn't read and write, but the business he was talking Santos had been doing so long it was like second nature. Also, the place—he looked away to see if anybody was watching or listening—was perfect for it. Everybody was digging away at something: their own deals, lunch, the waitresses, whatever. "Fuck it," he said, throwing out his right hand. "I fuckin' quit, you win. You keep your coke. I pack my shit and split. I retire."

"Down to PR?" Guy shook his head. "Not you. You don't know much more about Puerto Rico than I do. You're a New Yorker, a city boy, like me. The fuck we do down in some hot, flea-bitten country where you can't own a bicycle without worrying somebody might take your life for it? Why be successful, why have money, if you can't enjoy it? And need I mention your building and your girls? They allow that shit in Catholic countries? Nah, fuck it—I don't want to get into that. It's your business."

What, the guy have a crystal ball? That made three times he had tuned into what Santos was thinking and feeling.

"Look—Chino, may I call you that?" Guy reached out his hand that was steady as a rock no matter his red face; the hand then turned and the point finger pointed at his own chest, "—*me* go back to Ireland? Went there once. Rains all the goddamn time, and there's nothing to do but drink and count sheep, which can be done more effectively in here"—he meant the joint—"and in the subway. *Here* is where we belong." He looked into the dining room too, but like he owned it.

Yeah, thought Santos, here is where you belong on my money. And then the whole thing could just be some big bust to get the cop a promotion or something. Cops—they were the greediest bastards Santos knew, and lazy. They wanted everything easy with no work or nothing. Santos knew what *he* did. The profits were good, but the risks were high, and he worked for what he made. Fucking hard, man. It was sweat, twenty-four hours a day.

"Tell you what. I'm going to gift you—good faith, no charge—a little sample of what we've got. It's all the same, one big load. That way, you can test the quality of our product and know we're for real. You like, you call me at the number that'll show up on your beeper.

"Like I said, we're set up to do business whenever you can, but the sooner the better. We'll beep you sometime tonight, and we want you to get back to us, whether you want the deal or not. You wait"—he hunched his shoulders; he was an older guy in good shape everywhere but the gut— "we go elsewhere. We also jack up your heat."

He waited for Santos's reaction, but when there was none, he added, "I don't like threats, but so far you're just simmering. It wouldn't take much to bring you to a boil. Here I'm thinking of hassles, like the piece you got there under your belt."

Santos looked down, but nothing was showing.

"Or a little hard time for your girls. Who knows what Martita might come back with?"

Even hearing the guy use her name brought blood to Santos's ears.

"Oops—here's your salad." McCann's head swung to the waitress who had approached the table, plate in hand. "I'll let you eat in peace." He waited until she had left, then said, "Why don't you meet me down in the john in—say—five minutes." He checked his watch and stood.

Santos glanced down at his own on the wrist of the hand that was twirling the stem of the wineglass.

"Like that watch. Good investment. I got mine as collateral on a bad loan"—McCann flashed his own gold oyster shell—"I don't know, a dozen, maybe fifteen years ago for a couple, three thou. Now, what's it worth? Eighteen, twenty? Pays to invest long term, especially in commodities that appreciate." He turned and walked away, waving to somebody at a nearby table, stopping to shake hands with somebody else. He then reached out and pulled the waitress over to whisper something in her ear.

When she returned to Santos's table with the steak, he asked, "What he say to you?"

"Who?"

Santos pointed at the empty seat.

"Mr. McCann? He said I'm to send your check down to him in the bar."

"Mr. Mc—?"

"McCann."

"He got a first name?"

She thought a moment. "Guys at the bar call him Tug, but his platinum card says Edward."

Platinum card. Santos had heard of them; you could charge a fuckin' Porsche on plastic like that. "Bring me another bottle of wine."

She glanced at the table. "But you haven't finished—"

"Don' open it." Fuck her and this place, Santos thought. He'd take it home to Martita—pour it on her stomach, drink it out of her lap. It was a fuckin' stickup, cop style, was what it was.

Santos shook his head and looked back out the window, down at the limo in the street. If he wanted to go on, he'd have to do it. Like McWhatever said, a big load of product *would* make him independent from them zombie *máquineros* from Cali and Medellín. From the head-case Jamaicans he sometimes bought from. All the other jive-ass niggers whacked-out on crystal and rock. The *shit* he had to deal with, just to stay alive.

Santos sighed and wondered if the wine was getting to him. He looked down at the slab of scorched meat and decided he'd lost his appetite. He'd take it home too, feed it to his Dobermans, the ones who guarded his *loot*, like the guy said.

Back down in the bar, McCann said to Solange de los Páramos, "Sorry—I bumped into somebody," but he could see she had had no lack of company.

With smiling eyes she said, "George here was just telling me that he could get me all the tons I need somewhat below the six-eighty-five price we discussed."

McCann's head swung to the man who was a friendly competitor and now sitting on the other side of her. There was a bottle of Dom protruding from an ice bucket, like a gold-wrapped erection meant for her gold dress. You fucking shark, McCann's eyes said.

You better believe it, the other man's eyes flashed back over the barrel of an Upmann's.

Both were smiling, but when McCann began to chuckle, the other man did not join him. He was serious. I want your deal, the broad, your business, everything you got, and I'll get it too, if you're not careful, the message continued.

Tug shook his head. If George only knew. God, how McCann loved the place, his life, the city. Action like this. As he had said to their pigeon, Santos, he wouldn't know what to do with himself otherwise.

"Don't you have any response?" Solange de los Páramos asked.

"Is one called for?" She did not want anybody else's paper; of all the brokers in New York—big or little, like him—she had singled him out, which he still found kind of strange. "Remember Bozo, George?" He trotted out the story, which made it more credible, and even slid George the card she had given him.

"I didn't think you and Bozo were that close," George observed.

Nor had McCann, but you never knew what the other person was feeling. He nearly wrapped a friendly hand around the shimmering curve of the woman's hip, when out of the corner of his eyes he saw the bar door swing back and Chick's wide frame filled the opening. Behind him was First Deputy Police Commissioner Bob Brant, both of them looking, as usual, like media stars, which in a way they were. If McCann did not know about Cicciolino's uncle, the tailor, he would assume he was on the take.

Tony, the bartender, moved right down to them. "If it isn't Bill and Bob from the Bob and Bill Show. Where you been, strangers?" Celebrities were good for business.

"Ain't it obvious?" Cicciolino pulled Brant in close and turned them to the mirror in back of the bar. Both men were very brown. "We been down to the Islands, but don't get us wrong. *Not* together."

The others at the bar laughed, and Cicciolino pulled off his overcoat to reveal a pearl-gray combed-silk suit. His tie and pocket handkerchief were lavender, his shirt a pink blush. It was a combination that on any slighter frame would seem too much, but on Cicciolino's proportions, looked daring and elegant.

Brant looked properly British with a double-breasted blazer, a club tie, and pleated beige trousers.

The women in the bar—McCann noted—smiled.

Solange de los Páramos crossed her legs toward the cloakroom, as though expecting to be introduced. Cicciolino, however, was still speaking ostensibly to Tony. "Actually, we stopped in to 'parley vous.' Good news travels fast." He moved in on McCann and the redhead, who was even better, he thought, than McCann had said on the phone, and a perfect blind for the meet with Santos.

"Anything to drink, Bill?" Tony asked.

"Gee—I don't know. We on duty, Bob?" He turned to Brant, whose eyes were also on the woman.

"You are. Definitely. Me? I'm a civilian. I'm off. Scotch—please, Tony—rocks. You can get the chief a timber float."

Again the bar responded. George reached out to shake Brant's hand.

Said McCann, "Solange—may I introduce Assistant Chief Bill Cicciolino and First Deputy Police Commissioner Bob Brant."

Her eyes moved from his lips to Cicciolino's, who said, "My pleasure, if you're lucky."

"I beg your pardon?" she asked, not understanding.

Brant's hand lingered in hers. God, he thought, where'd McCann get her? She and Brant had the same red hair, though hers was finer, and almost exactly the same skin color except for his freckles. But she had something else in her, like Indian, he thought, and her face with the blond hair along her temples and the line of her high forehead reminded him of the meticulously crafted Incan death masks he had seen at a show at the Met not long past.

"Gee, Bob," Cicciolino said, reaching for the two pops of scotch that Tony had slid him, "you gonna give the lady back her hand, or what?"

Catching sight of Santos rounding the corner of the stairs down to the toilet, McCann eased himself off his barstool, "Excuse me a moment. I just remembered a phone call I have to make."

Said Cicciolino, "Permission granted, Brother Tug. Have a long one." He slid onto the stool. "Take a month or two. We'll mail you the check."

Down in the john, McCann waited, washing his hands until two other men, who were talking while they primped at a mirror, left. He then turned to Santos, who looked as if he were about to step into a tumbrel. From his suit coat McCann pulled a package that Arlene Gelb had gift-wrapped to look like a birthday present.

"What's that?" He meant the package.

"It's the sample I told you about. Me to you. You don't like it, you don't like the deal, you want to pull out—it's yours."

Santos weighed the package in his hands. "All stuff?"

McCann smiled and nodded. The little spic even had the right name for it.

"But is . . . is a *kilo* for crissake." Converted to crystal at five bucks a crack, it was $200,000 easy, maybe more.

"Call it good faith. We want you to know we're *serious*. Like I said, we got a bunch, and we want you to be happy."

"Yeah? Where you get it?" Santos didn't want to get in the middle of no coke war.

McCann's smile became more complete. "That, my friend, is none of your fuckin' business."

But it came to Santos that maybe the powder was from the police property room, one of them big busts he seen on the tube. In one raid out in Queens he'd seen, they grabbed fifteen hundred pounds of shit *and* $20 million in small bills. It was enough money to fill a van. Maybe a guy rank of chief could put his hands on shit like that and nobody know.

Still, he was worried. Sure, they were trying to stick him up. Sure, it happened, and had to him before, every once in a while. But there was something about this deal that was wild. Crazy. And he didn't like.

It began growing on him, though, when he slipped into a toilet stall. Using the straight razor that he kept strapped by a garter to the inside of his left calf, he slit open the kilo package. Because he did no drugs himself and he'd been buying regular now almost since he could remember, Santos didn't need no big test for good dope—weed, speed, heroin, or coke. Crack he would not touch; he made his own. Truth was, he hated coke, which made him jumpy, but he knew when it was good.

Sitting on the toilet in the john of the joint with all them business people upstairs, he wet a finger, touched it to the coke and then to his tongue. It had the taste, the way a hospital smelled, that he looked for. And when he snorted the precise amount with the little gold spoon that was attached to his key ring, Santos said, *"Sí. Ya lo creo."* It was good dope. It had the rush and head that pure powder brought on. His nose, his sinuses, the front of his face behind his eyes, blazed with fuzzy white light, and a kind of warm glow settled into the back of his skull, his head and shoulders. Carefully he resealed the package and wrapped it in his handkerchief, before fitting it in his jacket.

Every time Santos did coke, he could see how people got into it, but for him the downside—how it left you hopeless in no time— was too steep. And how much of his success, he asked his trim, shaped-up self in the mirror, was discipline and not feeling like he needed anybody or anything but himself? All of it, no question, which steeled him for the gauntlet upstairs.

With the steak and the bottle of wine for Martita in one hand and his trench coat and umbrella on the other arm, he turned from the cloakroom just as McCann was saying to the group around him, "Solange wants us to go back to her—get this—pied-à-terre for cocktails. She says the view of the park is fantastic." But the redhead said nothing. Her eyes were on Santos, and they spooked him, all hazel, slanted, and glittering like a poised cat.

He tried to step by the cops, but the big one—Cicciolino— reached out, grabbed his arm, and began walking him toward the door.

"See—what I tell you? Instead of a shit storm on your horizon, you got nothing but a big patch of blue sky."

"This you' deal. You gonna bus' me now?" The way he was dressed and the other cop, Santos could see a big TV bust with cameras and everything.

Guy shook his head. "Like I tol' you the other day, you got a choice—the shitter and fuckin' oblivion on one hand, pure product and no hassles on the other."

They were right at the door and the wall of frosted glass with the clear designs that formed the alcove with the telephone. Santos thought maybe he should phone his lawyer, tell him what was going down so he be in on it step by step. He glanced away at Brant, who was so high in the police he was like a god. "He in on it too?"

"I wouldn't want you to quote me."

Santos looked back at Cicciolino and met his eyes for the first time. "Can I say som'sin'?"

"Why not? It's a free country for those with the jack to pay. You're one of them. Fire away."

Santos regarded Cicciolino—the silk suit, the tie, the pocket thing. He didn't like what he saw. "Sure—jyou' big time. You can rip me off anytime you wan' or put you' foot down an'—" His eyes again flickered over at Brant, who was now deep in conversation with the redhead, although she was looking at them.

"Squash, I think is the word you're looking for. It's what you do to a cockroach."

"—but, jyou know?" Their eyes clashed. "You can get too cocky. If this ain't no big bust, I hope you do. You read me?"

"Like a death threat, *calabozo*."

It took only a few seconds that seemed like an eternity for their eyes to disengage, but both knew an understanding had passed between them.

Santos turned and left, and, when Cicciolino got back to the bar, Brant asked, "You know that guy?"

" 'Course, I'm a cop." He glanced at the woman, who was staring at his lips like she wanted him.

"What is he?" Brant pressed.

"Fuckin' scumbag, is what. Chicken hawk. Heroin pusher. Dope dealer."

"What you say to him?"

"Tol' him, get his fuckin' ass outa here and don't come back. This is my place, and I don't want guys like him around." Thinking of what the future held for him and Santos, Cicciolino decided he should add, "Guy like that—sometimes I almost feel like making him a crusade and busting his ass. Permanently." He glanced at the woman again. She smiled. Jesus—wouldn't he like to drill that? She looked like something out of a fashion magazine with the high-piled deep red hair and those eyes and all that gold. "You get my report?" he asked Brant.

"The one about the East Harlem drug dealer? I skimmed it."

Cicciolino pointed a finger at the door that Eva Burden had just opened, as though she would step in.

Suddenly she stopped, having seen the red-haired woman who, seated on a barstool, was staring at Bill Cicciolino.

Said Brant, amazed, "Him? In here?"

"What I thought too. You know you got trouble when the rats come at you in broad daylight."

"What?—he say something to you?"

Cicciolino cocked his head and smiled down into the woman's smooth-featured, upturned face. "The usual."

"You mean he threatened you?"

"Something like that." Cicciolino wrenched his eyes from hers and said to McCann, "We going sailing with Jay sometime soon?"

"I don't think there's a chance we won't."

"When you think? Thursday?"

McCann smiled and nodded, and Cicciolino turned to Brant, who, he knew, would be busy Thursday. "You up for a little voyage around the island, Commissioner?"

"Thursday?" Brant asked, though his eyes had returned to the woman—her neck and shoulders and the angular rest of her. "Can't. Meetings all day long."

"Some other time then." And to McCann, "We better make sure Jay knows we're on." That gave them only a day, and everything had to be ready. "You know who I think I just saw? Eva Burden."

"Where?" asked McCann, glancing to the door.

"Coming in. But—" Cicciolino swung his head in both directions.

McCann tried the nearer dining room, then asked the hostess if she had seen Eva. She had not.

Stepping toward the stairs to phone Gelb, he heard Chick say, "You a sailor, Solange? That's a nice name. French?" Son of a bitch, he thought, his best friend was trying to snake his date. McCann smiled. What a city. What a world.

"I know little about boats," she replied. "But I couldn't think of anything I'd like to do more than sail around Manhattan with you and Tug and—" She glanced off at the exit door.

Why not, Cicciolino thought. She might make a good blind. And then—hey—weren't the three of them on a roll sharing money *and* women? They'd have to work out a way to get Gelb laid, and not just by his wife, who was presently over in Jersey buying a new commercial van, the kind with no windows.

CHAPTER 22

EVASION

WHEN EVA BURDEN closed the exit door at O'Casey's and stepped back into the alcove, she did not know what to do. There they were at the bar, grouped around the woman—the *sicaria*—having a drink and talking about going sailing from the few words she had overheard, as though nothing had happened in the Islands, as though there would be no retribution. They couldn't know who the woman was, and as certainly Eva had to warn them immediately. But how, without endangering herself?

She realized her heart was suddenly pounding, and she was short of breath. She could confront the woman where she sat, demanding that she explain who she was, what had happened in Nassau, and what it was she wanted.

But what if the woman, sitting there among them in all her elegance, denied it, as she doubtless would? Where was Eva's proof? It would be her word against the woman's, and—she glanced through the clear lettering in the frosted glass—Bill Cicciolino was obviously taken with her. Cicciolino would not tolerate any mention of the Bahamas. And where was Tug? Suddenly he was gone from the barstool where he had been sitting.

The phone. She would use the pay phone in the alcove to call the bar and ask Tug to step out into the street. There she could at least tell him what she knew and what she had seen with her own eyes.

But when she turned around, she was met by the small, dark face of a man who was standing so close behind her that her forehead grazed the visor of his chauffeur's cap. Before she could scream, he clamped one hand over her mouth, another around her waist, and he hurled them at the push bar of the outer door. It burst open, and they tumbled out onto the sidewalk.

There, he scrambled up and, without taking his gloved hand from her mouth, began dragging her toward a limousine. Out of the corner of her eye Eva caught sight of two other Indians, who jumped out of a van that had double-parked and were running toward them. One opened the rear door of the limousine, the other bent for her ankles.

Santos had stepped into the street for a cab. Hearing the heavy door crack against its stop, he turned his head and said to himself, See—no difference downtown. Bitch getting mugged right there with people walking by. Other bitches was screaming, running away with their hands to their mouths. Guys moved forward like they wanted to get involved, but—hey—it was for real. They might get their suits messed up. "Stop!" one guy yelled. "Stop that!"

"Somebody call the police," Santos heard.

"They know each other? She drunk?"

Bitch's skirt was up over her legs, one shoe was off. Her purse was down on the sidewalk, everything in it scattered over the pavement. Out of habit Santos's eyes scanned for green.

The dark guy in the chauffeur's uniform pulled his hand away from her mouth, like he got bit, and the bitch—small, young-looking, blond—Santos's meat exactly—swung at his head and shouted, "Help! Somebody help me! They'll kill me!" Her fist caught him square on the nose.

He dropped her rough, and he was fast. With the same hand she had bit he smacked her once hard then backhand, knocking her head into the concrete. She went out. Her head dropped to the side, her body went limp.

Traffic had stopped for a red light, and Santos headed for a cab. When he reached for the door, some big guy nearly knocked him down rushing out. Santos jumped in. "First Avenue. Uptown. I tell you when to sop."

"Occupied," said the cabbie, bending to look out the passenger window at O'Casey's.

"Bu'shit! Nobody here!" It was hard to get cabs to take you above 110th Street, and you had to do, say, pay anything you could, specially with a kilo of blow in your pocket.

"My fare—" The cabbie pointed at the big guy.

"Fuck him. Wha' he owe you, I pay. Le's get oudahere."

"Three hundred bucks."

"Wha'? I look like a Jap? I'm takin' you' name, reportin' you downtown."

But the cabbie did not move, and Santos turned his head to see the big guy, who was sprinting and must've played ball, lay a block on the Indian in the white jumpsuit. He was bending for the bitch's ankles and got popped right off his feet. Spinning in the air, he tried to roll himself into a tuck. No luck. He came down hard, leaving a foot of face on the concrete.

The big guy pivoted, and with both hands thumped the chauffeur's chest so hard his head bounced hollow off the brick of the building. He melted down the wall.

"Hear that?" the cabbie said. "Sickening." He shook his head and smiled.

Nathanson rolled once and was back up on his feet in time to see the third Indian coming at him. He ducked a punch, then stuck him low, raising his body up on fist. As if shaking off slime, he dumped him in the gutter.

The first Indian, whose face was now blood, was on his hands and knees, reaching into his jumpsuit for something. Nathanson spun around, snapped a leg, and fed him brown shoe.

"There's lunch!" cried the cabbie.

Quickly Nathanson gathered up Eva's things, making sure he got all her cards and every scrap of paper. He boosted her up on his shoulder and carried her toward the taxi.

"Where you think they're from anyways, them assholes?" the cabbie asked Santos. "You ever see guys like that before? Cambodia? Nah—Cambodians ain't that blocky."

Santos did not answer; he was out the door and across the street. Fuck if he'd get involved. He had a steak, a bottle of red, and a package to get home safe, which might take some doing.

And maybe some business to take care of, once he thought about it good. The details.

Said the cabbie to Nathanson, "Man—where'd you learn that? Me, I woulda busted my foot." He goosed the cab to the corner of Madison, braked to a roll, then ran the red into the next block.

Nathanson eased Eva's head against the seat. He raised one of her eyelids to see if her pupils were dilated. She pushed his hand away and tried to clear her throat. There was blood flowing from the corner of her mouth, but except for the pain in her head she felt all right.

Eva opened her eyes, and the look of concern and—was it?— devotion on Nathanson's face both surprised and intrigued her. Not for years, not since she had first met her husband, had any man looked on her with such . . . subjection, and she was tempted to close her eyes so she could see it again. She knew something had passed between them down in Nassau, but she hadn't realized he had felt it too, and that it had been anything more than a momentary attraction. It made her smile, which hurt her lip.

"So, you're all right?"

"Except for my head."

"Those little bastards," Nathanson said under his breath. And then to the cabbie, "Swing back to O'Casey's and park."

"You gonna take another shot at them?"

They would not think he'd come back at them so soon. The chauffeur was the older Indian, the one who in Nassau had seemed like the redhead's right-hand man. Nassau. Just the thought of it—the flames, Creach, how he just sat there while they burned him out—made Nathanson's nostrils flare.

"Brian—she was in there at the bar, drinking with them."

"The *sicaria*? With—?"

"Tug and Bill."

"The guys from *Whistler*? The ones who ripped off my money and the dope?"

Eva glanced at the cabbie, whose eyes could be seen in the rear-view mirror. "Don't mind me. You got business, talk business. I can't remember my own name sometimes." He was a sallow, older man, whose hair had been imperfectly cut. He needed a shave.

With a handkerchief Nathanson dabbed at the corner of her mouth. She winced and extracted a flake of tooth enamel from her lower lip, which was puffy. She shook her head. "Damn, I've never even had a cavity." She glanced at him, and there was the look again, which curiously made her feel almost powerful. In all that chaos, destruction, and loss she had made a connection; somebody *cared* about her. Life was bizarre.

She looked into his pale green eyes. Her hand moved to his face. "Where's your . . . ?" He had shaved his Vandyke. "And your hair." In spite of which, she decided, he was a big, good-*looking* man.

"Tug and Bill. They were in there with her?" he pressed.

Eva nodded. "I thought I'd just come back here, collect my things, and go back home to California *before* anything could happen. I have my business, but—" She could lay that off either temporarily or permanently on Kitty. Failing that, she could just close the door and turn the key. She had no debts.

"I also thought I should at least tell the others what I know. That way, my conscience would be clear. I phoned Tug's office, but his secretary said he was at O'Casey's. I thought I'd just pop in, warn him there with other people around, say my good-bye, and leave. But there she was with them, like they were all in it together."

They were now, thought Nathanson. And as good as dead. The woman would discover what they had and where and take them out one at a time, which was probably what they deserved. Nathanson's own anger was still high, and his objective now was not much different from the *sicaria*'s, except for punishment, which never did any good. Who was he to play God? Or some *narcotrafficante* in Colombia, for that matter.

"How much was left in the cartons when they found the plane and the boat that morning? In the cove."

They were on Forty-first again. The cabbie pulled into a hydrant space and stopped. The limo was gone.

"I don't know. Cartons and cartons. I didn't want to look. Something sort of like this happened to me before, and I only wanted out." She glanced down at the chip of tooth that was still on her finger, and she tried to laugh before flicking it off onto the floor. "I should be so lucky." Only to have chipped a tooth, Nathanson assumed she meant.

"The money?"

"There was lots of it. A whole big suitcase. Bill"—she glanced at the cabbie and did not say Cicciolino's last name, which she knew was well-known in New York—"mentioned something about millions, I remember him shouting at me that my cut would be four hundred thousand."

"And you refused?"

Her eyes swung to his.

"Anybody else not go for it?"

"Gerri, I think. Bill's wife. But I can't imagine that Tug and Jay knew what they were getting into. Or Jay's wife, Arlene. I mean, I think they think it's like a big . . . game or something. A commodity venture. A gamble."

It was, the very biggest. Didn't Nathanson himself know personally? He could feel that he had torn the stitches in the wound in his side, which had begun to bleed again.

"I didn't say more in Nassau, because I didn't know who you were." Or are, her eyes added.

He looked away. It was as if they were onstage. The cabbie's face was riveted in the mirror, following every word. Only in New York, Nathanson thought. "Look—this isn't the time or place." He wasn't much for declarations, and he had something to do immediately. But he turned to her, offered his hand, and their eyes met. "Let's leave it that I want nothing to happen to you, and I'll make sure it won't."

The cabbie nodded, critiquing the line.

"How?"

The cabbie raised an eyebrow, as though to say, Ain't that just like a woman?

Nathanson opened the door. "Right now by seeing if I can talk to them."

Her hand reached for his arm. "But how will that help?"

Nathanson hunched a shoulder. He just wanted to eyeball the bastards, let them know he was out there and they owed him $2.4 million for starters. It would put a different spin on whatever deal they were developing to unload the dope.

And then the woman—he wanted to let her know that he didn't care what she called herself or purported to be or where she was from. She *herself* was responsible for her actions, and he held both Londoño *and* her accountable for the deaths of Jared and Deke, the burning of his house, the theft of his possessions.

But he said, "Wasn't that what you wanted me to do in Nassau?"

It was, but that was before she knew what they were really like. "But you're not just going to walk in there?"

"Why not? It's a public place. I don't think she'll risk her setup with them, however she managed it."

Eva didn't know, but then, of course, she did: Tug.

"Need any help?" the cabbie asked.

"I don't think so. Just keep the doors locked and the engine running." Nathanson had a rolling, big-shouldered gait, and kept both hands plunged deep in the pockets of his overcoat.

But, like the limo, they were gone.

"Just missed them," said the bartender.

"They say where they were going? It's important to get in touch with them."

"Her place, wasn't it, George? Her pied-à-terre, she called it."

The man named George drew on his cigar and regarded Nathanson.

"But where?" Nathanson pulled out a notebook and a pen. "I need a number or an address. It's vital."

"You a broker?" George asked.

Nathanson decided to nod. "Most often without the R."

"Then you're S.O.L., pal. He's got her all wrapped up."

"The redhead."

George nodded.

"But—wrapped up where?"

Said Tony in an aside to Nathanson, "Be there himself, if he knew."

And lucky he didn't.

Back out in the cab, Nathanson turned to Eva. "You said you have a business here in town?"

Eva nodded. "A little restaurant in Soho. Dinners."

"And I suppose there's *evidence* of that in your apartment?"

Eva thought for a moment and nodded.

"You check in there yet?"

She shook her head. "We're closed on Mondays, Tuesdays we only open for dinner. My plan was to go down there now."

"Not even a call?"

"No. Why?"

"Anybody be there now?"

"Kitty, my chef. She comes in early Tuesdays for deliveries and to do the prep work."

Nathanson sighed and looked away. "Maybe we ought to give it a look."

Thermidor was on Spring Street, one block north and five blocks east of Eva's apartment. Nathanson had the cabbie drive by and park a few doors away.

"How's it look to you?"

It was a storefront location with a sign in the form of a red three-dimensional lobster. The logo was repeated on silver drapes, which had been drawn across the windows. A shade on the door window said, THERMIDOR, in stenciled silver letters. DINNERS BY RESERVATION ONLY, TUESDAY THROUGH SUNDAY.

"Usually there's a Closed sign on the door, but otherwise—"

"How do I get in?"

Eva had her keys out. "We'll go in the front, of course."

Nathanson reached for them. "Why don't I check it out first?" When she didn't release the keys, he pulled them from her. "You've got a good right cross, but even the smallest of those guys has you by seventy pounds, a *penilla*, and probably a Mac-10."

"Be careful," she called after him.

The cabbie rolled down his window. "Hey, buddy—c'mere." When Nathanson got close, he motioned him to come closer still. "You packin' a piece?"

Nathanson shook his head.

"You want one?"

Nathanson searched the man's murky brown eyes. He was serious. "Not a bad idea."

The cabbie pulled back the newspaper in his lap and showed Nathanson a large-caliber automatic with a checkered walnut grip.

"How long you have that there?"

"From the moment I saw the first gook grab blond and beautiful. I could've cut off the limo with the cab. The rest would've been easy. If you do somebody in there"—he tilted his head at Thermidor—"wipe it and drop it. It's anonymous, if you know what I mean." He winked.

Fully loaded, a Colt Government Model weighed nearly three pounds and was a virtual pocket cannon that could blow through walls. Stuffed in the inner pocket of Nathanson's overcoat, its bulk was comforting.

Nathanson inserted the key in the lock, but the door was open. Stepping in, he left it slightly ajar and looked around.

The interior of the restaurant was also mainly silver: chevrons on the walls that were repeated in a dropped ceiling with indirect lighting, which was on. The tables and chairs were designer items with simple but futuristic lines that looked a bit Italian to Nathanson. Like the bar with its molded marble top and four tall, lightning-bolt seats. The cash drawer of a silver register was open and—Nathanson leaned across the bar to look in—empty.

Cooking smells were coming from the kitchen. With a hand between the lapels of his overcoat, he moved toward the open, swinging door. A large stock pot on the twelve-burner range had boiled down to a shallow ring of vegetables at the bottom. Nathanson turned off the gas and looked around. On a prep table in the center of the room were three piles of onions, carrots, and celery cut into julienne strips. A blue-steel chef's knife was nearby.

Somebody had also begun shucking a bushel of oysters that were immersed in running water in the well of a sink. Five had been opened and placed on a bed of ice. Cartons, which obviously had just been delivered, had been stacked inside the back door. Otherwise the kitchen was spotless, and everything seemed to be in its place.

Nathanson moved past the cartons and opened the door, which was also unlocked. He stepped into a dark, narrow alley and looked both ways. Nothing, and nobody above on the fire escapes. Back in the kitchen he found Eva standing in the open door to the dining room. "You find the register like that?" she asked. "The drawer open?"

He nodded. "Like the doors, front and back."

"The register should have a bank. You know, to pay the purveyors."

"How much?"

"A thousand dollars, minimum. We get most of our dry goods and liquor today."

"Could she—"

"Kitty," Eva supplied.

"—be in the head?"

Eva shook her head. "When I saw the open till, I checked."

"Maybe she stepped out. Some emergency."

"Not Kitty. Not without locking the place up. She's careful and competent." Eva turned and looked back out into the dining room at the open cash register, then returned her gaze to the kitchen: the julienned vegetables, the oysters, the deliveries. "What's that smell?"

"Stock pot. It had nearly burned down. I turned it off."

"Did the veg scorch?"

Nathanson moved toward the stove and peered into the pot again. "I don't think so. There's three or four inches of liquid in the bottom."

"Well, something did. Or is. But it smells like rubber or leather."

Funny, Nathanson thought. He only now became aware that he'd been smelling it as well. Veal, maybe. But rubber and leather too.

Eva stepped fully into the kitchen and began making her way toward the stove. Passing the pizza ovens, she felt heat on the side of her face, and she stopped. The wall oven had been there when she first leased the restaurant four years earlier. The unit was some old design, imported from Italy, that had neither a thermostat nor settings on its gas cock. You just turned it on and lit the jets. Once Eva and Kitty had learned its eccentricities, the oven had proved perfect for breads, pies, and cakes, and the occasional large roast.

But it was too early in the day for bread. Also, the smell wasn't sweet like from a confection. And finally they only served roasts on weekends.

Eva turned and reached for the silver bar of the oven door.

"Don't!" said Nathanson, now understanding what must have happened.

But Eva pried down the bar and tugged open the sliding rack of the oven before he could reach her. She looked down, not at first realizing what she was seeing.

It was a steaming, smoldering mass that had once been dressed in kitchen whites. Now the material, which was partially synthetic, had formed itself, like gooey icing, around the body of the woman on the rack. Her hair had been singed into a mass of wispy char, and the skin of her face crisped to a deep, abiding brown.

The red frames of her glasses, which also had plastic lenses, had melted and pooled in her eyes. Her mouth was open, her teeth exposed, and a jet of steam was venting from her throat. Having split in the heat, her kitchen work shoes were smoldering. Through the white leather, her toes protruded like black, shiny knobs.

"Kitty!" Eva screamed and dropped to her knees, her hands pressed against her eyes. "Not *Kitty*! Why?"

Nathanson looked down at the name on the apron. It said *Eva* in embroidered red letters. Reaching down, he bundled Eva in his arms and carried her out to the taxi. He tried to imagine what she was feeling, but he knew he couldn't. He did know that the killing had to stop, but how?

Hours later, when she had regained her composure, Eva tried to phone Tug at his office and home. He was not at either place, although he had called his secretary to say he would try to contact Eva later.

Nor was Arlene Gelb in her gallery, which her voice on a phone message said would be closed for the rest of the week. That left only the Cicciolinos. His office at One Police Plaza said he was out for the rest of the week.

Why? Nathanson wrote on his notepad.

They were in a suite of rooms that Nathanson had taken at the Doral on Park Avenue, only a few streets from O'Casey's. He had convinced Eva that, because of Cicciolino, any police involvement might tie them up permanently. "Kitty's dead, and nothing's going to change that. Let's think of the living."

"May I ask why?" Eva said. "I'm a personal friend. I hope there's nothing wrong."

"I wouldn't know, ma'am. Personal leave. But the chief's policy is to return all calls. If you give me your number, I'm sure he'll get back to you."

Eva did, though she had little hope that he would.

His wife, Gerri, was still in her office at UNION, the women's rights advocacy group that she had helped found and now directed. After a short wait, she picked up. Eva heard her ask her secretary to close the door, and then, "Yes, Eva?" Her tone was distant.

"I'm trying to get in touch with your husband." Eva paused. "About the matter in the Islands."

"I have no time for that. That's his concern, not mine. I'm sorry, but I'll have to hang up now."

"Wait," Eva nearly shouted, and felt pain in her swollen lip and the back of her head. She wasn't doing this just for herself anymore, she was doing it for Kitty and Jared and Deke. And for the others who had died on the planes and the boat and who would be taken down by the dope. "It's no concern of mine either, if you'll remember. I'm only calling you because I haven't been able to reach him at work, and he's in great danger." She waited. "Are you there?"

"I'm still here."

Eva thought she heard the woman drinking from a glass. She then explained how she had gotten off the cay, what had happened in Nassau, and that she had tried to contact Tug but had discovered him and Bill in O'Casey's "with the woman. The *sicaria*. This afternoon her . . . retainers murdered my chef."

Eva waited, but when nothing—not even surprise or disbelief—was expressed, she asked, "Gerri? Are you there?"

"I'm here." Her voice sounded tired and suddenly very old.

"I've tried to get in touch with the Gelbs," Eva went on, "but only a machine answers in the gallery. Would you have their number?" Eva waited, but when there was still no response, she added, "I think they should at least be warned, don't you?"

In her office Gerri Cicciolino reached for the glass of clear, colorless liquid that she had poured when her secretary had told her Eva Burden was on the line; in spite of her cool tone to Eva she had been worrying about her constantly from the moment Eva had jumped overboard. Bill had even shown her the telegram, but she had not believed any part of what he had said since the day in the cove.

Guilt was the cause of her anxiety, Gerri had deduced during the vodka-laced, sleepless nights that had followed their return. And envy. Like Eva, she should have been so sure of her stand against theft and drugs and greed and violent death that she could have stood shoulder to shoulder with her. Together they could have prevented the deaths of those men in the plane, of Monroe and some others, and perhaps now with what Eva had just told her, the deaths of all who had touched or had been touched by the corruption they had discovered that morning on the uninhabited island.

And the countless others, she now thought, who would consume the hundreds of thousands of vials of crack that over a thousand pounds of cocaine would produce. One night when Bill, who only came home to change his clothes and use the phone now, was gone, she had tried to compute just how much it would be. But she knew little more than what she had read about how it was manufactured, and she failed.

The next night she found herself in the car, somewhere up in the South Bronx in the Forty-fourth Precinct, which had been Bill's first precinct command given him by an Irish police commissioner who hated guineas and hoped he would fail. Gerri had thought that she would find a "spot," as they were called, where crack was being sold, and she'd call the seller over to her window and ask—pay—him for the information of how *exactly* crack was made from how much cocaine. But when she got his attention and he sauntered over, his hand in a jacket pocket like on a gun, he took one look at the fifty-dollar bill, dropped two sticklike objects in the front seat, and snatched the bill from her.

He then mumbled something like, "So, Mama, you messin' with Mr. Scotty now? You' the boss lady, but I tell you straight up—Scotty he a *mean* lovah. He treat you bad." It took Gerri days, playing his statement over in her mind while she sat in dark rooms, to figure out what the man had said and somewhat longer to understand what he meant. But when she got the two clips of five vials each home, she realized it was what she had wanted all along. She had taken them into the back bedroom, which was never used anymore except when Karen, their retarded daughter who was presently away at "school," was home, which wasn't very often. Bill didn't like having her around now that she was grown. And there Gerri experienced why it was called what it was.

The cracking of the burning crystal had begun almost from the moment she touched the lighter to the square of aluminum foil with which she had lined the pipe, one of Bill's father's that he kept as a memento on the desk in his den. Gerri had seen the aluminum foil and learned how it was perforated on the bottom in one of the "helpful" TV exposés on crack that were now standard fare in the media. Gerri smoked cigarettes. It was a habit that she had never been able to quell, and she inhaled deeply of the acid-tasting, rancid, heady fumes that rumbled into her body, as though her lungs were meant for nothing else. It then seared her brain with an

exquisite, deathly, blinding, euphoric rush that she thought at first
was going to be sexual—she was coming, she could feel Scotty
between her legs. . . . *Than like which*, she kept saying to herself
over and over. *Than like which* she had never felt and would not
again feel, she suspected, no matter how many times she tried. And
she did.

It was rough and brutal but also so totally, *systemically* plea-
surable it left her terrified. She had not believed what she had read
about crack, had thought the talk of brain transformation hyperbole. But in one brief period—how long? She glanced at her watch;
seven minutes—everything had changed for her. Radically. And
she knew what she must do with Mr. Scotty's aid, if he'd let her.

That was Monday. She had been with the man only two days
now, and she would need his awful strength often before Thursday, which she had overheard Bill say was The Day. *"Der Tag,"*
the party on the other end—obviously Jay—had suggested.

"Der what?" Bill had asked. "Spell that. Oh, yeah. *Tag.* As in
Whiskey, Whiskey One." Then, "What's your number there?" He
had listened and jotted down a number. "When's the cellular
phone getting installed in *Trekker?"* Another pause. "You sure?
It's essential to contact Arlene. It can't go down without coordi-
nation."

Go down, she had thought. Arlene. Gerri had an idea about
that too.

The phone number, she learned when she dialed it later, was
for a pay phone at the City Island Marina, and she now debated
whether she should tell Eva Burden the little she knew. Maybe they
were all better off dead. "Why?" she now asked her. "What can
you do to stop them?"

"Well—nothing, I suppose, except to warn them. I mean, to
convince them."

Of the error of their ways? She sounded like some sort of
Chautauquan. The wages of greed, Gerri feared, were far too
compelling for mere argument. As were the demands of Mr. Scotty.

She took a long drink from the glass. It contained straight
one-hundred-proof vodka, which had become a necessary refuge—
from the tyrant Scotty and his special pleasure—even now at work.
"All I know is Jay Gelb—I think it's Jay Gelb—is somewhere at the
City Island Marina, probably on a boat. A big boat, big enough to
have sailed here from the Islands. At least I know for sure he

arrived here on a boat—" When was the night Bill stayed at home waiting, she now realized, for a phone call from Gelb? She couldn't remember. "Last week sometime.

"Eva—you were right," she said, and hung up.

Said Nathanson, after Eva related what Gerri had said, "Well—I guess we've got two choices. To go back to your apartment and wait for McCann to phone you. Or to go out to City Island and try to find Gelb." Nathanson knew what he wanted to do: go for the boat. But it would soon be dark, and the City Island Marina was large. Would they have registered the boat under any of their names? He didn't think so.

Also, his side had begun to ache and needed attention.

"My apartment? Didn't you say they had followed me from there?" There was fear and anger in her eyes.

"I don't think they'll go back there, not now that they've located McCann and Cicciolino. Then, of course, they now think you're dead."

Eva lowered her eyes. She would never get over Kitty's death—what they had done to her, the way it had happened. *Ever.*

Another idea occurred to Nathanson. "You know, if I were the *sicaria*, I'd wait for the deal to go down. That way, she might come away with a hat trick." He pried back one finger. "The original money, which she could extort from them." Another, "The money from the new deal." And a third, "Possibly the dope too."

Nathanson felt the pocket of his shirt to make sure he had the photograph that Ochoa had sent him. He stood. "Come on. We'll stop by a pharmacy and get some things. I'll let you play nurse with me again."

Eva's hurt eyes widened. "What do you mean?"

Nathanson opened his coat and showed her the bright red patch on his white shirt. She looked relieved.

CHAPTER 23

CITYSCAPES

♦

THE VIEW FROM Solange de los Páramos's pied-á-terre was indeed spectacular. A penthouse on Fifth Avenue in the mid-eighties, it looked through tall atrium windows over Central Park.

At cocktail hour the balcony also caught the rays of the westering sun and allowed Cicciolino, McCann, and First Deputy Assistant Bob Brant to join their hostess in an arrangement of fanback wicker furniture with soft floral-pattern cushions.

Her staff served them fruity cocktails, which she insisted they drink. The concoction was delicious and hit Brant hard. Suddenly he could not relax what he knew was the silly smile on his face. Gazing over at Solange, he gave up trying.

With her golden color, her exotic racial background, her sophistication, and the ease with which she comported herself, she was so meant for him (and certainly not any of the others) that Brant believed he would willingly die for her. He had not felt that way in years.

Nor had Bill Cicciolino. After Solange excused herself "to freshen up," he pulled himself out of the low chair and moved over to the parapet. "I gotta get the recipe for this drink. If they make 'em everywhere like this, it's gonna become my beverage of choice because, shit, if I could feel, I'd tell you I feel good." He turned to the others, and there it was—the same stupid smile Brant and McCann had.

"This is some *peter tare*, ain't it?" Cicciolino went on, meaning the apartment.

Brant started laughing, but Cicciolino ignored him.

"She *own* this place, Tug? Or is it, you know, her company's?"

McCann was suddenly whacked. He could not actually bring himself to answer. He waved a hand to indicate the latter, or so he thought. He jerked back in the seat, trying to sit up, and managed to croak. "Beats—beats a hotel. Think about it"—he turned his face to Brant and knew his light blue eyes must look like marbles—"you shell out all sorts of jack for rooms, hospitality suites, the works, and where's it go? Up in smoke. Sure, you get the write-off, but . . ."

It was as if, now that he was speaking, McCann couldn't actually stop. He went on and on, until—thank God—Cicciolino interrupted. "How often she use it?"

"Use what?"

"I dunno. Whadawe talkin' about here? The place. The pad. Her digs here." Cicciolino was staring down into the glass, as though trying to see through the ice to the bottom.

" 'Course, I asked her how often she gets to New York, since it couldn't be often enough for me. She said not a whole bunch, so I guess maybe the place is used by—"

"Argentinians?" Cicciolino asked.

McCann nodded.

"How long she been here this time?" Cicciolino was catching a little breeze, there at the edge of the parapet, and it helped clear his head.

"Week, I guess."

Cicciolino turned his head and looked down over the parapet. Man, it was about a twelve-floor free-fall to the concrete below. The limo was still parked, like a Mercedes ad, in front of the marquee. There was a white van behind it that Cicciolino now remembered he'd seen following them from O'Casey's. He'd taken the jump seat so he could face her and make sure she saw him checking out her long brown, definitely dickable legs.

"Who're these mutts she got working for her? Where they from?" "Mutts" was a cop term and meant any shady character, black, white, or in this case, red.

McCann shook his head. "Beats me. Ugly fuckers, 's all I know."

"Andeans," Brant put in, so there wouldn't be any embarrassing racial allusions.

"That like Peru?"

"Or Bolivia. Chile." Brant didn't actually want another sip, but he couldn't seem to put the glass down. He'd drunk only half.

"Colombia?"

Brant nodded and was about to say that three great prongs of the Andes ran through Colombia, which he had visited back in '86 as part of an antidrug fact-finding mission, when Solange returned. "Well, *messieurs*—who would like another cocktail?"

She was wearing a dark sequin evening dress of the type that looked black at one moment, prismatic at the next, and was now patched with bursts of brilliant sun as the little mirrors flexed over her body. "It's such a lovely night—let me take you to dinner. Or, better yet, I can ask Maluko to set up a table here. Papel Porteños keeps a catering service on call. I've used them before, and they're excellent."

"I tell you what," she continued. "Why don't you phone up your friend who accompanied you on your holiday, Tug, and we can have a return-from-Nassau party."

"You mean Jay Gelb?"

"Is that his name?" she asked. "Why not? And your wives, if you'd like."

McCann traded a glance with Cicciolino. "Gee—that sounds like fun, Solange, the dinner part. But I'm afraid Jay is out of town at the moment. Something to do with work."

Brant watched her turn and glance into the apartment, where her chauffeur was standing in the shadows awaiting her orders.

"The university. Right over there." McCann pointed to the northwest corner of the park, and she followed his arm to the cluster of buildings that was the university.

"Also, as you know, I'm no longer married. Nor is Brant. And Bill's real ethnic in regard to women. He tries never to be seen in public with his wife, who is my sister."

Said Brant, "With a campaign manager like Tug, Bill'll never make mayor."

Everybody laughed but Cicciolino, who had crashed. Heavy

booze always made him nasty and paranoid, and something was bothering him. He didn't know what.

Like magic, a meal soon appeared and was far more complex and interesting than anything O'Casey's served, but only Brant ate much. Tug dived into the wine, which kept changing with each course and was excellent. He felt like a flagging long-distance swimmer who could not quite catch hold of the buoy of the food that was being set before him. He wanted to eat, he knew he should, but he did so much talking and drinking that the courses just kept appearing on and vanishing from his plate.

Cicciolino, on the other hand, ate, but not with any relish. He kept thinking that something was wrong, and he was preoccupied with thoughts of Gelb. Gelb was supposedly outfitting *Trekker* for the sail on Thursday and "any contingency," in Gelb's words, including the need to split from New York permanently. Then there was Arlene, who had to get the new van down to the Hoboken docks and spend the night aboard the Bayliner, as some one of them had since it had arrived. Tomorrow, all of them would have to hustle butt to make sure everything was ready for Thursday, which was only two days away.

But maybe the problem was right here. Cicciolino had like a sixth sense about some things, and he'd heard stories about the drug barons. With their beau-coup bucks, they could afford just about anything. *Beau-coup* was a Vietnam-era word that occurred to Cicciolino, looking at the French broad with the Spanish-sounding last name.

His eyes shifted to the stemware on the table, the china, the silver, then to the butler or chauffeur or whatever he was. The fuck had cold, dead eyes—killer eyes if he'd ever seen them—and Cicciolino decided to make a tour of the place.

Excusing himself, he made for the little sallow bastard and asked where the toilet was. The guy didn't just point but walked him down a long hall to the john, opened the door, flicked on the light, and closed it after Cicciolino stepped in.

Maybe that was courtesy in Paris or Argentina, but Cicciolino's paranoia was now stratospheric. He took a piss, flushed, and opened the door to find the guy still there. "Whoops—forgot to wash my hands." He showed them to the butler, closed the door again, turned on a tap, and waited for fucking ever until he heard the broad ring the little bell on the table. He counted to ten, then switched off the light and stepped out.

In the first room he came to, he found nothing. There was expensive period furniture and an Oriental rug, but the place didn't look, feel, or even smell lived in, which was probably because it was used like a hotel. The second door was obviously her room, with all her clothes in the closet and her perfume hard-on heavy in the air.

It was in the third room that Cicciolino thought he found what he was after. He opened the door, switched on the light, and discovered an Indian in a white jumpsuit sitting in the middle of the floor with like an Uzi in his lap. His face—one whole side—was a big scab haloed by bruise. His lips were puffed open, and Cicciolino could see he had lost teeth. "What happened to you?" The Indian's stare was a couple thousand miles long.

"May I help you, Bill?" It was the woman behind him.

"Got lost," Cicciolino said. "Who's that?"

"One of our retainers. He provides company security."

Not too effectively, Cicciolino thought. Whoever laid that trip on his face hadn't lost. "What happened to him?"

"While we were in O'Casey's, somebody tried to enter my car."

Cicciolino's eyes swung to her. "Call the police?" One thing being a cop had taught him was when somebody was lying.

"There was no point. The man fled."

"What he look like?"

"Tall, well-dressed, well-built. Brown fedora, dark overcoat." She wasn't lying about that.

"Where this guy get the pop gun?" He meant the Indian.

"Papel Porteños. Our executives have been kidnapped several times. Armed security is far cheaper than ransom."

Cicciolino thought of mentioning that automatic weapons were illegal, but fuck it, he wasn't going to be a cop much longer. He smiled, "What—no faith in the police?"

"On the contrary, I'm sure you're good at what you do. Perhaps we might get together sometime soon and you can explain in detail what exactly that is." Her smile worked even better than her perfume. Following her sure, graceful steps and the flex of the sequins over her hips, Cicciolino forgot all about the strange apartment and the little beat-up Indian with the machine pistol.

Also, the phone was ringing, and already Tug was on his feet.

"That's probably for me, Solange. I took the liberty of giving a client your phone number so he could reach me here tonight."

"But how did you know my number? You've never been here before."

McCann raised a fist and opened the fingers. In his palm was a beeper.

"Really! May I see it?"

McCann paused, glancing at Cicciolino, but he had no choice, and his hand came forward.

"You mean you can be someplace and punch in a number, and some other device like this will pick it up?"

"Well, the signal is sent to the paging service, then to the other party. It's called a Supah-Beepah, guy from Boston dreamed it up." McCann winked, but her eyes were on his lips.

"What's this button?"

"That's a memory function. It stores your ten most frequent contacts. Say I wanted Bill to phone me. I'd hit number one, then punch in the number of the phone I wanted him to call. If he had a beeper like this," which he does, McCann did not add, "the number would appear on his display. Then he'd call me."

"Marvelous! You Americans are wizards! And who are your *contacts*, Mr. McCann?" she said seductively, treating him to her deep green eyes.

"All business. Until you walked into my life, I was contemplating a religious vocation."

She laughed and turned, as though she would sit and admire the device.

McCann had to take it from her hands. "I should take the phone." He slid the beeper into a jacket pocket and moved toward the butler, who handed him the phone and left the balcony.

"This you?" Santos asked.

"I don't know who else it would be."

There was a pause, and then, "Jyou fuckin' there, or what?"

"Yes, Chino. It is I."

"We on?"

"Thursday."

"How it go down?"

"Haven't we discussed that?"

"Tell me again."

McCann debated going through it one more time, but the

background noise from the city and the street below was considerable. He doubted he'd be overheard.

"Like I told you this afternoon, first we'll pick you up and take you to where it is. You contact your people from there, have them check it out. If it's okay, you can even have them take it away. Then you tell us the location of your part. We send our guys around to pick it up. If it's all there and if everything goes well, they call us, and you go on your merry way."

"You mean, if it tests okay, my guys leave with it?"

"That's right, but not you. Any screw-ups in the payment, you'll never get to sell a nickel's worth of what you stole." More to the point, you'll never get away alive, McCann thought. "Are we agreed?"

There was a pause, and then, "*Sí*."

"I didn't hear you."

"Yeah, yeah. I said *yeah*."

"Your part should be in denominations that're easy to deal with. To demonstrate our continuing good faith, we intend to supply you with a van so your guys can take our part away."

"Who gets the keys?" Santos had done van deals before where things screwed up at key time.

"That's up to you. You like the stuff, you call that shot."

It made Santos feel a little better. He might have Justino check out the product, but he'd be fucked if anybody but him drove all that dope away.

"What about our part?" McCann said, meaning the money.

"Two nice boxes. Five each. I got it here."

"You're saying ten." The deal was for $12.5.

"Man, tha's all I got. Thousand-dollar bills—all used, all different—you can take to a bank."

"*Hector*—I thought we were *agreed*?"

What was this *agreed* shit? Santos wondered. Guy was too used to business downtown. Agreed was what you got in your hand when you got out clean. "Tha's it. High as I can go. I'm tapped out, can't go no more. You' asshole frien' with the heat cos' me money, man. If you non like, I fuckin' disappear, you get fuckin' nothin'."

"It's your choice, but don't plan on taking anything with you. Your ass-ets are covered."

"Wha' *you* think."

McCann waited, then altered his tone. "Hector—it's got to be at least eleven. If it's not eleven, I won't be able to sell it to you know who." He winked at Cicciolino, who was engaged in conversation with Brant and Solange but kept looking his way.

"Gotta hang up now," said Santos. "It's fuckin' ten fuckin' million bucks, you greedy pricks. Take it or leave it." But Santos did not hang up.

With his right hand McCann flashed ten at Cicciolino, who smirked and looked away. It was still $4 million more than they would have got had they not squeezed Santos and sold it on the street. He glanced at McCann and nodded.

"You know Seventy-ninth Street, the Baptist church there?"

"East or West?" Seventy-ninth Street, he meant.

"West."

Santos didn't know West Seventy-ninth too good.

"There's a phone booth across the street from it. Be there at ten sharp Thursday. I'll ring twice, hang up, and then call right back."

"I have my guys wi' me or what?"

"That's up to you. But when you meet us, be alone. We'll pick you up, tell you where our end is, and let you phone your guys to tell them where."

The plan was for Gelb to have *Trekker* in the Hudson River, standing off the Seventy-ninth Street Boat Basin, which was four blocks from the Baptist church. Once McCann and Santos got aboard, they would sail leisurely down to Piers 62 and 63, where the van with the dope would be parked. Santos would call his wombats and tell them where it was so they could check it out. When they called back, saying it was all there, Santos would reveal where the money was. Arlene Gelb, in her anonymous old Volvo station wagon, would pick it up. Her phone call to *Trekker* would release Santos, who from there would be on his own. "What about the keys?"

"What about them?"

"Who gets 'em and when?"

McCann paused. Santos was fixated on the keys, but there was no reason not to make him happy. Cicciolino would be watching the gate to the piers. "We can put them in the truck. We can *hide* them in the truck and tell only you. Or, when the time comes, we can give them to you."

"Yeah, you give them to *me*."

There it was, McCann thought—Santos didn't trust his guys.

"This truck, is it old or new?"

"Brand, spanking new."

"With a column lock?"

"I don't think they make 'em any other way anymore."

There was yet another pause. "This ain' no setup?"

"You take some time and think about it, Chino—how *could* it be?"

Again Santos pondered what had been said. "Ten o'clock then. This Bap'ist church—what it look like?"

"You can't miss it. It's the only Baptist church on Seventy-ninth Street."

Santos hung up.

McCann depressed the plunger and punched in the Gelbs' number. When the tone sounded on Arlene's answering machine, he said, "Know that little cruise Jay and I were threatening to take? All details in place for Thursday. We'll call you sometime after ten."

He rang off and said to the table, "Sorry—one more call and I'll be right with you."

Solange, seeing the others turn to him, waved, and McCann dialed Eva Burden's number.

With a large paper bag filled with Chinese takeout and a bottle of wine, Brian Nathanson and Eva Burden had returned to her empty apartment several hours earlier.

In the toilet, where a light wouldn't be seen, they closed the door and attended to the wound in Nathanson's side. Two stitches had ripped in his scuffle with the *sicaria*'s retainers. " 'Course I can't tell what might have happened with the internal stitches, but you'd be hurting if they'd popped." Eva's hands were still a little shaky from what had happened earlier in the day, but it was a relief to have to do something that took her mind off Kitty.

Deftly she ripped tape from a roll and applied a fresh bandage to the wound; with Nathanson backed against the sink, his large figure was looming over her. Only when she reached up to take the thermometer from his mouth did she see he was studying her. When she glanced at his eyes, she read in his smile quiet admiration and delight, and she remembered the concern and gentleness he had shown her in the cab and later at the restaurant. And the look.

She glanced down and saw he wasn't running a temperature. She shook out the thermometer and let her eyes sweep his face again before slipping it back into the solution case. Yup. There was no mistaking that searing look of . . . reverence, almost. Suddenly Eva was filled with a kind of joyful pride. Things weren't all that bad. Here when she felt so lost, she looked up to discover she *possessed* somebody. It was a complication, of course, and certainly not one that should be encouraged, her reason told her. But he was near, and she could feel the warmth from his body and his—was it?—anticipation.

She smiled too and, while discarding the wrappings from the bandages and tape, tried not to look into his eyes. But she did, and it was like trains colliding. Eva blushed and turned away. Suddenly her heart was beating wildly; she hadn't felt so ruffled in years. Nathanson had a big, full, rich smile—a warm smile—that puckered a single dimple, which was repeated, she noticed now that he had shaved, in his chin. It just made him more appealing to her. Physically.

She sighed. Something like this was best confronted. Left to smolder, it would only break out hotter at some other time, and given who he was, it was wrong. If she tried hard enough, she told herself, she could control at least her own emotions. After all, the world was filled with handsome men, and what was Brian Nathanson but a drug dealer and desperado of some sort. Pirate. Brigand. Probably a fence, the antiques business being just a blind.

Eva stepped toward him and wrapped her arms around his waist. Tilting back her head, she looked up into his eyes. "Why me?"

His smile grew a bit fuller; his light green eyes sparkled. "What do you mean?"

"You know what I mean."

"I do?"

Eva nodded. "Why are you falling in love with me?" There, she had said it and confronted the difficulty squarely. Embarrassed by her having exposed him, he would try to protect himself and would see her in a different light.

But he just kept on smiling, his eyes roaming her face.

"Don't tell me you're *not*? You look at all women this way."

"You seem to know more about it than me."

Eva didn't know why, but the possibility that he wasn't in

love with her made her almost angry. "Well—if you're not, there's no point in—" She began to move away from him, but he caught her wrists and pulled them behind him again.

"Is it because we have the same color eyes?"

He moved his head a bit, as though to say maybe. His smile, however, was still complete.

"That seems a little juvenile, doesn't it?"

Nathanson nodded. "That's just what it is."

"Or . . . what about your mother? Denny said I reminded him of your mother."

He hunched his broad shoulders. "Well, that's Denny, but I suppose the point is you're *not* my mother."

"Or . . . or, I'm the first *decent* woman you've ever been forced to be with for any length of time."

Nathanson laughed. "Now *there* you might have something. Denny would certainly agree."

Eva struggled to pull her arms from around him, but he held her close. "You're enjoying this, aren't you?"

He nodded. "Most fun I've had in some time."

Turning her head, Eva tried a look of sidelong assessment. "I want *you* to say something."

"About what? About your accusation?"

That too bothered her. "Well, about what I just said."

Nathanson waited until her eyes were firmly fixed in his. Somewhere in the tiny room a tap was dripping. A car horn sounded out in the street. "You look. You love. You're lost." His eyes dropped to her lips, his head moved toward hers.

Blood pounded in her temples, and all but his face became fuzzy. It *was* true; he *did* love her. She tried to avert her head. With her leaning back like that, their bodies were pressed together, and she could feel him against her. It was a situation that could easily get out of control.

And did. The next thing she knew, her mouth was on his, and he had released her hands, which were gripping the back of his neck. One of his, placed on the small of her back, began raising her toward him, and suddenly she found herself virtually on top of him, her legs wrapping his thighs, his hand up under the cable cardigan on her bare back.

Which was when they heard the phone ringing. Rushing for it in the darkness of the empty loft, she asked, "Why *lost*?" before picking up the receiver. Like a shout in a tunnel, her voice echoed off the bare walls.

It was Tug. "Eva? Jesus—it's been forever. Where've you been?"

She had to pause and think. "I—I stayed in the Islands for a while. How are you?"

"Jake, of course. And you?"

Nathanson now appeared at her side.

"Well, I'm alive."

"That's good to hear. Last time I saw you, I wasn't sure you would be."

Eva shook her head. It was exactly her present worry about him. "Tug—can you talk now?"

"If you mean *serious* serious, not really. I'm a little lit, and I'm in company."

"Where?"

There was a pause. "With friends."

"What about tomorrow early? Can I meet you for break-fast?"

"Gee, Eva, I can't. I'm chock-a-block tomorrow and Thursday. How 'bout Friday lunch? The usual place?"

"Tug, this can't wait. You know that woman you're with? I don't know what she's calling herself here in New York, but her name is Solange—" Hearing the dial tone, Eva took the receiver from her ear and handed it to Nathanson.

"We better get out of here," he said, dropping the receiver in its yoke. "Whoever cut him off might have a tracer on the phone, and, as much as I love her, Eva Burden has a flaw." Smiling up at the large, dark shape that she would somehow have to deal with *on her own terms*, Eva waited.

"No big, deep bed in her apartment. But"—with one strong arm he lifted her off her feet— "I know where one is."

When Eva awoke the next morning in the Doral Park, Nathanson was gone. A note said, *Out to City Island. Will try to call between 12:00 and 2:00. Don't—repeat—don't meet with shipmates. If you feel you must contact them, pay phones only. If you go out: hat, glasses, cabs. Leave key at desk.* Folded into the note were four crisp one-thousand-dollar bills with the explanation *Walking-around money*, which was crossed out. As was *Security money*. But not *Love notes from the accused.*

PART V

SQUEEZE PLAY

CHAPTER 24

BETWIXT AND BETWEEN

◆

THE DOCK MASTER at City Island Marina looked down at Nathanson's card. He twisted his head from side to side and made the chair squeak, as though he didn't like what he was seeing. "Doesn't say anywhere here you're a writer."

Nathanson had told him he was doing a piece on Island boats in U.S. waters. "It's nothing that instills confidence and respect."

"What's 'Island Trading' mean?"

"What it says. I live in the Islands. I trade."

The dock master was a stump of a man with a steely brush-cut and a plump chin that was creased like a baby's bottom. He gave Nathanson, who was standing beside his desk, another once-over that ended with a thorough consideration of his shoes. "Make a living?"

"I get by."

"I can see that. Them Nettletons?" He was staring at Nathanson's brogues.

"Wouldn't wear anything else."

"I wouldn't either, 'specially if I was getting by. What sumptin' like them cost?"

"This half of the century or the last, when they were new?"

Nathanson had inherited a closet full of them from his stepfather, who had been another large man. Nathanson took care of nice things, or at least there had been a time that he had. He thought of the burned-out shell of his house in Nassau.

The man's pale eyes were now on his face. "Can I tell you something, can you learn from my years?"

Nathanson looked away. It depended if the guy had spent his years on his ass, like now.

"Nobody likes a wise guy. Wise guys never get what they want. They think they do, but—" He shook his head. " 'Specially when they're nosy."

Me nosy? Nathanson thought. The guy had to be a former cop. First there was the certain practiced intimidation in his questions; second was the SEMPER FI tattoo on his left biceps. After their early training as self-righteous killers, there was no place else for them.

"What do you trade?"

"This and that."

"Oh, yeah? Really? You don't say." His popped eyes kept staring at the card. "That's great. People always need a lot of this-and-that. Vital commodity, 'specially when in short supply. I suppose the this-and-that fall into the category of the 'Collectibles' I see here."

Nathanson waited until the eyes rose to him again. "You trying to ask me how much I make and is it tax free? If a guy like you could retire in the Bahamas? Could you work? Would they send you your marine, Civil Service, and police pensions down there? Your Social Security? Is it expensive? Could you live cheap if you had to? Is the money interchangeable? Yes to all of the above.

"Now ask me if I know Bill Cicciolino, the assistant chief who's always on the tube. It's him who sent me. Where's Gelb at?"

The guy sighed. He shook his head, then waited maybe fifteen seconds. Windblown sea-gull shit had spattered the windows of his shack. "I was just trying to make conversation. You know, be friendly."

Nathanson waited some more.

"How do you know Cicciolino?"

"We're in business together."

It brought the guy's head back. "Oh, really? In what?"

"Finance. He borrows money from me. Then there's trade in the kind of this-and-that that's always in short supply. Can I ask a question?" Nathanson picked the Rolodex off the desk and pulled back the G tab. "How do you feel about niggers?"

"Hey—give that here."

"Could you live with them in their country? By that I mean, could you associate with them on a daily basis, meet them on the street, in business, invite them to your home? If you can't, don't consider the Islands." He tossed the Rolodex at the man's chest, then reached for his business card. "When Cicciolino comes by looking for Gelb, ask him about two-point-four-million dollars, the kind of this-and-that that's always in short supply, and me."

Gelb had changed the slip at which *Trekker*, the fifty-four-foot ketch, was docked twice. The present location was about as far from the dock house as he could get, next to a parking area and exit gate. Gelb also had a rental car, the registration and plate number of which were noted down.

Nathanson pulled his own rental car into a public parking area far enough away from *Trekker* that Gelb wouldn't be aware of his presence. After a few minutes he saw a thin, balding man with a full beard and wire-rim glasses appear out of the companionway hatch and step onto the dock. At the car he opened the trunk and began hauling cases of canned goods and boxes of foodstuffs aboard the boat. Lengths of line, two canisters of propane, and two plastic milk crates filled with what looked like books came next.

Why books? Because they planned on living aboard *Trekker*? Seemed like a good bet, Nathanson concluded, when Gelb added a portable television and a VCR, both still boxed with yellow receipts taped to the lids.

But no place local. With the help of a dock boy, Gelb pulled five bags of what Nathanson assumed were blown-out sails from the forward hatch. The dock boy shook his hand, then loaded them aboard a dock cart and pushed them to a smaller, older car that seemed like his own. If Gelb were going to remain in the area, he wouldn't give away what amounted to thousands of dollars of sails. Old canvas—or in this case Dacron—could be used in rough weather or made into sunscreens, hatch bonnets, boat covers. If nothing else, old sails could be sold as is; not everybody needed or could afford new, tight sails.

No. Gelb needed room aboard *Trekker* for the supplies he was bringing aboard. After the deal went down, he or they were leaving the area. Definitely, Nathanson decided, when Gelb left in the rental car and returned a short time later with more supplies.

How to proceed? Nathanson could board *Trekker* and confront Gelb. He didn't think it would take him long to learn their plans. But what would it get him? Not his money or the dope, which Cicciolino wouldn't have been dumb enough to store aboard the boat that had transported the dope north. Nothing would be aboard her now, and he'd only put them on notice that he was onto them.

But the arrival of a "NYNEX Installation Service" van an hour later as much as told Nathanson that *Trekker* would not be used for escape alone. A technician got out with a cellular telephone under one arm and a tool kit in the other hand. Gelb met him on the dock and ushered him below. Why bother getting yourself a traceable phone and number in what amounted to a regional system when you were planning to split? *Trekker* must be a part of whatever deal they were setting up. The telephone would help them coordinate details. Maybe Gelb's provisioning of the ketch was just a contingency plan in case things screwed up. Nathanson himself had always kept his jolly boat prepped for a survival run, and it had sure saved his ass.

It was late afternoon and overcast. A rolling grid of cloud, made pink by the setting sun, was racing east. Funnels at the edge were twining around each other in a complex weave that reminded Nathanson of a line splice. It would rain in a few hours, which would be both good and bad. Marina security would check the public parking area. He could say he was waiting for a friend in a boat, which was late, but he doubted they would let him stay very long. There was a sign in front of him that said, NO OVERNIGHT PARKING.

But the rain itself would cover his footsteps, when Gelb either left or Nathanson got him to leave the boat. He figured with all the provisions in the forward hold there'd be a dark nook for him to hide in, and when it all went down, there he'd be. On the scene.

Nathanson had plenty of time to ask why he, a man packing only a photograph, wanted that. Everybody else would be armed to the teeth, and nobody would tolerate the presence of a witness. Was it the money? After all, half of the $2.4 million they had lost was his, and all of his house, his possessions, and his pain. But Nathanson shook his head. It wasn't just the money. Over the years he'd been careful and smart, and he had eggs nested in places that couldn't be found by anybody who didn't know where to look. No, it wasn't just the money.

Then was it his pride? You know—that a cheap, thieving bastard had as much as set him up by contracting the Romeros to deliver the product and now dispatching a *sicaria* to take everything she could from him, including his life. Maybe, but the pain he had endured and the—was it?—joy he now felt at simply being alive were great enough to overcome angry pride. Also, there was Eva.

Nathanson rested his head against the neck brace of the car seat and reconsidered the night in the boat on the uninhabited island and the busted deal. It was as though another, better, more important trade had been done that night, which had been concealed from him and he had had to . . . discover. Had he not been receptive to who Eva was, had he not looked at and listened to her and tried to figure out what she was saying and what she could mean to him, she might have walked right out of his life.

Nathanson did not believe in God the way other people did, but he believed that Somebody or Something had been watching over him all of his life. It didn't seem to matter how dumb he was or the shit he got into, things had always worked out: in Vietnam, on the docks in Jersey, in South America and the Islands while he was dealing. This time, though, that Somebody or Something was trying to tell him something and—the way he was thinking about it now—Eva was the messenger. He liked her. More, he liked what she could mean to him, but there he was, acting as though nothing had happened and he was still taking care of business. He wondered how much stupidity one life could tolerate. One thing he knew from watching other guys who'd been in the trade and were now deceased: When your number was up, it was *up*. The punishment for a mistake was swift and sure.

Around eight o'clock, when it was fully dark and the cabin lights were blazing aboard *Trekker*, a security patrol car came by. The guy slowed and looked at him, then checked the three other cars in the public parking area and came back. He rolled down his window. "Nice night."

"For now," Nathanson said. "Looked like rain at sundown."

"That's what I hear. You planning on being here long?"

"I'm waiting for a friend. He was going to come by and pick me up for a weekend sail. Four, he said."

"Where's he coming from?"

"Noank."

"Sailing?"

Nathanson nodded.

"That's a long haul. Had the wind in his face all day."

It was the reason Nathanson had picked Noank.

"You want to make a call, there's a pay phone at the end of the parking lot. We got a curfew about people in cars. Midnight you'll have to leave. It keeps the kids out. Parkers. Vans and RVs overnighting in the summer."

Nathanson nodded. "By midnight I'll be long gone—either on the boat or back into the city. Any problem with cars in this lot?"

"Not with what you're driving." It was a midline Chevy with vinyl seats and an anemic engine. "Mercedes and BMWs I got to watch like a hawk. Don't know why anybody buys 'em. It's like hanging out a sign, 'Fat cat. Rip me off.' " Nathanson nodded and waved, the cop waved back. And again at ten-thirty.

By eleven it had begun to rain. Nathanson buttoned his tweed overcoat, turned up and fitted the collar under the brim of his fedora, and stepped out. Finding the tire iron in the trunk, he locked the car and moved toward the water.

His plan was to pace the dock, as though still waiting for his apocryphal boat, until he found the electrical-supply fuse box, which was a bothersome feature of every marina. Assholes were always pulling in with eighty or a hundred feet of complex electrical equipment; they'd hook up, throw everything on, and pop the circuit breakers up and down the line. If the box was locked, Nathanson would use the tire iron on the clasp, but he'd switch off the rheostat that supplied shore power to *Trekker*, which would bring Gelb running. Would he think to lock up the boat? Why, when he'd be able to see it while he wasn't futzing with the switch? And who was around? It was early in the season, and on a weekday evening he had the dock to himself.

But Nathanson had only just found the fuse box when headlights swept the dock area. He ducked behind the bollard on which the box had been hung and watched a taxi slow while its driver checked the numbers of the slips.

No need. In his yellow oilskins Gelb was out of *Trekker* and up into the parking area, waving to the cabbie. Nathanson heard, ". . . Hoboken."

"Aw, man—I don't *go* to no Hoboken. It's in another *state*."

Gelb ripped something in half and handed a piece to him. "You get the other half when we get back."

"What's this, a bad movie I'm in? I get fifty bucks just to go over the G.W. Bridge. It's seventy-five to Hoboken and back. If we're talkin' tip here"—he waved the ripped bill at Gelb—"get in. If not, I hope you got some Scotch tape."

"Fuck it and fuck you—I'll take my car." Gelb snatched the ripped bill from his hand and stalked toward his rental car.

"Wait a minute, wait a goddamn minute."

Gelb stopped.

"Way you're acting, you need a driver. You lit, or what?"

Gelb pulled out his keys.

The cabbie hopped out and shouted, "You can forget the fifty. I'm here already. It's seventy round-trip. *And* the C note that I get in Hoboken, when you get back in."

Gelb glanced up but he opened the rental-car door, as if he were going to get in. "*Fifty* and the hundred, you greedy prick. Any other hack would be shitting his shorts at the luck."

The cabbie turned his face up into the rain that was falling hard now. He sighed. "Get in, before I change my mind."

Gelb slammed the rental-car door, then locked the boat. "You sure I'm not putting you out?" he asked sarcastically, as he got into the cab.

"Don't know why you can't drive yourself."

"That's why you're driving a cab."

It was a typical New York exchange, but Nathanson's question was the same as the cabbie's. And Gelb seemed different from the professor of art that Eva had told him about. Here, he was hyper, decisive, even brash.

Nathanson waited only until the cab lights had disappeared to board *Trekker*. With the tire iron he prized off the hasp of the lock on the companionway hatch and went below. There, he found the new television and VCR, both of which he carried topside and dropped off the bow of the boat. The "theft" would explain the broken lock; Gelb would *not* notify the police.

Below again he picked up the cellular phone and dialed the

Doral Park. He figured the Three Musketeers wouldn't deny him a local call.

"Where are you?" Eva Burden asked.

Nathanson explained.

"Is Jay there?"

"Not at the moment."

"Have you spoken to him?"

In the dark boat, looking up through the companionway hatch, which he left partially open to simulate the carelessness of a thief, Nathanson watched the rain fall past a cadmium vapor lamp. Should he explain? *Could* he explain? "Not yet."

"Will you?"

Discuss with him how the $2.4 million was actually his and he wanted it back? And that the dope should be returned to its rightful owners, preferably with an apology? Maybe hiring a *sicaria* was the only way to go, after all. "I don't think I'll get the opportunity."

"Then what are you doing there?"

Which was *the* question exactly. Nathanson thought for a moment. Somehow the orange light had always made things seem artificial, timeless, and therefore unreal to Nathanson; it didn't help him think. "I don't know."

"Won't it be dangerous aboard the boat?"

Nathanson had an idea it would, especially if the *sicaria* joined them, as Eva had overheard in O'Casey's.

"I don't mean to belabor the point, but wouldn't it be better just to let the whole thing drop and come back here?" To me, she meant.

Nathanson did not reply.

"Do you *need* the money?"

His old self always needed money for the inevitable contingencies that were forever arising: new and better "equipment," which meant radars, infrareds, guns, etc.; bribe and hush money; legal fees; "south money" in case he had to support his Nassau operations from prison. His new self could make a perfectly acceptable living trading legal this-es-and-thats without the worry and care.

"I seem to be caught between what I used to do and what I

want to do," he blurted out. "I guess it's just something I'm going to have to work through."

Eva did not respond, but her "If you're lucky" occurred to him.

"I guess I called to tell you how much I miss you."

Still nothing.

"I could say I wish you were here, but, you know, I don't."

"And I wish you weren't either. Can't you simply put a period in the whole thing, turn the page, and begin fresh? What's keeping you from doing that? Is it pride or ego or your house and this *sicaria*? Or some combination? Maybe if you tried to figure it out, you could let it go."

"And that I love you." There, it was out; he said it.

Sitting up in bed with her other hand covering her ear so she could hear every sound, Eva flushed with joy and pleasure but consternation too. It made her complicated life, which was rushing forward at—*breakneck* speed was the phrase exactly—even more so, but it wasn't anything that could have been planned.

Nathanson heard only a slight pause, followed by, "Mmm-mm," as though she was agreeing with him. Then, "How much?"

"I hope you're not going to put conditions on my loving you."

"Well, stupid is stupid."

"So, that's what it is?" Loving you, he meant.

"The more you get to know me, the more accurate you'll see that is."

"What about you?" Do *you* love *me*? he meant.

"Is that a condition?" she asked playfully.

Nathanson waited.

"Shouldn't you be content to be in love with me? How will my loving you back improve that?"

"I can think of several ways."

"You can? Let me give you a piece of advice."

"Shoot."

"Love me. Be grateful for the little I give you, dutiful whenever I'm in need. Serve me like a slave. It'll make me think more of you and maybe better. Who knows, you might even be rewarded."

"What was that last night?"

"Exercise."

"I don't think you heard me. I said I *love* you."

Again Eva felt her blood surge. She didn't think she could hear him say it too often, which only made her reconsider their predicament. "Brian—this is all pointless, if you're going to go out and get yourself killed." When the stupid thing is you now know better, she did not add.

"Speaking of which, I've got to hang up."

"What's going on?" Suddenly her voice was filled with worry.

Nathanson had seen the flash of headlights in the parking lot, and he could now hear tires on the tar. Maybe Gelb had forgotten something, or it was the cop on his rounds again. "So—no affirmation, no glimmer of hope? Just give me a word, and I can die, if I have to, content in the knowledge that at least you cared a little."

"Don't even kid about that. I'll tell you *when* and *if* I see you."

"Mmmmm," he said before hanging up. The car had stopped near the stern of *Trekker*. He could hear the engine idling and see the rain slanting through the bluish glare of its headlights. In the darkness he made his way forward toward the fo'c'sle of the ketch where Gelb had stored his supplies.

Back in the suite at the Doral Park, Eva switched off the light on the nightstand and eased her head into the pillows. Wouldn't it be just her luck to have found somebody and have him taken from her before they could even begin to enjoy each other? Except for her daughter, everybody and everything that she had touched just seemed to come apart. Or worse.

She thought of her husband and her father and Kitty. Tears burst from her eyes. Eva had spent her day not answering police questions about who she thought might have wanted to murder and "bake"—their term—her chef. After she had learned that Bill Cicciolino was not in his office, she had phoned them and then Kitty's parents, who lived in Louisiana. Somehow the more lurid of the newspapers learned of the grisly murder, and she had had to ask a police captain to escort her to a taxi so she could get away from the reporters and their cameras. Late tomorrow she would have to meet Kitty's parents at the airport and . . .

More tears flowed from her eyes, and she wondered if she was just feeling sorry for herself and not Kitty. She was, she decided, and she repeated a prayer that she had learned when she had tried to get her husband to address his drug problem.

"I pray that whatever is good I may have," she said to the darkened ceiling of the hotel suite. "I leave to God the choice of what good will come to me."

CHAPTER 25

DER TAG

◆

AT 7:15 A.M. the next morning, PO Nunzio D'Amato knocked on the office door of Deputy Inspector Cliff Banks, commander of Precinct 25. He craned his head in. " 'Scuse me, Inspector. I was tol' bring this in myself."

Banks looked up from the log of Wednesday arrests. "What is it?" His eyes looked like hot, cracked coals.

D'Amato's first and maybe only love was sports betting, and he knew Banks had carried his rep as a tough-ass linebacker from Shea Stadium, where he had played for the Jets, into any police command he had ever been given. Banks was hard on his men and tough on perps. "A fuckin' role model for black Nazis," was how he heard one sat-on white cop say.

"You ain't gonna shoot the messenger, are you?" D'Amato had still not entered the office. Like a flag of truce, he waved a letter from Assistant Chief Bill Cicciolino, his boyhood buddy for who he now drove.

Recognizing D'Amato, Banks gave his approximation of a smile. To D'Amato he looked like a big black bear snarling at a piece of meat. "Depends on what it is, Nunzio. If it happens, we can always say you were aptly named."

And smart. D'Amato didn't like it when niggers were smart. With the way most of them were put together and could run and take shots, it gave them an unfair advantage.

"Me? I dunno what's in it," he went on, pretending Chick hadn't told him what it contained. "I didn't ask. I don't wanna know. I'm paid to drive and stay alive. Sounds like a rap song, don't it?" He stepped to the desk, placed the letter on the blotter in front of Banks, and smoothed it down with both hands. He stepped away. "Good seein' you again, Inspector. Have a nice day."

"Aren't you going to wait for an answer?"

Not if D'Amato could help it; he was already back at the door.

"Then why—" Banks continued, pulling open the envelope. Send it special messenger, he meant, if no answer was required.

"I was tol', in your hands and you know the chief." Chocolate and vanilla, D'Amato thought. It was like they broke Cicciolino and Banks from the same bear-shape mold.

D'Amato was halfway through the outer office when he heard, "Aw—*shit*! What? D'Amato. D'Amato, come back here!"

But D'Amato just kept on walking. Fast. Out in the corridor headed for the stairwell, he checked his watch. Way he understood it, Banks would be getting a phone call in a minute or two. Chick had explained, "I want it on his desk at seven-fifteen, no sooner, no later. I'll give him a minute to read it, and then I'll call. That way he won't try to catch me at home or the office."

When D'Amato had looked up for an explanation, Cicciolino had said, "The Santos thing. It was between Banks and me, the setup. Brant's calling it off. He wants to see what Santos will do when he realizes the heat's off. You know, where he'll go, who he'll deal with, shit like that. But Banks'll be pissed off, you'll see.

"Now, after Banks, I got something special for you. I want you over on the West Side." Cicciolino had handed D'Amato a slip of paper with an address on it and a license plate number. "Remember Jay Gelb's wife?" 'Course D'Amato remembered her. Hadn't they dropped in on her a couple weeks ago, about the time Cicciolino had stopped using D'Amato for driving and had put him on the Santos thing? "Remember what she looks like?" Together they had said, "Dale fucking Evans," and chuckled.

"With goggles," D'Amato had added.

Cicciolino had continued, "She'll be coming out of her place sometime after ten, but you know broads. She'll get into an old beat-up Volvo, which is the professor's car. She'll then drive out someplace, I don't know where, and pick up two cartons. I want you should follow her all day if you have to until she gets them to where she drops them off. Until they're out of her hands. Un'erstan'? After that, she's on her own."

D'Amato had understood, but he needed a reason.

"This is a personal thing you'll be doing for Gelb and her, but you'll be cruising as a cop. Anybody tries to stop her, hold her up, fuck with her in any way, you step in. Identify yourself, show your shield, get her going again with the stuff. Busts ain't important, and don't call for help. Like I said, it's personal. The important part is them cartons. They're to get where they're going, one way or another."

"What's in 'em?"

Cicciolino had shook his head. "Beats me. They asked, is all. I said, 'How 'bout Nunzio? If anybody knows the city and can handle a thing like this, it's him.' Gelb said, 'Nunzio D'Amato? Perfect.' There'll be an envelope in it. And maybe some pad after."

D'Amato's head had gone back. "Pad?" An envelope could be up to, say, a C note or two, but pad was big time.

But again Cicciolino shook his head. "Like I said, beats me. I don't know, and I don't wanna know. Art?" He had hunched his shoulders. "Some a' that shit is worth something, I guess. The Gelbs a' been at it long enough. It's time they made a score."

Back in his office Banks had only reached for the phone when it rang.

"Cliff? Bill Cicciolino here. Get my note?"

Mousetrap it was called, Banks thought: hit you high, hit you low, knock you out of the game. "Why *now*?" he asked. "Way I hear it, Santos went downtown Tuesday, and all we can figure is for a shrink. I know that asshole. He's coming apart, and it's only a matter of time before he blows."

Said Cicciolino, "What can I tell you? It's an order. Brant thinks we should let him off and see what he'll do, where he'll go first, who he'll see."

"But if we let him off, *how* will we know who he'll see?"

"Don't ask me. The usual way, I guess."

Banks swiveled in his chair and looked up into blue glare that coated his grimy office window like a cataract in an old eye. The only usual way he knew of was word on the street.

"The point is, I been told, it's not Santos that we're after, but, you know, Santos's *type*. The whole thing is an . . . exercise, a—what's the word I'm looking for? A—"

"Intellectual," Banks supplied.

"You got it, an *intellectual* exercise. Busting Santos for Santos's sake can come later."

Like when? Banks wanted to know. That sucker had been putting cleat marks on the face of the city for whole decades. In certain parts of East Harlem he was a kind of legend. Dumb kids, loser kids, admired him with his building that looked like a little fortress and his pigmeat, his dope money, and gang. "Chino," they called him, the word kind of glowing on their lips. Banks took what he did seriously; otherwise he wouldn't do it.

Said Cicciolino, "I feel the way you do. Guy's a fuckin' scumbag and should get exed. But until they appoint me Grand Inquisitor, I just take orders, like everybody else.

"You hear what he did on Tuesday?" With a towel wrapped around his waist, Cicciolino was standing at the telephone table in the hallway of his apartment on Ninety-fifth Street. He had spent the night with Arlene guarding the stuff aboard the Bayliner, and he was still hurting the way she had used him. It was as though she was so hyper because of what would happen today she needed the sex as an outlet, and she had even dicked *him*. It was the first time—"Your cherry," she kept saying with her tongue in his ear, "I want your cherry, Chick"—that had ever happened to Cicciolino, and he still didn't know how he felt about it. Wild then. Crazy. But now sore.

"Somehow the fuckin' yo-yo found out where the first dep and me was having lunch. Came in there all spiffed up in a three-piece suit and kissed me gentle." Cicciolino waited.

Banks pulled his head from the glare and found he had a big mother-of-pearl splotch in the center of his vision. "He *threatened* you?"

"In so many words."

"What you do?" The splotch was turning red, like Banks's mood.

"What could I? His word against mine. When was the last time you got threatened?"

Banks couldn't remember. Somehow he was not the type people threatened, but neither was Cicciolino. "You know, that pisses me off," he said in a small voice.

"Did me, but the place was packed. Brant was there though. Overheard it. I been told he wrote it up."

"A report or a complaint?"

"Report. Put it in Santos's file. Speaking about lunch, how does Tuesday next suit you? Brant's clear, I know for sure."

In the spring-back chair, Banks launched his body at the desk and looked down at his blotter calendar that he could not see. The spot before his eyes had turned to purple bruise. Fuck it, he thought. He was free. Anything that might get him where he could call the shots he'd do. "Perfect."

"I'll confirm Friday. Okay?"

"Gotcha."

"One thing about our erstwhile pigeon—he's smart."

Erstwhile. Cicciolino was surprising, and Banks reminded himself that the man had not made assistant chief by being stupid. They played hardball downtown, no two ways about it.

Banks liked the word "pigeon" better, and he wondered what he could do on his own, now that Santos was softened up. "I'll hear from you Friday then."

"For sure."

They hung up.

Cicciolino glanced up the hall toward Gerri's room and wondered if he should get dressed first before making the rest of his calls. He checked his arms and his chest for monkey bites and hickeys. After Arlene had strapped the thing on, she had been all over him, like it was a rape or something.

Cicciolino now turned and looked at his back in the hall mirror. It was a welter of red, mouth-shaped marks. As he had started to come, she had scratched and clawed at his dick the way he liked it and bit and sucked his back. He jerked and jerked, trying to get away from her. They lurched back into the head door, which burst open, and he let out this shriek he didn't think came from him. And he came so total and so long it felt like his guts were being pumped out through the end of his dick.

Even thinking about it now made him sweat, and now, as his cock began to swell, it hurt bad.

Fuck Gerri, he thought. If she saw his back, she saw it. They weren't long for each other anyhow. Soon as it was over, he'd shed her anyway. The fuck if he'd share anything with her she didn't want. Including his dick.

"Arlene?" He heard a kind of moan on the other end, and the picture of her getting it from somebody else popped to mind, which he'd like to watch. Banks, maybe. Or some other big nigger. "You alone, Arlene?"

There was a pause, and then. "Oh, please, Chick—let's not add jealousy to the list of your sterling qualities." There was another pause while she coughed or something. "But I'm flattered that you think I could, after last night."

With her pregnancy her belly was beginning to distend, but her tits were noble and, like, hard. Cicciolino had never had bigger, better-shaped tit.

Now, definitely, he had a hard-on; his cock was twitching in the towel that was wrapped around his waist. He thought what the hell, he'd take it to Gerri and see what she could do with it. It would make the contrast between what Gerri and a real woman could offer him more definite, make the split easier and more, you know, palpable. He hadn't dicked Gerri in—he couldn't remember when.

To Arlene he now said, "So—you're awake. Everything's in place, including your escort. He'll be outside waiting. Don't look back or in any way try to pick him off. He's good, so you probably won't anyway. You just wait there by the phone until Jay calls, then go straight to the place he tells you, count the stuff, load the car, and split. You know what to do from there."

"Yes."

Cicciolino didn't like her tone; something was wrong. "You all right?"

"Yes."

"You sure?"

"Yes."

"Long as you're *sure.*"

"I am."

He waited, trying to hear beyond her. "You alone?"

"Chick—please. You're like . . . you're like a disease. A *fatal* disease. I'm tired, is all. But I'm all right, honestly, and I know what to do. How many times do we have to go over this?"

"Okay," he said in a conciliatory voice. "Okay. Good luck, baby."

"And don't *baby* me!"

"You take care." He hung up.

Tug was next. He would be waiting by the pay phone on the dock in Hoboken where last night he'd relieved Cicciolino at midnight. Arlene had left by then, and Tug and he had had a pop and firmed up the plan.

Tug's youngest brother, Matty, was high up in the legal department of the "Port of Authority," McCann always said with a smile. Tug had told Matty he had a small load of contraband paper coming in, which wasn't far wrong. Could a discreet drop be arranged on Pier 63? "You know, behind the boat sheds where nothing'll be seen from the street? What I want is for nobody but me and the guys I'm doing the deal with to be there." Matty had told Tug not to worry. Since the days of Tammany Hall, it was the sort of thing that the McCanns did for each other, no questions asked.

McCann had selected the site for several reasons. First was the fact that Pier 63 extended far enough into the Hudson that any activity occurring on the wharf side of its sheds would be visible only to river traffic, especially if the gate into the pier could be controlled. Matty assured him it could.

Second, Pier 63 formed a kind of L with Pier 62 at the jog in Twelfth Avenue, which followed the east bank of the Hudson. There, the sudden curve created an open space in front of the gates of the piers. It was like a square and was even cobblestoned with a little tree-lined cul-de-sac of parked and abandoned cars leading off. Waiting there in an unmarked car, Chick could both surveil all city access in and out of the piers, and control traffic in or out, if need be. He'd be in touch with Gelb and him aboard *Trekker* by cellular phone.

Third, unlike so many other New York piers that were now abandoned, 62 and 63 were still fairly active with two cruise lines that were just beginning their season at this time of year. A little trading wouldn't attract the kind of attention as it might on some other, little-used pier. Actually police and Emergency Service Unit vans were now garaged on the other side of 63. With visible, uniformed cops around, it would make Santos less likely to pull anything stupid.

The scenario was for Tug to drive the dope from Hoboken through the Holland Tunnel and then up to 63. "I'll pull behind the shed of Sixty-three and wait until I see you park in the cul-de-sac," Tug now said. "I'll get out, toke the watchman a double sawbuck, like Matty promised him, and walk out through the gate. It shouldn't be too hard for me to catch a cab to Seventy-ninth Street," where McCann would phone Santos, and Gelb would have *Trekker* waiting for them. Cicciolino would then watch the van and the square for the first signs of Santos's mutts.

"What street is that again exactly?" Cicciolino asked. He wanted to be sure. He kept a mental map of the city, but with all the construction that was going on, there were always detours or closed-off streets. Also, at certain times of day large delivery trucks made certain cross-streets virtually impassable. Cicciolino wanted to plan out every possible route the dope vehicle might take, after the deal went down. He had his own plan about what would happen to it then.

"Twenty-third," said McCann. "There's a light there for traffic in and out of Sixty-two and Sixty-three. Across the street is that little park filled with drunks and bums. Shanties, homeless. You name it."

Cicciolino knew it well, but he wrote on the pad by the phone, "23rd St.," as he traced his way through the configuration of streets and alleys in that general area. Earlier in his career he had been captain of that precinct, the Tenth. "Gotcha."

"Hey, before you hang up—you take a memento from the Bayliner last night? You know, from *stock*?" McCann meant a kilo of cocaine. When it came to deals, he understood how small things could screw things up, especially for the buyer. When you were shelling out, you wanted *everything* there, and they were a package light.

"Not me."

"Must have been Jay."

Cicciolino knew addicts, and was surprised Gelb didn't take more. The question was when Gelb had taken it and what he had seen. The only time Cicciolino had, you know, let his guard down was when Arlene was with him. "I'm getting a little concerned about Jay. How 'bout you?"

McCann wasn't about to cast the first stone. "I'll speak to him *after*."

"Break a leg."

"The little one."

"You must be thinking of your own."

They hung up.

Gelb was next. Cicciolino had left the number of the new, cellular phone aboard *Trekker* in his wallet. Passing Gerri's room, he opened the door and looked in. Christ, he thought, there she was at seven-fifteen on a workday, still in bed and staring at the ceiling. Her eyes, which were dark and deep set and, like shining, made her look like the Old Lady Who Lived in the Shoe. Cicciolino scrubbed the idea of poking her before he left. Did he need bad when he had good? Who said he had to endure bad *for the rest of his life*? What, for crissake, had he ever done to her?

And the smell in that room—what was that smell? Like something hot and burning. Tinfoil? Ammonia?

He closed the door. He'd dress first, then call Gelb and split.

Gelb was standing at the helm of *Trekker*, which was plying the East River.

It was a glorious morning with the kind of light that Monet and Sisley had painted best when, like now, seasons were changing and the weather was in flux. The sun was hot almost, yet the air was pleasantly cool. Above him scudding cumulus clouds were being driven on the edge of a high-pressure system that promised fair weather for days to come. Yet Jay Gelb—art professor, skipper/owner of *Trekker*, husband of the fair Arlene—saw none of that.

He was wearing wraparound, polarized prescription sunglasses that he had had specially made for him since his return from the Islands. If eyes were windows into the soul, then Gelb wanted his with the shades drawn.

Last night, panicking to think that in a day he would have to provide himself with his own coke, Gelb had taken a cab to Hoboken to get more. He had seen Cicciolino's car parked by the Bayliner, but not finding him in the salon, he figured Chick had gone forward to rest.

It was dark in the boat, and Gelb had just untied the partial carton and slipped a kilo into his windbreaker, when the door to the head burst open. Gelb was then presented what seemed like a ten-second black-and-white clip from a skin flick.

There in the achromatic, fluorescent light over the sink stood Chick and Arlene, both stripped down except for her garter belt, silk stockings, high heels, and whatever else—it took Gelb whole seconds to put it together—Arlene was strapped into. She was standing behind Chick. With her head on his back and her hands reaching around his hips, she was grinding something into him.

Chick was gripping the sink so hard his fingers were white. His head was thrown back on his broad, hairy shoulders. Suddenly his eyes popped open, and he let out this deep, tragic groan, as though he were dying. Arlene swiveled suddenly and, reaching for the door handle, seemed to look directly at Gelb without seeing or acknowledging his presence. But she turned them just enough that Gelb saw what was going on, and what he saw frightened him.

The immense black dildo she was using on Chick was repeated but *larger*—was it possible?—in the great red shaft that Arlene was clutching in her left hand. It was enormous, far larger by a factor of maybe three than any erection Gelb had ever had, and he decided that if that was the experience Arlene could have with somebody else, who was he to keep her from it? Let her have Chick's dick and him too; Gelb just didn't want to have to compete. And lose.

It freed him, the thought: from her pregnancy and the baby she had got with somebody else entirely. Cal. From the necessity of having to do something about what he had seen. Or to worry about *Trekker* or the money or the deal or his addiction. There was simply nothing he could do about any of it anyway. Why strive? he had kept saying over and over to himself in the cab. Why?

The simple fact was that Jay Gelb had changed, become stronger, more able to deal with the environment that he could see in the murky water, the littered, decimated shoreline, the crumbling concrete overpasses of the FDR and the cityscape beyond. In such a way Gelb had become better, and if it had been the cocaine, as he suspected, that had worked the change, it was indeed a magic substance, and he had been rewarded doubly for getting more.

He was now entering the East River, and he looked up to see a Gray Liner, one of the many tourists boats that circled Manhattan daily, right in the middle of the channel, bearing down on him. Gray Liners were notorious for consistently breaking speed and safety regulations, and Gelb, who was sailing wing-on-wing with a following breeze, actually had right of way. Nevertheless, he eased over as close as he could toward the shore, keeping one eye on the fathometer and another on *Trekker*'s telltale, in case the wind suddenly shifted and the sails jibed.

"Hey, man—c'mere. I wanna talk to you. I wanna axe you somethin'," a voice shouted at him.

Gelb snapped his head to the shore. Standing up ahead of him maybe forty feet away was a group of five black teenagers.

"Yo, Cap'ain! We talkin' to *you*!" The largest stepped away from the others and waved. "Pull in here." He ran down through the weeds of the bank toward the shore. He was stripped to the waist, and his black, square body was glistening and looked slick and svelte in the hot sun.

Fifty yards farther a pyre of automobile tires was burning fiercely near a shack face covering a burrow in the riverbank. Black sooty smoke was drifting up over the FDR, which was packed with morning traffic.

Gelb kept half an eye on the Gray Liner, which would soon pass by, and the boom of the mainmast that was swinging dangerously close to the high bank of the shore.

"We got weed, speed, anythang you need." With a look of joyful predation, the kid turned his head and smiled back at the others. They banded behind him, jogging down a well-worn path as Gelb and *Trekker* slipped by them.

"Pussy?" Gelb's head turned to him. "Pigmeat. You like young? We got young, man. Babies. They suck you' dee-ick."

The Gray Liner now charged by, its diesels straining, and Gelb spun the wheel to turn *Trekker*'s bow to the wake. It was then that a gust of wind pushed the boom of the mainmast farther in toward shore, and the first boy sprinted forward and threw himself on it.

Trekker, however, now swung away from the embankment, and the boy, dangling from the boom, was carried with it. "Ah cain' swim!" he shouted. "Pull in, Ah cain' swim!" As the boat bucked through the chop from the Gray Liner, his flailing feet paddled the crests of the waves. He tried to pull himself up by lunging for the sail. He missed and nearly fell off.

On the highway above them a car slowed and honked its horn. The rest of his band were now shouting and waving.

"Jump!" Gelb yelled. "Jump, you little bastard, and swim or sink!" It was deep where they were, but the bank wasn't far. And, hey—Gelb had lived in New York long enough to know what "C'mere, I wanna axe you somethin' " really meant.

The kid now lunged for the sail a second time, caught it, and pulled his torso up over the boom. His smile at Gelb was a mixture of triumph and hate. Immediately he caught onto the main sheet and started pulling himself in, so that the boat began to heel over.

Gelb sighed. It had been a mistake for him to try to sail to the Seventy-ninth Street Boat Basin, he should have motored. But he had figured it might be his last solo sail, and *Trekker* sailed so well.

Gelb raised the waistband of his windbreaker and extracted the revolver that Chick—"Of the *big dee-ick*," Gelb said to himself—had given him, saying, "Necessary equipment in a deal like this. Things start happening, just point it and pull the trigger."

Well, *thangs* had. And the strange part was Gelb didn't brandish the weapon to show the boy he was foolish to pull himself farther in. No. Instead Gelb, who was left-handed, shielded the gun with his body and said, "C'mon. C'mon aboard, you little nigger. You wanna axe me somethin'? I got the question for you. Pigmeat? You're *it*. Let me see the size of dee-ick."

The kid's smile had fallen, and he had stopped trying to draw himself closer. "What you got in you' han'?"

Gelb swung *Trekker*, bringing her back to her original course. He turned and smiled at the kid. "Somethin' you ain'." He then fired *not* up into the air, no warning shot, no threat or bluster. It was as if somebody else were doing it. Gelb raised his right arm so he could continue to steer and with his left hand hugging his belt began squeezing off shots at the child—really, for that was all he was—on the boom.

The first shot thwacked into the anodized aluminum spar. The second tore a hole in the sail. The third passed off someplace else, maybe through the kid—Gelb didn't care—and he fell off into the water.

Turning only his head and shoulders, so the revolver would still remain obscured from any observer on shore, Gelb scanned the wake until the nappy head appeared. He thought of throwing him a life preserver, but the two close at hand were stenciled "*Trekker,*" and the moment he heard shouts and imprecations, all thought of assistance vanished.

All he could see was the boy's wide, angry mouth. "Muh'fuh! I fine you, I shoot you in you' head!" The boy then turned and stroked lazily toward shore.

The cellular telephone began ringing. Gelb picked it up. It was Chick. "Jay—where you at?"

The other Jay Gelb would have spilled his guts to Cicciolino. He would have begun first with the break-in last night, how the lock on the companionway hatch had been broken and his new TV and VCR stolen. Next he would have rambled on about the incident that had just concluded. He would have worried out loud if somebody had seen or heard the shots. Or that the boy had been hit. Or at least that Jay Gelb had changed and was becoming the kind of urban savage of the sort that Gelb had always condemned, feared, held responsible for the contagion of amour propre that had resulted in the decline of community, which was the root cause of the city's present malaise. The other Jay Gelb, having heard Cicciolino's voice, would have had to confront what he had seen on the night before. This Jay Gelb, however, said, "Just passed by the Harlem River."

"Everything okay?"

"Fine and dandy." Gelb slid the revolver back under his belt and pulled his sweater over the grip.

"How long you think it'll take you to get into the Hudson?"

"I'm right on schedule. Be there a half hour before you."

All dressed in casual street clothes and standing at the phone in the hall of his Ninety-fifth Street condo, Cicciolino tightened the phone to his ear. What was he hearing? Something different for sure. It hardly sounded like Gelb, and he wondered if it could just be the cellular phone and the fact that Gelb was outside. "You all right?"

Gelb said nothing. He didn't answer questions like that anymore.

"Jay?"

"I'm here."

"You come by last night and take another package of stuff?"

"I did." The *other* Jay Gelb would have added, While you and Arlene were in the head.

"Why?"

"Did you consult me when you and Tug lowered the price?" The *other* Jay Gelb would have apologized, made excuses, and felt guilty about something—his addiction or maybe being too Jewish. "I should have taken the carton."

Cicciolino's eyes searched the top of the telephone table. "You sure you're okay?"

"Maybe that's the question you should ask yourself."

Gelb dropped the phone into its yoke, set the wheel on autopilot, and went below for a minute or two to reload the revolver and stoke his nose.

While the phone in the hall kept ringing and ringing and ringing, it took Gerri Cicciolino whole minutes to push Mr. Scotty away. He was in her, on her, wrapped all around her. He had entered her nose, her mouth, her ears. He was sleeping, all balled up in a big painful knot in her stomach.

Finally she fell onto the carpet. She picked up the bedroom extension, but it was unplugged. She tried to fit the slotted clip back in, but her hand was shaking too much. Using the wall to gain her feet, Gerri staggered into the hallway and grabbed at the offending instrument. She stared at its silence for a while before putting it to her ear.

"Gerri? Are you there? Gerri? This is Eva Burden again. Hello, Gerri?"

Gerri made a sound. Whatever was wrong with her stomach was exacerbated by her upright position. She could not remember when she had eaten last. "What do you want?"

"The people I told you about from South America? The woman? They murdered my chef at my restaurant."

So what? Gerri thought. We all had to die sometime.

"Now I'm looking for a friend. His name is Brian Nathanson. He's the man who took me off that island. He's also the man who owns the money that Bill and Jay and Tug took."

"What's he want? His *money*?" Gerri's head was now spinning, and she needed something fast to cool the ache that began in her stomach and extended all through her body and head. Scotty had scorched her, and she needed something bitterly cold to soothe the burn: vodka in a big tumbler with lots of ice.

"Maybe. I don't know. But it *is* his money, and he's no killer. Not like the others. Yesterday he went out to City Island to see if he could locate Jay Gelb, but I haven't heard from him. Do you know where Jay is? Is Bill there? Can I speak to him?"

Gerri had to hang up. It was too much, the wild raging feeling in her stomach. She couldn't care less about killers. They could all kill each other, they could kill *her* for all she cared. "All I know is he's been on the phone to Tug and Jay, who's somewhere on a boat, I think. And that bitch, Arlene."

"He?"

"Bill, *Bill*," Gerri snapped. "He's written something down here." She had to close one eye to focus. "Piers Sixty-two and Sixty-three. West Twenty-third Street." She hung up.

The phone rang again while she was in the kitchen, and a third time while she was walking by it toward her room. She had only three vials left, and she wondered if the miserable, duplicitous bastard with the bite and suck marks on his back had taken the car on her.

If he had, she'd fucking kill him. She'd *kill* him.

Sitting on the bed in the suite at the Doral Park, Eva did not know what to do. Where was Nathanson? Why hadn't he called her as he had said he would? Because he had no access to the phone aboard Gelb's boat? Or because he and Gelb had run afoul of the *sicaria*?

The latter, she feared. Where could he possibly be that he wouldn't be able to use a phone? Eva had never been to City Island, but she could go. She had her car, which was parked in Queens, or she could take a cab. If Jay Gelb was out there, he couldn't be that hard to find. She'd knock on every door, pound on every boat, if she had to.

But what had Cicciolino's phone calls been about? she wondered. To Tug and Jay and Arlene, Gerri had said. Eva had been trying to reach Tug all morning, but she got only his machine at his apartment, and the secretary in his office said he probably wouldn't be in until Monday. "Exhausted from his vacation, I guess," the woman added nastily.

Bill Cicciolino's secretary was a man. "The chief is taking a long weekend. Sick leave. He picked up something in the Islands."

That he did, Eva had thought. Which could be terminal.

Now she glanced down at the information that she had gotten from Gerri. "Pier 62 and 63. 23rd St." Was that one place or two? Could they have arranged to sell the dope already? When, aboard *Whistler*, Bill Cicciolino had first announced that he planned to take it back to New York, he had promised a quick deal. Could that be why the *sicaria* was letting them live—to take them with their profits, after the deal was consummated?

Eva stood. She would first fetch her car, then decide how to locate Nathanson, who was all that mattered to her now. Somehow she'd convince him to let the whole situation go. After all, they could always start over again. Together.

CHAPTER 26

RIVER RUN

IN THE BEDROOM of his top-floor apartment in East Harlem, Hector ("Chino") Santos did not need nobody to help him dress. He'd been buying dope from every kind of *maricón* for almost twenty-five years, and he knew what to wear, how to get ready.

Martita was watching from the door as he tugged the rubber gloves over his hands. With a single turn of plastic electrical tape he bound a small silver gun to the inside of his left leg. He let the wide leg of his stylish trousers fall, checked for telltale bulges, then did the other leg with another exact same gun. It was a Compact Off-Duty Police .357 magnum that chambered four rounds, cost $225, and Santos bought a dozen at a time.

In close where things started and usually finished, a .357 magnum with a hard-to-see three-and-a-half-inch barrel was enough. It was easy to pull, and one right shot could stop a truck. All the noise about firepower and machine pistols, like stuff from *Star Wars*, was for killers, guys who wanted to get caught or get dead. Santos had killed when he had to, but he was no ice man. Maybe it was time he quit. Maybe this thing with the cop was a mistake, a way of trying to make the only life he knew last.

Santos let that leg fall and gave it a once-over. Perfect.

"Jyou do that good, Chino."

'Course. It's what he did. Santos was a professional and thought professional, which was why he done good at life. If the Compact he'd stuffed under his belt at the small of his back or the other two that fit, like prayers, in the side pocket of his blousy windbreaker failed him, he could always reach for the two on his legs.

It beat trying to finger up a clip, check for the bottom, stuff it in the magazine, and slam it home. One tug and the plastic tape busted, yet it was strong, with enough snap, like a rubber band, to hold the gun in place, long as he walked.

If he had to run, it only meant things had turned sour or there were cops and he just wanted out. Then it was like the tape *knew*. A block, maybe a block and a half of hard running, it ripped away from his skin and dumped the pieces, neat as shit, in the street. No fingerprints, no serial numbers, which had been filed off, nothing to say it was his or link him to any fence or gun dealer.

During the deal itself, Santos would wear other surgical gloves. Always. He now stuffed two pair in his right pants pocket, then added his own beeper to his belt, the one he had been given by the cop. He stepped toward the mirror to get the total effect.

There he stood, three ways, all five-foot-seven-and-a-half inches of macho man, he thought. He weighed 147 pounds, kept his dark hair cut short with just a trace of wave on top and his mustache trimmed square as a nail brush. His skin was olive tone and his dark eyes sharp. Except for the deep razor scar on his cheek, he looked through his own eyes five maybe ten years younger than thirty-seven, because he lived and ate good. He was careful.

There he stood, wearing a shiny "Caribbean Sky Blue"—the label say—bomber jacket that he liked a size too big, and a heavy-cotton baby-blue turtleneck sweater that was also loose. It covered a full torso-suit of Kevlar body armor that included a throat shield. His dark blue pleated pants were Polo, and he had a new pair of black Reebok Night Flyers on his feet that made him *go*, man, when he have to. He pulled off the gloves.

There he stood, with the straight razor he was never without in his right back pocket. In his left pocket was ten dollars in quarters; in his left back pocket was one thousand dollars in fifties. Otherwise Santos was bare. No Rolex, no big wad. It didn't do no good to carry money big enough some cop or crack head'd kill you for. If he couldn't get home with what he had, fuck it, he wasn't good enough to *be* home.

Which made him think, there he stood: older, dumb, rich PR guy no balls to say, No, you gotta change. You gotta cut the shit that will kill you, one way or another. The big, greedy cop, he beaded you in.

Another voice, the old macho voice, say back, But *what if?* What if it all works out and you sitting on all that coke, years of it, letting it out slow? When you *rich* rich, *then* you move. Cop come back then, you ready.

"Wha' you see?" he asked Martita.

"I see the han'somest man in Eas' Harlem."

Santos liked that. He preened.

"Han'somer even than Justino," she went on. "And he *han'-som*, man. All the girls say Justino a *hunk*."

Santos spun around on her.

She held out a hand. " 'Cep' Martita."

He went for her anyway, and she ran to the bed. But there she pulled him down on her, hugging him tight. "You listen to Martita," she said in his ear. "You listen good. Don' matter the money, the dope, the cop. *Nada.* You jus' tay . . . *cuidado, mio cariño.* You come back to Martita"—she pushed his head back so they were eye to eye—"who love you."

Santos clamped his hands on her shoulders and forced her down into the mattress. "*Never* say that to me! *Ever.* You don' love me, you don' know what love is."

He was off the bed and headed to the door, smoothing his hair back. He glanced at the cheap digital watch on his wrist. He had to check to see if Justino and the others were where they should, and he'd be late if he didn't hurry.

"But *you* do," she said through a laugh at the ceiling.

"Wha' you mean?" He started down the stairs, taking them two at a time just to test the tape on his legs.

"You *know* 's all."

By the metal door that led into the fourth-floor landing, Santos stopped and looked up at her. "Wha' you know 'bout wha' I know?"

"I know you love Martita, and I wan' you say it."

Santos looked up at her, that dark little girl who worshiped him—good mood, bad mood didn't matter, he knew; and he thought, why not. Maybe he wouldn't come back, and there was so much else he really should tell her so Justino or none of the others would get what he worked for.

Then, if he did come back, he told himself, he could always say he said it like a joke, so she wouldn't worry. "I love you, 'Tita," he said in a small voice; he didn't want nobody outside on the fourth floor to hear.

She smiled and like shook her head and giggled. "Say it louder, man. I wan' you say, I love *Mar-ti-ta*. Plain, like that."

Santos said it plain but low.

"*Bueno*. For now. When you ge' back, you write it."

"Wha'?"

"Palimony. Like Lee Marvin."

Or Rock Hudson, he thought. Way 'Tita was put together.

"Come back quick."

When Gelb docked at the Seventy-ninth Street Boat Basin on the Hudson River, he found a tall, striking-looking redheaded woman and what looked like her servant waiting for him at the slip Tug had reserved.

"Mr. Gelb?" she asked. "I'm a client of Tug McCann and a friend of Bill Cicciolino."

Gelb hopped out on the dock, and she handed him a card. "I'm early. I guess I heard eight-thirty, not nine-thirty."

Gelb secured the stern, then checked the dock boy's bowline. There was both chop and wind there, and he debated tying her off with a spring line. But *Trekker* was well-fendered, and they would not be there long.

Gelb glanced down at the card that announced her name, Solange de los Páramos, and the company for which she worked, Papel Porteños. Gelb had once protested against them for their wholesale destruction of irreplaceable rain forests.

"How pleasant of you to offer to take us for a sail this morning. I didn't know how well-provisioned you might be, and I took the liberty of bringing along a few supplies." She indicted the large hamper that her servant was carrying.

Gelb scanned her Negroid lips, her green eyes, the long, blonding sweep of her forehead and bright red hair that was pulled tight at the back of her head in a bun. She was wearing what looked like a loose-fitting white *ruana* or poncho—something South American in cut—over a crimson polo-neck cashmere sweater. Her slacks were also white, like her deck shoes, and in her hands she held a wide-brimmed sun hat with a crimson sash and a pair of sunglasses that she now slipped on.

The servant, whom Gelb recognized immediately as an Andean Indian, was also dressed in sailing whites, with a double-breasted service blazer and big black buttons that matched his naval-looking tie and the shiny black visor of his nautical cap. His eyes were dark, slanted, and watchful. Against the backdrop of *Trekker* and the boat basin, the two of them looked like mannequins who had just stepped out of a window at Sak's.

"May I go aboard? I believe that's the expression, is it not?"

The old Gelb would have wondered what, in the name of hell, McCann had in mind, inviting her along, but he would have stepped lively to help her aboard and to make sure she had every comfort.

The new Gelb said, "Please don't think me rude, but I'd prefer to wait until Tug gets here." He pointed to a bench near some dock boxes. "He ought to be along any moment now."

The woman said something to her servant in a language that Gelb did not recognize. Grasping a shroud, Gelb pulled himself up onto the deck of the ketch and heard her say something else. When he turned back on them, he found the servant's eyes on him. "What language is that you're speaking?" he asked, reaching for the boom crutch.

Out of the corner of his eye Gelb saw the servant nudge the woman, and she moved closer to the boat, lowering her sunglasses on the bridge of her nose. "I beg your pardon. There's so much noise."

Really? At the moment Gelb had been thinking how quiet it was there. For some reason little of the noise of the West Side Highway above them was reaching them there at that slip. Gelb repeated the question.

"Spanish, of course. Maluko is Argentinian, as am I."

"*¿Habla español?*" Gelb asked, and went on in Spanish, "Strange, it didn't sound like Spanish. Maluko, did you say?"

"*Sí*, Maluko."

"Isn't that the name of a Chibchan evil deity?" Gelb glanced at the servant. Having sat on a dock box, the man now opened the large hamper, which he had placed on his legs, and reached in, as though rearranging something.

"Why, yes. How perspicacious of you, Mr. Gelb. But then I understand from Tug that you're a professor at Columbia."

Colombia. It was now on Gelb's mind, along with what he thought was the refrain from a song he once knew. Gelb could never remember lyrics exactly:

> "She don't try,
> She don't lie,
> She don't die,
> Cocaine."

But Tug had arrived. He made a pretense of jogging down the dock. "Solange! Maluko! You guys introduce yourself to Jay Gelb, artist, ship's captain, and soon-to-be-retired ne'er-do-well and scapegrace?" His face, set off by a dark blue Greek fisherman's cap was an alarming shade of red, but his blue eyes, as always, were clear. He seemed very much up for the occasion.

He thrust out his arms and threw his head back on his shoulders. "Look at that sky. Look at that city. You order this weather?" he asked Maluko, who now closed the hamper, his furtive eyes canting away.

"Give us a break, Solange. Look at you! Don't you own a pair of jeans? Turn around."

She did.

"Don't you look like a million."

"That's all?" she asked.

"C'mon." McCann reached for her elbow. "Bill told me he can't make it. Ain't it a goldarn shame? But we got another guest coming. You'll like him. He speaks Spanish, I think."

"Can I have a word with you, Tug?" Gelb asked from the deck.

McCann looked up at him.

"Below, if you don't mind."

"*I* don't, but—" It was rude, his expression as much as said. His eyes traced Gelb's face for the reason, but none came.

"The fuck you want?" he asked, pounding down the companionway after Gelb. "Bill call you? Everything's set up at the Pier 63, like we planned. The truck with the stuff, Bill in the unmarked car watching it. I just called Santos. He'll be here in five minutes. All we have to do is sail down there, tell Santos where it is so he can phone his guys, and let them check it out. After he tells us where we can pick up the money, we wait for Arlene's call. It comes, we drop him off. And it's done."

The old Gelb knew the plan backward and forward, had gone over the *what if*s and *why not*s dozens of times. The new Gelb just wanted to be aboard *Trekker* tomorrow morning with enough coke and money to get him to South America, where, he had decided sometime last night, he could be free. "Who the fuck is she?"

McCann drew in a breath and let his eyes rest on the cabin ceiling for a moment. "What's it to you who she is? She's my date, a blind, a . . . beard, is all you have to know. People see us from the water they think, couple of lucky guys out with a gorgeous red-head. Big boat. A servant."

"What happens if things screw up? What's she then? A witness, right? Or maybe a victim." He shook his head again. "Son of a bitch, Tug—how'd it happen? Where'd you find her? How many drinks you have?"

McCann's jaw firmed. "Actually," he said in a small, tight voice, turning to climb back above, "it was Chick's idea, and don't you *ever* fucking mention substance abuse to me again, Mr. Sniff. Far as I can see, Chick and me are supporting and will continue to support your fucking habit, at least until the kilo you glommed last night is done."

"Then take it out of my cut, if it bothers you so much. But one thing that's wrong—and you know it—is her presence on this boat. We're trying to make money here, not cunt."

Cunt yourself, McCann thought, stepping out on deck. Gelb deserved everything Arlene was dishing out and more. After this was over, they were quits, no two ways about it. The guy was an ingrate, plain and simple, and McCann hated that more than anything: somebody who just couldn't keep score. They had spotted him the boat, two kilos of shit, and however many thousand-dollar bills he had slipped himself off the drug boat down in the Islands.

McCann turned his head toward the granite bulwark of the boat-basin retaining wall and the parking garage that lay beyond it. Santos was there, standing by a pay phone, as he'd been told. McCann hurried to get Solange and Maluko aboard. "Don't mind Jay. He's just a little jumpy, is all. Has to do with the boat insurance and guests. He's a worrier, has been since he was a kid.

"Whoops—there I see our other guest," he said when he had Solange seated comfortably in the cockpit. "Pardon me while I go get him." Jumping down onto the dock, McCann looked up on shore at the little Rican chili pimp who was going to make the rest of his life a hell of a lot easier.

Tomorrow McCann would be right where he should be—at the telephone end of O'Casey's bar. The only place he was going was in his mind, and the destination was filled with big, secure golden pillows stuffed with tax-free loot. He'd tell some of the *ganefs* who were always nibbling around the corners of deals to go jump. From now on he'd broker only for honorable clients, those who were as good as their word.

Santos didn't know what to make of it so far, except the suckers were on time, which was different at least. Santos had dealt with guys who had the right time but the wrong place, others who had the right place but the wrong day. Then some guys who came so paranoid and burnt, making the exchange was like playing catch with a hand grenade.

When he got to the phone in the booth on Seventy-ninth Street, it was ringing. He picked it up, and the guy say, "Just keep going west, Chino. You know the boat basin across the West Side Highway? There's a phone near the manager's office. Catch you in ten minutes."

Santos had rented two vans, like always, from a place in the Bronx. They kept no records, took cash not plastic, and had big, heavy-for-pushing, "real"-looking banged-up trucks with some name of some business on the side and papers that checked on the computer. He'd installed car phones on Wednesday and had Justino, who knew motors and could fix anything, make sure both were ready to roll. It was the only reason Justino wasn't dead.

They were behind him now, parked in the trees near the edge of the road that looked down on the basin. Santos didn't walk alone to no meet, not when he could have ten guys at his back.

It was then somebody came around the side of the building and tapped him on the shoulder. Santos spun around, both hands in his jacket pockets.

It was the Irishman, McWhatever, with the big boil face and a hat on. He had another in his hands.

"Ah, man, don' do that. Guys I know—you be dead."

He spread his hands. "But it's you and me, Chino, and we trust each other, remember? Also, we've got a beautiful morning, a big ugly city to further corrupt, and even the weather is cooperating. Here, I brought you something." He handed Santos a white captain's hat with a shiny black brim and a gold wheel sewed in the front. "I had to guess at the size. Go on, put it on. Show me I was right."

"Why?"

"We're going sailing, and you'll want to keep the sun out of your eyes. C'mon—" He reached for Santos's arm, but Santos whirled it away.

Nobody ever touched him, 'specially no guy who was trying to fuck him when he was armed and doing a deal.

"—boat's waiting." Like he didn't care, the guy looked around him for the first time. Santos wasn't sure about nothing no more. Guy was too cocky. "I see you brought your army with you. You gonna be able to get them to a phone, like we discussed? Out there?" He pointed to the river.

"I don' worry 'bout *my* guys," Santos said loud, but he was worried now about everything. "Wha' you mean, out there?"

McCann turned and began walking toward the docks. "We're going sailing."

"Nah' me. I came here to deal. You got the shit on the boat?"

"Chino, that wouldn't be elegant. For the money you're paying, we want things to be slick, cool, and smart. What would all these other boaters say if you and your people were to troop down here and mule a thousand-plus pounds of 'product,' I believe it's called, into your APCs?" By which McCann meant the battered delivery vans that he could see under the trees.

"Better we take you aboard our boat. We wine you, we dine you. We even have an interpreter along so there'll be no breakdown in communications. When the time comes, we tell you where our van is. It's a place where you can watch too. If it tests out? *Amigo*, you tell us where your half of the bargain is, we get our call that it's all there, and we let you off the boat anywhere you want. How many times do I have to go through this?"

Santos did not take his eyes off the river. With all that water out there, he could drown easy. Santos could not swim a stroke. He even freaked when Martita turned up the waves in the Jacuzzi.

"Look, we're honest brokers, we'll treat you right. Anytime you want to bail out, you just tell me, I'll put you ashore."

"But my guys . . . ?" Santos glanced at the two vans.

McCann stepped back toward Santos, as though herding him. "They know how to drive slow?"

Santos said nothing.

"If they know how to drive slow, they won't be far from you. Or the deal either," McCann decided to add. "C'mon, Chino—buck up. You can understand our caution. We need some security for the deal, and you're it."

Santos glanced at the boil face and clear blue eyes. At least that was honest. Maybe he was telling the truth about the rest of it too.

Santos strolled slowly back to the van and spoke for a while in the window. The first van with Justino was to follow the boat. The second van was to hang back and try to keep both van and boat in sight. "Don' let nobody see your phones. I don' wan' them think we can talk. I'll make like I callin' a pay phone when they tell me where the dope is."

At the wheel Justino shook his shiny head. "This deal is fucked, man." He was from California, and had so much oil on his hair it looked like a motor had come on his head. "I wouldn't do no deal like this."

"Tha's why you' a poor little Mex greaser and always will," said Santos, turning away from the truck.

"Yeah? But nobody'll never make me wear a fuckin' pop top like that," Justino shouted after him. "You gonna put the hat on or what, Chino? Don' you look *cool*! *El Capitán!*"

The others in Justino's truck laughed and catcalled.

That's it, Santos thought. Justino was fuckin' dead, the minute the deal got done. He'd work it in somehow. There he was, Justino, fuckin' shot in his fuckin' head close range with somethin' big. Santos wouldn't say, but the rest of them would know.

Down on the dock, Santos raised the hat and fit it careful over his head. McWhatever was right; he'd need it for the sun.

He heard some more shouting from Justino's truck and thought maybe he should go back and do him now. It would make the deal go smooth. From his end.

"That's more like it, Chino. You might even have a nice day in the bargain," said boil face.

Santos didn't think so, and even less when he saw who else was and wasn't aboard. The tall redhead from the bar was there, the one he thought was the guy's girlfriend, and her chauffeur from the stretch Mercedes who got knocked cold on the wall outside the joint.

It was him, some kind of Cartel mule or *pistolero*, that Santos didn't like. Less his eyes and what was in them: death and no mistake. They were hard black slant-eyes that didn't blink for maybe a minute. Guy was a fucking killer for sure, and Santos stuck both hands in the pockets of his sky-blue bomber jacket where he had his first two Compact .357 magnums. He wrapped his hands around the grips and put his fingers on the triggers. He mooched his ass against a rail where only the river was at his back. He watched them killer eyes close and worried.

Where was the cop, the big one, Chief Bill C., NYPD? Santos had shown Martita him and the other guy, First Deputy Brant, Saturday morning on the tube. What was the connection, them to the Cartel Indians and big dope? Were they all in it together?

Then why do the deal themselves? Why not let some mules—aliens, wetbacks, that didn't matter and wouldn't dare cross them? Because the deal was too big? Nah. Other, bigger deals happened every day. You saw them in the paper and on TV when they went bust.

Justino was right. The deal was fucked from the start. Sitting there on water with his hands in his pockets and his fears jacked up high as the Empire State, which he could watch every time the boat changed course, made Santos feel dumb, and more and more like a target.

CHAPTER 27

DEAL

◆

IN AN OLDSMOBILE Regency Brougham that wasn't more than a month old, Gerri McCann Cicciolino caught sight of the boat. She was driving south along the elevated section of the Henry Hudson Parkway, just before the road dropped down to pier-level on Fifty-seventh Street. What else but a boat on a dope run would be tacking back and forth when the helmsman could run with the breeze toward the bay?

And there was a certain grace to the way the yawl came up into the wind, fell back with the current, then jibed with hardly a ruffle in her sails, which was Jay Gelb's signature. He had missed his calling altogether, she thought, slowing to let the taxis, trucks, and vans, which claimed Twelfth Avenue as a commercial artery on a weekday morning, hurtle by her car.

There Gelb was, looking suitably nautical, she saw as the boat neared shore. He had on a Greek fisherman's cap, wraparound sunglasses, and a full beard. Tug, her brother, was standing behind him wearing a similar hat, but he, of course, had something to drink in his left hand, and his right was wrapped around the hip of some tall woman who was dressed in white with a wide sun hat and a blood-red band on her head.

There was another man, whom she did not recognize and who looked like he was cold, sitting against the taffrail with his hands in a shiny blue jacket. He was wearing a white yachting cap, like the third man, who now appeared from the companionway with a cocktail shaker in his hands. In all, it was a scene to quicken the pulse of even the most inveterate city dweller. Gerri had seen the boat only at night, but here from a distance it looked sleek and able, far more yare than any they had chartered in the Islands.

But she was soon distracted. After all, she was riding with Mr. Scotty, who now placed an insistent hand on her leg. Two sticks of five vials each were sitting on the seat beside her, and she needed someplace to pull in and light up. The traffic signal was green at Twenty-third Street, but the flow of traffic in the other direction was heavy. She waited until she had drifted around the sharp, narrow curve in Twelfth Avenue. Piers 63 and 62 were on her right, but she turned left onto Twenty-first Street. And a good thing too.

Gerri was blessed with excellent vision, which Scotty made sharper still. It was perhaps the only interesting side effect of the chemical, and she caught a glimpse of Bill, her husband, parked in the cul-de-sac that had been formed when the jog in Twelfth Avenue had been "improved" with concrete Jersey barriers. He was sitting in the unmarked car that he had garaged for days beside their Regency Brougham, slumped down at the wheel with some kind of soft hat pulled over his forehead.

The cul-de-sac was a sorry urban scene, a forgotten place, a traffic planner's mistake with four stunted sycamores shielding two rows of derelict automobiles and a muddy patch of bottles, trash, and old tires. But from there he could survey all the traffic entering or leaving Piers 62 and 63 without being unduly noticed by anybody on those wharves or loading docks.

Gerri drove around the block and parked the large, powerful Oldsmobile in the deep morning shadows of a bar on Twenty-second Street, which ran one-way toward the river. From there she could look across a small triangle of park, across a shantytown of homeless shelters, across the jog in Twelfth Avenue, and see her husband in *his* car in the cul-de-sac watching and waiting for . . . ? Gerri had a good idea.

With her tinted windows rolled up, she went down on Scotty again, sucking him deep into her lungs. She could no longer see the yacht because of the sheds on the piers, but she knew her husband all too well. He had to control everything. She'd keep an eye on him. When he moved, she would too.

Snapping her lighter, Gerri lowered her head and did Scotty some more. She didn't think she could get too much of him. Now.

Out on the afterdeck of *Trekker*, Tug McCann eased himself away from Solange de los Páramos and approached Santos. He had remained seated against the taffrail since leaving the Seventy-ninth Street Boat Basin. McCann sat beside him.

It was cool on the river, but every time they approached the New York shore, as they were now, gusts of hot city warmed them. "Recognize that smell?" McCann asked Santos, who did not answer. "Springtime in Manhattan. Hot tar, drying concrete, pools of fetid garbage pickling in restaurant dumpsters. It's not Paris, London, or Rome. It's not even Pittsburgh, it couldn't be. Not with seventy thousand homeless having pissed and shat on it for the past three winter months.

"But," he sighed, looking down into his empty glass, "I suppose it's home. For you, for me. Could you live anyplace else?"

Santos shook his head. *McWhatever* was a right name. Santos now had a .357 magnum pointed at his heart, and there he was cooing away, like a pigeon.

"See the white van on the wharf between those two cruise ships?" He pointed toward one end of Pier 63, where a small fleet of short-line cruise vessels was docked.

Santos followed his hand and nodded.

"That's it."

Only Santos's eyes moved to McCann. "How I contact my guys?"

"Phone. Below."

Santos did not seem to understand.

McCann pointed again. "Downstairs on the bar. You need privacy? Take the phone forward. To the front."

Santos paused and his eyes moved farther still to the woman, who had turned her head in the other direction. The guy at the wheel didn't seem to pay any attention either. The deal was weird, man, and they kept getting closer to the cruise ships. "There a gate?"

McCann nodded.

"How my guys get in?"

"They're expected."

"How 'bout them people on them ships?"

"Aren't any. Maybe some crew, but they mind their own business. It won't take long. It's all there, all pure. It'll make you and your cast of doubtless thousands *muy bienaventurado*." McCann had once dated a Venezuelan woman who told him it was how he made her feel—happy.

Santos looked at him hard, wondering what he meant. *Bienaventurado* meant simple, dumb, stupid. Fuck it, he thought. He was here with this asshole, the stuff was supposed to be there on the dock. He had the cash waiting in the back room of his sister's bodega on 127th Street, and there was water all around him. He'd feel better downstairs, he thought, until he got downstairs.

The Indian with the white suit and hat just like the one Santos was wearing was behind the bar, arms folded across his chest, his killer eyes on him. "Don' I know you from someplace?" Santos asked in English to see if he understood English, but the Indian said nothing. "I think I know you. You look . . ." Dead or something, Santos thought.

Keeping one hand in his jacket pocket, he reached for the cellular phone, which was on top of the bar, and then stepped toward the front of the boat. Santos walked all screwed up, like a junkie, because of the tilt, which then tilted the other way as the boat turned. Santos closed the door behind him, but saw it wouldn't cut the sound because of louvers. He kept going, closing another door and another until he found himself in a little cabin where the bow came together.

He dialed the number of the phone in van *Uno*, got Justino on the first ring, and told him the location. The two vans were right in front anyways, since they followed the boat. Santos spoke low in his jack Spanish in case McWhatever or the guy at the wheel could hear him. The boat could be wired.

"Park in front of the gates. *Don't* go in until I tell you. You, Justino, you walk to the new white van between the two ships at the end of the dock. You'll see it when you get past the gate."

"Alone, man?"

"You heard me."

"Aw, man—you hangin' my ass out to dry."

Santos could picture Justino, all grease and teeth, but the

conversation was being overheard by the others in van *Uno*. It was either do it or lose face. Santos spoke right over him. "If it tests, you get out of the van. Come to the edge of the dock, wave your arms over your head, and sit down on one of the benches there. Don't move.

"Now, what I just say?" Santos asked, quick, before Justino could begin bitching again. He wanted the others to know what he said.

While Justino said it back, Santos snapped his head and looked behind him at a little toilet like in a closet. The door to the cabin was still closed, but he had the feeling he was being watched. Fuck he be glad when the thing was over, glad to be alive with whatever came out.

"Jus' do it!" he said in English over more bitching. "Jus' do wha' I say or put Pepe on." He listened some more, then, "Put Pepe on."

Justino hung up on him.

Leaving the little room, he stepped into the toilet and looked around. Nothing but a sink, some cabinets, a toilet with like a pump on the floor, and a shower stall with a frosted-glass front. And all that wood, man, *everywhere* was maybe what Santos had been noticing without realizing because of the deal. It was so *fine*, like nothing he ever see before. He'd have to ask somebody, the guy at the wheel, what it was: two colors, all blond with little like shell patterns bordered by a dark, rich wood with a tight grain. Mahogany maybe, but like no mahogany Santos knew.

Fuck if he wouldn't get himself something good, like the boat, after the deal. Santos hadn't *lived* enough, and he wondered if they'd sell him the boat. He'd put it somewhere, like the boat basin, and just look at the patterns, one room at a time.

Him and Martita with one of them bottles of nice wine from the restaurant.

Sitting slumped down behind the wheel of the unmarked Caprice in the cul-de-sac, Bill Cicciolino watched the skinny spic mutt with the oiled curls get out of one of two battered felony wagons. Both were stopped and idling in the wide parking area in front of Piers 62 and 63.

Cicciolino watched the mutt approach the gate—shit-scared, nonchalant—his pimp roll exaggerated, his wide pants spanking the tops of his Reeboks. He spoke to the guard at the gatehouse, who pointed to the truck. Mutt then strolled in like he was checking out the boats, the dock, the bollards, the sky, even the fucking river water that was pea green and stank like old socks, before he opened the van door and slid in.

On the seat beside Cicciolino in the unmarked car, he had a Dan Wesson Super Mag with a six-inch barrel and a Mossberg 500 Security slug gun that would put holes through those vans the size of golf balls going in and jagged grapefruits coming out. He glanced down at the black, buttless finish of the shotgun with its ribbed slide that jacked shells slick as butter, and the thing Arlene had used on him last night came to mind. It was something he didn't want to think about too hard, but the inescapable fact was he had liked it. Too much.

After climbing in the new van with the dope on the dock, Justino locked both doors, slid into the rear compartment, and looked down. The sides were lined with nine large cartons and a partial tenth. They looked like hostages, he decided, about to be done. Like slick white pants, the plastic waterproof cases had been pulled halfway down the sides of the boxes. Strips of duct tape kept the flaps together.

Pulling his razor from the instep of his high-top Reeboks, Justino opened the blade, and, moving down the center of the van, slit every piece of tape. At the rear of the van, he replaced the razor, turned, and dumped one box after another. He alternated sides, until the floor of the van was heaped with plastic-wrapped bricks of cocaine with the empty cartons tossed on top. He straightened up.

Justino had run for Santos for three years, and he never knew him to make a deal like this. Bastard was cheap with everybody, even the little dark bitch, Martita, who he treated like a princess locked in a tower. It must be the heat the cops put on him, Justino thought. Santos was going big time, getting himself a stash. That way he wouldn't be shut down when it happened again.

Carefully inserting the toes of his sneakers under the kilos so he wouldn't bust none and get charged by Santos, Justino made his way to the back a third time. Justino didn't need no big test for powder. He'd been into cocaine since he was nine years old, but smart. He wasn't no addict. His nose knew pure blow by feel, rush, and head every time, no mistake. It was one of two reasons he was always in demand.

The other was his rock work. Out in California, where he was from, Justino was known as a "geologist." He could whip up a batch of base on a ring-top burner or with an acetylene torch even that was the same prime quality vial after vial, no waste. Add his talent with motors and shit, it was the reason he should be working for himself. Problem was, he needed a backer or a chance, and already he was thinking maybe here it was.

The trick in testing for pure was to use the exact same amount every time out, no matter when—business, like this; recreational with the guys; even partying with a chick—so it was like you were training yourself day after day. Justino had got so good he could tell Cali from Medellín from the independents.

Squatting down now, he broke open the seal of a kilo near the rear doors and scraped the little gold spoon on his key chain over the hardened white brick until he had separated enough small flakes and grains to fill it. What he had here—he leveled off the spoon and raised it to his nose, holding the other nostril and sniffing in—was—he waited, counting to ten for his face and ten more for his head—was Medellín, no cut, and just about as pure as he had ever sampled.

The same with the next and the next and the next bricks that he sampled random—seven in all—working his way down the truck to the front, making sure he resealed every package with a tab of strapping tape he took from the roll he carried in his jacket. By the time he slipped into the passenger seat, his head, neck, shoulders, and back were numb, and the plastic of the seat, which had been baking in the sun through the windshield, sent a slow, deep warmth through his body that made him want to do something wild, he felt so good. It was another thing Justino had trained himself to watch for. Instead he batted his hand at the rearview mirror, so he could look at the heap of white bricks while he chilled out.

But he thought—there it is, my stake. Santos was out on the boat, right? Justino could hot-wire the truck, drive it out of there, cut the others in if he had to, and split with most of the coke to someplace like Chicago or L.A., where he had contacts. There, he would stash it, scout out a location, pay in crack for muscle and runners, set up some spots, and there he'd be. A fucking rich man and no fucking hump, like Santos, living like a rat trapped in a box.

Justino tried to clear his mind. He asked himself if it was just the blow talking, making him dumb crazy, the way it could do. He shook his head. No, he decided, he had wanted to do Santos ever since that bitch of his, Martita, had started making fun of him in front of everybody: his hair, his clothes, him being Mex and not a fucking Rican like the others. She even had a name for him, *Aguadorso*—Wetback—that Santos's other bitches, the pigmeat he sold on the street, shortened to *Dors'*. Or Dork, when they were being Anglo.

Justino had made his first good money boosting cars in Chula Vista, and he still kept on him an electrician's stripping and crimping tool, not just for sentimental reasons. You never knew when you might need transportation, and since everything—alarms and shit—was electronic these days, it was just the thing.

But Justino would have to hurry. Already Santos was probably wondering what was taking him so long. Justino pulled the tool out and looked around to see if he was being watched. With the back of the van pointing toward the river, he could be seen only from the front, which meant the guardhouse, the gate, and the couple of cars parked down a little dead-end area in the parking lot. In the side mirror he caught sight of the boat maybe halfway out in the river, its ass end to him, sailing away.

Justino lowered his head below the glare of the windshield and peered down at the ignition that had some kind of GM lock on the steering column, he supposed. The thing was to defeat any electronic antitheft device first, get the van started and running, and then stick the column with another little gadget on his key ring that would let him steer as long as he kept it in, *baby*. Thanks to Santos for being such a tight ass, he had the roll of strapping tape for that.

But he also still had all the coke he done sitting right on the top of his brain. When he unsnapped the plastic column-wire clasp and separated out the wires, he couldn't remember which wire on GM vans was ignition and where he could cut into a pure hot wire to bypass any alarm.

On his first try Justino sounded the horn one long blast that scared him, and he banged his head on the bottom of the dash. Lucky the horn was one of the New York muted types that he hoped got lost in all the background noise. He tried another, but for some reason it didn't work until he decided it must be lights.

He was sweating now. The sun was hot on the side of the van, and his heart was beating wild, so fast it made his body jerk and twitch. Santos would kill him or at least try, just for the attempt. Maybe he needed a little more powder to steady him. But as he began pushing himself out from under the dash, his hand drifted into some other wires. There was a spark, and he got a shock. But the engine kicked over.

Santos did not hear the horn, but he saw the red rear lights of the van flicker on and off, on and off, maybe three, four times, as the boat came around and headed toward the New York shore again. Asshole, he thought, is probably wired on the coke, and his foot is hitting the brake pedal while he finishes up. You don't have to snort none of it, Santos had told him. We got other ways to tell if it's good.

But Justino had said no. He had to be *el Hombre*, the expert who knew everything there was about coke, like it was something he invented. And—hey—where Justino was concerned, Santos would let him screw himself up.

Until he saw the white backup lights go on too. His hands came out of his shiny blue windbreaker. The coke must be good. He jumped to his feet. "Lemme out!" he shouted at McWhatever. "Fucker's tryin' to steal my coke!" And leave me having to pay, he thought.

McWhatever looked up from the broad he was trying to make, as though Santos had dropped from the sky.

Santos took two quick steps toward the guy at the wheel. He grabbed his shoulder and spun him around. "There! *There!*" He pointed. "Hurry up. See them lights? Muh'fuck stealin' my shit!"

"How do you know?" McWhatever asked. Standing by Santos now, he had his own hand in his jacket, and Santos thought, Shit, they gonna think it's me. Justino, you dead.

"The backup light. You can't get no backup light— There!" The white lights popped on again. "See? You can't get no backup light without no key. Fuckin' fuck-ah! He fuckin' wirin' the column," he shouted. "I fuckin' *kee*-ill you, Justino! You' dead!"

And then to the wheel guy, "Go! *Go!* Ain' you got no motor?"

Said Gelb, "Why? You want us to drop you off?"

The lights had gone off again, then back on. Justino was having trouble getting it going, but it was only a matter of time. The way he was with coke, Justino was good boosting cars, the best Santos ever see.

"Where's the payment? No payment, no dock, *comprendes*?"

"Here. *Here*'s the *drop*!" From out of his pants pocket he pulled the card Martita had written the address on.

The guy took it from Santos and studied it, like reading a book.

"My sister, she own the bodega. In the back. Back room. She' waiting, no problem." He turned to McWhatever. "The motor! Get it going!" He looked down, but all he could see was a big dial, and some little levers with knobs on them. "This ain' no scam. I got too much to lose." Cupping his hands, Santos threw back his neck and shouted, "You fuckah, Justino, you fuckin' *dead*!"

Gelb turned to McCann, who hunched his shoulders and reached for the card. "I'll call it in." He gestured with the card at Santos and said, "Can't get far." He meant because of Cicciolino, who was waiting for Santos in the parking lot. "And—" He knows we know where to find him.

McCann turned his head to Solange to apologize before going below, but surprisingly she was gazing south, off toward Ellis Island and the Statue of Liberty beyond.

But not for long. McWhatever had only got down the stairs when Santos acted. There was no way he was just going to stand there with his thumb up his ass, while the little *Dors'* bastard ingrate cocksucker stole his delivery. Where was the cop, for cris-sake? At least with him no shit like this would go down.

He spun around, took three quick steps toward the broad, and glued a Compact to her head. "Up! Ged up! Ged you' hands out of the poncho. Now!" When her hands came free, Santos shoved her toward the wheel man. "The *motor*!" he shouted. "The fuckin' motor! *Now*!" He had to like reach to keep the stubby barrel on her head.

The guy bent someplace under the little well he was standing in and touched something. Somewhere down in the boat Santos heard an engine kick over and catch. The guy threw a lever and worked another, and they shot ahead.

Below deck, McCann reached for the cellular telephone on

the bar in front of Maluko and said, "Would you excuse me for a moment? I'd like to make a call." But the servant did not move; it was as though he had not understood him. McCann raised the phone to demonstrate and said it again, but Maluko's eyes did not even quaver.

He was standing behind the bar with his arms folded across his chest. On the low sink before him was the large hamper he had brought, the wicker top open.

McCann heard the high-pitched whine of the starter motor, and then the auxiliary engine sputtered, caught, and roared to a start. He turned his back and punched in the number that answered on the first ring. "Arlene? Tug here." He then read her the address. "From what I understand it's a bodega owned by the guy's sister. Break a leg."

Dropping the receiver in its yoke, McCann noticed a small round object with a little spring antenna that had been attached to the side of the phone. By Chick, he decided. Who else would be monitoring their calls? But Chick hadn't been aboard the boat since New Jersey, which was before they'd got the phone. Gelb? Why?

When he turned around, Maluko was gone, and even over the roar of the now-racing engine he heard further shouting up on deck.

"Tha's right," Santos said to McCann, as he moved up the companionway. "Slow, slow. The keys to the van. Put 'em there on the roof, or I kill you' pretty woman." When McCann hesitated and glanced at Gelb, Santos shouted, "Now! *Now*! I ain' fuckin' with you. Jyou assholes screw things up. If I gonna die, I gonna take you with me."

Again McCann's eyes met Gelb's. What could Santos know? Who could have told him? McCann pulled the new keys with the dealer's tag still on them from his pocket and dropped them on the cabin top.

Santos snatched them up. "Now—get over there with the mule." He meant Maluko, who was standing against the taffrail port side with something squarish and metallic in his hands. McCann blinked. It was an Uzi, or something like it. "Where'd he—" McCann began to ask Solange, when Santos reached out and shoved him. "Quick, quick—we nearly there."

Solange's smile to McCann was contained and seemed amaz-

ingly tranquil, but her eyes were moving from the boat to the dock
to Maluko and back to the dock.

"Jus' pull in, don' stop. Close, close. *Closer!*" With the gun
still to her head, Santos pulled Solange across the deck to the
starboard rail.

Nearing the section of dock between the two cruise ships
where the van was parked, Gelb swung the boat up around, dumping the wind from her sails, which spanked and snapped above
them. He disengaged the propeller, then shoved it into reverse and
hit the throttle while turning the wheel hard to starboard.

Trekker seemed to pause, as if deciding, and then gracefully
sideslipped toward a bollard while still maintaining forward way
that carried her within a yard or two of the dock.

Santos shoved the woman away from him and jumped off.

Maluko snapped up the automatic weapon and fired a burst
at Santos, who had ducked, and the bullets tattooed the brilliant
white side of the new van.

He fired again, but *Trekker*'s momentum now carried her past
the stern of the northernmost cruise ship, and he swung the barrel
at Gelb. To McCann he said, "You—get over there with him."

Moving beyond the lee of the cruise ship, *Trekker*'s sails filled.
She heeled over, paused once again, and darted off across the river.

Solange de los Páramos—now Solange Mercier La Guatavita—straightened the poncho on her shoulders and looked toward the dock, where she could see a man running from the van.
She had been taken by surprise by the turn of events, but the
situation was not beyond her control. If Maluko had installed the
device on the phone accurately, as she had taught him, they would
have the conversation with the location of the drop, as well as the
number called, which they could trace to that location. But she
would have to hurry.

Solange now slipped three fingers under the crimson cummerbund that had remained obscured beneath her poncho and extracted a Teac-38, a kind of modern derringer that fit in the palm
of her hand like a black wedge. She turned to McCann, since they
would need Gelb to get them back to the dock. She knew nothing
about boats, nor did Maluko. "Tell me who is picking up the
money and what happens after it's received."

McCann was stunned, confused. Suddenly, in two or three
minutes, no more, everything had got out of control and wacky,

and he wished from the bottom of his soul that Chick were with them. Tug had never liked guns, had never really cared for violence, and what was he seeing here? Was Solange actually pointing one at him? Why? "Jesus, what's this? We were just doing a little deal with that guy, and—"

Solange stiffened her arm and shot McCann in the middle of the forehead. The bullet was a .38 special with a hollow tip that fragmented in McCann's brain and blew off the back of his head. His Greek fisherman's cap, carried by the breeze, sailed out over the river.

Gelb pulled the gun from under his sweater, but the woman, quicker than he, pivoted and pointed hers at his face.

Maluko reached for McCann. Before his body could tumble off the taffrail, he extracted Santos's card with the address of the drop that he had seen McCann slip in the pocket of his windbreaker. He then pushed him overboard.

In spite of the gun that was on him, Gelb now shrieked to see Tug so finally and summarily dispatched. He dropped the revolver on the deck by his feet, launched himself down the companionway ladder, and rammed shut the hatch after him, throwing both side bolts.

But where could he hide?

His coke. He had stashed it in the fo'c'sle cabin, and suddenly he decided it was the most important thing in the world to him. He could face anything if he just had his coke. Already they were breaking through the companionway hatch. A stunning burst of gunfire riddled the ladder and filled the galley with smoke and dust.

Gelb turned and fled into the forward compartments of his beloved *Trekker*, closing and locking each louvered butternut cabin door after him.

CHAPTER 28

BUST TOO

♦

THE SLUGS FROM the machine pistol had ripped through the thin sheet metal of the van. Jagged slivers knifed into Justino's right leg, which was stretched into the back as he fiddled with the strapping tape on the column lock.

He hit the door clasp, fell from the truck, scrambled up, and began running toward the gate. There, he could see the two big, battered vans, idling in the wide parking area.

Santos stopped at the open driver-side door and pulled a Compact from his shiny blue bomber jacket. With his other hand, he steadied the small weapon, sighted Justino in, and squeezed the trigger.

The recoil of the small gun firing .357 loads produced extreme muzzle rise, but Santos forced his wrist down and fired again. And again and again until the four shots were spent.

Justino went down, but he got up again and made for the vans faster than ever.

Santos couldn't believe it. Here he had his chance with the weapon he'd been practicing on for years, but he only winged the little bastard, who was now too far to hit. It was not a good day.

Santos spun around, threw the empty gun into the river, and

hopped in the truck. Out of the corner of his eye he saw the bricks of coke scattered all around the back. It had to be good. Justino wouldn't risk his life for garbage.

The van was still idling, but the keyhole of the steering column was stuck with a twisted piece of some metal, and the wheel—shit—it wouldn't turn. Santos tried to calm himself. He glanced in the side mirror and saw that the boat had swung around and was sailing back out into the river. Good.

The trick was to pull out the skeleton Justino had used and stick in the key in one smooth pass. Whatever Justino had done to bypass the ignition Santos could never hope to do over, and usually it fucked the key start. He sucked in a breath, closed the door, and glanced up in time to see Justino push the driver away from the wheel of van *Uno*.

Santos stepped on the brake, shoved the gear selector into drive, then readied the ignition key in his right hand, while braking his left on the steering column for leverage.

Uno, dos, tres—he grabbed the skeleton, got a shock, grabbed again and tugged, but nothing. The fucker was jammed in the lock and hot. It was burning up, and he now realized he'd been smelling scorched plastic and hot wires since he got in. Now he could see smoke curling from under the dash.

It was then, looking down, that he saw Justino's tool, the electrician's pliers that he always carried, and Santos reached for them.

In van *Uno*, Justino turned to the four others. "Fuckin' van's loaded with coke. Tons. More coke than I ever seen. And *pure*. It's millions and millions, more than he ever need. You wanna be *rich*?"

The others just stared at him. He knew he'd been hit—there was blood on his right hand—but he didn't feel a thing, which was the coke. "Pepe—I axe *you*. You wanna be *rich*? You don't, get the fuck out, 'cause us other guys"—Justino threw the van in gear and turned the wheel toward the gate—"we gonna be *rich*!"

It was then that Cicciolino, sitting in the unmarked Caprice under the sycamores at the south end of the parking area, saw the brand-new van with Santos and the dope spurt forward. It hesitated, as Santos tested the wheel, then made for the same gate that the battered skell wagon with the little greaser who got winged was headed for. "Skell" was another cop term; it meant mutts, wombats, felons—anybody who was poor—or suspicious-looking, and probably not white.

It was time to act. Cicciolino had supposed the deal would go according to plan—Santos's crew would take the dope away; Santos would tell them where the loot was; Arlene would make the phone call that would release him. In the meantime Cicciolino would follow the skells to wherever they dropped the dope, and he would wait for Santos to arrive.

But this was even better. Santos himself would *leave* with the coke, and from all that Cicciolino could see, he was *alone*. More perfect still, he was rattled, and whatever piece of double-dealing shit that was going down between him and his dope tester was tailor-made. The second battered van had not moved, and it looked as if the skells inside were having an argument.

The gate to the World Tours dock was open, and Cicciolino hoped the gatekeeper in his kiosk was cool, as Tug's brother had said, since he was about to get an eyeful. It would be best if the whole thing was made to appear spontaneous, like something the mutts had done to themselves. The slugs in Cicciolino's shotgun would be untraceable, and with the two vans bearing down on him, the gatekeeper probably wouldn't catch where the shot had come from anyways. Cicciolino could not miss.

The cul-de-sac Cicciolino was in ran parallel to the front fence of World Tours, so he was approaching the gate from the flank. He tapped the accelerator of the Caprice, which nudged forward. On one side of the gate the battered felony wagon was charging forward at maybe a forty-five-degree angle. On the other side was Santos and the dope.

Cicciolino hit the power-control button, lowering the passenger window. He propped the shotgun on the sill, then eased the car to a stop and took aim. He waited until the battered van had nearly passed him and he couldn't miss the grill.

The shotgun roared, jumping off the door. The slug bucked through the van grill and burst the radiator. Coolant splashed the windshield and rose up in a green, steamy cloud. Yet the skell mobile kept rolling toward the open gate that Santos in the dope van had nearly reached.

Cicciolino jacked in another shell and took aim at the front tire. Santos and the dope had to get away from the pier and back up to East Harlem *before* Cicciolino made his find. Down here too many little things could be put together, especially now that the situation had become messy.

He squeezed off the second shot, which shattered the right front wheel of the van, stopping it cold, and the new white van with Santos jounced over the lip of the gate. It cut around the steaming van and sped off toward the exit of the parking area, as if Santos would cut right across Twelfth Avenue onto Twenty-third Street.

Until Cicciolino saw the long gray car with the black Landau roof, bearing down on Santos. It was an Olds Regency Brougham, just like Cicciolino's own new car. Behind the wheel was a woman with a shock of snowy-white hair. Fuck if it wasn't Gerri, his wife.

She had Mr. Scotty, larger than life now, sitting with her in the front seat of the car. She had waited where she had parked on Twenty-second Street, going down on him again and again until she had puffed him up into a palpable presence there beside her. He even urged her on.

"Go on, Mama—they be there," he said when they saw the two battered vans with what looked like Hispanics pull into the open area in front of the gate to Pier 63. "Any time's right. Don't make no nevermind to me." But she waited, tasting the rough and incandescent Scotty twice more while the thin boy with the dark, shiny curls walked through the gate to the new white van near the ships. He remained there for maybe fifteen minutes, only to come running back and be shot at—she saw the little puffs of smoke—by some other Spanish man, who then took control of the new van.

It was the death wagon, she decided, noting how her husband parked where he could command the entire wide lot, how he concentrated on it and prepared himself to protect it from the men in the other two vans. No, boys, really. They were just boys, like all the others all over the city who would never get a chance to become men. So when Chick started his car and began creeping like some predator toward the front of the gate, Gerri decided it was time to act. Direct intervention was called for.

But Scotty wouldn't let her alone. He pulled the wheel out of her hands. "Scotty don't need no chauffeur," he told her. "Scotty don't need no *guide*! Scotty, he be *Scotty*! What more could you want alive?" The car shot away from the corner and turned up

Eleventh Avenue against the one-way flow of traffic that honked, screeched, and swerved by them. To get to Pier 63, they had to turn onto Twenty-third Street, and then began a long, drifting skid that was checked by the side of a brown UPS truck. Glancing off, Scotty jerked the wheel and bolted for Twelfth Avenue, which was a blur of traffic speeding by.

Gerri's eyesight had never been better. Everything was clear and like frozen in a series of photographs that she was fanning through with her thumb. Up ahead of her now was Eva Burden, stepping out of a car. In the next frame Eva raised her hand, as though trying to signal Gerri to pull over. But Scotty said, "We ain't stoppin' for nothin' or nobody, Mama. Hold on!"

Twelfth Avenue is the major north-south West Side artery. Its road surface is also crowned high. Miraculously traffic ceased for the three seconds that it took Scotty to cross its four lanes, but the speeding car vaulted off the crown and sailed toward the parking area in front of Pier 63. When it came down on the cobblestones, the hubcaps burst from its wheels, but it shot directly at the new white van. The death wagon.

With arms stretched taut and her right foot pressed to the floor, Gerri Cicciolino surged right at it. "Tell me, Scotty—in your little jingle? What about dead?"

"Well, Mama—dead be *dead*."

Behind the wheel of the van with the dope, Santos did not know what to do, as the large gray car hurtled at him.

To his left where there was room to run stood van *Dos,* idling with three scared faces in the windshield expecting some signal from him. To the right was nothing but old junker cars, some trees, a little dead-end alley, and the concrete Jersey barriers that lined the curve on Twelfth Avenue. No escape.

Santos opened the door, like he would jump, but instead he pulled a Compact from the left pocket of his jacket and fired four quick shots at the driver of the car. He then cut the wheel hard, hit the gas pedal, and threw himself across the passenger seat.

He got her, he knew he did—some old broad—right in the face. He seen the blood. But something hit the ass end of the van, spinning it around, so that it teetered on two wheels and only its forward motion kept it from tipping over.

Santos then heard a loud crash and the sound of breaking glass somewhere beside him. He grabbed the wheel and pulled himself up. Turning to goose the van toward the green light at Twenty-third Street, he glanced in the side mirror and saw that the car had veered off and hit van *Dos* broadside, pushing it into the fence. He could see two, maybe three, of his guys on the ground and the rest running away.

But he was now out on Twenty-third Street, clipping down a line of trees in the little park where the lights on Eleventh and Tenth were in his favor. He had to stop at Ninth Avenue, and he scanned all three mirrors to see if somebody was on him. Traffic was light there, and he could see nothing behind him but a single taxi dropping off a fare and a tour bus going the other way.

The dashboard was still smoking, and the damage that the van had taken in back might catch a cop's eye, 'specially the bullet holes in the side. But Santos, who was trembling now the exchange was over, nearly rejoiced. *Jesús Cristo*—was he out of the thing alive *and* with the coke?

Justino? If he wasn't dead, he would be, and anybody else too who wanted to try. Santos would tell the others he set the whole thing up, like for a test. The guy with the shotgun was his backer.

The cop. Cicciolino. He wouldn't want any of the others in van *Uno* taken in either. His saving Santos from Justino showed he was sincere, and it was no cop buy/bust sting. Where had he come from? It was like he was waiting for him. A fucking big, ugly dark angel with firepower. Question was—where was he now? Could Santos count on him if there was more trouble?

Cicciolino was on Twenty-fourth Street, one block above Santos, following the homing device he had placed in the van the night before. He had seen what had happened to Gerri, but he hadn't considered stopping. Why? There was no way she could have survived that crash. The engine of the Regency Brougham had been driven into the backseat. And anyways, she had only been trying to screw things up. She had always been a busybody, a perfectionist, and she got what she deserved.

She must have overheard him or something, when he was standing in the hall of their apartment talking to Tug on the phone. Frankly Cicciolino felt relieved, having her out of the way. Also, there was the bonus that it would make everything else seem doubly justifiable, and he only hoped Santos had dropped the gun he had fired at the scene or it was still on him.

The boat. He wondered how things had gone there. Too fast, it had seemed to him. *Trekker* had only just arrived at the dock when Santos was off her, into the van, and pounding out through the gate.

And why hadn't Gelb split, as they'd agreed? The last glimpse Cicciolino had of *Trekker* as he turned down Twenty-fourth Street, she was out in the middle of the river, creeping north, not south, her sails luffing in the breeze.

In the fo'c'sle cabin of *Trekker* with the door locked behind him, Gelb had not known what to do or where to go. Gone was the New Gelb of the coke heroics; the old, sorry, weak Gelb had returned with a vengeance. To die, he feared.

The coke, which could help him, was so well concealed in a net above a utility locker that it would take him whole minutes to retrieve. And then his hands were shaking so badly he could never ready some lines before they got to him.

He could hear the Indian pounding and shooting and hacking at *Trekker*, breaking his way through the companionway hatch and the three cabin doors Gelb had locked in back of him. For a moment there was silence, and he figured out they were making a call on the cellular telephone in the main salon. In the welter of vowelly sounds that was Chibchan, he guessed, he distinctly heard his wife's name, "Arlene Gelb," followed by his address.

Another stunning burst of automatic-weapons fire followed, and Gelb snapped his head toward the bow. The only other place he could flee to was the fo'c'sle head, which at least had a door, but, stepping in, he caught sight of himself in the little mirror over the sink—gaunt, haggard-looking with the beard, bloodless—and he stopped. He pulled off the wraparound sunglasses and considered his eyes, which he had always thought—and his mother had said—were among his best features: hazel, bright, and compassionate. Yet he could scarcely see them.

In front of Gelb's vision, like an image initialized on a screen, was the picture of Tug standing there on the deck with the little spot on his forehead and his hat discing off over the river. He was dead on his feet so quickly that only his eyes—which had fixed

Gelb's—had acknowledged the change. Suddenly they had muted from the lively light blue that Gelb had always thought of as "Tug's Eyes," like no other vibrant shade, to some dull color as opaque as agate.

Something heavy hit the second cabin door, which splintered and fell, and he could hear the woman's voice directing the servant again in Chibchan. Colombians. They had come to claim what was theirs, and Gelb could only think of poor, simple Arlene who—like Tug and Bill and he himself—had tired of the limitations of their own good lives and had tried for more. She with her lovers and her baby and her myth of her cowboy father who had been a nasty, self-righteous gambler and drunk. Tug and Bill who, each in his own way, had been so consumed by the city that they had lost all perspective on good and bad, right and wrong.

And he himself—sailor? Fuck. Pistol-packing coke addict? Double fuck. He had let the picture get blurry. Things had got out of whack, and he had lost balance.

He could hear them making their way toward the door, quietly, cautiously, not knowing if he had a gun. Gelb lowered his head to the sink, the porcelain of which was emblazoned gold in a shaft of bright sun through the polarized, double-glazed hatch light.

Violence. Violence nauseated Jay Gelb. How had he got caught up in it? Gelb had never cruelly killed any living thing, and until this morning he had never tried. Even if he still had his gun or possessed the means of killing the two people who were coming for him, would he be able to live with himself afterward?

What was he thinking—two? There had been Monroe and the others who had been killed in the plane that had attacked them on the uninhabited island where they found the stuff. Gelb tried to retch, he felt so awful, but he failed even at that.

He looked up. There was the forward hatch itself, but Gelb had bolted it from above to prevent Santos from coming up on them suddenly when he went down below to make his phone call. Or from escaping, which was an irony not lost on Gelb at the moment.

Faintly he could hear the auxiliary engine still idling, and from the sound of the water cutting by her aluminum hull, he could tell that *Trekker* was sailing herself. Without anybody at the helm, she had turned herself up into the wind and current. A good boat, strong and true.

"Professor Gelb," the woman now said through the louvered door. "Professor Gelb, do you know who we are?"

"Yes," he heard himself say. "I think so." It occurred to him now that he had read somewhere about the assassins who were sent out by the drug cartels to recover their losses. In South and Central America, the article had stated. Seldom in the United States, unless the loss was large. There was a word for such operatives, but he could not quite think what it was. Though he would.

He heard the Indian mumble something before the woman went on, "Then you must know that we're here to reclaim the merchandise that you and your friends appropriated in the Bahamas. Can we talk?"

Gelb watched the door handle slowly turn, as one of them tried the door. "We are, aren't we? What would you like to know?"

Again the Indian mumbled before she spoke. "Well, to be frank—we're now interested in the payment you and your friends are receiving for our cocaine. If we had that and the address of Señor Santos, we would be satisfied and believe ourselves 'made whole,' as it were."

Not from what Gelb had read. In addition to taking anything and everything they could, the procedure was to slay everybody concerned. To make an example and to leave no witnesses. Again Gelb thought of Arlene, whose understanding of the world had always been so *oblique,* Gelb now decided. It was that which he had fallen in love with first. The . . . central mystery of Arlene that he had still not even begun to solve. Maybe if he had been a better husband to her she would have revealed more of herself and not have sought out the—*company,* he supposed, was not quite the word—of Cal, whoever he was, and Chick, who could take care of himself. "I can't do that."

Yet again the Indian spoke.

"Because of your wife? Is her telephone number"—the woman paused—"555-1122? It was she whom Tug called earlier, wasn't it? To pick up the money."

There, they had it. Gelb thought of the ease with which they had tracked them north and the woman had insinuated herself among them. Had Arlene any chance at all?

"I must tell you, Professor. You either cooperate with us now or there is no hope for you or your wife. What say we make a deal.

You give us what is ours and we seek, and you and your wife keep this boat and your lives."

Still Gelb said nothing. He couldn't. He knew what he had to do now and what it would mean. The only hope Arlene had was to get away, and his "cooperating," whatever that would mean, would only lessen her chances.

Gelb stepped farther into the head and closed and locked the door. He would get into the shower stall, which was like a kind of upright sarcophagus—an exquisite construction of multicolored Moroccan tile and bleached teak. There was even a little port where he might get a final glimpse of the city, but he would tell them nothing, he vowed, no matter what they did to him personally.

He reached for the door of the shower, which was made of opaque frosted glass so that one cabin occupant might use it while the other shaved. Shipboard life, he mused, was so different. And better.

"Professor Gelb." The woman's voice came to him faintly now through the two closed doors. "Professor Gelb, you'll either have to come out now, or we'll have to come in. This is your last chance to make a deal. Do you have a weapon?"

With his eyes at the level of the port, Gelb opened the shower-stall door and fully expected to step in, but—he jumped back—there was a large, tall man already in there, who raised a finger to his lips.

"I'm Brian Nathanson," he whispered. "The money? The two-point-four million?" He waited until Gelb nodded. "It was mine. It was also in my boat that Eva Burden got off that cay. You listen close and do everything I say. Maybe I can save your life."

Gelb blinked. Nathanson was a big, broad-shouldered man who seemed to fill the shower stall, and all Gelb could think was that he had to have been there since the night before, when Gelb had gone to Hoboken to get more coke. Somebody had broken in and stolen his new TV and VCR, but maybe not.

The man was wearing street clothes—a tweed overcoat, shirt and tie—and was maybe six-four or five. He had short brownish hair, well-tanned skin, and light green eyes that reminded Gelb of Eva Burden. There was a dimple that formed in the side of one cheek when he spoke. It was repeated in the center of a large, round chin.

"You got a gun?"

Gelb shook his head.

Nathanson looked away. He had not wanted to get into guns again, but he now wished he had. Killing the woman might bring the renewed wrath of the Boyacas on him, but it might also stop them cold. He wondered how inconspicuous or efficient they would be on their own here in New York.

"You said you know who those people are. Do you really?"

Gelb blinked.

"I hope you do. I also heard what she said about your telephone number and your wife. The phone call McCann made? I heard that too. What's she doing, your wife? Taking the drop back to your place on West End Avenue?"

Gelb was amazed. There he had been sure he was part of a tight, discreet operation, known only to four people. He now thought of Eva Burden again, whom Arlene had said was back in town and trying to contact them. And of Tug.

"That single shot I heard, after the first burst at the van on the dock. Was that McCann? They take him out?" he asked.

Gelb closed his eyes and nodded. "The woman did." The difference was, he decided, that the others, like this man, were professionals. Eva had been right. How much better off would they have been not to have touched a thing, not even the money, which was—given who they were—unrealistic to expect. Even now, close to death, Gelb knew he would be hard-pressed to pass up $2.4 million in found money. It just wasn't in him to see money as good or bad or clean or tainted. Money was money, and as long as *they* hadn't killed or corrupted for it . . . but, of course, they had now.

It was why Gelb had never been able to get into his father's religion. It was too taxing and inhuman, like being a reformed alcoholic. You were a weak, corrupt, basically vile creature who had to struggle mightily on a daily basis—reading the Scriptures, performing obeisances, and questioning yourself at every turn—to be good. And you were either good, that is, *utterly blameless in everything,* or you were bad. As God had wanted all along.

"Where's Cicciolino? He on the buyer's tail? He gonna bust the guy who bought it and become a hero in the bargain?"

Gelb only looked away.

Nathanson shook his head. People always wanted too much.

It was what had got him and Creach all jammed up with themselves. The whole one-more-deal bit when they already had plenty, and all the fun and adventure was out of the business for them.

To Gelb he now said, "I want you to step into the cabin and tell her you're unarmed, you're opening the door." When Gelb did not move, Nathanson added, "Now. Quick. Before they begin firing."

Backing out of the head, Gelb tripped over the doorsill and wondered if it was the coke still and was he imagining the man? "Wait. *Wait!*" he shouted. "Don't shoot. I've thought better of it. I'll let you in. Don't shoot, please."

The Indian spoke yet again, and then the woman said, "We won't shoot you, I promise."

"Good. Now—I'll slide the bolt and then step well back from the door. My hands are up." He glanced at the man, Nathanson, who was now standing in the doorway of the head, and nearly added, "I'm not alone," but decided against it. In case he was.

Gelb did as he said, and slowly the door, which opened in, came toward them, swaying with the boat. It was dark along the passageway, and Nathanson thought he saw the face of the Indian for an instant someplace in the shadows. They obviously knew what they were doing and were taking no chances. Nathanson then heard the Indian speak.

"Who's with you, Professor?"

"My name is Brian Nathanson. I believe you know me. If you come to the door where you can read my lips, we can talk."

That too was translated, and the woman then asked, "Are you armed, Mr. Nathanson?"

"No."

There was a pause, then, "I want you to raise your arms in front of you, palms out."

Both Nathanson and Gelb complied, and suddenly the Indian, Maluko, appeared in the doorway. He slipped into the cabin, the stubby barrel of the automatic weapon pointed at their chests.

The woman was next, and she looked as unruffled as Nathanson had seen her in Nassau. In her hand was a silver automatic. "Mr. Nathanson. I missed you in Nassau. How altogether tidy that you decided to meet me here. There must be a reason."

"I'd like to stop all of this, if I could."

Her smile was strangely pleasant. "And not to seek your money? Or revenge?"

Running his eyes down her angular body that looked stunning in the white cotton slacks and red sash, Nathanson thought, Mantrap. Hands still out, he only stared at her.

"And how, may I ask, do you propose to make things right by my client?"

"Pachito Londoño."

Her pleasant expression remained unchanged, but the way she stared at his lips was unnerving.

"By showing you the most important document you'll ever see in your life."

Her eyes rose to his and became more complete. "After Nassau I respect you, Mr. Nathanson. But what possibly could you know of my life and what I have and have not seen?" She had a deep but entirely feminine voice that sounded vaguely French.

Nathanson inclined his head. "You have not seen this. If you had, you wouldn't be here. May I?" He meant his hand, which he moved toward his lapel.

The gun she was holding followed it to his heart.

"Remember, now. I'm purchasing our lives. Mine and Professor Gelb's."

Gelb attempted a nervous smile, but she said, "Let me be the judge of that."

Nathanson drew out the envelope and handed it to her.

Slipping the nickel-plated .9-mm Llama under her cummerbund, Solange Mercier La Guatavita looked down at the photograph she found in the envelope.

"Recognize anybody?"

She did immediately. Her nostrils flared, and she breathed in the damp, warm air of the cabin. Anybody else would not have affected her at all. It was the edge that she had in her profession: no loves or hates, passions of any kind that might deflect her from the completion of her contracts, on which she prided herself.

Apart from this man, Don Pacho Londoño. It had been because of him that she had taken the assignment from his son. She wanted to prove to herself and to others, who knew her story, that she had put aside her anger at how the old man had treated her. And had moved on—personally, emotionally. But this was different. If the brooch stone in the picture was real, it could mean only one thing—it had been Don Pacho himself who had murdered her parents and stolen the gem.

Something like it was dangling from the scrawny neck of Doña Dolores. "When was this taken?"

"Spain. Three years ago."

"I don't believe you. It's a fake, a . . . mock-up." The brooch stone or the photograph, she meant. She flipped the picture over, but the other side was blank.

"The gemstone? I can only tell you that it was described to me as magnificent. The photo? Study the background. See the Mercedes? It's an F-series. They weren't made until '85."

She asked herself if that was something that could be accomplished in a photo laboratory. She studied the photograph, but did not think so. Everything seemed too sharp, too clean-edged, and too real.

Her heart was pounding now, and she could feel that her face was flushed.

"What is it?" Maluko asked her in Chibchan.

She did not answer.

Said Nathanson, "When the Londoños arrived at the table in that restaurant, the other Colombian guests recognized the stone immediately. Doña Dolores was mortified. Don Pacho, who had insisted she wear it, was drunk. He said, and I quote, 'What—you afraid people might find out your husband wasn't a fool after all?' I'm told it ruined the meal. Nobody could take their eyes off it. It was assumed Don Pacho was just a little too drunk to be cautious, or had just wanted to let the party know."

Her eyes, which were nearly the same deep green color as the stone, snapped up at him. "What party? You were told by whom?"

Nathanson shook his head. "That I can't tell you. I called in a favor, is all."

She studied his face, then nodded her head once. She had called in favors of her own before, when in extremity. She stared back down at the photo. If it was genuine, it meant that Don Pacho had murdered her mother and father for the stone, then fabricated the story of labor unrest and a raid by thieving Indians. Solange had suffered post-trauma amnesia after the blow to the head that had deafened her. She could remember very little of her life with her mother and father.

"I'm going to say something to you, Mr. Nathanson, only

once. This—" she raised the photo and shook it at him—"has bought you your life, but it had better be real. If it's not, I will employ all my resources and find you and make you eat—am I understood?—*eat* a stone the size of that emerald. *Before* Maluko kills you this way."

"What about the others. How about them?"

"You mean, those *others* who stole from my client, who then transported the stolen goods here to New York, and have sold them for ten million dollars? Please, Mr. Nathanson, don't try my patience."

A nice round figure, Nathanson thought; they had managed things nicely. "But your client is Pachito Londoño, son of the man who did all these things to you and your family. How could he not have known what his father did, when the man who gave me that picture was a distant cousin on his mother's side?"

So, an Ochoa had sent Nathanson the picture, she thought. Jorge Luis, she was willing to bet. It meant that he had or would soon declare open season on Finca Los Llanos, after Solange had exacted her vengeance and Londoño was dead. It was his way both to allow somebody else to clear the way for him, and to cop for himself the bigger prize. She would have her parents' brooch stone; he would take possession of the *finca*.

She turned suddenly and began speaking to her servant in Chibchan, her eyes flicking from Nathanson to Gelb and, when she had finished, back to Nathanson.

The only two words Nathanson understood were *contrato* and *profesionalmente,* which, he assumed, had no equivalent in the Indian dialect she was speaking and therefore had to be said in Spanish.

She drew out her handgun again, which she aimed at Nathanson's head. "You lead. Aft, I believe the term is."

Nathanson did not move.

"The wheel. Take us to the dock. There, you'll be free to go."

Nathanson glanced from her to the Indian, whose dead, dark eyes had suddenly become enlivened. Even the corners of his mouth had turned up in what approximated a smile. "What did you say to him?"

"I told him to finish up here professionally."

"Here?"

"The contract. New York."

"But for the *Londoños? Why?*"

"Because I have my reputation to maintain, my *pureza,* if you like." She did not add how much better it would look in Colombia. It would be said that even when she had understood the totality of the Londoños' treachery to her, she had completed what she had agreed to do *before* she settled the score.

"But we had an agreement."

She shook her head. "Don't tax my patience, Mr. Nathanson. Had we killed you, we would have removed the photograph from your corpse. With it you have protected your own life. Barely. Or have you something else to show me?

"Now move, and don't think for a moment that I won't kill you."

Nathanson turned to Gelb, whose eyes were terrified but who said, "I don't care about me. Really. I don't care. But my wife, Arlene, she's pregnant. She didn't know what she was getting into. She thought it was all some big—" He looked away; all Gelb could think of was the thing he had seen her using on Cicciolino. It surely was big. "Please, not Arlene. Not my wife."

Said the *sicaria* in Spanish to her servant, her voice dripping with irony, "No, *not* the woman who is taking possession of the money. She's guiltless. Certainly not she."

But the Indian, impatient now, reached out and shoved Nathanson, who saw him draw from under his white blazer a long bush knife. A *penilla.*

"Oh, no. No," Gelb pleaded. "Shoot me. Please, shoot me."

Up at the wheel with a gun virtually in his back, Nathanson took the wheel of *Trekker,* which was barely making way in the middle of the river. He kicked down the throttle of the engine and hurtled the yawl toward Pier 62, where the *sicaria* had said she wanted to "disembark. Or is it debark? I can never get those terms straight in English. Could it be they're synonymous? You're a man of learning—or at least of books—Mr. Nathanson. Which is it?"

But even the roaring of the engine could not expunge Gelb's shrieks.

"Do you know about Boyacas, Mr. Nathanson? They delight in forestalling their victim's death until the last possible moment. The supreme requirement is to perform at a single stroke a death cut. Anything less dishonors both parties, but the longer the victim then remains alive the better. Or, rather, the more graceful the act that has delivered death."

Suddenly the Indian appeared in the companionway, smiling. He was holding the handles of a picnic basket in one hand, the *penilla* in the other. Its bright blade was patterned with fresh blood. He stepped onto the deck and moved away from the hatch, as though wanting them to look below.

"We are indeed fortunate this morning," she went on. "It must be a death worthy of an audience." Below they could hear Gelb like keening, his voice high, faint, and pitiful, while he flopped around on the floorboards of the salon like a gaffed, dying fish.

Nathanson tried not to look. He forced his eyes toward the dock, which they were approaching. There, several smallish cruise ships were moored at intervals along the L-shaped pier. The pier itself was fenced with a gatehouse at its farther end, beyond which he could see the rotating beacon lights of police cars and at least two ambulances.

But Gelb himself now appeared on the companionway ladder. "¡Mira!¡Mira!" the Indian demanded, turning to them a radiant, smiling face.

Standing at the wheel, Nathanson had a view that was not enviable. He could look directly down the companionway, and there Gelb was on hands and knees on the ladder, his face craned up at Nathanson. His eyes were pleading for help, but as he crabbed his way up the steps, his feet kept slipping on something that made him utter the doleful, horrible sounds.

The Indian waved to the woman, as though wanting her to come closer. He snapped his head to her and said something in Chibchan. He glanced at his watch.

Standing away from the taffrail, she explained, "Later, when Maluko describes this event to his tribesmen, he will need corroboration."

Gelb had now reached the final step, but there, with the effort of trying to stand, his eyes floated up into his skull. Still he managed to mouth, "Arlene," before he began falling slowly back.

Releasing the wheel, Nathanson took a step to reach for him and keep him from toppling the ten or so feet down into the cabin, but his hands froze, appalled at what he saw.

Gelb had no stomach, only a bright magenta cavity from which dangled a white, squidlike appendage that was his intestine and a flap of bloody skin. But he was gone, falling heavily into the shadows of the salon. Nathanson wrenched his eyes away.

"Oh, bravo, Maluko. First rate!" She paused a moment, as Nathanson loosed the sheets yet more so the yawl would not heel as he cut between two of the cruise ships. "Say it, Mr. Nathanson. Humor the man. Commend his technique."

She waited. "Above such savagery, are we, sir? Then consider the facts for a moment. Maluko only does with a *penilla* what you and your Mr. Creach have been doing to the children of this city with a spoon and a needle or a pipe for—how long have you been in the trade? Ten years? Fifteen?

"But please don't mistake me. I draw no invidious comparison. Maluko is a mere amateur when judged against you, and much too honest and forthright in his blood lust. Your victims are doubtless legion, whereas he kills selectively, with the courage to meet his victims face to face, eye to eye.

"Also, his victims are exclusively scum, would-be mass murderers, like our Professor Gelb or his partner Assistant Chief Cicciolino, and others I might name who simply desire quick, obscene profits so they might flee in style to some tropical paradise. I'm reminded here of Water Street, Nassau.

"It rather puts Professor Gelb's exquisite death in perspective, wouldn't you say?"

Nathanson eased the yacht toward a bollard, and then left the wheel, reaching for the stern line. Below them Gelb was still moving. Nathanson could hear a foot or something kicking out against a locker. The Indian was leaning on the cabin trunk, peering down into the shadows with the same pleased smile on his face.

"Since it seems you can't," she added, slipping the automatic under her poncho, "at least tell him you consider his feat memorable. Or that he's added to your sum of experience. That much is obvious from your pallor and indignation. Or could it be outrage? *You*, of all people."

She turned and said something to Maluko, who reluctantly turned away from his handiwork. He picked up the hamper and made his way to the rail, where he hopped off onto the dock and waited for her.

"Happy hunting, Mr. Nathanson. Thank you for the snapshot. It rather puts my life together, does it not? Here's hoping we don't see each other again."

Once on the dock, she began walking quickly toward the kiosk, looking like a tourist from one of the cruise ships. Or perhaps the wife of a captain with her bearer.

Yet again Nathanson heard a noise from below. "Jesus—least you could do is finish him off," he called after her. "You've had your fun. Where's the point?"

The Indian translated.

Almost girlishly she turned and, walking backward, said, "You ask Professor Gelb that. See what he says. I'm sure by now he has an answer. If you're so inclined, look in the galley for a knife. Maluko tells me there are several that will suffice. He recommends the throat, if your sensibilities will allow. Angle the blade down and cut in."

In the main salon Nathanson found a shark bat lying in the blood under the companionway ladder. And there, slipping on Gelb's guts which were spread out over the floorboards, like offal, he struck him once very hard on the head.

Moments later he found himself at the galley sink; the smell of the boat was now like nothing he had experienced. It was some noisome mix of blood, fear, excrement, and suffering that had attracted—immediately; where had they come from?—a horde of fat, river flies.

He watched them crawl over the palms of his hands, which were sticky with blood, before he vomited into the sink until he was too weak to stand.

From the corner of Twenty-third Street and Twelfth Avenue, where she had parked her car, Eva Burden watched the *sicaria* and one of her Indians stroll out the gate of the Word Tours pier toward the long black limousine that had just pulled onto the edge of the parking lot. The only police notice she attracted was admiration. Several of the very same cops who had just given Eva such a hard time now turned and watched the woman pass. They smiled at each other. One pursed his lips and made kissing sounds. Another grabbed his crotch and gave it a shake.

Eva thought for a moment that she would repeat what Gerri Cicciolino had done. She would start up her car and aim the hood at the woman. If she were quick enough, she could get to them before they reached the car. But Eva was distraught in addition to being angry and confused, and she reminded herself it was not her way.

She had run to Gerri's car the minute that the white van and Bill Cicciolino in the unmarked car had left the parking lot and the others—the Puerto Rican or Hispanic men in the two damaged vans—had fled. Or at least those who could had.

Gerri had been shot once from above through the left cheek. The bullet had smashed her jaw and exited at a point below her left ear. Her chest was crushed, or at least a number of ribs were broken, but she was still very much alive and breathing when Eva got to her. It was only a matter of moments before police cars arrived, and shortly thereafter police emergency vans, dispatched from the Pier 63 garage that was only a hundred yards away, arrived.

But nobody—neither the police nor the ESU personnel—would help her with Gerri.

The two cops who first looked at Gerri shook their heads.

"Don't you have a hurst tool in the trunk?" Eva demanded.

"What's that?"

"A hurst tool. A jaws of life."

"Whadawe look like, state troopers? Traffic cops? And it don't matter anyhow. Look at her, she's dead." Then, to a third cop, who was eating a sandwich and had a can of beer on the dashboard of a battered police car, "Hey, you—asshole. Call Central. Tell 'em we need a jaws here." The cop in the car, his cheek bulging with food and his hat cocked back on his head, gave the finger and kept eating.

"But"— Eva twisted her head to Gerri—"maybe we don't need them, if you help me. The wheel looks broken, and if we could just get it off her chest . . ." She scurried back to the car. "Look, it's loose."

The one cop who seemed most interested shook his head. "Not me. I touch her and she dies, I get sued."

"She's alive. Can't you see that? We can save her. Look, listen to her—she's breathing."

It was a noisy sound, like air being drawn through wet straw. Either the blood from the wound was flowing down into her lungs or a broken rib had pierced a lung or both.

"How you know? You a doctor?"

"No, but I've been an emergency nurse and a physician's

assistant. I've worked in trauma units, I know what I'm doing."

The cop shook his head again. "I don't do nothin' without no doctor. Those guys need our help more." He meant the two young men from the van who were lying on the cobblestones. He turned as though he would walk away, and Eva ran for him.

She grabbed his arm and spun him around. "You know who she is? She's Gerri Cicciolino. Assistant Chief Bill Cicciolino's wife."

The cop's eyes seemed to clear for a moment. "You in the car with her?"

"No."

"Then how you know?"

"She's an acquaintance. I've sailed with her. I was to meet her here."

"For what?" asked some other cop who was looking in the other side of the car.

"Chief who?" the one closest to her asked.

"Cicciolino. Quick, you have to help me now. She'll choke on her own blood like that."

"The cop on television? Bob and Bill? She Chief Bill C.'s wife?"

"In a pig's eye," said a cop, a sergeant, on the other side of the car. "She's a fuckin' crack head. Look—" He held up a clip of crack vials and a pipe that was sheathed in aluminum foil. "Take care of them others first. You call for some jaws yet?" he yelled at the cop in the car, who nodded and raised the microphone of the radio, his mouth still filled with food.

Eva rushed to the car and tried to pull or push or twist the broken wheel that had clamped Gerri to the seat, but it was no use. She then rushed to one of the arriving ESU vans and tried to pull the hurst tool kit from a storage cabinet, before she was restrained by attendants. She explained what was needed, and they helped her carry it to the car.

But before they could position the mechanism, Gerri's breathing grew more violent. She began what seemed like coughing that brought up blood, and then that stopped.

"Gerri!" Eva shouted, and tried to jounce the wheel to start her breathing again. "Gerri!"

But the wheel was not flexible enough, and because of the twisted metal she could not get her hands on Gerri's chest.

With her fingers pressed to the side of Gerri's neck, Eva stood there in the full morning sun, tears streaming down her face, powerless to help the woman. She felt the pulse fade, then stop, and she turned and walked toward Twelfth Avenue and her own car on the corner.

"Hey, you. Come back here," the sergeant called after her. "Were you a witness to this thing?"

Eva shook her head and kept walking.

Back in her car, trying to summon the will to leave, she watched the black Mercedes limousine with the woman, the *sicaria*, ease out into traffic.

Eva turned the key and was about to pull around the corner when she saw Brian Nathanson on the other side of the avenue, trying to hail a taxi.

She honked, then opened the door and stepped out so he could see her.

When he got in, he noticed her red eyes and the tearstains on her cheeks. "What happened?"

"Gerri Cicciolino," she said, pointing to the wreck of the new gray car across the street, and she told him what she had seen.

Nathanson shook his head, trying both to clear it of his own experience aboard the yawl and to put together the sequence of events. "A grab?" he asked out loud. "A group in one of the vans trying to rip off the delivery?"

Eva filled him in about the clip of crack vials that the sergeant said he had found in Gerri's car, which at least explained what had happened to her. Or perhaps put what happened to her beyond explanation.

Nathanson turned to Eva, and without mentioning details explained that Tug McCann and Jay Gelb were dead, murdered with utter indifference by the *sicaria*. "I might have done something about Gelb, but she had a gun to my head."

"Why'd she let you go?"

Nathanson explained that too, mentioning his phone calls to Ochoa, the photograph, and the significant details of Solange Mercier's past.

"Won't she just leave now?"

Nathanson nodded, but he also told Eva about the woman's orders to "finish things up professionally. Interpreted by Maluko . . . ?" He hunched his large shoulders and looked away. If nothing else, Maluko was a *professional* savage.

"Who's in danger?"

"Anybody who was aboard *Whistler*." Their eyes met. "After all, they've tried for you three times already. Luck like that can't hold."

"But, you know, in *immediate* danger."

"Arlene Gelb." From what Nathanson had overheard McCann discuss with her on the phone, she had been sent to a bodega in East Harlem to pick up the payment for the dope.

"Alone?"

"Probably, with Cicciolino following the buyer, as Gelb had as much as admitted on the boat. You know, to *bust* him. Terminally."

"Can I ask a favor?"

Her eyes swung to him again.

"Let me use your car. I'll drive you back to the hotel. Or, better, we'll change hotels."

"And then you'll make a stab for the money?" Her expression was assessing.

Nathanson was asking himself the same question. Or did he merely want to keep what had happened to Gelb from happening to the wife, who Gelb had said was pregnant? He looked away, not wanting even to imagine that. "I don't know. Maybe. But there's been too much . . . savagery." And the *sicaria* had been right about Nathanson's own participation; without a doubt he was more culpable than Maluko, who killed only selectively, under orders, and in a way for cause.

Nathanson shook his head again. He could still taste bile in the back of his throat. "It's got to stop. Cicciolino can take care of himself, but I wonder if Arlene Gelb can."

"I'd prefer to go with you."

"It might be dangerous."

But not as nerve-racking as waiting in a hotel. Eva started the car and headed north. It was an ice-blue vintage BMW 633, with low miles and a blond leather interior. Tug, who had had good taste, could never resist a bargain, and had got it for her nearly a year ago for what he described as pin money.

Eva shook her head and sighed. Tug.

PART VI
STRANGE FRUIT

CHAPTER 29
HARLEM SHUTTLE

◆

DEPUTY INSPECTOR CLIFF BANKS, commander of Precinct 25, was still scorched over Downtown canceling just when he was sure the Santos squeeze would draw the little viper from under his rock. He was burnt and smoking.

He had driven all the way down to the Purple Palace—the tall red-marble building at One Police Plaza—for a tête-à-tête with his rabbi, who was a deputy chief, only to learn that the guy was in Florida on vacation. Even Bill Cicciolino had taken off. "Gone for the day," was the way his secretary put it. "We can schedule you for tomorrow, Inspector. At your convenience. I'm sure the chief will be sorry he missed you."

Not likely, Banks had thought, and by tomorrow he would probably have lost his anger. It was like that with Banks—fierce while it was on him, and forgotten once it was gone—and he lost it best while driving around, seeing other perps, places, and things that angered him more. So on his way back, Banks, who was officially off-duty, began cruising his own personal car through the western limits of his command.

An old Checker Marathon, the car with its high, boxy shape was so much a part of the New York cityscape that Banks never drew a second glance from the ignorant skells he collared in his spare time. They thought it was just another of the gypsy cabs that served the black and Hispanic communities citywide with some big spade behind the wheel. Those who did, however, called it the "Clean Machine" you had to watch for. Like everything that Cliff Banks owned or managed, it was shaped-up. Its old blue paint gleamed, and inside it smelled like a new-car dealership.

From his vantage behind the wheel a foot above more modern cars, Banks could peer down whole streets. He could also control the locks on the rear doors from a button on the dash. A steel mesh separated him from the backseat, which was large enough to hold a half-dozen mutts.

Banks was on Lenox Avenue just above 112th Street. He was stopped at a traffic light, scanning a smoke shop across the street that had begun dealing "EXXXSTACY." They sold it in neat-looking glassine envelopes shaped either like tits or dicks, depending on your predilection, with the brand name spelled like the X-rated cable channel. The idea of equating drugs with sex was not new, of course—heroin had long been called "boy" on the street, cocaine "girl"—but the packaging was catchy. Or, rather, addictive.

It was then the light changed, and drifting across the intersection, Banks passed a familiar face in a white van that was stopped for the light one car back on the west corner. Banks pulled the brim of his pork-pie hat a little farther down on his forehead and shifted the fat shill cigar he never smoked to the side of his mouth. He signaled and pulled over, as if he were letting off a fare, then glanced in the wide side mirror and studied the van.

It was so new it sparkled, but the back end had been smashed, and recently too. In the noon-hour sun, the streaked sheet metal shone like silver. And what were the little pips in the side of the van? Bullet holes? Sure as hell looked like it, even from afar. The license plate was baby blue and beige, and all Banks could think was dope run. Having decided to chance it, Santos had set something up in Jersey and was now attempting to sneak it in the back door. Even the street he chose—112th—was quiet and little-used by crosstown traffic since it dead-stopped at Jefferson Park.

The taillight was gone, which was reason enough to pull Santos over, but Banks decided he would wait and see where the little asshole brought the shit. A skell with *his* money had contacts.

Maybe he'd heard the heat was off, and he'd drive it home to his slum castle keep that was the envy of every aspiring spic knight errant in East Harlem. And then bingo, Banks would call for backup on the radio under the dash, and they'd confiscate everything, including the gold in the teeth Banks would make sure Santos lost.

Fuck First "Dip" Bob Brant. Banks had his own friends in the media, and Downtown would be hard-pressed to discipline a black ex-NFL hero cop who had personally taken out one of the major mythmakers in the East Harlem drug trade. They could dredge up Santos's pigmeat and heroin sidelines and the gang of thieves, cutthroats, and murderers he housed in his building. By the time they were through, Santos would look like a nastier, Hispanic version of Nicky Barnes, the infamous drug dealer. Or Brian de Bois-Guilbert, the villain in *Ivanhoe*. Banks's escape was reading; the more distant and romantic the book, the better.

The light changed, and Banks watched Santos motor slowly across the intersection, as though he would continue past 112th Street; but, committed now with two cars behind him, Santos had to wait while a large delivery truck backed down an alley midblock. Good. It gave Banks a chance to pull a U-ey and get a look at the other side of the new van, which was dumb and unlike anything the usually careful Santos would use. It was conspicuous, a target for theft if nothing else, and could be seen from a half-mile away.

The delivery truck had disappeared, and Santos now moved forward. Banks was about to force the grill of his Checker into the stream of traffic and follow Santos when Assistant Chief Bill Cicciolino, slumped down in the seat of an unmarked car, moseyed past him. It could be nobody else. Framed in the window of the unmarked car like that, his head, crooked nose, and dark, wavy hair looked like the profile of Caligula. Banks let another car go by, then slipped in behind to see what Cicciolino would do. Santos turned at the next block. So did Cicciolino.

Curiouser and curiouser, Banks thought. What was he seeing here? Had Brant called off the saturation surveillance of Santos because he knew Santos was about to make a big buy and he wanted Cicciolino to have the honor of busting him? Rumor had it that Brant and Cicciolino were as close off-camera as they appeared to be on their Saturday morning TV show. They ate, drank, and chased broads together. All the kidding around and bonhomie were real.

But where was Cicciolino's backup? Banks had had his police radio on all morning, and he had heard nothing, not a hint of any operation like that; and it was common courtesy—and good sense—to inform a commander that you were about to operate in his precinct. That way you lowered the odds of cops shooting cops and increased your chances of success. Precinct cops knew their turf and the cockroaches in it far better than blow-ins from the Palace, and having a couple of locals along at least as observers was always smart.

Then it occurred to Banks that he had not actually heard from Brant. Was Cicciolino trying to buck for bureau chief by making a grandstand play that would get him headlines? Maybe he had something bigger in mind, say, politics. Hadn't Mario Biaggi used anticrime heroics to launch a political career? What better now in the present political climate than busting a major player? In such a light the whole Santos squeeze looked like a setup from the start.

But Banks could not understand what Cicciolino was doing. He was hanging back so far he was in danger of losing Santos. Banks himself could no longer see the white van.

Could it be Cicciolino hadn't seen Santos, and it was pure coincidence that he turned down the same street? Or—Banks straightened his back and flicked up the brim of his hat— Cicciolino *knew* where Santos was going, and didn't want to chance tipping him off?

How? He knew the location of Santos's stash house? No. Why follow Santos if he knew that? Better to hide there and wait. A homing device? Cicciolino would have had to get close enough to the deal to plant it, and nobody—buyer or seller—would have allowed that. They would have been watching the van like hawks.

In any case—Banks again eased himself back into the seat— Cicciolino obviously didn't think there was a chance of *his* being followed. He had not run a single red light nor was he glancing unduly in his rearview mirror.

Fifteen blocks to the north, PO Nunzio D'Amato— Cicciolino's driver—was. Waiting a few doors down from the bodega on 127th Street where Jay Gelb's wife, Arlene, had just entered the store, he kept turning his eyes from the three mirrors in his unmarked car to the sidewalks in front of him, the windows of the buildings above, and any cars coming at him down the street. He couldn't be sure, he hadn't seen anything, but he had a strong feeling that something was screwy about the setup.

When Chick had asked him to ride shotgun for the Lady Gelb, D'Amato had thought, What could it be? Some art or something. He was on-duty anyways, he'd make a couple of extra clams, and it'd be a milk run from beginning to end. But when Chick mentioned the possibility of pad, it got D'Amato's attention, which was now 100 percent.

D'Amato knew the bodega. It was a bad place where bad cops and lazy cops from all over Manhattan North cooped. In the back room they drank beer, fenced the stolen goods and drugs they ripped off skells, but mainly fucked around, told stories, traded bullshit, and hung out. The owner, some spic broad, loved them, since it made her immune, and she could deal just about anything she liked right over the counter.

The live action was cockroach racing, which D'Amato himself had once been aces at, and he enjoyed maybe more than the nags, since at least you could afford to own your own. He once had a stable of four or five that he kept in a little terrarium and were simply fucking unbeatable. On his days off, or when Chick let him, he had toured the roach parlors the city over and cleaned up, which was how he knew about the bodega. It was a fun place, but with armed, drunk cops and big money down, it was also dangerous and no place for a lady.

Maybe Chick had got a tip and put Gelb wise to some art that was being fenced there, he thought, as he watched Mrs. Gelb—Dale fucking Evans with granny glasses and reddish hair put up in a zany bun—step out of her beat-up Volvo station wagon and saunter, no cares, toward the door. Maybe that was why she needed protection. Nah, couldn't be. Chick would have asked D'Amato to go right in there with her, make sure she got what she was after.

On the sidewalk she stopped, it seemed, to check the address on the rolled-up awning of the store with a slip of paper in her hand, and the loose raincoat she was wearing open enough to give D'Amato an eyeful. Fuck if she wasn't pregnant. How old could she be anyways? Gelb was D'Amato's age almost exactly, which was forty-eight. And Dale there had to be at least forty to forty-five, though she looked good. Cheeks nice and pink, good tits. She always had zoomers, and her belly just getting that high fullness D'Amato had always liked seeing in somebody else's gash.

Jesus H., he thought, wasn't life strange? He could imagine Gelb as a father, worrying the living shit out of a kid. Making his life barely worth the hassle with good schools, music lessons, improvement courses, and all that Hebe shit that made Jews the Jews they were.

Arlene was surprised by the inside of the store. She had imagined the grocery filled with plantains, cassavas, yams, and mangoes, and all the yucca root, pinto beans, and blue corn that the denizens of an ethnic neighborhood preferred and were not readily available in supermarkets. Instead she saw a few rows of dusty canned goods and a deli case filled mainly with large cheeses that were stamped in purple letters "USDA NOT FOR RESALE." There were cigarettes, cigars, and every other type of tobacco product, beer and wine in another large glass refrigerator, and a Lotto machine near the cash register.

Positioned in a rocking chair behind the counter was a young dark Hispanic woman who was wearing so much bright, primary-color makeup she looked like an Emil Nolde watercolor. "Jyes?" she asked. "You huh?"

Arlene said she suspected she was, and she was led through a beaded curtain down a dark hall toward a closed door from which she could hear men shouting and cursing. Opened, it revealed a fug of dense smoke and a clutch of mainly policemen in uniform who were gathered over a large, open cardboard box. They were grasping wads of limp bills and bottles of beer, as they pointed into the box and laughed and shouted.

"Dere." The woman moved a foot to indicate two sizable boxes in a corner. Both had been wrapped so completely with yellow strapping tape they looked lumpy.

Arlene had been told by Chick she need not check the contents. "Santos wouldn't dare stiff us. He's got too much to lose. Just get it and get out of there." Arlene now moued her resignation and bent for the top carton, which was bulky and heavy. In turning for the door, her ankle snagged on a corner of the other carton, and she staggered, nearly falling.

"Don' look a' me," said the woman, who was grasping her elbows as though she wanted nothing to do with the cartons. "Ba' back."

"She'll need it tonight," said one of the cops, who were now exchanging money, kidding and kibitzing with each other in the hall. "Heavy date." Obviously he had won, and he looked up from his stack of bills, which he had been arranging. "Hey, Red—whatcha got there?"

Arlene didn't know how to answer, but none was required.

"Need a hand with that?"

The other cops objected. "Fuck no. She don't need no help. Look at her—big strong girl. You stay right here until we get our money back."

But the cop was insistent. "Will you listen to yous guys? Maybe we should play for bottle caps instead? Me—I ain't going no place till I got your every last cent." He moved toward Arlene. "Let me take that for you, hon'. Where you want it anyhow, your car or mine?"

Said another cop, "Where they get these roaches anyways? I collared five last week quicker than these."

The others laughed, but the oldest cop said, "Somebody go with that No-Response. Make sure he comes back."

"This yours too, babe?" yet another cop asked Arlene, snatching up the second carton. "Shit—what's in here, bricks?"

"Don't you wish," somebody observed. "And bring back some beer when you come."

Out on the street just as Arlene was leading the two cops with the cartons to her Volvo, D'Amato watched a new van that was moving toward them stop suddenly, as though the driver, who was some kind of spic Injun, didn't know what to do. They had people from everywhere in neighborhoods like this. Another definite Injun in a white jumpsuit—kind of small and squat with a bodybuilder's chest and shoulders—hopped out, but the others said something to him, and he got back in.

Coasting by, three of them turned their heads to watch the cops loading the cartons into the back of the car. D'Amato couldn't swear it, but he thought he saw a face at either blackened back window as the van moved away. When it turned in at a hydrant by the corner and waited, idling, with the driver's foot on the brake so the lights in back stayed lit, D'Amato knew he had trouble.

He zipped down his beige windbreaker so he could get at his weapon, which he kept in a shoulder holster, and he thought about getting out and having a word with the Mrs. But with a puff of blue smoke and a wave to the cops, she was off in the old wreck, the van jerking out from the curb to fall in behind her.

No technique there. Whatever they wanted, she had, and dollars to doughnuts it was in them cartons.

It took a few blocks, but Arlene saw them too—how could she help not?—right on her tailgate: three Andean faces in the front windshield, their eyes jumping from her to the neighborhood, as though looking for a place to pull her over, or so she supposed. She did not want to be paranoid, but when she turned sharply into 124th Street, then turned back uptown on Third Avenue and over again on 127th, she knew her supposition was correct.

At the corner of 125th and Lexington, she paused slightly at the corner and, as though a stranger from out-of-town not acquainted with the city proscription against right-hand turns on red, pulled out. The van followed too and another car behind her, which she assumed was the tail Chick told her he would hire for safety. She threw the all-door latch lock, just to make sure she was safe, and opened her purse, which contained a large-caliber pistol that Chick had also given her, "Just in case. Anybody—I mean *anybody*—tries to take that money off you, blow them away and get it where it can't be found. We'll take care of the sordid details later."

Good move, thought D'Amato, when they were out on 125th Street. Stick to the main drags and don't let them get ahead of you, he coached like she could hear him. The best route would be straight over to Lenox Avenue and then west again on 110th to West End, all heavily traveled, well-peopled thoroughfares where only a smash-and-grab might work, which D'Amato could bust up, if he had to.

He considered pulling the van over and tossing the mutts, but he was no hero, and there was always the possibility that the van was not alone. And then Chick's words came back to him: "The important part is them cartons. They're to get where they're going, one way or another."

But when she turned left on Park Avenue and caught green lights right down to Ninety-sixth, where she turned right, D'Amato shouted, "No! Not the fuckin' park. Anyplace but Central Park. They'll fuckin' *stomp* you in Central Park!" He goosed his car to pick up on the skell van that now leapt after her. It wouldn't take them much. They could force her over, hop out, and in them jumpsuits pretend they were helping her out. Breakdown. Flat tire. Shit like that.

If there was pad money in this the way Chick had said, D'Amato hoped it was good, because with the odds like they were, he planned to shoot first and find dead felons after, which meant paper work if he wasn't dead himself. D'Amato despised paper work. And court.

In the Volvo wagon that could hit maybe eighty tops without something flying off, Arlene Gelb's assessment of her situation was far more optimistic. After all, she had walked, jogged, exercised, and recreated in Central Park for nearly half of her life, and knew this Ninety-sixth Street section, which was closest to her home, like the back of her hand.

True, the road was narrow and tortuous, with several twists and turns, but she was thinking in particular of the arched brownstone underpasses that were narrower still. She was willing to bet that her old Volvo station wagon with its large, sluggish, six-cylinder engine had far more steel and was heavier than any new van. Certainly it had a lower center of gravity, and the steel cage they advertised as a safety feature.

Stopping for the traffic light at the intersection of Ninety-sixth and Fifth Avenue with the entrance to Central Park just across the street, Arlene watched one of the Andean-looking men get out of the van and approach her window. Her hand moved across the seat to her open purse and pulled out the large pistol, which she shielded in her lap under her wide-brimmed sun hat. Holding it in her right hand, she aimed it at the window.

It had the feel, if not the look, of the six-guns she had fired as a girl with her father, and in a curious way she was anxious to use it. She did not know who the men were, but she imagined they had something to do with the cocaine or knew what was in the boxes, and the point was to lose them any way she could.

The man rapped on the window and pointed across the street at the park. "Pull over. In the . . . *bosque.* You mus' pull over. There." Again he jabbed his hand at the new spring green across the street where toddlers with their nannies and old people on benches were sunning themselves against the park wall.

Arlene rolled down her window. "Pardon me? I'm afraid I couldn't hear you."

The man stepped closer and bent to the window. He zipped down the front of his jumpsuit to show her the cross-hatched walnut butt of a handgun no smaller than her own. He then repeated more vehemently what he had said, and a vivid memory flashed into Arlene's mind of having come upon a Hopi Indian, sitting at a fire and feasting upon a calf that her father and she, then still a child, had been searching for.

"Why?" she now asked.

The light had changed, and behind her cars were now honking.

The man had no answer beyond the evident mayhem she could read in his dark, quick eyes, and she remembered her father's words. "It ain't pretty, but you gotta cut them odds, girl, whenever you can."

"POW!" the gun spoke. It was a huge, shiny silver thing that Arlene had examined, felt, and even polished since getting it from Chick the night before—a Colt Python with a long vent-rib barrel—and the noise it made was bigger still.

She pulled the trigger again, just to hear it repeat the sound. "POW!" just like that, just like an onomatopoeia in a cartoon noise balloon.

Arlene shook her head in amazement, wondering if it was life mirroring art, and she hit the gas. Her old Volvo stuttered, then caught, and rattled across Fifth Avenue into the park with the van and the security car right behind her.

Lying on the crosswalk with two holes nearly epicentric in his forehead was a dead Injun skell who had no identification, no money, no nothing on him—the cop who answered the call would later report—not even labels in his clothes that might hint at an identity.

*   *   *

Up in East Harlem three-and-a-half blocks exactly from his five-story fortress, Hector ("Chino") Santos Cabrón pulled the new white van with the bullet holes, the damaged rear panel, and nearly a half-ton of pure coke in off the street.

He aimed it down a narrow alley beside another building that he also owned through a dummy corporation his high-priced lawyer had set up, which reminded him. He'd have to call the sucker first thing he got home and set up a meet. Fallout. Damage-control, in case things screwed up. You never knew with cops. Santos had got what he needed at a right price, now the deal was over, and the point was to keep himself from getting dead. Or in jail.

It was a three-story former baled-goods warehouse with a wide covered loading dock and big arched windows that had been busted out and Santos had replaced with iron bars and plywood. Inside he had a security system that rang in his fifth-floor apartment, and he saved the place as his stash of last resort, the place where he put things his life depended on, like now. Worse came to worst, he always had it to bargain with.

But Santos was still feeling good about how the deal went down. Even the job of loading the coke back in the boxes before he skidded them out on the platform and then quick into the building was no big thing, and he set about it with a kind of inner joy, humming to himself, even singing a few bars of "There Is a Ros' in Spanish Hah-lem." Dah-ah-dah, dah-ah-dah, dah, dah.

The van? He'd dump it down the street with the other wrecks, then drop a dime to a guy he knew. Two hours and it be gone, at least all the good parts. Then Santos would have nothing left but Justino, if he dragged his shot ass back, and Santos was hoping he would.

Cicciolino, having located Santos down the alley, idled his unmarked car quietly along the litter-strewn street. At the corner he found himself in a graveyard of chopped and trashed cars, old wheels and fenders that he had to weave around. He traced a circuitous route through the debris toward the edge of an open rubble lot maybe 150 yards from the warehouse.

From there, with the binoculars he'd brought along for the earlier part of the deal, Cicciolino was able to peer in the windshield of the van and see what Santos was up to, which was all elbows and asshole. Good. That way Santos would save the city the cost of manpower it would take to box up the coke and eliminate any chance of loss, which was inevitable whenever you put cops near too much loose money or drugs.

Cicciolino smiled and imagined how nice it would look stacked on a table with all the television lights making it look like a white brick wall, and he pulled in the focus to examine the terrain he'd have to cross to get up alongside the van. Santos would never expect anybody to come at him from there. Cicciolino hoped he wouldn't get a flat, but how much would it matter if he did? The whole thing would stop there, at least for Santos, and Cicciolino would lament the fact that he hadn't been able to make a clean collar.

Tenements had once circled the lot, and for years before they were ripped down, the niggers and shit who lived in them couldn't be bothered even to put the garbage and trash out on the curb for the sanitation trucks. Instead they just tossed it out windows and over porch railings into the middle. Even now after the buildings had been flattened, it remained in a twisted, rusting pyramid, like a monument to the kind of wrongheaded thinking that supposed all people were equal and would be good, productive, law-abiding members of society, if given a chance. Gerri's kind of thinking.

Maybe years from now some archaeological dig could find the courage in all the busted bottles and HIV-positive syringes to label the people who lived here what they were: barely human scum that didn't deserve a chance and had dragged the city and the rest of the country down. Hadn't he seen it with his own eyes?

Well, at least in her death—and he hoped she was dead— Gerri had done one thing right. She had provided him with the perfect excuse. He reached for the shotgun, fitted two slugs in the slide, then rammed them home. Picking the two spent shells he had fired on Pier 63, he tossed them out the window and decided the angle he'd take: angry white husband and cop, justifiably aggrieved, who had sought and successfully wreaked the only vengeance worth the name with the courts and justice system in the shape they were.

Hey, if Goetz and Gotti could make the public judge and jury, why not him? Cicciolino was a respectable, well-liked public figure, whose stand on crime and bias had been documented weekly for two years on television. He was already etched into the mass mind, and to have him act out their not-so-secret aggressions? With the money he now had, there was no telling where it might lead.

Cicciolino decided he would not even need to get out of the car. Once the boxes were out on the platform, he would pull up to the van with the window open and plink Santos, like a rat in a can.

Cliff Banks, watching Cicciolino's unmarked car hobbyhorse slowly across the vacant lot, tacking this way and that to avoid hazards, understood what Cicciolino had in mind. He would take Santos unawares.

Banks did not know why Cicciolino had not radioed in a ten-eighty-five with backup of at least two units. It was wrong and against everything in the book, but one thing was certain. If it did not work, Santos in the van could always get back out the way he came in, and Banks, concealed behind a row of double-parked cars, now moved his Checker toward the alley to eliminate the possibility.

Hurtling through Central Park, inches from the bumper of the van driven by the jumpsuit spic Injuns, which was inches from the bumper of the Volvo with Lady Gelb behind the wheel, D'Amato could hardly believe what he thought he'd seen.

Sure, he *saw* it. Wasn't the Injun dead there on the street when he passed him, eyes staring up at the buildings and his forehead a mess? D'Amato had seen dead people before. With two big bullets in his brain, that sucker was a stiff before he even hit the pavement. What was it she did him with, a cannon? The thing sounded like a pipe bomb going off.

People were surprising, D'Amato thought as he kept trying to jockey the unmarked Taurus he was driving out into the other lane every time a car going the other way passed. The road was narrow, and he could only get a glimpse of the Volvo lurching over the uneven road, spewing out a cloud of dirty blue smoke. Just when you thought you had people all pegged and down pat, they up and went and did something wild. What could be in them boxes that she would kill so easily?

Suddenly the rear doors of the van burst open, and there was one jumpsuit Injun being held by the legs by two other, kneeling wombats. In his hands he had some kind of stubby black auto-matic weapon, and D'Amato only just hit the brakes and threw himself across the seat when the windshield blew out and the back of the seat felt like it was being whacked with a bat. Glass and big chunks of seat material flew everywhere. When D'Amato thought he could, he raised his head and was amazed to find the Taurus still in the middle of the road. The windshield was gone, but maybe it was a good thing.

It had become a hot, shitty day with lots of dishwater glare and no breeze, and this way he'd have a clearish shot at the van's wheels. Jerking the steering wheel to look left at oncoming traffic, D'Amato hit the gas. A blowout at eighty miles an hour would be acceptable. The van could never stabilize itself on such a narrow road, and would make a big mess tumbling at oncoming traffic.

D'Amato pounded the accelerator into the floor, raised himself and the gun off the seat, and aimed at the rear left wheel of the van. They were approaching an underpass. D'Amato was right alongside the van now. He was about to squeeze off a shot at the rear wheel when out of the corner of his eye he saw the Volvo slow up and swing suddenly to the left, smacking into the van, which caromed into him. Was the fucking bitch trying to put both of them into the solid block of the tunnel wall?

D'Amato dropped the gun, grabbed the wheel, and hit the brakes. The van careened by him, angling off toward the solid brownstone abutment of the underpass. Again the rear doors opened, and there were the two wombats holding the third with the gun as if he would shoot at D'Amato again. But when the van hit the wall, the three of them vanished toward the front, like they'd been sucked down a tube.

D'Amato cut the wheel, and hurtled through the tunnel with the Volvo in front of him bounding from one side to the other, sending sparks and molding and hubcaps everywhere.

In the sunshine at the end of the tunnel, the station wagon did a complete one-eighty before its wheels caught on something and it rolled over once, landing upright with a little, like, hop and jounce. It then rolled up a grassy embankment, where it stopped.

The old Volvo was all new dents and scrapes. Steam was coming up from its grill, but there she sat—the Mrs.—*with,* get this, the straw hat still on her head. D'Amato stuffed his service revolver back in its holster, got out of his car, and hustled over to her.

Up above them on the bridge, all the strollers, joggers, and bicyclers had gathered to gawk down at the smashed van, and whatever unique sight was there to be seen. A couple of cabs in true New York fashion now came barreling in from the west, horns blaring at the big twisted piece of what had just been the van. D'Amato could just see it at the other end of the tunnel.

He wrapped a knuckle on the passenger window and gestured the Mrs. should lower it. She hit the button and gave him about four inches.

"You all right?"

She nodded. She had her left hand on the wheel, her right around the fucking huge *pistola* that was resting on the seat, sort of pointing at him. D'Amato wondered where she had got it.

"How 'bout the car?" which was the major point. They had to get out of there fast.

She nodded. It was still ticking over.

"Them boxes okay?" D'Amato brought his head nearly in the window to peer toward the back where he could see the yellow tape that somebody had wrapped them with.

His eyes met hers again, which were some strange shallow gray color. "You don't know me. I'm Nunzio D'Amato. I'm okay. I went to school with your husband, and Chick asked me—"

"POW!" the gun roared such that Arlene's other hand jumped to her ear. She thought for sure it had deafened her, it was that loud.

The shot had passed through the window so cleanly the hole looked like it had been cut with a diamond tip. It had also lifted the man off his feet and set him down at least a yard from the car on the grassy bank.

He was clutching his chest, and his torso now fell forward so that his dark, glossy head lolled down onto his legs. It was exactly the *Paschimothanasana* position in Yoga, which Arlene practiced, and she wondered if he had always been so supple. From a black hole in the back of his tan windbreaker a red aureole was quickly spreading.

She shifted the lever into D, and the old car rolled across the grass, the sidewalk, over the curb, and out onto the road. For all the smoke, Arlene could scarcely see what she left behind.

Chick. He was nowhere in her plans, nor was any potential witness or tail.

*   *   *

Santos thought he was alone until he heard the scrunch of a tire beside the dope van. He had just slid the tenth and final carton out the open back doors, and instead of showing himself, he put an eye to one of the bullet holes in the side of the van and looked out.

It was the cop, Cicciolino. Santos wondered what he want now. Kiss him maybe? Or tell him he can't sell no dope in New York, like the deal was for some other city like Minneapolis. No rules for cops; they made them up as they went along. Maybe he want to shake hands. Maybe he want some dope, now they were both in the business.

Santos was about to turn away and go out and see what, when his eye caught on something: the way the cop had backed the car in so it couldn't be seen from the street, the open window, and the black thing resting on the sill.

Fuck is that? Santos asked himself, raising himself up on the toes of his Night Flyers to peer down, when it exploded and rocked the van twice, blowing through the other side. Santos tried to run toward the open doors, but that was where Cicciolino fired next, "walking" each of the next seven slugs in quick succession toward the cab.

Santos thought about it for a split second before he threw himself down. He flattened his body and tried to dig into the hard corrugated-steel liner of the van, hoping the motherfucker would keep shooting high.

It was then another slug blasted through the side and everything went very white on Santos, a blinding, horrible, painful light that turned red and then rainbow colors and finally black. He scrambled up, he had to get out of there; but which way? He hit something hard, like the side of the van, and went down. And right above his ear the van exploded again, and his whole head was filled with pain.

Deputy Inspector Cliff Banks was out of his Checker, which he had left parked across the opening of the alley, sprinting toward the van. He vaulted the loading dock, but by the time he got to the open rear doors, Cicciolino was standing there looking into the back of the van.

Santos was in there, crawling toward them. His face was streaming with blood, and one of his eyes had nearly been torn from his head. "The paper," Banks would remember him saying. "You mad at the paper? Paper non my idea. Was Martita's."

Cicciolino didn't know what he meant, nor did he care. He turned to Banks. "Good, you're right on time." He was holding his service revolver outstretched, the barrel pointed at Santos. "What's that in that perp's right hand, Inspector?"

It was a small stainless-steel automatic.

Cicciolino didn't wait for Banks to answer. He squeezed off a shot into the top of Santos's head, then kept pulling the trigger as quickly as he could until the cylinder was empty. The back of the van was filled with gunsmoke. He batted it away from his face, stepped out, and began reloading with rounds that he pulled from a pocket of his windbreaker.

Banks let out a kind of groan and shook his head. He swung his body around and walked toward one of the cartons. He sat and looked down at his gun, which he replaced in his kidney holster. His hands were next. He looked at them front and back, then folded them in his lap.

"What's wrong with you?" Cicciolino demanded.

Banks shrugged. "I don't know. You tell me?" About why you called off the surveillance only to show up on his tail the next day? About where you picked him up, why you were following him alone, how the bullet holes got in the van, why no notification, no backup, no Miranda? And now this, which was an assassination, plain and simple. Banks had so many questions he didn't know where to begin.

Said Cicciolino, "I see a dead drug pusher, child molester, chicken hawk, killed in a dramatic gun battle with two veteran cops. Whatever you want, he had, including, if my guess is correct"—Cicciolino stepped into the van and eased the small automatic from Santos's limp fingers. He walked back and stood over Banks—"that huge, motherfucking load of cocaine you're sitting on, Cliff."

Cicciolino turned and fired the four .357 magnum rounds in Santos's Compact into his unmarked car: the door, the side window, and two in through the open window. He then moved back into the van, wiped the gun off on a unbloody section of Santos's jacket, and fit it back into his dead hand.

"I also see, since you really want to know, the man who just murdered my wife."

Banks's square head rocked back on his shoulders. He blinked. "You' shittin' me."

Cicciolino closed his eyes and shook his head. "West Side. Pier Sixty-three. I don't know what the fuck she was doing there. Maybe she overheard me on the phone. She's had some emotional problems of late, and—" He looked away.

There was a long pause in which faintly now they could hear sirens approaching.

"Way I see it," Cicciolino went on, "you got two ways to play this, Cliff. What I just said, or whatever the fuck it is you want to do. What we got here"—he kicked a carton—"is plenty of glory to go around. I'm on my way out, but you're on your way up. You know about the department," and about cops who squealed on other cops, he meant. "I just paid the motherfucker back, is all. For Gerri and for all the others.

"Tell me you wouldn't have done the same, and I wouldn't have helped you."

Brian Nathanson and Eva Burden got to the Gelbs' West End Avenue condo just as Arlene was walking under the marquee, past the long black Mercedes that was parked in front of the marquee. "That's her," said Eva. "And that's the *sicaria*'s limo."

The day had turned almost hot, and Arlene had removed her jacket, which she carried over one arm. In her other hand she had a sun hat that she was swinging, like a little girl.

"Is she *pregnant*?" Eva asked, looking away for a place to park her BMW.

Nathanson's mind again flooded with images of Gelb's death and the prize of his wife's pregnant belly. "Let me out. Park around the corner and keep the car running. If that limo or any of those Indians even comes near you, don't hesitate, just go." He remembered the *sicaria* telling Maluko to "finish up professionally."

"I think they're on a kind of . . . murder run. One of them might remember you from Nassau."

"What about you?"

He cocked his head. He could take care of himself, or at least he thought he could. "I'll meet you back at the hotel. Make sure you're not followed." He opened the door.

She reached for his sleeve. "Brian—be careful."

His eyes lingered on hers for a moment. They squeezed hands, and he hopped out, sprinting past the grill of the Mercedes and under the marquee. Both doors of the building were open to the fresh spring air, and he waited inside an interior arch to see if anybody would get out of the Mercedes to follow him in or if the car would move off after Eva.

Neither, though he thought he saw the limo rock, as though there was somebody in it.

"He'p you?" a voice asked. It came from a large black man dressed in a doorman's uniform. He was slumped down in a chair before an array of black-and-white TV monitors. Mirror sunglasses wrapped his upper face, Walkman earphones were stretched over his uniform cap.

"Arlene Gelb. Where's she live?"

"Ain't in."

Nathanson moved toward him; he was in no mood for a bribe. "That's bullshit. She just walked in, or did the Indians in the limo pay you not to see her?"

There she was anyway, on one of the screens that surveilled the elevator. On the seventh-floor landing in the stairwell and in the seventh-floor hall were two Indians, both dressed in black chauffeur uniforms.

"Aw—man—I gonna have to bounce you, nice day like this?" said the doorman, beginning to pull himself out of the chair.

"I wouldn't if I were you."

The mirrors eyed Nathanson.

"Insurance. You're about to lose your job, and you won't be covered for any liability. See those two men there?" He meant the two Indians. "They want to rob her, sure. But mainly they're here to murder her, and you're gonna be an accessory. I promise you I'll make that stick."

The doorman eased himself back into the seat and regarded Nathanson. He shook his head. "Won't happen."

"Why not?"

"Because she ain't goin' to no seven where she live."

Nathanson waited.

"She goin' "—he wagged a big finger at the screens—"*down*."

They now watched Arlene Gelb step out of the elevator and walk along a hall. Neither of the two Indians on the other monitor moved.

"That be C. Sub-basemen'. Boyfriend live there. Mr. Cal. Mr. Calvin"—he leaned over to check a list on the desk—"Boltman. Young man a actor. Pretty, know what I' sayin'?"

They watched her knock on the door and knock again. "Funny—I know he in."

Suddenly an Indian appeared in the same hall Arlene Gelb was in, and the two other Indians on seven began to move, one rapidly down the stairs, the other toward the elevator.

Said Nathanson, "How many of them are there?"

"Today?"

"Why? They been here before?"

"You a cop?"

"How many!" Nathanson barked, watching Arlene Gelb. She turned from the door and, seeing the Indian, raised her arm that was covered by her jacket.

"Three today. Other times they came, they was mo'. A week ago. Week and a half."

That probably made four, *if* they left a driver in the limo, which was smart on a hit. They had come for the money, but failing that, they would take out everybody they could.

But not the Indian on C. His hands now flew up to his chest or his throat. His hat flew off before he fell and rolled into a wall. Arlene Gelb's arm jumped once more, and the sounds that came to them were deadened and faint, like somebody tapping lightly on the concrete slab beneath the carpet under their feet.

"See that?" asked the doorman, pulling himself out of the seat. "What she do, off tha' sucker? She got a gun there, under her coat?"

She now stepped daintily over the man and moved up the hall toward the stairwell.

"Where's she going?" Nathanson demanded.

"That way to the parking lot out back." His hand moved to another monitor that pictured a door, at which Arlene now appeared.

"Can you stop the elevator here?" Nathanson asked. Stepping toward it, he saw the sixth floor lighted on the panel and now the fifth.

"Override," said the doorman.

"Well—do it. And keep the Indian on it here, if you can. Tell him something, anything. The limo. Tell him it's been hit."

"The key. Le's see, I got the key here someplace—"

Nathanson reached out and hit the down button, which at least would stop the elevator in the lobby briefly, and he turned to the stairwell door, opening it a crack first to listen. He heard footsteps above and below, the former louder, heavier, taking the stairs down at a furious pace. He also noted that the door swung open nearly to the newel post of the stairs.

He eased the door nearly to and waited, while the doorman conducted a brief, profane search of his desktop. Finally finding the key, he then took two long steps to the elevator, where he inserted it in the lock.

But the door of the elevator slid open just as the Indian on the stairwell reached the lobby landing. Nathanson shoved open the heavy fire door, which caught the rushing Indian in the face and head. The blow was stunning, and Nathanson threw his body into the door again and again, loading his 230 pounds into the hard gray metal. Yet the Indian, falling, managed to lash out with his *penilla;* the blade bit into the tweed of his overcoat.

Nathanson cried out. He pivoted and stomped at the wrist of the hand that held the knife, pinning it to the floor; and with the heel of the other shoe, he crushed the Indian's knuckles into the concrete. And suddenly in anger and rage at all that he had seen and felt and what had been done to him and others, he had the man up in his arms, the black, slick head in his hands, which he twisted once sharply to the side. Like green wood snapping, the vertebrae in the Indian's neck cracked apart, and Nathanson dropped the limp figure to the floor.

Behind him he heard the doorman shout, and he turned to see the second Indian bolt out of the elevator, something black and boxy in his right hand. It was a machine pistol that now winked light at him, and filled the lobby with a harsh clatter like from a rivet gun. But the doorman, pivoting gracefully, swung a large foot between the Indian's ankles, and he went down, skidding across the polished tile floor toward the stairwell door.

Nathanson stomped on him twice too—the neck again—then reached down and pulled the weapon from his grasp. The *penilla,* which the other one had dropped, was next. Nathanson tossed it to the doorman. "Maybe they'll get up, maybe not. Call the cops."

"Where you learn that?"

In a rough, thoughtless life that was still a big mess, Nathanson thought.

"Where you goin'?" the doorman shouted down the stairwell, but Nathanson was on B, headed for C.

Arlene Gelb was already out in the parking lot of the building that was situated on a hill.

Eva Burden, stopped on the side street across from the parking lot, watched Arlene run toward the battered Volvo that Eva knew was the Gelbs' car. She had caught a ride with them to the airport when they had flown down to the Islands together. Thinking that perhaps Nathanson had missed Arlene in the building, Eva got out of her BMW and moved toward the lot to warn Arlene about the Mercedes and the danger she was in.

Arlene had opened the rear cargo door of the station wagon, which was parked beside a Winnebago RV. She was trying to heft one of two cardboard boxes off the tailgate but was hampered by the coat she was carrying over one had.

"Arlene?" Eva called out. "Arlene?"

Arlene straightened up and released the carton, which fell off the tailgate.

"Arlene—I've been trying to call you. Didn't you get my message on your machine?"

Arlene spun around and held the jacket at arm's length, as though pointing it at her.

Eva saw too late the nickel-plated barrel protruding from under the coat.

Arlene pulled the trigger, and the gun jumped. She pulled it again, but it still did not fire. The material of the coat had snagged between the hammer and the cartridges. She tried to tug it free.

But Eva was upon her. "Did you just try to shoot me?" She didn't wait for an answer. Her hand lashed out in a wide sweeping arc that caught the taller woman on the side of the face. It snapped Arlene's head back and sent her spectacles flying. Eva had witnessed too much violence, had been subjected to too much fear over the past few weeks. She was tired of people acting like greedy motes or murderous zombies.

She struck her again with her other hand, and the wide sun hat fluttered down onto the tar. Eva wanted to punch her, to throw her down—all the techniques she had learned in the navy, but she kept thinking, I can't. She's pregnant, and at least the child is innocent.

It was then she heard the squeal of tires. Turning, she saw the Mercedes limo bearing down on them. It screeched to a stop, and one of the South American Indians dressed in a black chauffeur's suit hopped out. The side of his face was a black scab, and she could see, when he muttered something, that he had lost his front teeth.

He had a short black automatic weapon in his hands. With it he gestured that she should stand beside Arlene.

No, Eva thought. He would kill them anyway, and she would not go meekly.

The Indian had moved to the fallen carton, and when he lowered his head to look at it, Eva took one quick step and lunged at him.

He snapped up the automatic and fired a burst at her, then turned the gun on Arlene Gelb, who was fleeing toward the open cab door of the Winnebago. The pattern of fire burst across her shoulders and neck, the base of her skull, and she went down.

Nathanson, seeing Eva on the tar and the man firing at Arlene Gelb, jerked up the weapon he was holding and squeezed off the clip. The flurry of shots spun the man around, knocked the gun from his hands, and spiked him on the hood ornament of the limousine.

Then Nathanson had Eva in his arms. There was blood flowing from her shoulders and neck, her chest. An arm.

He looked wildly around, and seeing the door of the Winnebago open, rushed her there. Arlene Gelb was next. And the two cartons. Why did he think to take that? he wondered, as he backed the large, lumbering vehicle out into the lot and then with a glancing blow cleared the rear of the Mercedes from his path. Would his having stopped—how long?—ten seconds, fifteen at the outside?—now make the difference for Eva or the other woman?

He was out on the street now, and he swung the Winnebago south toward St. Clare's. He switched on the emergency lights and kept his hand on the horn the full twenty blocks to the hospital. There, Nathanson remained with the two women, who were still alive, until he was satisfied everything immediately possible was being done for them. He then made three phone calls to three New York friends, calling in favors they owed him from the past.

One was to a doctor for doctors. He needed a skilled surgeon, a trauma specialist, who could get to St. Clare's as soon as possible. The emergency-room staff would probably have to work on Eva before the specialist could arrive, but he wanted the best in attendance, should her wounds require. Nathanson had also been told that the Gelb woman, who was brain dead, would need an obstetrician. They estimated that she was some eight months pregnant, and the baby was uninjured and had a strong heartbeat.

Two, Nathanson needed a secure garage to park a Winnebago.

And three, he wanted to get hold of a silencer and at least two clips of 9-mm ammunition for an Ingram Model 10 A1S. He had been a fool to think he could settle what he had begun armed only with a photograph and a changed attitude. He had gotten soft and forgotten the early lessons, the only ones that made sense in the world he knew. Maybe if he had acted forcefully sooner, Eva wouldn't be lying down the hall beyond the green curtains.

He would finish what they had started, *then* quit. Something such as this was either ended well or not at all, and for a good, clean finish he would have to act fast, while events were still confused and in turmoil.

From what he could determine, only the cop, Cicciolino, had escaped with his life, and that was an outrage. Nathanson was no killer, but it would gnaw on him for the rest of his life if Eva died and Cicciolino did not. At the very least, he wanted to talk to the man.

When he opened the door of the phone booth, he heard his name being paged. At the nurses' desk two men were standing, looking toward the green curtains. Detectives, Nathanson guessed.

He unscrewed the bulb above his head and closed the door to wait until they moved toward the waiting room. There would be plenty of time for explanations after it was all over. His way.

CHAPTER 30

SO-LONG!

◆

ON HIS LUNCH BREAK a few hours earlier First Deputy Commissioner Bob Brant suddenly found himself in a cab that took him uptown for some impromptu shopping. Everybody else—Cicciolino, Commissioner Ward, even Mayor Koch—had taken the day off, from what he had been able to determine after trying to contact them. Cicciolino was sailing with McCann and Jay Gelb, Ward was "getting a haircut," and Koch was simply "unavailable, and will be for the rest of the day. Please call back on Monday."

Why, then, was Brant punishing himself by being in the office on such a beautiful spring day? Because he was still hung over from Tuesday night and feeling depressed or sorry for himself? Because his divorce, which in effect had estranged him from his children, made him feel guilty, as his therapist had suggested the night before? Or because he simply had not enjoyed the—company was not the word—of a beautiful woman in . . . he could not exactly remember when, but it had been a long time? Months and months. Almost a year.

Which *definitely* was one of his problems, and he speculated that his condition in that regard was exacerbated by the change in seasons. He was merely responding to the difference in light and climate. A few off-the-rack purchases and a new pair of shoes always cheered Brant up and would enhance his image for his inevitable sortie into the fairer sex. The problem was, Brant was not thinking of women in general but in the particular, which always frightened him.

He kept wondering if his libido or subconscious had worked it all out before he even left the office, for he could not find anything to his liking and he kept wandering north. From Marc Jeffries on Forty-third Street he walked over to Paul Stewart on Forty-fifth, and then up to Saks on Forty-ninth. He was about to hail another cab to take him back to the Purple Palace, when he remembered a salesman in Jeffries telling him that they still had poplin blazers in his size on sale in their Seventh Avenue and Fifty-eighth Street store. On the way back he could ask the cabbie to drive through Central Park and then down Fifth Avenue, which was one-way southbound. And there—not quite miraculously—he would be on the street where she lived.

Oh, the towering feeling, he nearly began to hum, thrilling to direct his conscious thoughts to Solange de los Páramos, the recollection of whom he had been avoiding now since he left his office. Why? Because he felt foolish, like some callow youth seized in the throes of an impossible infatuation. He had even gone to the library and looked up *páramos,* which he discovered was the name of sweeping plateaus so high in the Andes they were treeless and barren.

That was Wednesday night when he could not sleep, thinking of her: her strong but entirely feminine, angular shape; her proud—haughty, even—Incan/French/Negroid features; her deep green eyes that seemed to hold so much hope and promise. She was more meant for him, he had decided, than for Tug McCann, who was one of the whitest white guys Brant knew.

In addition to a certain taste that was apparent in what they chose to wear, how carefully they spoke and handled themselves, she and Brant shared almost the same racial background. Brant's maternal great-grandfather had been a white, Louisiana Roman-Catholic priest; a grandmother on his father's side had been a full-blooded Cherokee Indian. The rest of him was black.

The question was, had McCann bedded her? Brant didn't think so. If she had only met him on Tuesday at lunch, then had lunch with him on Wednesday and the dinner that Brant himself had attended, then McCann had not yet bedded her. Tuesday he had no chance, and Wednesday he was too drunk. But Brant knew Tug, who would try today after the sail, when no further social outing would be necessary.

Would he score? Tug was charming, and he certainly had a facile line with the ladies, but would a woman so cosmopolitan and seemingly . . . worldly-wise fall for a man who, while successful, was so overwhelmingly white working-class New York that he was in effect a provincial archetype? Brant didn't think so.

"You know, I've changed my mind," he said before the cabbie could cross to the West Side. "Could you drive up Madison as far as the low nineties, then take me down to One Police Plaza?"

"Anything you say, Commissioner."

Brant glanced in the mirror, and the man, who was black, smiled.

"Nice day for a ride," Brant explained.

"You mean, they don't give you a car and a driver?"

They, of course, did, but even back in his office before setting out, Brant had known where he was headed, and he hadn't wanted to spark the tender of the gossip that was always ready to ignite around a single senior official at Police Headquarters. But the evasion and now the excuse to the cabbie only made him feel more foolish.

Until he saw her again. There in front of the royal-blue marquee of her building on Fifth Avenue opposite the park, he saw her Mercedes stretch limo pull into the curb and the driver hop out in a hell of a hurry. He opened the door, and there she was dressed in sparkling-white *ruana* and slacks, cinched with a blood-red sash that matched the ribbon around her white sun hat. But as quickly she was gone into the building, her chief bearer—Maluko, Brant thought he remembered from two nights ago—in her train, also dressed in yachting whites and carrying a wicker picnic basket.

"Stop the car," Brant said without giving himself time to think it over; if he did, he knew he'd chicken out. "I just saw somebody I know."

"Ain't you lucky, if you mean who I think you do. She maybe the best-lookin' woman I see all week."

Brant wanted to catch her before she got into the elevator. He'd say he saw her, wanted to thank her for her hospitality. Had she had lunch? A drink? Maybe she'd like to take a stroll in the park? He figured she'd decline, and he'd ask her to dinner, which is what he really wanted. McCann couldn't comprehend the moves Brant could lay on a *lady*.

But he never got the chance. She was already in the elevator and was "temporarily indisposed" when Brant got into the foyer of the sumptuous apartment. "She'll be with you momentarily, she wishes me to say." It was Maluko, who was reading from a card. "Mademoiselle asks if yours is a personal visit, Commissioner Brant, or business?"

Brant blinked and studied the man's opaque black eyes. She must be confusing him with McCann, he decided, but then why the *Commissioner*? "Personal, of course."

"Then she asks if you will be kind enough to take a seat on the terrace and that I provide you with a drink. Would the same as on Tuesday be acceptable?"

"I don't care for a drink." Brant didn't want her to think he was a lush, like McCann.

"Are you sure? She says she already has a head start and —"

"No," Brant stated flatly, walking toward the terrace. "As I said, I don't care for any." Let her have her head start; it would give him the advantage this time.

The terrace of the twenty-third-floor penthouse apartment was nearly wild with wind. It beat the vents of his jacket and ruffled the finger waves of his reddish, kinky hair. He had to struggle to move toward the edge and look down over the parapet into the deep shadows of the side street below. The Mercedes had been moved there; parked in front of it was a white van, the back of which three of her Indians in white uniforms were loading with suitcases.

Brant moved out of the blast, back to what looked like the most protected seat near the sliding glass doors.

Maluko soon appeared there. "Are you sure I can't get you something to drink?"

"Positive, thank you."

"Coffee, tea? A soft drink?"

"Nothing, *thanks*."

The butler waited before nodding, his eyes studying Brant. He then walked toward the edge of the terrace and looked down, as though checking on the loading of the van. Turning back, he waved at Brant.

Brant was confused. Did he want him to join him there, or was he waving to somebody behind him? Brant turned, and there in the open sliding-glass door were the figures of three other Indians, who were also dressed in white jumpsuits.

They advanced upon him, one moving to one side of his chair, another to the other. The third stood behind him.

"Yes?" Brant asked. "What do you want?"

Reaching down for the chair, they picked him up.

"What are you doing?" At first Brant thought it was merely some elaborate South American courtesy; they were going to move him to a sunnier, more protected part of the terrace. Until, as they approached the middle of the terrace, they began to gain speed, running almost.

"No, wait—" Brant clamped his hands on the arms of the chair and began pushing himself out. But they were already at the parapet where the butler, Maluko, stood, smiling. He pointed over the edge, and the three Indians, holding on to the chair as they would a container, chucked the flailing Brant out into the blast that nearly buoyed him. *"So-lange!"* he shouted in the moment before he plunged the twenty-three stories to the street below.

There, three other Indians were waiting. They snatched up his pulverized remains and threw them into a plastic sheet in the back of the van. They closed the doors and drove off toward Kennedy Airport, leaving a splotch on the pavement where Brant's head had been.

Four days later, when the penthouse apartment was searched and the incident investigated, several residents reported having heard a man scream "So-long!" around the time that a pathologist estimated Brant had been defenestrated.

CHAPTER 31

WHAT GOES AROUND

IT WAS EARLY midnight by the time Nathanson got back to his hotel room. He phoned St. Clare's and was told Eva was still on the critical list in "guarded" condition. He was given the number of the specialist that his doctor friend had got for her, but an answering service said the man would be unavailable until nine in the morning. "If you care to leave your name and number . . . ?" Nathanson did not.

He showered and fixed himself a drink from the complimentary bar in the suite, but it did not help. The television news was full of early, lurid reports of "a day of drug-related death that has touched the lives of one of the city's most-respected couples."

Gerri Cicciolino's murder and her husband's subsequent "megabust" of an East Harlem drug dealer, who had been killed in a gun battle with him and a precinct commander, was the lead story. The details were still "sketchy," but the short news breaks, which Nathanson caught at one-thirty and two o'clock, conjectured that the shooting deaths of Cicciolino's driver, Police Officer Nunzio D'Amato, and "an-as-yet-unidentified foreign man, possibly of Colombian origin" on Ninety-sixth Street, could be connected to the deaths of four other men in a van in Central Park.

Also possibly related were the bodies that had been found in a West End Avenue condominium. Police responding to an emergency call from the doorman discovered four other dead "possible Colombians." Two had been shot, two others had had their necks broken. On further investigation the police had also discovered the body of one Calvin H. Boltman, age twenty-eight, which had been discovered in his basement apartment at the same address. He had been bound, gagged, and shot execution-style in the back of the head. The doorman was being held as a material witness.

There would be a press conference at eleven o'clock at NYPD Headquarters on One Police Plaza. Commissioner Ward, Assistant Chief Cicciolino, and Deputy Inspector Clifton Banks would be present to explain what they knew thus far.

"And, finally, this just in," the Channel 2 anchor added. "We have an as-yet-unconfirmed report that two Manhattan women, one of whom resides at the West End Avenue condominium, were admitted to St. Clare's Hospital sometime yesterday afternoon, suffering from multiple gunshot wounds. The resident of the address is Arlene Gelb, an East Side gallery owner and wife of a Columbia University professor. She is pregnant, and is presently being maintained on a life-support system."

"The second woman is Eva Burden, owner of the Thermidor Restaurant in Soho, where she also lives. Her condition is listed as critical. The police speculate that they somehow ran afoul of the violence at the West End Avenue condominium."

There followed an editorial about the shocking increase in the level of drug-related violence in Manhattan, which formerly had been confined to the boroughs, and "yet another call—a *plea*—for a concerted city, state, and national effort to get guns and drugs off our streets."

Which would never happen, thought Nathanson, pressing the remote button to turn the television off. It would take more money than the rest of the country was willing to shell out. Guns and drugs were the only high-profit possibilities open to a good half of the city, whom nobody who counted cared about anyway, until something like this happened to some of their own. And the whole truth had yet to come out.

Nathanson picked up the telephone and asked for a wake-up call at eight o'clock, a full breakfast, "and all the city papers, please." He was asked if he would be staying longer. "Yes, I guess

I'll be with you for a while." Then could he stop at the desk tomorrow morning? Money again, and for the first time in hours Nathanson thought of the Winnebago and its cargo.

BRASS BUST
HARLEM
DRUG BARON

Banner capitals of the *Daily News* read. Below was a split picture, one half of a bullet-riddled van with a body sprawled inside, the other of the bullet holes in an unmarked police car.

The articles inside—Nathanson counted seven separate stories —detailed all of what he had watched on television the night before, along with the new discovery of two additional bodies: that of Tug McCann, which had been found floating off Battery Park; and Professor Jay Gelb of Columbia, "husband of the pregnant woman on life-support at St. Clare's Hospital.

"Gelb was discovered in his yacht, which was tied to Pier 63, the scene of the murder of Gerri McCann Cicciolino, founder of UNION and wife of Asst. Chief Bill Cicciolino of the NYPD. Police at the scene used words 'savage' and 'barbarous' to describe the condition in which Gelb's body had been discovered. They would speculate only that he had been cut with a large knife."

Nathanson searched the other papers, but as yet there was no suggestion that McCann and the Gelbs had been close friends of Cicciolino.

There was a small article on page 17 of the *Post*, however, saying that one Martita Cruz Sanchez, who describes herself as the common-law wife of Hector ("Chino") Santos Cabrón, had contacted the Spanish-language newspaper *La Prensa*, alleging Santos had *bought* the drugs from Cicciolino and some other white cops. They then murdered him to make themselves look like heroes. *La Prensa* would be out in the afternoon.

Upon first awakening, Nathanson had phoned Eva's doctor, and now tried again. "He's in surgery right now, but he'd like to speak to you about Ms. Burden. If you will just leave a number—" Nathanson declined, saying he'd get in touch later.

After his short stop at the desk, he found that at least the weather had changed and was cooperating. It was a dark, dreary day with a cold wind sweeping in before a storm front to the west.

At Lord & Taylor's on Fifth Avenue, Nathanson bought an inexpensive trench coat one size too big and in the men's room on the seventh floor transferred the Intratec machine pistol, the silencer, and two clips to the deep interior pockets of the new garment.

Back out on Thirty-fourth Street, he gave his Burberry tweed overcoat with the slashed forearm to the first homeless man he spotted, then caught a taxi downtown.

But try as he did, the cabbie could not get within three blocks of One Police Plaza. "Look a' that," he said pointing to the wall of television trucks that were lining St. James Place. "This is gotta be the biggest thing since Bernie Goetz."

"What happened?" Nathanson asked, to get the word on the street.

"You ain't heard?"

Nathanson shook his head.

"White cop—a *chief*—gets a line on this drug pusher who's going to make a big buy. Somehow the cop's missus overhears what's going on and, scared for him or something, shows up there. Doesn't she get whacked by the drug dealer, and the cop takes off after him. Another cop—Cliff Banks, 'member him from the Jets? Big black guy, linebacker. Mean as shit—he's an inspector now, and he sees what's going on. He throws in with the chief, and they get the guy cornered with a *half-ton* of coke. Imagine it, half a fucking ton! Turns out the guy is also into kids. He's got a string of little girls he's shacked up with and rents out.

"You think they read this scumbag his rights? Guy's murdered the chief's wife, right? And who's around to see? The papers say they found the guy with a gun that had been fired into the chief's car. That's maybe right, but I'd have to see videotapes to believe it.

"Meanwhile, crosstown the chief's driver is following the Colombians who sold the guy the shit. They waste him, but not before he gets a bunch of them. Four, five—I don't know. They're still counting.

"They're having a press conference about it there in the Palace in a half hour." The cabbie pointed out the window at the red stone building they could see in the distance.

Said Nathanson, "Oh, yeah—it was on the tube while I was shaving. What about the women who got shot? And the guy in the apartment?"

The cabbie hunched his shoulders. "Got caught in the middle,

I guess," which Nathanson judged was the truest word on the street.

Nathanson got out, and after locating the parking-garage exit, he avoided One Police Plaza. With a crush like that, security would be tight. Only reporters with valid press passes would get near the conference room, and Nathanson's concern was with afterward anyhow—where Cicciolino would go and where he could be got alone. He searched for a bar where he might wait until it was over.

It was an old saloon on East Broadway that was patronized by cops and other government workers from the nearby courthouses and municipal buildings. It had a high tin ceiling, paddle fans, and a long Victorian bar. There was a crowd mainly of cops from the night tour, Nathanson guessed, and their heads were turned to the large television screen at the end of the bar.

Nathanson slid onto the last stool near the door and ordered a beer. When it arrived, he asked the bartender, "Bill Cicciolino drink here?"

Three heads turned and regarded him. Said the bartender, "Chiefs don't drink, or at least drink in public. But him? If he does, he's got a reason."

"Who wants to know?" asked one of the cops.

"A concerned citizen," said Nathanson.

"Aren't we all." And they turned back to the television screen, where a podium with the shield of New York was pictured.

Nathanson had only sipped from his glass when the dais began to fill with the mayor and police officials.

"Can we have some fuckin' quiet?" one of the cops at the bar bawled. Then, "Turn that thing up," to the bartender. It was not a request.

Mayor Koch spoke first, saying that maybe the "atrocious events of the past twenty-four hours will compel legislators in state capitals and Washington to hear the plea of the cities of this nation to provide funding to strengthen the court system and build more prisons. There simply is no other immediate solution than to get these death-dealers off our streets."

Commissioner Ben Ward praised the courage and professionalism of his department from "the very highest level—I speak here of Assistant Chief Bill Cicciolino and Deputy Inspector Cliff Banks—to the uniformed police officers on foot posts or in radio cars. I ask now for a moment of silence for Chief Cicciolino's wife, Gerri, who after having devoted herself to a range of just causes, has now given her life for this city.

"Also for Chief Cicciolino's driver, Police Officer Nunzio D'Amato, who after thirty-one years of service went above and beyond the call of duty and took on a small army of murderers. Like seven other police officers to date this year, he gave his life for this city."

"Close them ranks," somebody said. A murmur passed through the bar, and with the persons on the screen the bar crowd observed the commissioner's call for silence.

"Chief Cicciolino has a written statement to read," Ward went on, "and then, acting in his capacity as police spokesperson, he will take questions. Chief?"

It was the first time Nathanson had actually seen Cicciolino, and he was surprised by both his size and his demeanor. He was a big, well-constructed man in obvious good shape. His blunt-featured, Italianate face was well-tanned, and his black curly hair, which was neatly trimmed, was a match for his tailored black suit and tie.

He placed a folder on the podium, opened it, and paused, glancing about the room as strobes flashed and motorized shutters whizzed and snapped. "I'd like to begin with a little background on what transpired yesterday. I hope you can appreciate that we're still trying to sort things out, and what I tell you here might be amended later on. The details."

The television panned to present Cicciolino's face in close-up, and his large, clear, and unblinking brown eyes were most apparent.

"Look a' that fucker," one of the cops said. "They stung him bad, but he won't give 'em an inch of satisfaction. Not an inch."

Nor did the eyes waver as he said, "As you know, my wife, Gerri, is dead. Yesterday was a day off for us. We had planned to go sailing with our friends, but it seems that certain people had other plans for us. A drug dealer, one Hector—("Chino")—Santos Cabrón"—Cicciolino paused, and his nostrils flared, "—targeted me, my family, my friends and associates, for death. As we know from the media, this is something that often happens in certain South American countries. Presidential candidates, supreme court judges, law-enforcement officers, have all been murdered by hired killers. To my knowledge it's only happened a few times here in the United States, and never before in New York.

"Up until Wednesday of this week, this Mr. Santos was the subject of a surveillance operation initiated by First Deputy Commissioner Brant and commanded by Deputy Inspector Banks and me. Over a three-week period we had virtually shut down his cocaine, crack-cocaine, heroin, and child-prostitution operations in East Harlem. Far be it from me to assess Mr. Santos's motives, but either out of a fit of pique that we had shut down his operation or some other reason, we conjecture that he hired a group of Colombian contract killers to murder First Deputy Commissioner Brant, me, and those around us.

"The first part of that operation occurred at Piers Sixty-two and Sixty-three, where I was to meet my wife to go sailing aboard Professor Jay Gelb's boat with another old friend, Tug McCann. Somehow Santos had learned of my plans, and he and some of his accomplices were waiting there, already having murdered Jay and Tug. Gruesomely, I might add.

"When I arrived on the scene, Santos fired on my unmarked police car. I returned the fire with a riot shotgun that I had been carrying for contingency purposes during the surveillance operation. I shot at the grill and the wheel of one of three vans that Santos had with him, disabling it. Mr. Frank McNabb of Kearny, New Jersey, a watchman at the pier, is a witness to all of this and has made himself available to our investigation.

"It was at that time my wife, Gerri, appeared on the scene." Cicciolino paused and reached for a glass of water on the podium.

Nathanson drained his beer and signaled for another. Cicciolino's story required fluid to choke down.

"It's impossible for me to assess her motives, but I'd like to believe she thought me in danger. I was being fired on, and she tried to intercede. She was shot once by Mr. Santos, who was driving the van with the cocaine. The bullet entered her face slightly below the left nostril. It exited at the back of her head. Her car crashed into a third van that contained two men, known drug dealers, who have admitted to being in the employ of Santos. Those two men—a Mr. Gonzalez and a Mr. Rivera—were injured and have been taken into custody. The others in that van fled the scene.

"As did Mr. Santos, who I followed back to his operation in East Harlem. At One-hundred-and-eleventh Street on that journey, Deputy Inspector Banks saw both Mr. Santos in the van and me in my unmarked car, and he too followed, assuming—he has stated— that I had some reason to be pursuing Santos. My reason was that I had just witnessed the incredible level of violence of which he was capable, and I thought it prudent to wait until he reached some less well populated place to make my arrest. I also had it in the back of my mind that Santos might flee to some place of concealment that we did not know of.

"He did. He drove the van to a commercial building that we have since determined he owns. He proceeded to unload a large amount of cocaine that was in the back of the van he was driving. Once he got the cartons out of the van and onto the loading dock, I identified myself as a police officer and attempted to arrest him. At that point Deputy Inspector Banks rushed to my aid, also identifying himself, and Santos fired a .357 magnum—the same type of weapon, if not the weapon, which he used to shoot my wife. I returned the fire, striking Santos with six of the six rounds in my police revolver. Deputy Inspector Banks did not fire his weapon."

"Didn't have to," one of the cops at the bar observed. "Six out of six in the squash—game's over."

Cicciolino paused and rearranged the sheets of paper before him. The reporters in the room, thinking he had finished, began shouting questions simultaneously, but Commissioner Ward held up a hand and quieted them.

"Meanwhile the hit team of Colombian nationals contracted by Santos attacked and killed my driver, Police Officer Nunzio D'Amato. But not before he personally accounted for five of them. The killers then proceeded to Professor Gelb's address, where they either murdered or had already murdered a Mr. Calvin Boltman, and then shot Arlene Gelb, the professor's wife, and Eva Burden of Soho, a friend of Mrs. Gelb and a woman my wife, Gerri, and I also knew. Had not a Good Samaritan happened by, Mrs. Gelb and Ms. Burden would now be dead. He seems to have interceded and . . . dispatched certain of the hit team, then he drove the women to St. Clare's. We're still searching for the man, and we ask him to come forward."

"Finally, in a development that is only minutes old, it further saddens me to tell you that First Deputy Brant has also become a victim of these people. His body was discovered in the back of a rental van at Kennedy Airport."

"*What?*" one of the off-duty cops at the bar asked.

"Son of a *bitch!*" said another. "We're gettin' our asses kicked by them greasers."

There was further clamor at the news conference, and Cicciolino had to wait until the crowd of reporters in front of the podium quieted. In a performance worthy of an Oscar he stared unblinking directly into the cameras for what must have been an entire minute.

"Bob sustained massive injuries to nearly every part of his body. A police pathologist speculates that he fell from some great height before his body was placed in the van."

"Or was pushed," yet another off-duty cop said.

"The document used to rent the vehicle was forged, and the description of the person who signed the rental agreement fits that of a man who left this country last night aboard an Avianca jet bound for Medellín.

"I think that explains what we know so far. If you have any questions, I'll attempt—"

They were shouted thick and fast. Ward kept having to ask for order. The first were about Brant, but neither Ward nor Cicciolino had anything to add. The next question was about why there was no record of Cicciolino's having radioed for assistance from other police units. "I was so distraught I didn't think of it." About why Santos tried to kill him, with a van loaded with coke. "To be honest, I'm the last guy you should ask about Santos's thought processes." About where exactly D'Amato had been shot and by which Colombian firing what type weapon. "I was across town at the time. With Santos." About reports that it had been a woman wearing a sun hat and driving an old car who had shot a man on the corner of Ninety-sixth Street. Cicciolino hunched his heavy shoulders. About a description of the Good Samaritan. "A police artist's rendering will be distributed at the close of the press conference."

He answered the questions easily and well, until he was asked about an ambulance attendant's claim that crack had been discovered in his wife's car. Cicciolino's ears went back. He said that his wife's record as a courageous humanitarian who had championed the causes of women, the homeless, the poor and unemployed, the disabled and disadvantaged, the addicted, and AIDS victims was a matter of public record and personal pride; and he would like the individual who had made that claim to come forward and make a public statement. "We've all heard that talk is cheap, but in this situation talk like that is very cheap."

Again he bristled and nearly lost his aplomb when he was asked by a woman reporter with an identifiably Spanish accent about the claim of one Martita Cruz Sanchez "that you and several other white policemen actually set up the drug deal and *sold* Hector Santos Cabrón the vanload of drugs for a payment of ten million dollars. She claims that was why you did not call for assistance from other police and why you murdered him."

"Fuckin' spic bitch," muttered one of the cops at the bar.

Suddenly the press conference was very quiet. Cicciolino looked away and shook his head, and when he returned his eyes to the audience and the camera, they were glazed with fury. "Isn't it bad enough that the man murdered my wife and set up the murders of my friends? Now we have one of his prostitutes trying to denigrate me and—"

It was then that Commissioner Ward stepped forward. He was holding a sheet of paper in one hand. "I'd like to add something on that point, if I may. Deputy Commissioner Brant was with Assistant Chief Cicciolino two days before this tragedy when this Hector Santos Cabrón sought them out while they were having lunch in a midtown restaurant. Santos could not have known where they would be dining unless he or one of his Colombian henchmen had followed them. There, he threatened Chief Cicciolino with death if Brant and he did not curtail our surveillance of his drug operation in East Harlem. The next day, Wednesday, Brant dictated this report" —Ward waved the sheet of paper— "and had his secretary place it in the file that Brant had developed on Santos. Copies will be made available to members of the press at the close of this proceeding.

"But let me add this. If we had had the resources and manpower to maintain the pressure on Santos, we might have had sufficient police personnel in place to have avoided the gross loss of life and personal tragedy that lamentably occurred."

Ward then turned to Cicciolino and thanked and commended him for "your courage in taking time away from your family at this sad hour."

As the conference broke up and yet more questions were

shouted, a voice-over explained that Assistant Chief Cicciolino was the father of four daughters, the youngest of whom was severely retarded, and that he would now be leaving One Police Plaza to be with her at this time.

A police artist's composite rendering of the man Cicciolino had called the Good Samaritan—"created after a description given by the doorman at the West End Avenue condominium"— was flashed on the screen and bore a remarkable likeness to Nathanson. He raised the glass mug to his face and finished his beer.

The cops at the bar had turned their heads away from the screen and were conversing in low, gruff, and angry tones.

Standing to leave, Nathanson glanced at the screen again. Cicciolino was now out in a hallway, moving through a cordon of police in blue uniforms who were keeping back a crowd of "the press who could not be accommodated at the news conference, administrative personnel, and other interested people with the clout to have gotten beyond police security guards."

There were reaching out to touch Cicciolino's arm or to say something to him. Like a politician or a celebrity, Cicciolino was working them. Now and again he recognized somebody, he stopped and shook hands, nodding his head and thanking them, while the voice of the television commentator summarized the press conference.

Nathanson turned his back and started for the door when he heard what sounded like three quick pops, followed by shrieks, and a fourth pop. Pandemonium—at the bar, on the screen— broke out. "Holy shit!"

"What?"

"I don't fuckin' believe it!" A cop was up on his feet, pointing at the screen. "They done him right there in the Palace!"

"Shut up and watch!" somebody else shouted from the tables.

All of the cops were on their feet. One had even drawn his service revolver.

The television camera was still being jostled, and backs and heads filled the screen. But suddenly a space was cleared, and it focused on a thin, raised arm, the hand of which grasped a small silver automatic that Deputy Inspector Banks now pried from her grasp.

"He kee-ill Chino," they kept hearing a girl's voice say. "Martita kee-ill *heem*!"

"Rican cunt!" a cop in the bar yelled.

They saw more heads and backs on the screen, while the voice-over explained that Chief Bill Cicciolino had been shot three, possibly four times at close range, and was down on the floor of a hallway at One Police Plaza.

The screen showed a picture of two burly white cops leading away what looked like a child—a dark little girl all angry teeth ringed with bright, lurid lipstick as she shouted her message at the camera.

"How they let her in there?" one of the cops at the bar demanded.

"Press pass. Look—" one of them pointed at the screen.

"Shit—I know a place you can get any ID you want for a double 'buck."

"And that metal detector they got at the door?" yet another observed. "It'd take only two people to defeat that, one inside the barricade, the other out."

The camera shifted to a stretcher that was being rushed down a hall from which civilians were being kept back by angry, rough police. It focused on a cop with a wide, square body who now turned and walked up the hallway toward the camera and the lights.

It was Deputy Inspector Cliff Banks again. His eyes were red and truculent, the front of his shirt bloody. He still had the small silver gun in his hand. Like flashes of lightning, strobe lights kept illuminating the shadows of his stormy face.

Some of the reporters began asking him how Assistant Chief Cicciolino was. Where had he been shot? How many times? Who was the woman? Whom did she represent?

Banks only kept walking. He did not have to clear a space for himself.

Said one cop in the bar, "There goes our future."

Said another, "You hope."

Said a third, "If somebody like him can't clean the place up, nobody can. Point is, is it worth it?"

Which seemed to Nathanson like the question in Banks's eyes.

*　　*　　*

Out on the street Nathanson found it strangely quiet in the direction of One Police Plaza. He flagged a cab and asked to be driven uptown to the West Side, two blocks from the garage in which he had parked the Winnebago.

There, in the deep shadows at the back of the building, he opened the doors of the RV and stepped in. Instead of switching on the lights, he found a flashlight in a utility locker and a large, sharp knife in the kitchen area. There was a six-pack in the refrigerator. He unsnapped a can and removed his trench coat, which was heavy with the machine pistol. He advanced on the two large cartons concealed under the folding bed at the back of the van.

Arlene Gelb had not planned to return to New York. She had packed every interior space with artwork, mounted and framed photographs, cameras, small antiques, and curios. There were jewelry boxes, a music box, even a yard-square strongbox of the kind that could resist fire. Nathanson tasted the beer and turned his attention to the cartons.

It took him some time to work the blade of the knife through all the reinforced strapping tape, but at last he got to the inner flaps, which were sealed with duct tape. He placed a flashlight where it would shine into the box, severed the tape down the middle, and there it was—a sight to quicken any pulse—neatly stacked rows of banded thousand-dollar bills.

Until—Nathanson began to chuckle—he dug down past the top two layers and discovered that the rest were shill bundles with thousand-dollar top bills and green cut paper below. He laughed. Nathanson tilted back his head and began roaring at the irony and absurdity of all that death for—he opened the second box—just under $2.5 million, when he added the thousand-dollar notes from each shill stack. It was the same amount to the penny that Creach and he had planned to pay for the delivery, and, really, all that the dope had been worth in the Bahamas.

In the jewelry box he found a nice collection of turquoise and silver Navajo jewelry, the stones of which were just the color of Eva's eyes. He had to screw the silencer onto the barrel of the Intratec and shoot into the lock of the strongbox. There he found $800,000 in sixteen more stacks of fifty $1,000 bills each—the Gelbs' share of the $2.4 million that they had found on his boat.

Nathanson drained the can of beer, and on the idea that he

had considered earlier—ending the thing right—he decided that
the contents of the strongbox should be Eva Burden's too, *if* she
did not accept his other offer. He dumped the contents of a suitcase
that contained a weird collection of night apparel, and packed it
with all the available money, the jewelry, the Intratec, its silencer,
and what was now the spare clip.

At the hospital he learned that Eva had been removed from
the critical list and transferred out of intensive care to the private
room that he had arranged for yesterday. At the door he met her
doctor, who told him she was out of danger but would require
long, careful recuperation. The bullet that had been removed from
her chest had damaged a section of her left lung and had nicked
her aorta. "A millimeter difference, it would have killed her. And,
of course, her bones must mend." Left arm and left collarbone, he
meant.

Nathanson also asked about Arlene Gelb, and was told that
she had expired after giving birth to a six-pound baby boy who
was in surprisingly good condition. "Miraculous, really. A pree-
mie, of course, but perfectly healthy. He would have been a big
baby if allowed to come to term." Nathanson wondered if the
Gelbs had any near relatives and just how difficult it would be for
him to adopt the child. But first things first.

Nathanson opened the door, stepped into the room, and slid
the suitcase into the closet. He placed the trench coat and his hat
on top of it. He locked the door and slipped the key in his pocket.

The room was dark, and filled with flowers from—Nathanson
checked the cards—restaurant purveyors, a restaurant trade association, some individual friends whose names he did not recognize,
the Police Benevolent Association, and even Assistant Chief Bill
Cicciolino.

Nathanson turned to the bed and found her eyes on him.
"Hi," he said. "Regret you're still living?"

Her smile was thin. She raised her hand. He took it and sat on
the edge of the bed. Her left shoulder and arm were in a cast that
angled out from her torso.

"Doctor talk to you?"

She tried to say yes, but her mouth was dry; Nathanson
reached for the water.

"He says you'll need a long recuperation."

She closed her eyes and nodded.

"I told him we'd have to wait until you came to—for a professional opinion."

She drank from the straw, then eased her head back into the pillows and looked at him again. Her hand put pressure on his.

"You too weak for a proposition?"

Watching her eyes trying to read his features, he was reminded of the jewelry in the suitcase. "Proposition?" she managed to say.

"There's another word for it, I know, but it's never been a part of my vocabulary."

"Charity?" She closed her eyes, as though fighting pain.

He waited for them to open again. "No, wait, I think I've got it. I had in mind more the word 'proposal.' "

She blinked and regarded him further.

"I know you're weak and hurting, and I guess I got you into all of this. You don't have to answer now, I can wait. But it's all over now. You don't have to worry about anything."

Nathanson reached for the clicker of the TV. Most of the channels were still covering "the crisis at One Police Plaza," and the update was just as Nathanson had expected. Cicciolino had been a big man, but three .357 magnum slugs in the chest and one in the right temple had taken him out. ". . . dead on arrival at Cornell Downtown Medical Center."

Eva closed her eyes again. Nathanson switched channels to the composite photograph of the "Good Samaritan," and he clicked it off.

He waited. Through the closed windows the city was giving off what sounded like a distant groan. From time to time he could hear voices from the hall.

When she opened her eyes again, she asked, "You were saying?"

"I was?"

She squeezed his hand, encouraging him. "Make my day. I'm good at refusals."

"Remember what you were talking about the other night at your place?"

She rolled her eyes and tried to smile. "My accusation?"

"No, wait. This is serious. It occurred to me that you're right. You *do* remind me of my mother, and I have an idea that you can cook. I'm thinking of rebuilding my house in Nassau, and this position will need to be filled. I can't pay much, but the fringe benefits—" Nathanson felt her squeeze his hand, as though wanting him to stop.

When she opened her eyes again, she asked, "Why *lost?*"

"Why not? It's what happens. Happened."

"What about 'nature'?" The grip of her eyes on his was almost tangible.

"If you mean, what about dealing—all done. Gone."

"And anything . . . illegal?"

"Are these conditions I'm hearing? How 'bout a straight answer?"

She hunched her good shoulder and closed her eyes. "You said you've got time." But she lifted her head slightly and puckered her lips.

Nathanson was just lowering his head to hers when they heard a sharp rap on the door, which opened. In it stood the two plainclothes cops he had seen the day before at the emergency-room reception desk. Between them was the doorman from the building on West End Avenue where the Gelbs had lived.

"That the man?" one of the cops asked.

The tall black man looked at Nathanson and winked. "Ain't him."

"Whadaya mean, ain't him?" one of the cops demanded. "This is *him*." He smacked a paper in his hand. "Stand up, you."

Nathanson didn't move.

"I said, stand up!"

"You got a hat?" the other cop asked.

Nathanson shook his head.

"What's he to you?"

"My . . . fiancé." Eva drank from her water cup, then touched her chest, as though what she had said was hard to swallow.

"You the one brought her in?"

Nathanson nodded.

"Where'd you find her?"

"Can't we take this outside?"

"Sure—but we got two cops dead, and we want answers."

"Back soon," Nathanson said to Eva, returning the pressure he felt on his hand. "Want anything special?"

"Details. A contract. And two witnesses that'll swear you're lost."

PART VII

SOUTH MONEY

CHAPTER 32

COMES AROUND

◆

It took David Creach a week and a half to slip through the informal security net that Solange Mercier La Guatavita had surrounded herself with in Medellín's notorious Barrio Antioquia.

It was early autumn in Colombia, and the weather in the city on the flanks of the Andean highlands had grown wet, if not yet cold. Once a day a frigid wind swept up from the south and brought a hard, driving rain that chilled Creach to the bone. His recently amputated fingers bothered him most, but he kept the hand exposed and visible to passers-by in the warren of narrow laneways that was the city's most squalid ghetto.

He wore only the cheapest shirt and trousers and the standard fedora hat that marked him as a *campesino,* a hick. His only concession to the elements was a *ruana,* another native item, fashioned from a square of coarse woven wool with a hole in the middle for his head. It was wide, and its heavy fabric readily concealed his second, and last, two-barrel Saturn 2-22 that he was now never without.

Even the neck of the garment he refused to secure, preferring instead to leave the new scars on his throat visible. He wanted to be seen as just another small, sorry black *amputato* who could no longer make a living as a laborer in the fields and had come to the city to drink and die.

Creach worked his way slowly from bar to bar toward the section of the barrio where the *sicaria* lived surrounded by her Boyaca Indians. Since his speech was little more than a hoarse whisper, Creach could only look and listen, but in a way that was better. Although he could understand Spanish, his accent was heavy, and his ignorance of the local idiom would mark him as a stranger.

And he didn't want anybody to suspect he was one pissed-off *Norteamericano* who had come to settle a score any way he could. From what he had gathered whenever her name was mentioned, La Guatavita was looked upon as the reigning queen of Medellín's underworld. The tone was always respectful, and often reverential.

So Creach drank, or, rather, he swished his mouth out with *guarupo,* a harsh native brew made of molasses and wild yeasts. It kicked like a mule, especially when mixed with *aguardiente,* the Colombian anise brandy.

He drank *guarupo* on boards stretched across barrels down dark alleys where usually something—a dog, a cat, a rat, a baby—had recently died. He drank it in rusting corrugated-metal shacks with urine-wet mud floors so foul his eyes watered until he could breathe the fumes of his drink. With his back always to some wall, he usually kept the cup there where he could see without being noticed, where he would look like just another *borrachón* making love to the vessel that would claim him.

On steps, in doorways, any place dry he could find, Creach offered his always-handy bottle to anybody who sat near him. Across the rivulets of mud and filth that flowed down the steep hillside of the barrio, he would point toward the compound of laneways and painted, substantial cinder-block houses. There, mainly Boyaca women, who were even uglier than their men, could be seen coming and going, and he let whoever was with him talk.

The Boyacas, he learned, were strangers themselves from the mountains to the southeast near Bogotá. They literally worshiped La Guatavita, he was told, who was like a kind of huntress. From time to time she departed with the Boyaca men and returned with vast riches that she shared, not always equally, with her small, fierce community. In addition to good, dry houses, they had running water, plumbing, and their own electrical plant, and seemed to come up with automobiles, trucks, and guns whenever they needed them.

They were feared, envied, and respected, and any thief caught in their quarter was brought out into some more public street to be cut open by their women as a lesson to others. "The police don't bother them, not with her connections. And some say they are afraid. The Boyacas are like her army. Losses don't matter to them. They're not people, they're ants. Expendable. And they breed like them. There's always another to fill a place."

Most recently La Guatavita and a large contingent of her Boyacas had gone away on some trip or other, leaving a small guard of men to protect the compound. She had then returned but had left immediately, taking the guard with her. "But don't get any ideas," the old Medillíno who was speaking to Creach advised. "The women are worse than the men. At least they will kill you quickly. The women will cut off your *cojones* and make you eat them one by one before—" He had then imitated the killing stroke that Creach himself had nearly seen too close.

Creach bought another bottle and waited for the old man to pass out. Creach was not without his own skills, and he decided to make his move now, before the *sicaria* or any of her guard returned.

The rain had stopped, the skies were clearing. He would use the moonlight to stage his assault on the Boyaca compound.

You *can* go home again, La Guatavita thought, especially when home is not really home, you are armed with new truth, and you lead a small army.

From afar, Finca Los Llanos looked like an Antioquian dream of the best possible life. Across the fertile plain of recently harvested fields that had given the estate its name, the house could be seen, standing at the base of the Cordillero Central and nested in a demesne of gardens, some of which dated from the eighteenth century.

An avenue of towering cypresses, imported from Tuscany, led up to the entrance. Under a sparkling windblown sky with a full moon, their massive bowls flickered like lambent silver flames. Beyond lay the house, which was of Spanish colonial design.

Severely simple, with a terra-cotta roof sloping to massive

stone walls that had been stuccoed white, it was *de pura cepa*—the real thing, she thought. An arched veranda wrapped the entire structure, which contained an interior courtyard that was fourteen rods on the diagonal, she had once heard Don Pacho brag.

Set deep in the walls of the front facade were double casement windows with moorish, multifoil arches. The leaded glass had been shaped in a diamond pattern. In all, it was a handsome package, she decided not for the first time, holding only vileness within. Tonight she would rid the structure of its smirch.

As the three Land Rovers drew near the house with their headlamps extinguished, La Guatavita could see lights in the study, where Pachito would be reading, and the glow of others leading along a hall to the house servants' quarters on the far side. There were other lights and smoke rising from the kitchen, which was a separate building set off from the house, but it was nearly midnight, and both Don Pacho and his wife, Doña Dolores, would have long since retired.

La Guatavita waited while her Boyaca retainers secured the compound, one group stealing off toward the stables and barns, the second toward that kitchen and *finca* offices in yet another building set up on a hill where agricultural operations during the day could be monitored through binoculars. The third group moved toward the house and chapel. Only when Maluko flashed her two quick signals did she climb out of the Rover.

As she approached the house in which she had known so much pain, she realized that she would pass through its immense front doors for the first time. Whenever she had been with the Londoños and they had returned to the *finca*, they had entered the front door, and she had been made to walk around to the rear.

She had been seven years old the first time, and still very much suffering from the cerebral damage that had deafened her. Her vision was blurred, and she had become nauseous from the pounding headache that was with her day and night but had become more severe after the bumpy car ride into Medellín. Wandering off the veranda to vomit, she had been stricken with what she now imagined was reverse peristalsis. In her weakened condition and still trying to heave, she fell in the sun on the granite drive that led toward the stables. It was January, and full summer and torrid.

When Pachito, who was only two years older than she, had run to help her, Don Pacho had held him back. "If she dies," he said, "it is God's will. He has meant for only the strong to survive," a servant told her years later. She passed the test and somehow she survived that day, though with all of her exposed skin blistered, she lay near death for a week. And she also weathered the other, sundry tests to which the man had subjected her—the rapes, the beatings, the humiliations.

So be it, she now thought. Don Pacho knew how the world worked; she wondered how deep was his knowledge of pain. Tonight she, an expert, would tutor him in depth.

The immense oak door squealed on its hinges as Maluko opened it for her, and her heels rang on the patterned marble stone of the darkened hall. Pachito met her—book in hand, pipe in mouth—at the doorway of the library. "Are you back already? How did it go?" He looked down at her hands as though he expected her to have something for him.

From under her white *ruana* she produced the photograph that Brian Nathanson through Jorge Luis Ochoa had provided her. While Pachito took it to the lamp by the chair where he had been reading, she glanced around the room with its floor-to-ceiling collection of leather-bound first editions, its magnificent mahogany tables, and supple leather chairs with brass tacks that the Londoños' servants, who were given nothing but food and shelter and were therefore slaves, kept bright. Everything—even the ponderous beams of the twenty-foot ceiling—gleamed and smelled of lemon oil and wax. It was another room that she had never entered; but, then, when she had last been here, she had not been La Guatavita.

With his back to her, Pachito slowly straightened up.

She could tell from the way he didn't turn to her that he had known. "Turn and face me, Pachito." She waited until he did.

"Did you know about the brooch stone before you hired me to recover your shipment?"

Londoño nodded, then lowered his eyes. He was a tall, dark well-built man, who suddenly looked old and bent. He had to know that an Ochoa and only an Ochoa could have taken the picture, which meant that her arrival at Finca Los Llanos was sanctioned by los Dueños del Cupo.

"And yet you had the gall to ask me to do this thing for you."

"I had no choice, I was desperate."

To maintain your lifestyle, she thought. Apropos of the referent of his surname, he was wearing a loose brown cardigan sweater over what appeared to be cricketing whites. The trousers were linen and pleated, the shoes white buck.

"And for that you sacrificed the truth and our friendship."

"As I said, I was desperate."

La Guatavita allowed her eyes to sweep the collection of books, the sprawling plantation master's desk that was made of iron wood and so heavy it had taken four men to move into the library the day Don Paco bought it, probably with the proceeds of other emeralds that he had stolen from her parents. Through the open door to the music room she saw the gleaming black expanse of the Bechstein grand piano that she had sent Pachito back from Nassau. "And weak."

He nodded. "I never claimed to be strong."

And therefore you hid behind your weakness and the excuse of having a father like Don Paco she thought. "Tonight I'll give you the chance to try. Where is it?"

"The brooch?"

La Guatavita waited, hoping he could read her eyes. He would have to dissimulate only once and he'd be dead.

"In the safe in my mother's room."

"What about the other safe?" In Don Pacho's study, she meant.

"I don't know, I won't learn the combination until . . ."—the old man dies, he meant.

"Get the brooch stone. I want it now. Maluko will accompany you. And, Pachito, know this"— from under her white *ruana* she drew a shiny *penilla;* with a finger she touched its honed blade—"you are a man on the edge. Any slip will be fatal."

While she waited, she toyed with the idea of trying to secure the *finca* for herself, but short of marriage to Pachito it would be an impossibility. The Ochoas would never allow her, a Creole bitch, to possess an estate as *rich* in history as this. And why own it? Possessing property only made a person vulnerable, a target, as she had seen in her present profession. And could she live here? Not with her memories.

The stone was contained in an exquisite jade case with an ornate M carved into its top. La Guatavita ran her long tawny fingers over the figure. "For Mercier, I assume?"

"I never saw the case before tonight."

"Like you never saw the emerald."

"I never said that."

"That's right. You never said anything."

With two fingers La Guatavita pushed up the lid and gazed down on the Mercier brooch stone, which was sitting in a plush of red silk. In the direct light of the desk lamp it glowed with a color that was unlike any other. It was simply what it was—a pure green flawless emerald the size of a goose egg.

"Who cut it?" The stone had been masterfully shaped. Its facets sparkled and winked as she turned it in the light.

"I once overheard him say . . . your father."

"Really?" La Guatavita drew the emerald from its silken pocket and squeezed it in both hands. Closing her eyes, she tried to summon some impression of her father, but beyond two photographs that she had discovered in the files of a Bogotá newspaper, she could remember nothing of either parent. "So, you've known about it for some time, Pachito?" She handed him the stone, wanting him to fix the clasp of its simple gold chain around her neck.

"Until I actually saw it, I thought it was just another fabrication of his. You know how he is, always puffing himself up."

"And when did you see it? First."

Londoño did not want to answer, and he averted his eyes.

"Come now, Pachito—isn't it about time you became a man?"

He sighed. "On my twenty-first birthday. He took me into his study, which was where he was keeping it then. He showed it to me and said it would be mine someday. 'Everybody thinks I've been a failure, and look what I have,' is how he put it."

For which he had murdered two innocent people and maimed a third. Well, she thought, turning to admire the emerald in the reflection from one of the glass-covered bookcases, Don Pacho had only returned to first-impulse wealth-gathering in the Americas— rape, pillage, and plunder. Her problem was that she was just too close to the victims of his greed. She simply couldn't bring herself to view his selfish acts with any dispassion.

"Come," she said to Londoño, pointing toward the door where Maluko was standing with a machine pistol at the ready, "we shall proceed with step two in your rehabilitation as a gentleman. It's not enough merely to understand that you must tell the truth when your life depends on it. No. You must also be initiated into the difficult part of the maturation process as we know it in the New World. Granted, it's a blooding, but all societies must have their rites and rituals."

Out in the hall she asked, "Did I tell you that I'm thinking of writing a book on the subject? It won't quite be Castiglione, but then, times have changed." Her voice echoed off the marble and stone. "Does the 'don' still sleep in the master bedroom?"

Londoño did not answer. With the muzzle of the weapon Maluko was nudging him along.

"Alone, I hope. I view your mother more as a victim than an enabler, but I wish only you to be the witness. It is a male thing that we do, and there is a lesson in it for you."

In the Barrio Antioquia Creach waited only until the hour of curfew to make his move. Every night for the week and a half of his reconnaissance he had watched a powerfully built Boyaca woman make a nightly circuit of the perimeter of the compound, yipping for Boyaca children. It was the signal that it was getting dark and they should come home. The sound was chilling, like a she-wolf calling in a pack of cubs, and they came quickly. Those who were only minutes late had their bare legs whipped with a switch. Creach had seen two who dared to make her linger beaten with her fists.

Creach concealed himself in the shadows of the stairway, and when she passed by, he fell in behind her, walking into the compound until she noticed he was there. Switch cocked, she spun around, but he had something to show her. He raised the Saturn 2-22, so she could see what it was. He then aimed its double barrel at the heavy door that he had watched her lock and unlock on four separate nights now. The three-second burst destroyed the door and left a gaping, smoking hole where the lock had been.

Creach then raised his *ruana* to show her the bundle of plastic explosive that was strapped to his chest. He ejected the spent clip and inserted another from his stock of an even-dozen clips there. He nodded to the door, and they moved toward it.

Inside he found a pleasant arcaded cloister with plants and a stream that tumbled through rocks into a quiet pool. There were benches, tables, and dwarf palms for shade, but Creach directed the woman toward a pair of large double doors. There, days before, Denny—watching from a hotel room window through binoculars—had seen La Guatavita on her brief return enter that room and summon what Denny had assumed were her captains. It would be there that Creach waited.

But the moment she understood what he wanted, the woman began shouting in some language Creach did not understand, which was okay with him. The more of them who knew the better. He had to make all of them understand the danger they were in; that way, there would be no mistakes. But her bitching like that also gave him an idea that the room was special. Maybe it was where the loot was kept, which was half of what he had come for.

And maybe not. The walls were covered with what could only be gold leaf, and there was an enormous solid-gold like platter on the wall behind the desk. Raised on it was the figure of either a man or a woman with long, flowing hair. It was turned three-quarters away from the viewer. He or she was standing on a raft or barge in the middle of a lake, looking toward a rising sun, and poised as if to dive into the golden water. The platter alone was a prize worth having, but he wondered how many men it would take to carry it away.

With his stump Creach pointed to the carpet and made the woman sit in the middle of the room, facing the desk. He then showed her the detonator attached to the thumb of his ruined hand. He also made sure she saw the scar on his throat. There was now a crowd in the doorway, mostly women and a few old men with weapons, and she spoke to them in their language, evidently warning them against attacking him.

She then turned and asked in Spanish what he wanted. With his stump Creach touched his lips and then pointed to the figure on the platter above the desk.

"There are other ways to do that, *señor*. You need not put all of us in danger."

Creach only smiled to show he had understood.

When Maluko, La Guatavita, and Pachito Londoño entered the master bedroom at Finca Los Llanos, they found the old man, Don Pacho, sleeping in a canopied bed that had been set close to an open window. A shaft of moonlight was falling across his face, and he appeared to be smiling, as though experiencing a pleasant dream. But for his age and the gray in his mustache and hair, it could as easily have been his son lying there. Both had the same high forehead, prominent Roman nose, high cheekbones, and deep-set eyes.

La Guatavita herself smiled and positioned Maluko at the head of the bed, Pachito near the window where he could see, and a third man—another Boyaca who had appeared immediately upon Maluko's whistle—in the doorway. She then sat on the edge of the bed and turned her body into the moonlight so she would be visible to Don Pacho when he opened his eyes.

With one hand she pulled back the covers. Don Pacho was wearing silk pajamas of nearly the same color as the emerald they had just viewed in the library and that was now concealed beneath her *ruana*. How old could he be? she asked herself, looking down at him. Sixty or sixty-five, no more, and whereas his face testified to his years of debauchery, his body still looked strong. And felt strong, as now with infinite care she lowered her hand to his inner thigh so he would not wake until she was ready for him.

Slowly, working only with the tips of her fingers, she moved the hand up his thigh toward his groin area and back again. Then up and back a second time. On the third pass she allowed her fingernails to graze the head of his penis, which had become prominent and visible through the thin, slick silk. And again around the ridge of the cap.

In his sleep Don Pacho smiled more completely, and twisted his head from side to side. He muttered something and spread his legs. Now his penis was bulging in the silk. As she had remembered, he was well-hung—certainly too well for a seven-year-old—and she let her fingers dally with the shaft, plucking at it, teasing, and tickling him. Again he groaned, and she directed it up and out through the vent in his pajamas, which she pulled down so his gonads too were visible in the moonlight.

And there it pulsed while she continued to work it up, the object that had kept her enslaved until her fifteenth year. She wanted it big, as big and vile as it had felt whenever he had wakened her with it from her sleep.

But when now he began to climax, she squeezed it as hard as she could.

His body jerked, his eyes opened, and he sat up. His hands fell on hers. "Who is it?"

La Guatavita turned her face to the moonlight and smiled.

"Solange? Is it really you?" he asked, the fear melting from his face. "I dream about you. But—" His hands worked on hers, feeling her.

With her other hand she pulled off the *ruana*. There, hanging from her neck, was the emerald, the Mercier brooch stone that he had slain her parents to steal. In her lap was the shiny *penilla* that she had shown his son earlier.

Suddenly it was in her hand, and with the other she pulled up his penis as far as it would extend. In one quick cut she had it off. Blood jetted across the bed and splotched the front of her dress.

Don Pacho tried to scream, but, as if with a punch, she silenced him, stuffing what she had cut off into the open orifice. Maluko had grabbed hold of Don Pacho's head and now forced the mouth down until she had it all in. Looping a strap under the jaw, he then twisted the leather thongs at the back of the head, sealing the mouth.

La Guatavita did not leave the bed. Instead she sat there smiling silently, her hands folded in her lap, until the old man— Don Pacho, her nemesis—choked on his own *macho*.

He dreamed about me, she thought. But then she supposed *he* would.

For Creach, who was waiting for her, the hours passed slowly. Around midnight he heard footsteps, many hushed voices, and then silence as the guard at the door backed away.

La Guatavita entered the room proudly, triumphantly even, alone and unarmed. Except for a splotch of something that looked like blood across the front of her dress, she was dressed all in white. Around her neck hung an enormous green stone that could only be an emerald from the way it shone. With all the gold in the room it looked especially fiery, and Creach wondered at its value.

She paused, as though sizing up the situation, and told the woman sitting on the floor to go. "And close the door behind you," she added in Spanish.

To Creach she then spoke English. "You must be the fabled Mr. Creach who 'don't take no shit.' " She advanced on a computer terminal, switched it on, and after a short wait punched the keys, and a color likeness of Creach came on the screen. She hit some other keys, and the machine began scanning through page after page of a dossier that included Creach's U.S. Army files, his International Longshoreman and Warehouse Workers' Union

cards, and his U.S. arrest record. There was also a list of sales that
Nathanson and he had been involved in, and another of the weapons that Creach possessed or was known to have used.

"Need I ask why you're here?"

When Creach said nothing, she went on, "Oh, that's right.
You took a little shit in the Islands, and now"—she opened her
hands and closed them—"somebody else must be to blame."

Creach smiled. It was the principle her clients operated on.
They *never* were wrong, and somebody else *always* had to pay. He
wished he still had his voice and could say something about pi-
geons roosting.

"Well, you found me. Don't you think I or one of my com-
rades will be able to find you?"

He raised the wedge that remained of his left hand, then
moved it to his neck. He hunched his shoulders and smiled more
completely. He wanted her to know he didn't give a fuck.

"And failing that, we can always locate your comrade, Mr.
Nathanson. Like a lemming to a cliff, I'm sure he'll return to his
beloved Nassau."

Creach closed his eyes and shook his head, as in, That settles
it. Now you're dead.

It gave her pause. When he looked at her again, her eyes for
the first time shied, moving away from his to the platter on the
wall in back of him and to the computer monitor. Her hand rose
to the emerald on her neck.

When she turned back, her smile was warm. "But you don't
really want to kill me. Certainly we can make some accommoda-
tion, find some middle ground. I have money." Her hand swung to
the platter above him. "And connections. We can work something
out. Perhaps we might even set you up."

Set him up? Creach raised his left hand to show her his own
connection. The cord attached to his thumb was as immediate and
direct as any. He need only try to make a fist to take out at least
him, her, the room, and a good part of the compound.

"And, you know, we're really not that much different, you
and I."

Which was news to Creach. He was not now, nor had he ever
been, a contract killer or a scavenger. The worst he'd ever done
was run coke wholesale.

"Slaves." She waited, then nodded. "Yes, still. We are slaves, both of us. Would you care to hear my explanation and my proposal?" She stepped toward the door. "Come, we'll take a drive. That way, if you don't care for what I have to say, there'll be only the two of us. There's no need for anybody else to lose his life. These people here are guiltless, as are, incidentally, you and I. Interested?"

He was. In spite of the *plastique* strapped to his chest, Creach still had hopes of getting back to Nassau alive, which would not be possible if they remained in the compound. There were simply too many Boyacas and too many miles between him and Denny at the hotel, and between Denny and him and Nathanson's yacht, which they had docked in Barranquilla. Or even, say, the Medellín airport.

"I can see you are," she went on, raising her hands to her neck, as though she would remove the brooch stone.

Creach shook his head.

She smiled. "Did you mean to say, leave it?" She lowered her hands. "You see, we're a lot closer than you thought. Because of our disabilities, we can communicate better than with others. You want me to leave this on?"

Creach nodded.

"Do you know my story and what it means to me?"

Creach didn't care about her story, and what the emerald meant to her didn't matter.

"Well, I suppose just a symbol, but I've grown rather fond of the thing, as you can imagine. And then one can't ignore its intrinsic worth. Tell you what—why don't we make it the guarantor of my proposal. If you don't care for my terms, well—you can always take this. But you will, you'll see.

"Ready?"

Not before he made her lean against a gold wall, and he patted her down.

"Your touch is gentle," she whispered, as he moved down her legs. "Perhaps we might add something like that to our deal. I have not had a man willingly in—" She tossed back her head, as though thinking, but did not complete the thought.

Walking out of the compound, which seemed deserted, Creach kept her close. They found the Boyacas grouped under the

canvas awnings of some stores on the other side of the muddy
street near the perimeter. Creach nudged the *sicaria* and, when she
turned to him, mouthed, "Speak Spanish only."

"Or English. Would you prefer English? Maluko knows English."

Creach recognized him from Nassau as the older Indian with
the hard, shifty eyes who gave the orders. He was wearing combat
fatigues.

She told him to gas up one of the Land Rovers that they could
see just inside the gate. "We'll need some jerry cans too. And do
not follow us. Mr. Creach and I have some matters to discuss, and
I would like him to concentrate."

Before they left, Creach conducted a careful, patient search of
the vehicle: for a hidden gun, a homing device, a bug, anything
that might make him a target. She took the wheel and he the
passenger seat, which he extended to his maximum reach so he
could watch her every move.

She drove all night, north out of Medellín, then northeast and
finally due east, according to the compass on the dash.

They climbed over the Cordillera Central. It was a main road,
but poorly marked, with many sudden turns and zero visibility, as
they plunged through heavy mists toward the Magdalena. They
crossed that river at Porto Berrío. The Rio Carare was next. From
there they began a long, winding climb up the steep flanks of the
Cordillera Oriental into Boyaca, Creach saw on a small, battered
sign that the headlights flashed over.

While she spoke, Creach wondered at the possibility that the
journey was some contingency plan that she had established in
advance. Or that she had had time to discuss where she would
attempt to take him before she had entered the gold room. Would
it matter? No, he decided. Not from what he had seen on the gold
platter. The figure on the raft in the lake was hers—her wide
shoulders and thin waist; her long, well-shaped legs—even down
to the length of her hair. They would not make a try for him as
long as he kept her close.

She spoke first of the Antioqueños—"all that riffraff from
Medellín and hereabouts"—whom she called upstarts, thugs, and
hooligans. Having been transported from Europe for "thievery,
villainy, and other noncapital crimes," their ancestors had arrived

in Colombia as paupers and had been banished to the mountainous, rocky regions where the land was not readily exploitable. The hope had been that they would perish.

"But they were weeds, and, like other, hardy, noxious growths, they thrived. Like your New Englanders, Mr. Creach, who were also prominent in the slave trade, a time came when they decided they should develop a myth of themselves as a people. A *raza,* if you will. You know, who they were and where they came from and who was most pure. And so forth.

"I don't deny people their myths. We need them to live by. We know they're not true, but they're not exactly false either, and they explain dramas larger than just one person or set of persons. Dramas of peoples and history. But we can judge those myths and know a people by what it dreams of its past.

"Think here of the myths of your own country, the claptrap that you learned about its origins in school. The Europeans who settled it yearned for religious and political freedom, toleration, and the space—a new playing field—on which to grow and prosper. That was the myth. The reality?

"Once in the saddle they did and are still doing everything they can to keep the reins of power, the limits of freedom, the standards of acceptance, and even the conditions of life of all lesser beings, in their hands. They even practiced slavery—the total, unconditional bondage of other human beings—for fifty years after the rest of the so-called 'civilized' world declared the vile practice anathema.

"Why? Because there were big, enormous, obscene profits in that trade, so big it took a horrendous, bloody, divisive civil war to curtail overt slavery, if not put an end to the issue, which took other forms. As you know, it is still with you today.

"It was different here only in its directness. In South America things have always been more conspicuous."

It was getting to be first light, and the Rover had climbed so high, so fast that Creach was feeling a bit light-headed. They had to be well above ten thousand feet, he guessed, and had passed into the *páramos* of Colombia, the treeless upland wastes that offered little more than tussock grass and treacherous bogs.

Now in early autumn, with the harsh Andean winter nearly upon them, the barren looked stark and oppressive. The sky overhead was no better, freighted with dark storm clouds. From time to time they caught a glimpse of somber black mountains that climbed an additional five thousand feet into the clouds.

"Have you heard of the legend of El Dorado?" Swinging the wheel of the Land Rover, she pulled them off the main road down a narrow mountain track of furrowed ruts. It led toward a kind of cup formed by the flanks of three mountains that met there. In it was a small, clear lake.

"Scholars claim that there are several sources to the myth, but this is the original." They had come to the shore of the lake, and she stopped the truck. "Shall we get out and stretch our legs?" When he turned his head to her, she added, "Please, Mr. Creach. After all these miles, here in this barren, could we not be alone? You hold all the cards, as it were. What could you possibly be afraid of?" She opened the door and got out.

Creach pulled the key from the ignition, locked her door, and then locked his own before following her.

The wind was stiff, a steady, roaring buffet that staggered them and made Creach feel momentarily cold, until he pulled the *ruana* closer to his body.

And yet, hands in the pockets of her white, blood-stained dress, the *sicaria* tossed back her head, and her nostrils flared as she breathed in the thin and cold air. Her red hair, beating behind her, was the color of the sunrise that was just becoming visible through clouds between two of the mountains.

"This is Lake Guatavita. It's deep. The Boyacas say it has no bottom. It was sacred to the Chibchas, my ancestors on my mother's side, who were the original people of this area. Bogotá, for instance, is a corruption of the Chibchan word for the house of the Zipa, who was the ruler of the Chibchas. The Guatavita was their priest, and this was his lake."

She began walking toward the shore, and Creach—checking behind them and to either side, his good hand firmly on the grip of the Saturn—followed.

"The Chibchas, like most Andean mountain tribes, worshiped the sun. But they deemed the sun too splendid to receive gifts and offerings from mere mortals in some low place, and so every year after the harvest was over, they would journey up here and make their formal offering in this sacred lake."

They had stopped at the water's edge, and La Guatavita, as Creach reminded himself she was also known, now reached down for some flat stones. She began skipping them over the lake, which was serene and still, with the surrounding mountains shielding its surface from the winds.

"The whole tribe would ring its shore, carrying with them little objects crafted in gold, which they considered to be the sun's metal here on earth, and fiery emeralds, the clearest in the world, that can still be found in these mountains." Her left hand touched the stone on her chest.

"Out on a sacred barge in the middle of the lake, the Guatavita, who was the sun god's representative here on earth, would be standing naked, his oiled body coated with gold dust. When the sun could be seen—*there*"—she pointed between the mountains where the thinning clouds showed the sun rising from the lake— "the Guatavita would plunge into the lake, and the tribe would toss its offerings, giving back to the sun its sacred substances in the hope that the diety would return the gift in heat and light in the coming year.

"As often happens when word is carried, the report of the event became exaggerated. When the Spanish first heard of it, they were told by coastal Indians of a 'Gilded Man'—literally *El Dorado*—and his mountain of gold. The streets of his city were lined with gold, his public buildings and royal houses built of it. Three complete raiding parties set out simultaneously—one from the Atlantic coast, another from the Caribbean coast, and the third from Peru—looking for what?" She paused until Creach turned to her. "That one, big, quick score which—you're not alone to blame—is the worm at the center of *your* civilization's ethos. You know, the thing beyond right or wrong that is dreamed about, the thing of adventure, the thing which can solve all life's problems at one fell swoop.

"But it didn't for the Spanish. Whatever gold the Chibchas possessed had already been given here in offerings, and it wasn't much. Certainly there was gold hereabouts and emeralds, and so—enraged now that myth and reality were so disparate—they enslaved the Chibchas, who were gentle, advanced people, and forced them to produce the riches their greed demanded. To do this, coca, which had been another sacred item, was employed immoderately, and only the strong who were used to these severe mountains, like my Boyacas, survived.

"Well, as on your continent, overt slavery is now gone, but

the instrument of South American slavery—the cheap, abundant coca leaf—remains." Yet again she bent for more flat stones to skip. There were none around her, and she moved a few steps farther for others.

Again Creach glanced behind him and along the shore. He wondered what she was getting at, and if she had brought him all this way for a lecture on myth and history.

"Coca." Her arm snapped out, and a stone darted across the lake, skimming over the surface in a long staccato arc. "As a leaf it helped to enslave my continent. As a powder it is now enforcing the covert slavery of yours. At the center of its trade is that same desire for the big, quick, clean score. Greed, some would have it, but greed is too simple, it's more than that. It's El Dorado all over again in a modern form, the quest for the big adventure with the prize of enormous, undreamed-of riches for the victor, be he *cartellero, transportador,* middleman like you and Mr. Nathanson, cop, or the dealer on the street. It's at the center of the myth of your civilization, which conquered mine and the world and is therefore undeniable. And unchangeable.

"My part in all of that *was*"—yet again she waited until his eyes met hers—"lamentable but necessary. I did those things, I performed my part, but never gladly, willingly, with any . . . heart. I did them because otherwise I would die. As a whore there in the Barrio Antioquia some disease or affliction or some client would have killed me. As a madam one twisted personality tried. He was rich and powerful, and after he failed, I had no choice but to become a feared *sicaria,* if only to protect myself and what was mine.

"Perhaps I would not have died immediately. But it would have happened, had I faltered. Now with this and all that it means to me"—she reached to her neck and lifted the emerald over her head—"it's over, which brings me to my proposal."

She bent and picked up a stone about the size and shape of the brooch stone, which she was holding in the palm of the other hand. "Here we have two stones of approximately the same size and shape. They are probably of roughly equal antiquity and ultimate value. By that I mean what they will be worth to us after we are dead, which is the only way to judge things.

"Another way to look at it is that both stones could kill us."

She hefted them in her palms. "If thrown, they have the size and the weight to slay. This one, however," she raised the emerald so that she was staring across it at Creach, "*will* kill us, as surely as any cancer. You quickly, if you take it from me. Me, whenever I grow weak, which is inevitable. In either case, it will claim us and warp the rest of our lives.

"My proposal: that we take these two stones and cast them as far as we can into this bottomless lake as an offering to the giver of life." She nodded toward the sun, which was now fully above the mountains and veiled only slightly by the thinning clouds. "And as a way of settling the enmity between us. Finally. With no recriminations. No revenge." She regarded him.

Creach did not know how to answer, what to say. She sounded so sincere, so convincing, that he didn't doubt that it was a turning point in her life. But his own life experience told him that no sane person would willingly throw away the object in her left hand. Also, he could not keep himself from thinking that he knew the lake was bottomless only by her say-so, and the entire proposal—hell, her *proposition*—could be a riff to get him to walk away from her empty-handed.

"You hesitate. Why?" she demanded. "Cocaine is slavery, Mr. Creach. Just another aspect of exploitation that has obtained since the white man first invaded this hemisphere. The modes of servility have changed, but the pattern is the same. The money generated from this slavery has a life of its own. People are expendable, especially the little people on the low end of the trade—the mules, the pushers, the users. It's the money, the *gold,* that lives. The green fire in this stone." Between thumb and forefinger she raised the stone so that Creach could look through it toward the sun. She trained the beam from it into his face.

The emerald was magnificent, really, like a great green sparkling eye. The light bursting from it was gold at the center, like the sun behind, with prismatic radii shaped like brilliant rainbow-colored swords and daggers.

"I assume from your silence that you reject my offer. So be it." With the other hand she lobbed the other stone into the lake not far from shore, then turned and began striding back toward the Land Rover.

It was then that the four men burst from the surface of the

lake, drawing Kalashnikovs or some type of assault rifle with them. They were obviously over their heads and treading water, and they had to clear their eyes and aim before firing. Two managed to get off a few wild shots before Creach threw himself down to present less of a silhouette against the horizon. The gun of the third would not fire. The fourth resubmerged and began swimming underwater toward shore.

Creach waited until the two who managed to get off the shots came up again before he treated them to the special firepower of his double-barrel weapon. It hammered the water, sending up a wide geyser of spray in the three seconds that the short clip allowed him to fan the weapon from one form to the other.

A third man now appeared and trained his weapon on him. With his good hand Creach fumbled for another clip and rolled himself away from the fire that now came as two shots, a pause, a curse, and two more. Creach jacked the clip into the Saturn, and raised his head just in time to roll again. The *penilla* of the fourth Boyaca bit harmlessly into the thick wool of the *ruana*. Creach snapped up the loaded Saturn, popped the trigger once, and three quick bullets smacked into the Boyaca's bare back, spilling him over onto his side. Three more in the chest flopped him down flat like a big yellow sunfish.

Creach glanced toward the water but could not see the final Boyaca. One of the other two had bellied up, and blood and bits of hair and skin spangled the clear, sunlit water.

At the Land Rover the *sicaria* had discovered that the doors were locked, and she now opened a tool storage box and looked in.

Swimming away, the last Boyaca surfaced but was nearly out of range, and Creach let him go.

He took his time walking back to the Land Rover, watching the woman scurry from one box to another, trying to find something to pry open a door. But when he got close, she simply turned, faced him, and dropped the tire iron in her hands.

The emerald was back around her neck. She raised her wide shoulders and let them fall. She then removed the emerald from her neck and looked down at it. She smiled. "Nice, isn't it? Magnificent. Pity I couldn't have kept it longer. But it's enough to buy a life, I suppose. Like Brian Nathanson bought his from me in New York."

Creach's head went back.

"You didn't know that? It's recent, and perhaps you two haven't spoken since the debacle at his house. He gave me a certain photograph that proved key to my understanding of who possessed the stone and why. It occurred in a situation similar to this, and I let him walk, as you would say. I ask only that for myself. You get into this vehicle with the stone and drive away. I'll find my own way back.

"Don't worry, I won't come after it. Fair is fair."

Like her fair proposition of five minutes past, Creach thought. He did not believe for one moment that she would let him just drive away. They were in her country, in fact her province. Bogotá with its airport was also her city, and Barranquilla or the border with Venezuela were hundreds of miles of slow, winding, mountainous roads away. Somehow she or that Maluko had got word here, and he did not doubt they could similarly waylay him before he could get out of the country.

And finally she had led Creach to this desolate spot to kill him, not for the first time. All the "claptrap"—her word—about cocaine and slavery and a truce was only just that: jive, which was his word.

Could he believe what she had said about letting Nathanson off in New York? Maybe. Nathanson had been making call after call to contacts in Colombia about the time Creach made his play for the Indians in Nassau. But not even that changed things, either here and now or in the future.

Creach shook his head.

And if he took the emerald and let her off, he'd have to run and try to hide. He had already seen how quickly after the busted deal in the Islands she had got herself and her team of Boyacas to Nassau.

Creach shook his head again.

Or if, say, he let her walk *with* the emerald, would even that make a difference? Creach didn't know. After all, she murdered for a living, and that alone was not understandable to Creach.

For the last time Creach shook his head.

He raised the barrel of the Saturn. It was time to settle things.

The *sicaria* smiled gamely. "One last wish?"

He waited.

"I want you to see what you're about to destroy. It's yours

too, of course. If you want." She reached behind her neck and undid the snap of her white dress. In one movement it was off her, and she was naked, as if she had planned for the moment.

In the slanting light of the newly risen sun, her skin was a rich golden color, and Creach did not think he had ever seen a more beautiful woman. Her body was tightly defined but full, and her nipples had the same bronze glistening color of the dew-wet *páramo* grass, there by the shore of the lake.

CHAPTER 33
PAYBACK

◆

FOR BRIAN NATHANSON'S first on-site meeting with his architect nearly a month later, the weather did not cooperate.

It was a turbulent, muscular early summer morning of the sort that is peculiar to the Islands. Everything *seemed* perfect, with a limitless, cerulean-blue sky, a strong sun the size of a dirigible, and gusty, obstreperous winds. Combined, however, those elements proved too much. Like a squadron of smarmy sailors bound for shore, they took you by the collar and demanded, "Look, you— ain't we pretty?"

Under a canopied table on the terrace of Nathanson's gutted building, Denny had arranged a brunch of conch salad, smoked kingfish, spicy squid in red wine, and char-broiled fresh halibut. But there was simply too much fresh wind that was too hot and too wet. It threatened to bluster the canopy right off its stanchions, and although it beat the architectural drawings around, like loosed sails, the paper itself was wet and felt slimy.

Also, the sun was too powerful. Looking up at the brown-stone walls to count how many framing timbers remained in the burned-out house, Nathanson and the architect could tolerate only a quick peek at the eaves before having to duck back under the canopy. And yet it was Creach's kind of weather exactly, the sort that made him glad he had settled in Nassau.

His present plan was to set himself up in the antique gun and small-arms trade. Creach was sitting at one end of the table with copies of *Antique Weaponry* and *Whittaker's Small Arms of Yesterday* spread before him. To one side was a tall, weak rum drink. In his right hand he held a thin dark cigar that he was smoking in spite of Dr. Southworth's admonition to quit because of his throat.

Creach was scheduled to be admitted to a hospital in Toronto. Southworth believed that Eva, who was working temporarily as his assistant, had found a doctor who might help Creach regain his voice. The whole group of them—Nathanson, Eva, Denny, and Eva's child, Sandy—would fly up there next week. On the way back they would stop in New York to be interviewed about adopting the Gelbs' baby.

Sandy, who was four, was now pedaling her tricycle around the patterned flagstones by Creach's feet. She was a tiny blond girl, who looked like a miniature of Eva and seemed content with her mother's new situation here. She played easily with Nathanson, Denny, and Mr. Bert, the Dalmatian dog, and she was the only person Creach allowed to call him Dave. Creach liked that. Contentment was now something that he found himself working on. It wasn't easy to say, Well, I'm lucky, and I've got enough. From now on I'm going to reef my sails and ease off the wind when it blows strong. Somehow he hoped the urge wasn't permanent.

But he guessed it was time to pay back his debt. For over an hour he had been listening to Nathanson and the architect discussing the details of the restoration and how much items like cut-and-shaped marble for kitchen counters and teak flooring now cost. Whenever Nathanson said, "Well—maybe there's something a little cheaper that will serve as well," Creach shook his head, meaning they should spring for the real stuff. Nathanson had only raised an eyebrow and moved on to something else.

A corner of the architectural drawing was snapping in the wind, and Creach waved Sandy over. From the pocket of his jacket he pulled out a velvet pouch that contained a small but weighty object. "Do me a favor?" he whispered.

"Sure," she whispered back.

"Put this over there on those papers that're blowing around. We don't want 'em to rip."

"What is it?" She could barely hold it in her hand.

"You'll see soon enough."

Talking about mullions and double-glazed windows and the price of custom—instead of ready-made—frames, the three others returned to the table.

"Shall we go on to the second floor?" the architect asked. He reached for the velvet case so he could remove a drawing from the pile. "This is heavy. What is it?"

Nathanson shook his head.

Opening the drawstring, the architect slid the Mercier brooch stone into the palm of his left hand. He was standing in the sunlight, and the emerald was almost too much to look at directly. It had been cut by a master, and its facets, clarity, and fiery green color were dazzling. "My God, is it real?" he asked. "No, it's too damn big. But look at it. It's like it's lit from within."

Nathanson turned to Creach. "David—what's this about?"

"Windows and doors," Creach whispered.

Said the architect, "You mean it's a *real* emerald? It must be the biggest damn thing in the world. And clear! It looks . . . flawless. Where'd you get it, David?"

"Yes, David—*where*?" Eva asked. "It's outrageous."

Creach stood and began walking away. It was nothing he was proud of, and he needed another drink from the basket that was lying in the cool shadows under the grape arbor. "Ask Denny," he whispered, passing the table.

Denny didn't look up. He continued busying himself with the arrangement of the brunch.

"C'mon, David—I can't take this," said Nathanson. "It's priceless. I don't know, but I can imagine, what you had to do to get it. Whatever it was, it's yours."

With a fresh drink Creach returned to the table. He reached for the emerald, then squatted down in front of Sandy, who had been squinting at the brilliant thing in the architect's hands.

Between thumb and forefinger Creach held the emerald before Sandy's eyes and whispered in her ear.

"What do I see?" She looked back at the emerald. "Green fire," she said without hesitation.

Creach whispered again.

"A *what*? A house?"

He whispered one more time.

"A *new* house? Where? I don't see a new house."

But Creach did, and a new life. Standing, he tossed the emerald to Nathanson, who barely caught it.

"David!" Denny admonished, advancing on Nathanson. "Don't you ever learn? That thing could have fallen and chipped or, worse, cracked. Then what would it be worth? You haven't settled down a bit. Gimme that damn thing, Brian. I'll keep it safe." He had the velvet case open. He took the emerald from Nathanson's hand, explaining to Eva, "Two fools. They should think what it already cost them. Girl—you don't know what you got yourself into."

On his way toward his hamper he added, "But I'm sure glad you' here."